Charles de Montzey

Life of the Venerable John Eudes

With a sketch of the History of his Foundation from A.D. 1601 to 1874

Charles de Montzey

Life of the Venerable John Eudes
With a sketch of the History of his Foundation from A.D. 1601 to 1874

ISBN/EAN: 9783744747165

Printed in Europe, USA, Canada, Australia, Japan

Cover: Foto ©Raphael Reischuk / pixelio.de

More available books at **www.hansebooks.com**

LIFE

OF THE

VENERABLE JOHN EUDES.

WITH A SKETCH OF THE

HISTORY OF HIS FOUNDATIONS,

FROM A.D. 1601 TO 1874.

BY

M. CH. DE MONTZEY,

ANCIEN OFFICIER D'INFANTERIE, CHEVALIER DE LA
LEGION D'HONNEUR, DE L'ORDRE ROYAL ET MILITAIRE DE
L'EPEE DE SUEDE, DE ST. GREGOIRE LE-GRAND,
DECORE DE LA TROISIEME CLASSE DU
NIKANI IFTIKHAR.

WITH A BRIEF OF APPROVAL FROM

HIS HOLINESS POPE PIUS IX.

OBEDIENS USQUE AD MORTEM.
Servire Christo et Ecclesiæ, in sanctitate et
justitia coram ipso, omnibus diebus nostris.—
Motto of the Congregation of Jesus and Mary.

SECOND EDITION.

1883.

BRIEF OF POPE PIUS IX.,

TO THE

WRITER OF THE LIFE OF FATHER EUDES.

TO OUR DEAR SON THE CHEVALIER C. DE MONTZEY.

Dear Son, Health and Apostolical Benediction.

Your position in society, my dear son, has made the more welcome to Us the work which you have written concerning the life and good deeds of your great-uncle, John Eudes, that most Apostolic Missionary. For We have considered it not a slight proof of your religious sentiments, that amidst military cares you have preserved that relish for spiritual things, which has made you consider preferable to all worldly glory the noble virtues of a servant of God, his zeal, his apostolic labours, and the new institutes which he founded for the salvation of his

neighbour; of which institutes experience
has proved the value.   We therefore congratulate you, that, looking to the glory of
God and the salvation of souls, you have,
after great research, presented these to the
piety of the faithful in a copious narra-
tive ; and We pray that your work may
have abundant   fruit.   In   assurance
whereof, and as a pledge of Our paternal
favour, We give you with sincere affection
Our Apostolic Benediction.

Given at Rome, at St. Peter's, on the
9th day of February, 1870, in the 24
year of Our Pontificate.

Pius PP. IX.

The life of the priest, like that of the soldier, is a warfare. Courage, endurance, self-abnegation, and perseverance, are the special virtues of each calling.

Differing, as they do, in education and habits, they find a point of contact in sacrifice: the minister of the last sacraments has often met his death on the battle-field, as he knelt beside a penitent who had fallen to rise no more.

A close relationship exists between these two careers, and they are united by common sentiments, which shine forth in all their greatness in the midst of the most terrible scenes.

A soldier now ventures to take up his pen, hitherto devoted solely to military subjects, and to relate, as best he may, the life of his great-uncle, the holy Father Eudes, founder of the Congregation of

Jesus and Mary; of the order of our Lady of Charity of the Refuge, and of the third order of the Daughters of the Sacred Heart of Mary. The traditions of that life still direct the steps of his spiritual children; we see them still devoting themselves to the education of the youth of France, and ever burning more and more brightly with the fire of charity and the love of God.

The illustrious Bishop of Orleans tells us that a rare combination of qualities is required in order to write the life of a saint, and that special qualifications are needed to narrate it in such a manner as to satisfy the claims of piety and to avoid the delusions which he has often remarked in such works. The summary which he gives of these circumstances and qualifications might well fill us with alarm, did we not remember that he who fights valiantly, is even in defeat worthy of honour. "In the first place," says Mgr. Dupanloup, with his exquisite perception of what befits the subject, "in the first place, there must be *love for the saint;* then the requisite time and labour must be employed in a thorough study of his soul and life, by means of contemporary sources and documents ; that soul must be delineated, its struggles described, the different workings of nature and grace discriminated, in a simple, truthful, clear, and dignified style, with all those details which bring the saint and his times vividly before the mind, always giving him the prominent place; artistic skill is needed for the arrangement of the facts."*

Can we in our first undertaking of the kind hope to reach such a standard ?

We have placed our work under the patronage of Jesus and Mary, and we hope also for that of the eminent prelates whose dioceses were for so many years the scene of Father Eudes' labours, particularly the Bishop of Bayeux, who directs the enquiries for his beatification, and the Bishop of Séez, one of whose parishes was the birthplace of this great servant of God. We cannot refrain from here expressing our feelings of devotion and veneration for Mgr. Fillion, our Bishop, by whose good will and precious affection our courage has been sustained.

* Lettre de Mgr. l'Evêque d'Orleans à M. l'abbé Bougaud auteur de l'histoire de Ste. Chantal ; Orleans, 15 Mai, 1863.

The Very Rev. Father Gaudaire, superior-general of the *Eudists*, and representative of their holy founder, has given us access to the manuscript Annals of the Congregation, dating from the year 1643; we have thus enjoyed the privilege of intimate acquaintance with religious who have long passed away from this earth, and have been able to trace the ever onward march of the Order of Our Lady of Charity of the Refuge, and the Order of our Lady of Charity of the Good Shepherd, whose principal monastery, founded in 1829 at Angers, from that at Tours, was made by Gregory XVI. the mother-house of the Order, and is the head of all houses which may hereafter be founded throughout the world.

We beg the Very Rev. Father Gaudaire to accept the expression of our heart-felt gratitude, not only for the paternal kindness with which he received us at St. Sauveur de Redon, but also for having put us in a position to celebrate the virtues of our ancestor, by a record of "facts and actions," such as is recommended by Abbé Fleury,* and for having enabled us to

* Letter of the Abbé Fleury to Father Costil, annalist of the

retrace the course of that eventful **17th** century, which calls forth the astonishment and enthusiasm of every student, and one of whose wonders was Father Eudes.

Our undertaking is a daring one, but duty requires it. Sursum Corda!

C. DE MONTZEY.

La Flèche, 9th January, 1869.
(Sarthe.)

Congregation of Jesus and Mary, on the manner of writing the lives of pious persons:

"I have always disapproved of the method of modern authors, who, after writing the life of a saint or other illustrious person, give a treatise on his virtues as a separate thing. They ought to be exhibited by *facts and actions*. It is not worth while to write a life of mere thoughts and reflexions. Facts must be given as circumstantially as possible. I have done this according to my power in the notices of the Lives of the Saints, contained in my Ecclesiastical History. You have gratified me and done me honour by consulting me on this important subject, and I hope you may deem my reply satisfactory. Recommending myself to your pious sacrifices, I remain, sir, &c.,

"FLEURY, THE KING'S CONFESSOR."

In obedience to the decree of Urban
VIII., we declare that, wherever we have
spoken in this book, of Father Eudes or
any other as *holy*, *venerable*, or a *great
servant of God*, we attach to these expressions no other meaning than that which
they bear in theological language.

We have no intention of forming a
judgment on any question whatsoever,
reserved by the Holy See, to which we
shall always consider it an honour to be
entirely subject.

NOTICE TO THE SECOND EDITION.

Since this volume was written the cause of
the canonization of Venerable Father Eudes
has made rapid progress. In the matter of the
canonization of her saints the Church generally
moves with no hasty step. She waits in her
wisdom the march of events, and the development of what may throw light on the path she
should pursue. It is only a few years back,
that is, on February 7th, 1874, that the first
step towards the canonization of Father Eudes
received its completion, by his being solemnly
declared *Venerable* by Pope Pius IX., of happy
memory. In 1867 this holy Pope, when reading
the life of the servant of God, had been struck
with a great admiration for the grandeur of his
work, his character, and his virtues. In the
following year he received to an audience some
of the Eudist Fathers, and he then urged them
to make no delay in setting on foot the cause of
Father Eudes' canonization.

Words from such a quarter naturally came
with weight, like a command; so, in the April
of that same year, 1868, Father Gaudaire,
Superior-General of the Eudist Congregation of

Jesus and Mary, in the name of his own Institute, as well as of the Order of our Lady of Charity of Refuge, and of the Society of the Admirable Heart of the Mother of God, appointed one of his fathers as Postulator of the cause of canonization. The demand for the first process was addressed to the Bishop of Bayeux, in whose diocese was the tomb of Father Eudes. The opening of the process was announced for August 19th, the anniversary day of Father Eudes' happy passage. The first sitting took place in the chapel attached to the bishop's palace, and the oath was then administered to those who were to give evidence. The second session was held in the same place, and the Postulator then gave into the hands of the commission a statement of the different things which he was intending to bring evidence on, which might be summed up in these three: first, that Father Eudes had always had the reputation of sanctity; secondly, that his virtues were heroic; and thirdly, that divers favours had been obtained through his intercession.

In the ordinary course of matters it would be a considerable time before the Venerable Father Eudes would receive the additional glory of *beatification*. But Pope Leo XIII. casts a pitying eye on the prevailing miseries of France, and is anxious to give her new advocates and protectors, by raising some of God's servants belonging to that nation to the honours of canonization. Amongst those distinguished servants of God His Holiness has designated in a special manner the Venerable John Eudes, for from his intercession he expects much for the salvation of France. The Congregation of Rites has lately concluded a long and important examination into the cause of Father Eudes, and it has declared that this venerable man was regarded as a saint during his life, and that his memory has been held in veneration in the Church. It has proclaimed, in fine, in a general manner, that it is clear that this great servant of God has practised all Christian virtues in an eminent degree, and that God has deigned to grant, through his intercession, many truly miraculous favours. This sentence of the Sacred Congregation of Rites was approved and signed by his Holiness on the 10th of May, 1883. This is a matter of real joy to all the children of the Venerable Father Eudes, and indeed to all Catholics, and we may hope soon to see this holy man added to the glorious list of the beatified servants of God.

CONTENTS.

BOOK I.

CHAPTER I.

1601—1615.

CHAPTER II.

1615—1625.

CHAPTER III.

1625—1632.

CHAPTER IV.

1632—1641.

CHAPTER V.

1641—1642.

BOOK II.

1642—1658.

CHAPTER I.

1642—1644.

CHAPTER II.

1644—1648.

CHAPTER III.

1648—1651.

CHAPTER IV.

1651.—1658.

BOOK III.

CHAPTER I.

1658—1660.

CHAPTER II.

1660—1666.

CHAPTER III.

1666—1677.

CHAPTER IV.

1677—1680.

FIRST APPENDIX.

1680—1782.

SECOND APPENDIX.

FATHER EUDES' FOUNDATIONS.
1792—1869.

ERRATA.

Page 20 line 43, note, for *Historie* read *Histoire.*
— 22 line 35, note, for *Bulle* read *Bull.*
— — line 40, note, for *propriæ* read *proprie.*
— 24 line 23, for *neques* read *nequeo.*
— 43 line 33, note, for *Visconti* read *Vicomte.*
— 46 line 25, for *satis dicitur* read *satis discitur.*
— 50 line 32, note, for *religiousus* read *religiosius.*
— — — — — *spiritu vi* read *Spiritus vi.*
— 74 line 27, for *Lilii* read *Liliis.*
— — line 36, note, for *Françaus* read *Français.*
— 97 line 1, for *cordi,* read *corde.*
— 106 line 22, note, for *exercices piete,* read *exercices de piete.*
— — line 45, note, for *Vie de La ou,* read *La vie de.*
— 153 line 25, for *Mazazin* read *Mazarin.*
— 239 line 39, note, for *Pius Pape* read *Pius Papa.*
— 252 line 27, for *ready ty* read *ready to.*
— 256 line 16, for *le janenisme* read *le jansenisme.*

FATHER EUDES,

APOSTOLIC MISSIONARY,

AND HIS FOUNDATIONS.

BOOK I.

CHAPTER I.

1601—1615.

INAUGURATION OF THE MEDALLIONS OF THE THREE BROTHERS
EUDES, AT RI, THEIR BIRTH-PLACE, 1853.—STATUE OF EUDES
DE MEZERAY, PERPETUAL SECRETARY AND MEMBER OF THE
FRENCH ACADEMY, IN THE PLACE DU LOUVRE.—MONUMENT
ERECTED TO THE THREE BROTHERS IN THE PLACE AT AR-
GENTAN, 1866.—ISAAC EUDES AND MARTHA CORBIN HIS WIFE.
—BIRTH OF JOHN EUDES, OF HIS BROTHERS AND SISTERS.—
HIS CHILDHOOD AND EARLY EDUCATION.—HE ENTERS THE
JESUITS' COLLEGE AT CAEN.—HIS CONDUCT, HIS SUCCESS.—
HE RETURNS TO RI.—HIS VOCATION.—OPPOSITION OF HIS
PARENTS.—HE RECEIVES THE TONSURE AND MINOR ORDERS.

The principal people of the neighbourhood, and
the members of the family of Eudes, were invited
by the Comte de Vigneral to assemble at his
chateau of Ri, in the canton of Putanges, on the
11th of September, 1853, for the inauguration of
the medallions of the three brothers Eudes, on the
largest gable of a school-house, close to the little
church, where, in the early part of the XVIIth
century, they had been made Christians, and
under the shadow of an ancient elm tree said to

have been planted by Mézeray on the day that Louis XIV. was born.*

Why was such honour paid, after the lapse of two hundred years, to these children of the commune of Ri? John Eudes, the eldest, was founder of the Congregation of Jesus and Mary, of the Order of our Lady of Charity of the Refuge, and of the third order of the Daughters of the Sacred Heart of Mary; he shines with a glory like that of Cardinal de Berulle and St. Vincent de Paul; the second made the name of François de Mezeray illustrious by his indefatigable labours; he became historiographer to the king, member and perpetual secretary of the French Academy. The third, Charles Eudes du d'Houay, clung to his native soil, and lived in sight of his own church tower; followed, with much honour, his father's profession of surgeon,† dwelt in the town of Argentan, made a happy and advantageous marriage, saved money, bought a house, and kept his paternal inheritance intact; he was ever ready for the labours, as well as the honours of municipal authority, and defended small privileges and small liberties of his native town as a sacred trust committed to him.‡

---

* A medallion by the author, in which these three are reproduced, gained a silver medal at the Avranches Exhibition, 1854, and was sold on behalf of the monument since erected on the Place at Argentan. It bears the legend, *predicat, scribit, et ego defendam.*

† Speech of M. G. Levavasseur at the inauguration of the monument of Mezeray, on the Place at Argentan. (Sep. 1866.)

‡ Comte de Grancey, Marshal of France, and governor of Argentan, wished to demolish a certain tower at Argentan. It contained a clock which had been given to the town by Mary of Spain, Countess of Alencon. The inhabitants were much attached to the tower and the clock, on grounds of *public defence* and utility. The proposed measure caused general dissatisfaction, but no one presumed to take the initiative in opposing so powerful an authority. Charles Eudes, alone, had courage to present the petition of the inhabitants to the governor, and to

Public gratitude has always associated the old magistrate with the venerable religious and the illustrious author.

The fête at Ri was a prelude to yet greater honours, and now, when the descendants of those three brothers cross the Place du Louvre, they bow before the figure of him who is called, in the world of literature and art, old Mezeray; there he stands, with his style in one hand and his tablets in the other, as if watching from that height the course of passing events, and ready to write them down for the benefit of posterity.

The erection of a monument to the three Eudes on the principal Place at Argentan had long been under contemplation, and at last, after many difficulties, it was completed in September, 1866.

The life of Father Eudes has a special interest for those who dwell in our beautiful Normandy, where he went about preaching the Word of God, and spent himself in labours, undaunted by distance or by the complete want of means of communication, which made travelling in those days so full of difficulty.

Let us bear in mind that these monuments are not mere ornaments of our public squares; they read a great lesson to youth, which, in its impatience to reach the goal, never calculates the intervening distance. They seem to say, Be like Eudes de Mezeray, whose first law was labour. Be like Father Eudes, whose spiritual children are still preaching the Word of God, while the Daughters of Charity continue to succour souls in peril,

maintain their rights with undaunted energy. *Illi robur et æs triplex circa pectus erat.*

The governor was enraged, and asked in astonishment who it was that dared to gainsay his orders? Charles Eudes then made an answer, worthy of the best days of Athens or of Rome: " We are three brothers, who worship truth; the eldest preaches it, the second writes it, and I will maintain it till my last breath." —Speech of M. Berrier Fontaine, Mayor of Argentan.

and to raise up souls that have fallen. Be like Charles Eudes du d'Houay, whose memory is joined with that of Eustache de St. Pierre, and of Alain Blanchard, as an example of readiness to sacrifice life itself on behalf of the great truths which uphold the present and future destinies of our race.

And we, in our turn, are about to defend these great truths, by relating the holy life of Father Eudes. It seems to us just now as if we could more easily die for them. More than ever does our own weakness come before us, but from the south of France a voice we love reaches our ears. It exclaims,* " You will not give way." Forward, then ! To yield would not be like a Frenchman.

" A traveller," says the author of St. Chantal's life, " who sets off very early in the morning, sometimes sees a beautiful light on the horizon before sun-rise, and such a dawn is to him a token of mid-day splendour. So is it with the historian, as he beholds the first appearance of those great luminaries the saints."

And so is it with us, as we trace the rise and growth of this soul, which, from the first, seems so advanced in Divine things.

God wished to save the XVIIth century from the evil heritage left to it by the XVIth, and therefore He spread out His forces, as we do when we would make the fire of our battalions take full effect. One after another He sent forth those who were to become its leaders. Cardinal de Bérulle was born in 1565 ; St. Francis of Sales in 1567 ; St. Vincent de Paul in 1576 ; Father de Condren in 1588, and M. Ollier in 1608. Father Eudes, their disciple and friend, in 1601.

At that time a worthy surgeon was living in a village of the parish of Ri, in the diocese of Séez, Lower Normandy. He had originally been destined

* Baron G. de Flotke, Catholic writer and poet, Marseilles.

for the priesthood, but when all his brothers were carried off by the plague of 1585, his self-devotion found another channel in the practice of medicine. He soon married a young woman, named Corbin, of good understanding and decided* character. They were both full of faith, and fervent in the practice of their religion. Isaac Eudes, indeed, had retained from his former vocation the custom of saying his breviary every day.

But their happy union was not blessed by children; and it seemed that an honoured, though lowly name, was about to die out.†

Then they turned their thoughts to God, and promised to make a pilgrimage to our Lady of Recouvrances, in the parish of Tourailles, if He would graciously grant them posterity. Some time after this, Isaac took his staff and set off for Tourailles, accompanied by his wife, for they both longed to kneel before Mary's altar, and fulfil their vow, which had been accepted.

This was in the month of February, 1601, and on the 14th of November, in the same year, a son was born, who was baptized by the name of John.‡ In course of time they had two other sons and three daughters; the latter were all married.

* A relation of Martha Corbin's having been unhappily killed in a duel, the authorities took measures to investigate the affair, according to the king's orders. Martha Corbin caused the body to be buried in a field belonging to her, and had the field ploughed with such diligence that the officers, who arrived at Ri the next morning, could not make the necessary investigations. (P. Costil, Annales de la Congrégation.)

† No officer or nobleman dared to offer any insult by word or deed to any girl who was with this good couple. It is said that Isaac Eudes, in consideration of his services to the royal cause, had obtained from Henri IV. free entry for certain goods into some towns of Normandy.

‡ "If," Father Herambourg remarks, "If physicians are correct in their opinion that the soul is united to the body of a male child on the fortieth day after conception, the soul of Father Eudes must have been created on the 25th of March, the day on which the Word became incarnate for our salvation; and the Blessed Virgin was raised to the honour of Divine Maternity."

The posterity of Martha Corbin is not extinct; their blood soon mingled with that of very noble families, and these same families are still glad to ally themselves with it : " Maxima in minimis."

We learn from M. Levavasseur that " John Eudes, the child of predestination, always received his mother's pious instructions with docility ; he never knew the storms of youth; the cares, the rivalries, and tumults of the court and town; or the temptations of ambition."

For John had chosen the better part ; and although he met with much opposition in carrying out his pious purposes, yet before he was called to give an account of the actions of his saintly life, he saw the field of his mission enlarged to an unexpected degree.

In his pure childhood, as in that of Francis of Sales and of St. Chantal, were seen the germs of those virtues, hereafter to become so glorious in the sight of God. Like them, he had that faith that can move mountains ; and his faith, like St. Chantal's, was joined to a strength of soul capable alike of conflict and of resignation, to a generosity and divine ardour, which united him to those who were most holy as well as most distinguished by their position in the world.

Madame de Chantal had not at first any presentiment of her future vocation, but St. Francis of Sales and John Eudes had but one desire in their childhood, one steadfast purpose in their youth, to devote themselves to God, to adore the Heart of Jesus, and to honour His Blessed Mother. There is a striking similarity between the early lives of these two chosen servants of God ; one a scion of a noble house in Savoy, and the other the son of a village surgeon.

The opposition of their families had to be overcome in both cases, and the desired victory was gained by submission and filial respect, such as is little known in the present day.

Let us borrow from one who is richer than ourselves, and use the words of Abbé Bougault :* "No doubt many elements of dissolution were already and had long been at work; the general relaxation of morals so often pointed out by councils ; the wild cry of reform, which, by proclaiming the liberty of the flesh, had kindled all its passions ; the long and violent religious wars ; the writings of the 'infamous' Rabelais, as St. Francis of Sales called him, and of all his disciples : these causes and many others had unsettled society; nevertheless, at the period of which we write, the family preserved its integrity. It appears in all its strength, in the ancient and virginal beauty which Christianity had given it. Strong and generous fathers, energetic and fruitful mothers, numerous children, respect paid to paternal authority even in old age, by those who themselves had reached the prime of life, devotion to duty at any cost, domestic purity and joy ; all these were the sweet and holy results of Christianity. Alas ! they have vanished, and where shall we now look for them ?"

How seldom do we see the son bow to the father ! How rarely is the widow's will respected, as if the family had not lost its natural head ! How often those, whose lawful authority is set at nought, are driven back to painful memories of their own earlier days !

No doubt we have made progress in many ways; but while we willingly acknowledge this, we shall never fail on fitting occasions to point out the great and noble lessons to be learned from the errors of the past !

Let us return to the early years, during which

* Histoire de Ste. Chantal.

John Eudes was being prepared for his future work. He was a child of prayer, a special gift of God, and already he seemed to wish to give himself wholly to God; he watched over his baptismal innocence, and, according to the testimony of his ordinary confessor, he never lost it. He was distinguished from other children of the same age, by acts of unusual virtue. When he was but nine years old, one of his companions, M. d'Esdiguères, struck him.* John fell upon his knees, and turned his other cheek. The offender blushed, and showed his sorrow by making known this admirable instance of obedience to the counsel of the Gospel.†

One day his parents were made uneasy by his long absence, and went to seek him, as Mary and Joseph went to seek Jesus; they found him kneeling beside one of the pillars of the church, where he had gone to pray, and forgotten everything else.

At this time the intention of his parents was to bring him up to the hardy life of a husbandman, which was considered better suited to his delicate constitution than any calling involving great mental labour.

But his vocation carried all before it. Isaac Eudes ended by yielding to his entreaties, and it was a happy day for his son when he was entrusted to the care of an old priest of the same canton, named Jacques Blavette. The master was soon astonished at the rapid progress of his pious pupil.

---

* The d'Esdiguères family still live in the neighbourhood of Argentan.

† St. Francis of Sales one day begged that a servant in the Jesuits' house, who had behaved very insolently to him, might be forgiven. As he continued to urge this request with much warmth, notwithstanding the refusal of his preceptor, M. Déage, the latter gave him a blow as his only answer. The holy youth, who had fallen on his knees in the eagerness of his charity, rose up as calmly as if he had gained his point.

Important public events were now taking place in France. Henry IV. had been assassinated on the 14th of May, 1610; the people in general mourned for him, and no one felt his death more deeply than Isaac Eudes.

External tranquillity still prevailed, but a leaven of revolt and insubordination was already at work, and the government of a queen regent was unable to arrest its progress.

At twelve years of age John Eudes was allowed to make his first Communion. He felt the full importance of this act, and it was the beginning of the *undeviating* course which he followed with so much constancy and firmness. He wished, like the Jews of old, to gird up his loins for the Paschal Feast, and it soon became necessary to hold him back from the premature engagements by which he would fain have bound himself. Every month he drew near to the Table of the Lord, giving an example little followed in those days of indifference.*

Day by day his health became stronger. In 1615 he completed his fourteenth year, and his parents, who had no longer any reason to fear the effects of study, decided to send him to the Jesuits' College at Caen. His master, Father Robin, very soon proposed him as an example for the imitation of his fellow-students. He surpassed them all in wisdom and piety, and they all looked up to him, Father Herambourg tells us, as if he had been one of their teachers. The charm of his goodness was felt even by the most hardened. He was holy, Father Herambourg† again tells us,

* No record is to be found of the date of Father Eudes' Confirmation, nor or of the name of the Prelate who administered that Sacrament to him.

† Father Herambourg entered the Congregation of Jesus and Mary in 1682, at the age of twenty-one. The novice-master who formed him to the sacerdotal and religious life, was Father de Bonnefond, the best-loved disciple of Father Eudes. For years

from the beginning of his life. He was gifted
with that excellent nature, called by the wise man,
a good soul, and considered by theologians as one
of the chief signs of predestination, inasmuch as
it is a predisposition to virtue, and facilitates its
acquisition and practice. From this time forth,
those who watched over his soul rejoiced to see
his fear of sin, his docile obedience to his superiors, and his great attraction for *purity, prayer,*
and *charity,* the virtues which were to shine so
brightly in his after life.

During his holidays, John Eudes refreshed his
heart and mind by devoting himself to exercises
of piety. He recalls to our mind St. Francis of
Sales, at the College of Annecy, where his companions used to say, as he drew near, "The saint
is coming, let us be good."

Such was his course till he attained his
eighteenth year, when he began to seek for guidance concerning his future life. He thought there
could be no surer way of gaining light than by
entering the service of Mary in the Sodality
established in her honour amongst the scholars,
where he gave general edification by his gentle
piety, his perfect innocence, and his unfailing
regularity.* From this time, the tender devotion
which he had always had for our Lady grew
deeper and stronger, so that it filled his heart till
the last moment of his life. It is to be seen in
all his writings. His thoughts constantly turned
to the Blessed Virgin. To hear of her glories
made him happy, and soothed his greatest sorrows

he had the privilege of the direction and companionship of those
who had been most closely connected with our holy apostle.
Father Eudes died in 1680; he therefore saw the traces of his
life while they were still recent, and has transmitted to us many
most precious traditions.

* St. Francis of Sales was admitted into the Congregation of
the Blessed Virgin existing among the Jesuits.

and pains.* He promoted devotion to Mary amongst those with whom he came in contact, especially amongst priests, because of their peculiar relation to her. Father Costil† says, "He chose the Blessed Mother of God as his Mother, or rather as his spouse, and that he might never forget her, and might constantly keep this spiritual alliance in mind, he placed a ring on the finger of her image. We learn from his journal,‡ that from that day precious graces were bestowed upon him, and that it was made known to him that his Divine Patroness ratified the alliance."

John Eudes went through his course of rhetoric and of philosophy with the greatest success. "It was not then the custom to make light of this important science, whose object is to lay the first foundations of all belief, to direct the mind in its search for truth, to give those habits of accurate thought and solid reasoning which are a preparation for acting and speaking well, and a safeguard against the sophisms and false judgments which inundate society, and are the source of all kinds of evil. Four years were given to philosophy, and the most competent teachers were chosen to direct the study.§

The four precious years which complete the physical and intellectual development of youth, are now spent, even in the best institutions, in a mere preparation for examinations, whose requirements are so onerous, that, when the candidate is no longer obliged to think of them, nothing is left in his mind, and his profession, with or without a vocation, is irrevocably decided. The sad results of this system are to be seen in the deep distaste

---

* P. Herambourg, vertus du P. Eudes.

† Annales de la Congregation de Jesus et de Marie.

‡ Father Eudes' journal is called "Memorial of God's benefits."

§ Vie de St. François de Sales.

for serious reading so prevalent in France, in the absence of power of resistance, and in the great influence gained by books which pervert all principles of pure morality, and turn history into a wretched romance.

The authentic attestation of Father de la Haye, prefect of the college at Caen, informs us that J. Eudes studied humanities for four years with great distinction, that he went through his course of philosophy, maintained his public theses with general applause, and that during this whole period his general deportment, his uprightness and modesty were most exemplary.*

Despite the representations of his friends, he refused to take his degree; he looked on it as unnecessary, and his only ambition was for the favour of God. Besides which, his humility shrunk from praise, the words of our Saviour, "Woe to you when men shall bless you," filled his soul with fear. *Mihi confusio et ignominia, tibi autem honor et gloria*, was often on his lips, and yet more often in his heart. He wished that he might become as nothing in the sight of all creatures, and that God alone might be seen in him.† His family anxiously looked forward to his return home, and had their own reasons for wishing to keep him far from the honours he so little coveted.

Francis of Sales, the son of a noble in Savoy, followed step by step the directions of his father, who had every reason to hope great things from him. After he had completed his studies at the University of Padua, and received from Pancirola, the celebrated prince of jurisprudence, the ring and the privileges of the university, together with the doctor's crown and cap, he returned to his father's

---

* Annales. '

† P. Herambourg, vertus.

house, and contented himself with the title of advocate of the senate, in which he never took his seat.* He, like John Eudes, had found his vocation, but he kept the precious secret until the moment came when it was God's will that he should make it known to his family.

On John Eudes' return home, he was assailed by prayers not easily to be resisted. The germ of lawful love is to be found in every heart, and a strong vocation was indeed required to silence the voice of passion, and to withstand the entreaties of a mother. But, as we have seen, John had already given his heart and soul to one who never has known, or can know, a rival in beauty and dignity.

Isaac Eudes and Martha Corbin had wished to bring about their son's marriage with a young person whose suitable fortune and good qualities seemed to promise a happy future. But they entreated in vain, and, at last, remembering that John was a present from Heaven, they left him free to follow the designs of Providence, hoping, however, still to keep him with them.†

But John saw very well that the same thing might happen again, and, after having consulted a prudent director, he resolved on entering the ecclesiastical state, and thus securing the vow of chastity, which he had made at the age of fourteen, against any further parental persuasions. A high idea of the priestly state, and of the apostolic life, was the ruling principle of his actions; he used often to say, " The greatest perfection, the most

* Vie de St. François de Sales.

† A similar circumstance is recorded in the Life of St. Francis of Sales. M. de Boisy, his father, in ignorance of his purpose, wished him to marry Mlle. de Suchet, only daughter of the Lord of Végy. He brought Francis to her house, but, notwithstanding his father's reproaches and her great attractions, he remained cold and unmoved. " As for me," he wrote to a friend, " God alone shall be my portion for ever."—(Vie de St. François de Sales.)

exalted holiness, is binding on priests, especially
on such as are called to the direction of souls;
what, then, is to be said of those whose vocation
it is to form priests?" This was his abiding feeling; by virtue of his holy calling, he considered
himself as under an obligation to aim at the
highest perfection.*

Mgr. Le Camus, his bishop, who was consecrated in 1614, and died at Séez in 1650, gave
him, after careful examination, the tonsure and
minor orders, with a firm conviction that the
Church was gaining a valuable servant. His engagement was not yet irrevocable, but to him it
was a step from which no turning back was possible. John Eudes had but one idea, *to strengthen
his vocation.* This included everything, *a desire
to learn, to study theology as thoroughly as possible,
to arm himself for the conflict,* and then *to take the
field* as God might direct him.

He determined to spend three years in preparation, and to lose no time in adopting the mode of
life best suited for the accomplishment of his
purpose.

What do we seek for in a life which is worthy
of record? We have already answered, instruction for posterity. We try to scan the future,
but we too seldom apply to the past for its examples of piety and strength. "What age ever
needed them more?" asks the biographer of St.
Chantal; "where has more feebleness of character
ever been seen? When were weak souls more in
want of the bracing air of such examples?"

It is true that we do meet with many fallen
souls, with many degenerate hearts, impotent even
in evil; yet generous sentiments and noble impulses
have not forsaken the youth of France: We have no
need to despair, for, by the side of those who make

* Constitutions de la Congregation de Jesus et de Marie;
memorial de la Vie Ecclesiastique par le R. P. Eudes.

a parade of their ignorance, their lawlessness, and their idleness, there is another band, often thinned by contagion, yet marching steadfastly on towards the future. Too often the state of society, the overcrowding of all careers, keep many from following that path in life to which they have the strongest attraction. A thirst for the quick and easy gains of hazardous speculation creates a distaste for that serious labour, which, amidst all the varying tendencies of ages, ever remains the great law of humanity. But the other day M. Thiers spoke the following words: "When young men ask for advice from my experience, I answer, *work:* if you are ambitious you will succeed according to the measure of your ability. *Work!* labour will make pleasure sweeter, and grief less bitter to you. *Labour is the greatest blessing God has bestowed upon man.* It is the greatest object to be kept before nations as well as individuals."

Too seldom do we meet with these children or predestination, radiant from the very dawn of their existence with a divine glory which shines on all things near them, showing their wondering teachers and school-fellows how grace can lead all ages to perfection.

CHAPTER II.

1615—1625.

STATE OF SOCIETY IN FRANCE AT THE BEGINNING OF THE SEVENTEENTH CENTURY.—JOHN EUDES' PARENTS PERMIT HIM TO FOLLOW HIS VOCATION.—HE IS ADMITTED INTO THE CONGREGATION OF THE ORATORY, MARCH 1623.—OBJECT OF THIS CONGREGATION.—M. DE BERULLE MAKES HIM PREACH THE WORD OF GOD.—HIS SUCCESS.—HE IS ORDAINED SUB-DEACON ON THE 21ST DECEMBER, 1624, DEACON IN LENT, 1625, AND PRIEST IN THE FOLLOWING DECEMBER.—HIS FIRST MASS.—FRANCIS EUDES DE MEZERAY, AND CHARLES EUDES DU D'HOUAY.

The final decision was made.; henceforth John Eudes bore the marks of Jesus Christ. His future battle-field was already stained by sanguinary religious wars, which continued to rage during part of the XVIIth century. "France had been too long led astray by the charms of novelty, licentiousness had paved the way for heresy. She had fallen from the frivolity of Francis I. to the intrigues of Marie de Medicis; from the weakness of Charles IX. to the wickedness of Henry III., and was on the verge of Protestantism. Happily, she had just awakened from her slumber, and, horror-struck at the abyss open before her, was preparing with characteristic ardour for the great battle between good and evil. The glare of the storm made manifest, not only the greatness of the peril, but the causes which had produced it. People were ignorant of religion, manners were corrupt, institutions in decay, scandals dishonoured the altar and invaded the cloister, prelates without zeal opened the sanctuary to priests without vocation, holy things were despised by the people, because they were profaned by unworthy ministers. Wounds like these could not be hidden; they drew sighs from many hearts, and roused others to a holy jealousy. Councils and assemblies of the clergy were gathered together to provide remedies. The fiery and impassioned harangues of the League were succeeded by preaching equally ardent and popular; but coming from holy lips, and appealing only to men's consciences."*

And now, this hand to hand combat against heresy, ignorance, and corruption, is waged by St. Francis Regis in the Cevennes, by Father Eudes in Normandy, by Michael Noblez in Brittany, by Blessed Peter Fourrier in Lorraine, and by the great Cardinal Duperron in Paris. The Cardinal, with his sword at his side, had preached Mary Stuart's funeral oration, by order of the king, and we see him with surprise already master of a style which did not become general till sixty years later. César de Bus promoted the education of poor children by founding the Congregation of the Fathers of Christian Doctrine, and the Venerable de la Salle's admirable Institution of Brethren was soon to arise, founded on the most perfect rule.

It was necessary to defend every point of the line of battle. Works were said to be of no avail for salvation; Catholics multiplied them a hundred-fold. Thousands of Christians gave up all the pleasures of the world; rich men made themselves poor, changed their costly apparel for serge, broke their knightly swords, and, with the cross in their hands, gathered round the Catholic banner, which the Dominicans, Jesuits, and others had planted on the breach.

It seemed as if the Reformation would have destroyed the monastic life for ever, but it rose

---

* Vie de Ste. Chantal.

from its ruins: everywhere, and under many different forms, it was to be seen, acting, teaching, and consoling; everywhere it resisted heresy *verbis et scriptis;* and many new orders were founded, each one with its own special mission.

Such was the general state of the Church in the beginning of the 17th century, which was destined to heal the deep and fearful wound left to it by its predecessor.

Let us now confine our attention to the general moral condition of the parishes of Normandy, the future scene of Father Eudes' constant and successful labours. Here is to be found the ruling motive of all his important decisions throughout life, and the answer to the many attacks made against him. "The ignorance of the clergy, and the general desolation introduced into the province seventy years before by Calvinism, caused the grossest ignorance among the people, and this in its turn led to a wide-spread corruption, such as will seem hardly credible to posterity. The clergy lived in continual idleness, and disregard of all the rules of external propriety: they dressed like laymen; the poorer among them entered into business, and worked as journeymen; the rich and well-born spent the revenues of their benefices in banquets, play, and other vanities. The people knew nothing of their religion, because sermons were very seldom preached. Aged persons remember the time when morning and evening prayer, and examination of conscience before confession were unknown; when people only went to church for mass on festivals, and considered this practice and abstinence from meat on the prescribed days to be the essentials of Christianity. They went to communion only at Easter, and few confessors deferred absolution even in the case of habitual sinners. The most absurd superstitions gained ground, and the most horrible crimes and most shameful excesses were fearlessly committed."[*]

The pure soul of John Eudes could not but be deeply touched at the contemplation of this sad state of things. He saw that the ecclesiastical order had fallen from its ancient splendour in consequence of the causes we have mentioned, and he resolved to leave his father's house, and to join a new institution which seemed to possess all the advantages he could desire as a priest, while it was exempt from many perils to be met with in the world.

This institution was the Oratory.

The shining virtues of their son had been a source of daily edification to Isaac Eudes and Martha Corbin, but the work that had been going on in his soul was hidden from them, and when he told them of his design, they resolved to prove a vocation which appeared to them too sudden, for they knew not that John's strength of purpose had been gained by constant intercourse with God in holy Communion and in visits to the Blessed Sacrament.

They therefore refused their consent.

But his vocation was so real that it outweighed his hitherto unfailing filial obedience. A few days after this refusal, which he considered irrevocable, he left his home on horseback, but his horse having been ridden more rapidly, and to a greater distance than usual, stopped when he was some leagues beyond Ri, and could not be induced to go any further; John had perhaps reflected on the hastiness of his conduct, he went back to his parents, who were at length convinced, and left him free for the future.[†]

* Annales de la Congregation. (P. Costil.)

† A somewhat similar incident is related in the life of St. Francis of Sales. As he passed through the forest of Sonaz, on his return from Chambéry to Annecy, his horse fell down three times, and three times his sword was loosened from his belt, and

On the 16th of May, 1623, M. Berulle, after due trial, gave John Eudes the ecclesiastical dress, which, although he had received the tonsure, he had not yet adopted, a custom then unhappily too common even among priests. From that day he always wore it, looking on the cassock as an emblem of His Master's death and an image of his own burial.

Again we must pause, for the Congregation of the Oratory claims a few words. It bears the traces of St. Francis of Sales, and we love to dwell on the different points of similarity between his life and that of Father Eudes.

The Duchess of Longueville wished to establish in France Carmelite nuns of the reformed rule, which St. Theresa had introduced in Spain. She invited St. Francis, (at that time coadjutor of Claude de Granier, Bishop of Geneva,) Doctors Duval and Gallemant, and Fathers de Bérulle and Brétigny, to assist her in carrying out this pious project.

The Coadjutor of Geneva and M. de Berulle thus became acquainted, and learned to venerate each other. Francis of Sales, struck by the great clearness and precision of M. de Berulle's mind, urged him to undertake a work which he believed to be greatly needed in France. The training of the clergy was one of the chief objects of his solicitude; he had made many ineffectual efforts for the establishment of a great seminary, and Rome

crossed its sheath so as to form the sign of our salvation. Francis thought that perhaps the moment had now come for following the unvarying attraction which had ruled his heart from childhood. When he reached home he told his mother of his desire to enter holy orders. Mdme. de Boisy believed it to be from God, and had a cassock made ready for him to put on, as soon as his father's consent should be obtained. This was a work of difficulty. M. de Boisy, with all his strength of character, could not resist the sight of his son weeping at his feet. "Do what God requires of you," said he; "who am I to resist Him?" On the 15th of May, 1593, Francis of Sales put on his cassock.—*Historie de St. F. de S.*

had not answered his repeated prayers, but, during his intercourse with M. de Berulle, the idea of a society entirely devoted to the education of the clergy had occurred to his mind. This was the original object of the Congregation of the Oratory.

Many and heterogeneous causes may have promoted the progress of civilization in capitals, but throughout the country, and especially at that period, the clergy were necessarily the chief instruments of its diffusion. It was most needful that their moral tone should be raised, and their sentiments refined. Father Eudes fully understood this necessity, and made it the business of his life to supply it.

Father de Bérulle, founder of the Congregation of the Oratory, was born in 1575, at the Chateau of Sérilly, in Champagne. His father was Claude de Bérulle, councillor in the parliament of Paris, and his mother, Louisa Ségnier, aunt of the chancellor of that name; after her husband's death she entered the Third Order of Franciscans, and ultimately became a Carmelite. Queen Mary of Medicis, with several princesses and great ladies of the court, attended her funeral.

M. de Bérulle is said to have made a vow of chastity at seven years of age. Father Eudes had the same desire at a very early period, though he was not permitted to accomplish it until he was fourteen.

We need not wonder that M. de Bérulle thanked God for having sent him such a neophyte. The holy founder determined on the establishment of a Congregation after the model of that of St. Philip Neri at Rome. St. Francis of Sales, St. Vincent of Paul, and the venerable Cesar de Bus, favoured the project; and it was carried into effect with the approbation of Henry de Gondi, Bishop of Paris, uncle of Paul de Gondi, better known as Cardinal de Retz, whose sister, the Marquise de

Magnetay, had already provided a sum of fifty thousand livres for the foundation.

In 1611, M. de Bérulle gathered several priests together into a community, in the Hotel du Petit Bourbon, faubourg St. Jacques, whose site is now occupied by the Val de Grâce.

The first who joined Father de Bérulle were Father J. Bance and James Gastaud, a doctor of theology of the faculty of Paris, Paul Metezeau, bachelor of the same faculty, Francis de Bourgoing, afterwards General of the Congregation, and Father Cazan, parish priest of Beauvais.

Louis XIII. granted letters patent to the new Congregation, and Pope Paul V. approved it under the title of the Oratory of Jesus, naming Father de Bérulle general.*

When M. de Bérulle asked for the Bull of Institution, the Pope would not allow him to exclude *the instruction of youth in polite literature.* This fact clearly shows the founder's intention ; he did not mean to *establish colleges, nor to undertake their direction.*†

His purpose was to form a society of ecclesiastics, practising evangelical poverty while they retained their possessions, performing the functions of their calling, without seeking benefices or positions about the bishops, to whom, however, they were to be in complete subjection. Some of these ecclesiastics were *associated,* and others *incorporated* to the Congregation. The general was to choose the directors from among the former, the latter belonged to the Congregation only during the time necessary for their train-

* Bulle of Institution of the Oratory, given by Paul V., 1613. "Primum est, ut principale et præcipuum institutum sit, perfectioni statûs sacerdotalis totaliter incumbere......Tertio, sacerdotum et aliorum ad sacros ordines adspirantium instructioni, non tam circa scientiam, quam circa usum scientiæ, ritus et mores, propriæ ecclesiasticos se addicere."—Vie de M. Ollier.

† Vie de M. Ollier.

ing in ecclesiastical life and manners. The study of theology or of profane literature did not enter into the original purpose, which was simply to lead priests to fulfil their holy functions with all possible perfection.

The Oratory was, therefore, a purely ecclesiastical body. This was formally declared by Father de Condren, the worthy successor of Cardinal de Bérulle, at the first general meeting of the Congregation, in the following words : " As the Congregation has been chosen by God, and established on earth, by our late revered father, principally to honour the priesthood of the Son of God, this assembly decides that its condition is purely ecclesiastical, and that it must adhere to the institution of the priesthood, as given by our Lord to His Church, without any addition or omission, so that its subjects can never at any time, or in any future assembly whatever, be obliged by any vows, whether solemn or simple ; and those who may endeavour to bind them by the said simple vows, or who themselves make the said solemn vows, even should they be the majority of the Congregation, are to be considered as separating themselves from its body, and are bound to leave all the houses and temporal goods of the Congregation to those who continue in the merely ecclesiastical and priestly order, even if they should be the minority."*

Here is a precise and positive declaration : we shall have hereafter to use it as a defensive argument ; it shows us clearly what the spirit of the Oratory was ; and this spirit Father Eudes, who left it, gave to his own Congregation.

In the funeral oration, preached by Bossuet, for Father de Bourgoing, third General of the Oratory, he speaks of it as a " Congregation to which its

* Vie de M. Ollier. Notes.

founder wished to give no other spirit but the spirit of the Church, no rules but the holy Canons, no vows but those of Baptism and the Priesthood, no bonds but those of charity."

The fathers of the Oratory afterwards directed a considerable number of schools with success.

Difficulties raised by the Procureur General of the Parliament of Normandy obliged the fathers of the Oratory to make a formal declaration that they were not religious, but merely priests living in community, and in absolute dependance on the Bishops in whose dioceses their houses were established.*

Their principal house was in the Rue St. Honoré; and on the 2nd of October, 1629, their founder died there, at the age of 54, while saying Mass in the Oratory Church: he sank down as he pronounced those words of the Canon, " Hanc igitur oblationem." Being unable to complete the sacrifice as *priest*, he completed it as *victim*.

> " Capta sub extremis neques dùm sacra Sacerdos
> Perficere, ac saltem Victima perficiam."

Cardinal de Bérulle, (as we see from the missive letters of Richelieu,) was often employed in important negotiations. On several occasions he served as an intermediary between Mary de Medicis and her son Louis XIII., he was also sent to Rome to obtain the dispensations necessary for the marriage of the Prince of Wales, afterwards Charles I., with Henrietta of France, he accompanied her to England, and there won universal esteem and veneration.

The Congregation of the Oratory, which was suppressed in 1790, was re-established in Paris in 1853, by Father Pététot, under the title of the Oratory of the Immaculate Conception. Many dis-

* Ordres Monastiques, l'Oratoire.

tinguished men have belonged to this Congregation;
amongst others we may name Malebranche, Massillon, Mascaron, Niceron, La Blatterie, Fonce-
mayne, and Dotteville; but in course of time it
was tainted by Jansenism, and its latter end was
less glorious than its beginning.

These details are necessary to throw light on
the path we have to follow. We must, so to
speak, enter the Oratory with John Eudes, endeavouring, according to Fénélon's directions, *to take
his portrait from nature, to represent him as he
was at all ages, and in all the principal circumstances of his life.*

Happily he had found his vocation; he possessed the virtue of *fortitude* in a very high
degree; it was, in fact, the distinguishing virtue
of his character, it inspired all his undertakings,
made him follow throughout life one undeviating
course, it was the secret of his mission, and the
true reason of his appearance in the XVIIth century.

It made the practice of every spiritual exercise
belonging to his holy calling easy to him. Father
de Bérulle and his immediate directors were soon
surprised at his rare fitness for that calling, and
we have abundant proof that in his case fortitude
was accompanied by tenderness and prudence, in
the fact that the good opinion of his superiors was
shared by the whole community, and no jealousy
was felt by any of its members on seeing the
youngest of their number become the favourite
child of Father de Bérulle. This wise general
thought it well to bring forward a disciple whose
mind was so strong and character so stable; therefore, although he was only twenty-four, and still in
minor orders, he made him preach the word of
God publicly. The hopes of his master were
fully satisfied, and the zeal and dignity with which

he acquitted himself of this duty gave promise of his future success.

Similar reasons induced Mgr. de Granier to appoint St. Francis of Sales, while also in minor orders, to preach in the Cathedral on the Feast of the Blessed Sacrament.

And now the eagle's wings were fully grown, and he was about to soar to the highest regions, and to descend and seize with his powerful talons the evil which was devouring society like a contagious leprosy. Natural eloquence, which the habit of preaching improved, was accompanied in Father Eudes by those exterior advantages which assist an orator's talent; he was well-made, and had that imposing air which, as time goes on, becomes venerable; his action was easy, and his voice good. But, above all, he, like St. Francis of Sales, was himself an image of all the virtues he recommended to his audience. Is not this ever one of the chief conditions of success?

In the month of December, 1624, Father Eudes went to Seez, where, on the 21st of the month, he was ordained sub-deacon by Mgr. de Camus. In the Lent of 1625, Mgr. d'Angennes, Bishop of Bayeux, ordained him deacon, and in the following December he was admitted to the priesthood, by Mgr. Boivin, Bishop of Tars, and coadjutor to Mgr. de Pericard, Bishop of Avranches. John Eudes had then completed his 24th year. He had spent a whole year in preparation for the priesthood, with a fervour which increased with every bond that drew him closer to the altar. He was more than ever impressed with his own nothingness, and therefore in his first Mass, which he said the night before Christmas day, in a chapel dedicated, as he remarked, to the Blessed Virgin, he seemed to be quite filled with God, and with the holiness of the Sacrifice he was offering. Sweet consolations and never-to-be-forgotten graces were granted to him on this occasion.

Henceforth, the light that had shewn him the excellence of the holy Mass led him to unreserved devotion. "We should need," he said, "three eternities to say Mass aright; the first, to *prepare for it*, the second, to *say it*, and the third, to make our thanksgiving for it.*

Father Hérambourg tells us that one of the graces he most earnestly asked of God, was to be able to say Mass every day of his life. He was not like some who feel full of zeal the first time they have this great honour, but whose ardour grows cold as it becomes familiar to them. Notwithstanding his grievous illnesses, his toilsome journeys, the overwhelming amount of business which occupied him, he hardly ever failed to satisfy his devotion. He knew what purity is required of the hands that offer the Immaculate Host, and of the heart that receives It, therefore, before hearing or saying Mass, he used with the deepest humility to confess all the sins of his life inwardly to God and the angels and saints. We can scarcely enter into the fervour with which he offered the Holy Sacrifice, his desires were unbounded, they were inflamed with love. We read, (Fleurs. L. 2. §§ 21.) that "Father Eudes could not understand how any priest could hurry through his Mass." One day he observed that a member of the Congregation had said it in a quarter of an hour; he could not conceal his indignation, and said, in presence of the whole community, without, however, naming the offender, that "unless he amended, one or other of them must leave the Congregation; for that it was enough to make him die of grief to see his Master served so badly."†

* Vertus du P. Eudes, note du P. Le Doré.

† Père Herambourg, vertus du P. Eudes. Fleurs de la Congrégation.

He also considered the act of serving at Mass as most honourable, and used to say that it was sharing the office of the Mother of God, of St. Joseph, and St. Gabriel, who ministered to our Lord while He was on earth, and that the same Sacrament which was instituted to give Priests grace to offer the Sacrifice, was also intended to give grace and dignity to those who serve.*

He was very anxious that people should hear Mass with befitting modesty. He once said Mass at Versailles, before Louis XIV.; the King knelt devoutly, but those about him stood. When he came to the offertory, the holy apostle thought it well to congratulate his Majesty on the respect which he showed to the King of Kings, before Whom all earthly Sovereigns are but dust, and added: "But, Sire, I am astonished to see that while you are performing your religious duties so perfectly, and worshipping God with so much humility, those around you are behaving in a very different manner." The courtiers were thunder-struck, every one became reverent, especially when the King began to turn round to see who were standing.†

Such were the deep and holy impressions which the young Priest's first Mass left in his heart.

St. Francis of Sales was admitted to the priest-hood at the age of 26. Some one said to him afterwards, that the Altar does not make the priest impeccable; but that he may be overcome by failings after receiving orders as he was before. "Those who speak in such a manner," he answered, "little know what it is to be a priest, to handle and receive the Body of Christ daily; no one is worthy of the name of priest, who is not as pure as an angel."

* Vertus du P. Eudes.

† Annales de la Congregation.

We must not completely lose sight of the two
brothers, who are associated with Father Eudes in
the honours paid by a populace grateful for their
good deeds, or proud of their glory.

While John was beginning to preach in Paris,
Francis and Charles were growing up beneath
their father's roof; there was but one year between them, for Francis was born in 1610, and
Charles in 1611. No doubt John, who was to
evangelize so many districts, cast the good seed
into these young hearts. He must have spent at
least two years at home with them. "Be this as
it may," says M. Levavasseur, in his notice of
the three brothers, "Francis soon left home and
went to Caen, to pursue those studies which afterwards led him, by a very different path from his
elder brother, to far greater glory and renown."

It is but too true that John Eudes, bravo
champion, holy priest, eloquent missionary as he
was, had no glory in this world : like Jesus he was
buffeted and calumniated. This gives a peculiar
character to his life ; when we speak of what
touches him personally, we have to relate constant
suffering. But it is this specially that makes us
love him with all the love that a biographer can
bear to a saint.

It seems probable that Charles accompanied his
brother, and after completing his education, returned home, and studied medicine and surgery
under his father, who no doubt laid the foundation of the devotion and self-sacrifice by which
he was hereafter distinguished. Father Costil
tells us, in the annals of the Congregation, that
Charles Eudes du d'Houay, served for some time
with the army, and then practised medicine at
Argentan. Possibly he may have been one of the
surgeons appointed to regiments by Cardinal de
Richelieu, in 1629, when he gave to each regiment
a hospital and a chaplain.

It is certain that he settled permanently at Argentan, and left a posterity which has now become very numerous, and is represented by the families of *Mallevoue, Le Cousturier, de Beaulaincourt, Chappe d'Auteroche, d'Achon, de Montzey,* and *de la Porte.*

Of Father Eudes' sisters, Mary is the only one whose descendants are still living; she is represented by the family of *Lautour* of Argentan.

CHAPTER III.

1625—1632.

POLITICAL MOVEMENTS.—RICHELIEU.—FATHER JOSEPH.—AUSTERITIÉS OF FATHER EUDES.—HIS ILLNESS.—RETREAT AT THE SEMINARY OF OUR LADY OF AUBERVILLIERS.—STUDIES DURING THIS RETREAT.—THE PLAGUE IN FRANCE.—AT ECOUCHE.—SELF-DEVOTION OF FATHER EUDES AND OF FATHER LAURENS, PARISH PRIEST OF ST. CHRISTOPHE.— THE PLAGUE AT ARGENTAN, FATHER EUDES HASTENS THERE. —THE PLAGUE AT CAEN.—HEROIC CHARITY OF FATHER EUDES.—HE TAKES UP HIS ABODE AMONGST THE PLAGUE-STRICKEN.—THE SAINT'S MEADOW.—THE PLAGUE IN THE HOUSE OF THE ORATORY AT CAEN.—ILLNESS OF FATHER EUDES.—LETTER FROM THE CARMELITES AT CAEN.—FRANCIS EUDES DE MEZERAY, CHARLES EUDES DU D'HOUAY.

John Eudes, Jerôme Vignier, J. F. Senault, afterwards General of the Oratory, and other distinguished members of that celebrated Congregation, were preparing themselves for future conflicts, not merely by a profound study of theology, but also by a study of the public with whom they would have to deal, and of the means best adapted to convince and convert them, and by trying their strength in the pulpit.

When Henri IV. was suddenly removed from

the world in which he had played so conspicuous a part, the supreme power devolved upon the Queen, whose party was naturally hostile to the Protestants. The Duke of Sully was recalled with expressions of favour: he consented to remain in office, but his fellow-Protestants bitterly lamented the King's death, and organized themselves for the defence of the rights conceded to them by the Edict of Nantes. Philip de Mornay, the most ardent champion of the Reformation, exclaimed: "Let there be amongst us no more talk of Huguenots and Papists; these names are forbidden by our edicts...we must have but one badge; whoever is a good Frenchman, is to be looked on as a good citizen, and a brother."*......
Such were his words in public, but when he opened his heart in private, he said: "I fear that we shall be like brothers, who, after their father's death, fall on each other's necks, and weep together, but when the first grief is over, return to their old quarrels, and are ready to come to blows for a dollar."† The forebodings of Henri IV.'s old comrade were correct, but even his experience could not yet guess who was to prove the most formidable enemy of the reformation. The consideration with which it was at present treated, seemed to his mind the sign of a coming tempest. The clerical body, wishing to overcome by persuasion, was now deeply occupied in study, and Richelieu was silently becoming great. He had been originally destined to the profession of arms, but had received holy orders, and at the age of twenty-two was consecrated Bishop of Luçon. He was deputy to the States General in 1614, and attracted the notice of the Queen and the Marechal d'Ancre. In 1615, the Queen made

---

* Assemblée du 19 Mai, 1616.

† Bazin.

him her chaplain, and in 1616 caused him to be appointed Secretary of State for War and for the Interior.

In 1617 he accompanied the Queen-mother, (then out of favour,) to Blois, probably with the tacit consent of the king, and afterwards he succeeded in the delicate mission of bringing about a reconciliation between them. By his influence the treaty of Augoulême was concluded in 1620, and that of Angers in 1621; he received the Cardinal's hat in 1622, became a member of Council in 1623, having left all his rivals, and especially old Villeroi, at a distance. He ultimately became Prime Minister, and under a king like Louis XIII., almost absolute master of the destinies of France.

This minister was unquestionably one of the greatest who have ever governed France.

He pursued his course with one aim ever in view, ruthlessly bearing down all obstacles; that aim was to destroy the power of the nobles, to crush heresy, at least as a party in the realm, and to bring down the greatness of the house of Austria.

He appears from afar like a brilliant meteor, a giant form which we cannot measure; and we may not venture to condemn or to acquit him.

In the course of this history we shall have to mention one of his most active and trustworthy agents, who has been invested with a kind of legendary interest under the name of his grey eminence. Father Joseph, (Francis Le Clerc de Tremblay,) became celebrated under a religious habit, though he probably would have remained unknown if he had merely followed the career which lay before him as a nobleman. Imagination has made of him a kind of familiar demon or evil genius; all sorts of crimes have been laid to his charge; romance has taken hold of his life and stained it with blood. This is a calumny, and if there is anything more infamous than calumny against the living, it is calumny against the dead, who can no longer answer it.* Father Joseph was a man of counsel and of action, whom Richelieu often employed in most important affairs, and who was devoted to the minister long before he had reached the summit of power.

Chastity and mortification are sisters. Father Eudes was chaste, and mortified to the highest degree. He had a peculiar love for chastity; he lived an angelic life in a human body, and his very flesh became spiritualized; it was, as Tertullian says of virgin bodies, angelidata caro. He ever guarded this hidden treasure with a kind of shame-facedness and modesty. He feared the very shadow of impurity more than hell itself; and he closed the doors of his heart against this monster, by complete mortification of the senses, especially that of sight; he would not look at women, even when he spoke to them. He never transgressed the rules of temperance, and recommended it as the surest means of preservation from temptations of the flesh. Not only did he sometimes deny himself necessaries, but he inflicted strange mortifications on his body. "This miserable body," he would often say, "will do

* Letter from Richelieu to Father Joseph, end of April, 1624. (Missive Letters of the Cardinal.) "As you are the principal agent whom God has made use of to lead me to my present honours, I feel bound to give you the first news of them, and to tell you that the king has been pleased, at the queen's request, to appoint me his prime minister; at the same time, I beg you to hasten your journey, and to come as soon as possible to share with me the conduct of affairs; there are important matters, which I will not entrust to any one else, nor decide without your opinion. Come quickly, therefore, and receive the testimony of the great esteem which Cardinal de Richelieu has for you." Father Joseph was then a friend from the first, and not one of those tools whom a tyrant always finds ready, and with whom Father Eudes would never have treated of the concerns of religion.

3

nothing if it is not well cared for, and often refreshed. This wretched carcase gives me a great deal of trouble." Such complaints were made when he was obliged to take any food more strengthening than usual. He practised every kind of penance. Father Hérambourg tells us that from his sixteenth or seventeenth year he constantly watched and fasted, took the discipline, used a hair-shirt and iron chain. He continued these practices till he was past forty, and with so much severity that his health was ruined and his life endangered. His directors were obliged to restrain his rigour, that he might be able to undertake the work of missions. He was absolutely commanded to take care of his health, because God wanted him as an instrument to promote His glory.

In the midst of his labours Father Eudes had a long illness, resulting in some measure from excessive austerities. Experience taught him the necessity of moderating his fervour, not merely for his own sake, but for the sake of those who might at a future time be placed under his direction.

It was thought that his native air would be the best remedy, but he derived no benefit from it, and was sent to the seminary of our Lady of Aubervilliers. This was a celebrated place of pilgrimage, in the neighbourhood of Paris, and the seminary there was one of the first houses given to the Oratory.*

* The pilgrimage to our Lady of Virtues at Aubervilliers, owes its origin to a miraculous picture of the Blessed Virgin, which attracted multitudes as early as the year 1338. Philip de Valois and his queen, the Duke of Alencon, Count d'Estampes and many other persons of consideration visited it, and left tokens of their munificence. Many miracles were worked there, which gave it the name of our Lady of Virtues, miracles in the XIVth century being called virtues. In order to provide a sufficient number of clergy for the needs of the pilgrims to Aubervilliers, the spiritual charge of the town was given to the priests

The two years which he spent at Aubervilliers were devoted to a profound study of the Holy Scriptures; his method is worthy of notice, because, as he told many of his disciples, it gave him a clear insight into his subject. After prostrating himself before his crucifix, and imploring the Holy Spirit to give him light, he remained on his knees as long as his strength permitted. In this humble position, which he did not willingly change, he read the sacred text straight through, without making use of translation or commentary. When he met with passages easy to be understood, he did his best to fix the facts, the meaning, the proofs, and even the very expressions used by the inspired writers in his mind, endeavouring, at the same time, to foresee the different occasions on which they might be turned to account for his own benefit or the instruction of others.*

Was not this storing up treasure for the future? Studies of this kind are most important to an orator, and they gave Father Eudes such ease in speaking, and such power of reasoning, that he was never at a loss, and was able to speak often, and at length, without exhausting his subject.

But he was even more admirable when he met with those obscure points which seem to be covered with an impenetrable veil; instead of exalting his own reason above the question, he humbled himself before God, and worked on with calmness and entire confidence in Him who gives light so freely when the soul is not blinded by pride.

We shall not be understood by all, certainly not by those who are wearying themselves in a useless

of the Oratory. The Seminary of St. Sulpice used to go there in a body on Whitsun Tuesday; this custom was abolished in 1629, but many of the ecclesiastics of that house still perform the pilgrimage during their vacation.—(Vie de M. Ollier, notes.)

* Père Montigny.

pursuit of the unknown. We, in our simplicity, possess this unknown, for our faith is founded on the acts of Jesus Christ, on the writings of the Fathers of our ancient·Church, who, before everything was made clear to them, had also their doubts and cruel·uncertainties, but those doubts were the secret of their cells, and when at length they spoke to the world, it was to declare truths which will remain unmoved through time and eternity.

And now we have theories, always theories. Woe to those who would tamper with the faith which our children have learned at their mother's knees, but which they may not perhaps be able to hand down to their descendants. Woe to them, for the Father of the family raises His hand to curse them. But let no one fear that we shall remain behindhand. Our Church cannot grow old: she ever is, she ever will be young and active; she would have her children march onwards, she would have them explore the fields of science, she applauds their victories, she·blames the laggards.

Father Eudes was restored to health. He is no longer to remain in apparent inaction; he is to work, to earn the praise which has just been bestowed upon him. " Pertransiit benefaciendo." The soldier is about to take the field.

"During the fearful plague which, towards the end of 1628, fell upon France, Savoy, Piedmont, Italy, and the whole world, and continued its terrible ravages during the three following* years, the supernatural power of grace and the marvellous spiritual transformations of which we have given a faint picture, were seen in all their glory.

"The epidemics of the XIXth century can give

* Details which we shall give regarding the plague in Normandy, prove that it began in 1627.

no idea of what the plague was in those days.
The want of cleanliness in towns, the entire insufficiency of remedial measures, the absence of a
regular police capable of restoring some degree of
order in the midst of the general confusion, the
contagious nature of the malady, (which was considered even more contagious than it really was,)
combined to increase at once mortality, fear and
despair.

"People were afraid to see anyone, or touch
anything, for the plague was communicated by
the touch or the breath of the sufferer, and anything that had come in contact with him might
transmit it. Towns were forsaken, and for months
together became like deserts; the grass grew in
the streets, and great bands of wolves ranged
through them, attracted by the odour of the un-
buried corpses.†

This scourge had visited France several times
since 1585, and though religious foundations had
been interrupted more or less, a greater number
of souls had been brought back to the true faith
by each visitation, than would have been won by a
hundred preachers in a century.

The record of the heroic devotion of Father
Eudes shews us that even in 1627 the plague had
reached some parts of the rich province of Normandy, where so many now go in the beautiful
summer days to seek the health and strength that
has been impaired by worldly pleasure, instead of
by the austerities to which he so nearly fell a
victim.

On learning that the plague had reached Ecouché, and was drawing near to the place of his
birth, but one thought took possession of the
young priest's breast; he longed to brave all dangers, that he might give the sick courage to en-

† Abbé Bougaud. Histoire de Ste. Chantal.

dure, and provide as far as possible for their necessities.

Father de Berulle consented to his departure, imposing only one condition, that he should take every prudent precaution consistent with the exercise of his perilous ministry. Father de Berulle desired Father Allard, Superior of the Oratory at Caen,* to direct his movements, and he accordingly gave him a letter to the vicar-general of the Bishop of Seez, requesting him, in the bishop's absence, to give him the necessary faculties for that diocese. Before leaving Paris Father Eudes had provided himself with a portable altar and all other things needed for the celebration of the Holy Sacrifice. The faculties were readily granted, and he lost no time in going where the plague was at the worst.

In our military archives we give the first place to those written orders which may be called death-warrants; and which the French officer always receives with a calm heart and a smiling countenance, though he little knows whether he shall ever return from the peril which he must meet. Side by side with those orders we might lay that which Father Costil has transmitted to us containing Father Allard's letter to the Vicar-general of Seez. The original is in Latin, and we give a translation. "In accordance with the orders of our Rev. Father General, I, the undersigned, priest of the Congregation of the Oratory, and superior of the house at Caen, testify that our well-beloved John Eudes, priest of the diocese of Seez, and highly esteemed in our Congregation, has always, in your neighbourhood and amongst ourselves, been adorned by virtues, science, modesty, and purity of manners, that his life has

* The Oratory at Caen was established on the 10th June 1622. M. and Mdme. de Repichon founded it in Rue Guillebert.

been edifying, and that he is impelled to go to
you solely by Christian charity, by a desire for the
glory of God and the salvation of souls.

"These things considered, the care and instruction of the faithful may safely be entrusted to
him, as well as the office of preaching the word of
God, and the administration of the Sacraments,
especially in those places where the present misery
and the plague cause a deficiency of priests, (in
his locis maximè, ubi pro temporum calamitate et
epidemiæ morbo desunt et absunt sacerdotes). We
could not withstand his earnest and repeated entreaties for this favour, and now make them known
to your wisdom. The order of charity required
that his talents should be employed in the service
of that province where he received life, grace, and
ordination, and that his own diocese should be
the first to gather the fruits that may be expected
from his ability, his piety, his wisdom, his work
and his life. We who are your servants in Christ,
after having given him our blessing, take the
liberty of sending him to you, that he may receive
from you one greater and more abundant, which
will enable him to provide for the wants of his
people and of yours also, if occasion require. As
he will freely give everything in his power, we
hope you will not refuse him what is necessary.

"Given at Caen, the 13th of August, in the year
1627.*

"ALLARD."

Furnished with this favourable certificate, to
which we shall have occasion again to refer, Father
Eudes immediately obtained from the Vicar-general of Seez powers for exercising his ministry in
all parts of the diocese.

The panic was general, and the minister of the

---

* This date fixes the time of the beginning of the plague.

plague-stricken was dreaded as they were. No gentleman or priest would give him lodging. To use Father Hérambourg's words, "He was like his Master, who when He left His throne of glory to comfort men and deliver them from their infirmities, was shamefully rejected by them : *In propria venit et sui eum non receperunt.*" After the example of his Saviour, he had devoted himself to the service of all men ; he considered that nothing belonged to him any more than to a slave ; that he had no right to make any use of himself, to employ his body or soul, his means, his time or his life, except for Jesus Christ and His members.* No difficulty was able to daunt him. A single priest, however, Father Laurent, of St. Christophe, offered to share with him his small remaining means, and to assist him in his labours. At this time all business was at a standstill, the markets were closed, and those whom the plague had spared were suffering from famine. We read in the history of this period, that the monasteries were the only houses in the towns whose inhabitants remained in them, and that they were often destitute of food and medicine, and deprived of confessors.

The heroic charity of Father Eudes was only equalled by that of his companion, whose name has happily been handed down to us. For two months they went to and fro through the infected parishes of St. Pierre, St. Martin, Vrigny, Avoines and others. Like the High Priest Aaron, who went forth, with his censor in his hand, between the living and the dead, Father Eudes passed from one scene of misery to another, under the protection of the Body of Christ, veiled in the most Holy Sacrament, which he bore in a pyx round his neck. Thus the saint of Savoy travelled

---

* P. Herambourg. Vertus.

throngh a country laid waste by heresy, to give the sacraments to the few Catholics who had escaped the fury of the Bernese. And like him again, Father Eudes and Father Laurent drew the great courage and never-failing strength which made them insensible to danger from the Holy Sacrifice of the Mass.

From the altar of the neighbouring chapel of St. Euroult, they went from cabin to cabin, from hut to hut, to the poor forsaken sufferers, who looked on them as angels come from heaven.

In the fulfilment of their arduous and self-chosen task, they not only did all that ardent zeal could do for the salvation of souls, but they bestowed on the sick all the temporal assistance that their diligent charity could command. They both forgot their own danger: we know, indeed, how little the wisest precautions often avail in such a case, but God preserved them. Soon the plague ceased: it had lasted from the month of August to the Feast of All Saints, and we cannot but attribute its cessation to the labours and fervent prayers of these two devoted men.

Father Eudes was soon engaged in similar labours at Argentan, where the plague had broken out; he advised the citizens to put their town for ever under the protection of our Lady, by a public and solemn consecration. They did so, and soon experienced the effects of her power with God. He made them place the image of the Mother of the Afflicted at each of their gates, and it was still to be seen there in 1778.*

All danger being at length at an end, Father Eudes considered his further presence as uncalled for, and bidding farewell to his faithful and virtuous companion in arms, he returned to Paris to receive further orders from his superior. He

* Vertus. Note du P. Le Doré.

arrived there about the time of All Saints, 1627,
and was soon sent to Caen, where for three years
he spared no pains in bringing the people back to
the Sacraments, in teaching them and preaching
the Word of God daily.

The plague had remained for some time latent,
but in 1631 it suddenly seized with fury on the
town of Caen, and God permitted it to make
terrible havoc.   On its first appearance efforts
were made to prevent its further spread by the
complete isolation of those who were stricken.
The despair of these wretched beings may be more
easily imagined than described.   Nothing but
heroic, heaven-born charity could save them, and
fear had paralyzed all the noblest feelings of
nature.

But Father Eudes soon appeared; most of the
inhabitants had already seen him in the pulpit,
they were now to know him by his deeds.   He
met his old enemy face to face.   His friends
vainly tried to dissuade him from encountering
a danger, which in our days the noblest women in
France have dared to defy.   But none of their
arguments could meet that which he used at once
as an answer and a justification: "What have I
to fear? am not I the strongest, for I am quite
full of corruption, and more evil than the plague
itself?"   This argument was wondrously plausi-
ble; for he feared for his dear companions the
perils which he made light of when he himself
was concerned.   "Did you not know," answered
St. Francis of Sales, when his father begged him
not to expose himself to the violence of the heretics, "did you not know, that I must be entirely
occupied about my heavenly Father's interests?"

Father Eudes, therefore, left his brethren, and
their farewells must have been solemn, for he was
going into the very jaws of death.   His only lodging was a cask, which he had rolled into a meadow

near the Abbey of the Trinity. This place was lately known as the *Saint's field*. In like manner St. Athanasius, Patriarch of Antioch, lived for four months in a tomb, that the friends who had offered him shelter might not be exposed to the danger of persecution from the emperor's emissaries, who were then searching for him.

The young Oratorian devoted his whole days, and a part of his nights, to the care and consolation of the sick, cheering their miserable abode as if by a heavenly light. He only returned to his strange and humble abode when nature positively asserted her rights. Worn out as he was with fatigue and hunger, it would have been impossible for him to procure even the coarsest food, if Providence had not provided for him. Mdme. de Budos,* abbess of the Trinity, sent the necessary provisions every day, and probably in sufficient quantity to enable him to share with the poor. This was a great act of charity, at a time when every one was in want. Father Costil had these facts from a nun of the Abbey of the Trinity, at Caen, who repeated them again in a letter to Father Hérambourg.

While Father Eudes was himself preserved unscathed in the midst of the dying and the dead, he heard that notwithstanding all the precautions taken by the fathers, the plague had reached the house of the Oratory; all the inmates were attacked. Nothing less could have torn the holy priest from his poor; he now shut himself up

---

* Laurence de Budos, daughter of the Visconti de Portes, was a member of one of the most illustrious families in the kingdom. Henry IV., at the request of the Constable of Montmorency, her uncle, gave her the Abbey of the Trinity at Caen, when she was thirteen years of age. When she had attained the required age, she received the habit from Mdme. d'Aumale, at the monastery of Chelles, went to her Abbey, and reformed it thoroughly. She died there, in the odour of sanctity, on the 13th of June, 1650, aged 66.

with his brethren, and lavished on them all the care to which all his dearly-bought experience gave such value. He saved them all except Father Répichon, the superior, and one other father, both of whom died in his arms.

He was not without consolations in the midst of his labours and fatigues. An old Protestant was struck down by the plague; Father Eudes was soon at his bed-side, giving him encouragement and support, notwithstanding the moral gulf which separated them. The sufferer was touched by such generosity, more than he might perhaps have been by the most eloquent words; he abjured his errors, made his confession to his charitable benefactor, and died a most sincere Catholic. It is believed that this convert was the first whom Father Eudes had the happiness of receiving.

Although he had been so miraculously preserved from contagion, he almost fell a victim to an illness which the natural delicacy of his constitution made more dangerous, especially as it came after he had undergone so many privations. He thought his last hour was at hand, but God still wanted His servant, and gave him back to the fervent prayers of the Carmelites, the Benedictines, and, it may be, of many other unknown and grateful suppliants.*

His self-devotion had been like that of St. Francis of Sales during the ravages of the plague at Annecy in 1599, and during his illness he, like that saint, was more than resigned; he fervently

---

* St. Francis of Sales being dangerously ill while he was studying at Padua, his tutor, M. Déage thought it right to tell him that perhaps he would soon be called to appear before God, the holy youth exclaimed:

"Sive me mori, Christe jubes,
Seu vivere mavis;
Dulce mihi tecum vivere
Dulce mori."
Vie de St. Fs. de Ss. de 1586 à 1590.

longed to go to the Master whom he had served so well. But he feared that the powerful prayers of the pious Carmelites at Caen would deprive him of that happiness. They knew it, and nothing can be more touching than the letter which they wrote to him when his illness was at the worst. " Very Reverend Father, We have heard that you are much afraid lest we should snatch you out of God's hands. O, no! do not fear anything of the kind. Our charity towards you is not so small.... We do not pray *absolutely* for the continuation of your life, but only for whatever may be for the greater glory of our dear and only beloved Jesus... ......If Jesus Christ still wishes to be glorified in and by you in this vale of tears, there is no help for it, father, you must have patience ; if you were at the very gate of heaven, and about to enter, *we would still bring you back.*"......

Father Eudes had reason to fear these holy virgins, who beatified him beforehand, by begging him with beautiful simplicity, if he should die, to " bear their greetings to the Blessed Virgin, to their mother St. Theresa, to St. Joseph, their Blessed Father, and to all their friends and relations."

Does not the preservation of his life from 1627 to 1631 seem like a miracle ?

With returning health his ardent desire to devote himself immediately and without reserve to his neighbours' salvation also returned. His love for his neighbour was of that kind which had both bonds and wings, which sometimes arrests the steps of apostolic men, and sometimes makes them fly. At first it had led him to seek the solitude of his cell and his oratory, that he might be filled with the Spirit of God ; afterwards it led him forth to sow the seed of the Gospel in many provinces. He had the zeal of which St. Chry-

sostom speaks, a zeal which enables a man to undertake everything for the glory of God.

"His zeal," says Father Hérambourg, "was
immense in action, and courageous in enterprise.
He considered every opportunity of working for
the salvation of souls infinite in value, and would
have blamed himself much if he had neglected a
single one." Such he was already, and such he
ever continued to be.

As soon as he had recovered, he wished to give
missions in the towns and country places. His
motto was *Verba et acta.* His superiors could
not refuse him permission to give himself up to a
work for which his persuasive powers so eminently
qualified him.

The poor peasants were, as we have said, in the
greatest need of ardent words like his, for they
had been beset for sixty years by the temptations
of the Reformation, and their ignorant and care-
less pastors did little for their guidance or edification.

"Believe me," said St. Francis of Sales, "there
can never be enough preaching: *nunquam satis
dicitur quod numquam satis dicitur;* and especially
now in presence of heresy, which only holds its
ground by preaching, and can only be overcome by
preaching."

Father Eudes became a missionary.

The parish of Ri is at no great distance from
Ecouché, and all the other places where the son
of Isaac Eudes and Martha Corbin had become
so well known by his devoted labours in 1627.
Perhaps the old physician may have met him beneath the roof of the plague-stricken, and while
his heart was wrung with cruel anxiety at the dangers to which he was exposed, he must also have
rejoiced that he was the father of so holy a son.
Again, in 1631 his devotion to the people of Caen
must have reached the ears of his family, and

doubtless often formed the topic of their fireside talk.

Let us take up the history of his two brothers. As M. Levavasseur remarks, "When simple parents give their children a superior education, it does not tend to acclimatize them to their home, and so the ambitious Francis, when he was hardly grown up, left the modest hamlet in the parish of Ri, and went to seek his fortune in Paris, taking with him from his native place nothing but the name of *Mezeray*, of which we have already spoken, and which was more likely to make a favourable impression on the great men and wits of the capital, than his simple patronymic.*

He gave to this name much more than it gave him ; a stern and noble lesson to those who, despising that of their forefathers, alter it or give it up, and die insolvent debtors to their usurped honours. At Paris, Francis Eudes de Mezeray found the Abbot des Yveteaux, brother of Francis of Vauquelin, Lord of Ri, Baron of Sassy and other places. He naturally sought his protection ; the Abbot had been tutor to the Dauphin, and by his influence Mezeray obtained the appointment of army commissary. He followed the army in two campaigns, of which as historian he preserved the record.†

We shall soon meet Charles Eudes du d'Houay, at Argentan, following John's example of sublime self-devotion.

---

* Three spots in the commune of Ri still bear the name of Mezeray ; a field, a paddock, and a common which is divided into several lots. The hamlet of d'Houay is in the same commune.

† Richelieu wrote thus in May 1624 to the Abbot des Yveteaux, whose house was but a doubtful school of manners : " You are so well accustomed to steer your course through this world, that I receive the intelligence you have sent me as coming from one who is able to judge of the future by the past."

CHAPTER IV.

1632—1641.

Father Eudes was now to devote himself to
the ministry of preaching; this work inevitably
involved great bodily fatigue at a period when
regular means of communication were us rare as
great roads, and the smaller roads were often impracticable. Future generations will never know
the difficulties of all kinds, and the immense loss
of time attendant on travelling in those days.
But Father Eudes feared no amount of trouble or
labour, and determined to go wherever his presence seemed necessary. Convinced that God had
called him to preach His word, he took up for his
motto the apostle's words: "*Væ mihi, si non*

evangelizavero;" " Wo is unto me if I preach not the Gospel."[*]

" Eudes preached sufficiently well for an age in which pulpit eloquence had not reached its present standard; his talent caused him to be sought after, and his Congregation gained by it."[†]

To form an idea of the state of eloquence in the beginning of the 17th century, one must read the sermons of that time, which are full of conceits and plays upon words.[‡]

Father Eudes' great glory is to have been "one of those rugged Norman husbandmen, who broke fresh ground and cleared away brambles and gaudy weeds; one of the brave apostles who prepared, and founded and inaugurated the 17th century.[§] The testimony of Mgr. Camus, Bishop of Belley, with regard to Father Eudes' eloquence, may be looked on as unprejudiced.

This old friend of St. Francis of Sales had retired to the Oratory at Caen, and after having heard a sermon by the young preacher, he felt his own apostolic zeal revive, and thought that he could produce a far more striking effect by the employment of those flowers of rhetoric which Father Eudes rejected as useless. To his great surprise his audience seemed unmoved. Mgr. Camus soon confessed that his rival was right,

* Annales de la Congregation, P. Costil.

† Dictionnaire historique, 1789.

‡ Mgr. Camus, Bishop of Belley, was fonder of preaching than of hearing confessions, but his sermons did not satisfy St. Francis of Sales. He recommended him to make a more sparing use of the riches of his imagination, and of the flowers of rhetoric; to give Catechism, retreats, and subjects for meditation in preference to grand discourses. " I fear," said he, " that your flowers will not bear fruit; it is time to prune your vineyard, and to free it from irrelevant ornaments, *tempus putationis advenit :* it is well to use the vessels of Egypt for the decoration of the tabernacle, but it must be with moderation.—*Spirit of St. Francis of Sales,* 2nd part, section xxxvi.

§ M. Gustave Levavasseur, discours.

and the celebrated preacher, whose talents were of no common order, took every opportunity of doing due justice to Father Eudes. "I have seen," said he, one day, as the servant of God was leaving the pulpit, "in the course of my life many preachers, and I have heard all the best in Italy and France, but I must say, I have never heard any one who touched the heart so deeply as this good father does."

Yet Mgr. Camus could not but remember St. Francis, whose penetrating words had conquered a heresy supported by force of arms.*

Mgr. de Cospéan, Bishop of Lisieux, wrote to the Holy Father that he knew no one who preached with more unction, who better implanted Jesus Christ in people's hearts, or gained more souls to His service.†

Any object of charity which Father Eudes undertook to recommend, was sure of success. When funds were wanted for the general hospital at Caen, a work of which M. de Gavius was the chief promoter, Father Eudes preached his daily sermon for a week on these words from the 40th psalm : "Blessed is he that understandeth concerning the needy and the poor ;" money came in so rapidly, that there was soon more than enough for the completion of the building.‡

* P. Montigny, 1787.

† Mgr. de Cóspéan to the Holy Father :
" Nihil nosse optimo isto viro (Fr. Eudes) aut sacris ejus concionibus, religiousus ; nihil quod majori æterni spiritu vi atque energia Christum Christianorum inserat pectoribus, quos tanto numero ad se trahit, in odorem ejus quem prædicat, ut id unice nobis sit credibile, qui testes habemus oculos."—*P. Heram-bourg, vertus.*

‡ In the list of witnesses who appeared before the commission, entrusted with the first enquiry made by order of the Holy Father with regard to the beatification of Father Eudes, we observe the name of Mdme. de Montpinson, superior of this same hospital of St. Louis, whose foundation was assisted by Father Eudes' sermons.

Such was Father Eudes' power in the pulpit; what was its source?

He looked on the office of a preacher as far more holy and useful than that of a prophet, inasmuch as the teachers of the ancient law gave their hearers nothing but the letter, while those who have the honour of preaching the Gospel impart its spirit also to their hearers, if they present no obstacle. He used to say that priests shared the apostles' labours, and that they both worked in common with our Lord : "As My Father sent Me, so I also send you ; *going, therefore, teach.*" He considered preachers of the Gospel as angels of the Lord, messengers from heaven, heralds of the Most Blessed Trinity, trumpets of the Eternal Father, ambassadors of the Word, organs of the Holy Spirit, fellow-workers with Jesus Christ in the greatest of all His works, the salvation of souls. He always spoke as *from God, before God, and in Christ;* "*Sicut ex Deo, coram Deo, in Christo loquimur.*" (2 Cor. ii.) As a preacher, he assumed a position above that of kings and princes ; boldly and respectfully proclaiming the Word of God in their presence. "*Loquebar de testimoniis tuis in conspectu regum, et non confundebar.*"

But, above all, his wonderful success was due to the force of his own example, to the conformity between his preaching and his practice. "His word was thunder, because his life was lightning," as Father Hérambourg expresses it. He believed that if a preacher failed to regulate his own actions by the truths which he proclaimed to others, his own words would prove his condemnation, and overwhelm him on his death-bed, according to the saying of St. Prosper: "Benè loqui et malè vivere, quid aliud est, nisi se sua voce damnare?"

He always put the poor before the rich ; he preferred the most miserable villages to opulent

cities : "Pauperes evangelisantur." (Matt. xi.)
He sought not praise or glory; he was never discouraged by the smallness of his audience, for he
knew that one of the most beautiful sermons recorded in the Gospel was spoken by the Son of
God to one poor woman.*

God had specially chosen him for this ministry.
"I give myself up to preaching," said he, "though
it is against my own inclination, because I see
that it is the will of God, which I must never
resist."†

In the present day, the eloquent men who have
taken the place once occupied by de Frayssinous,
de Ravignan, and Lacordaire, at Notre Dame, see
a crowd around them; an ardent, educated, often
an uneasy crowd, gathered from the highest classes
of society, from the army, from the different seats
of learning, assembled there to draw fresh strength
from the preacher's arguments, or to listen with a
view of meeting them, or of weakening their effect
by means of those well-known journals, which are
dangerous in proportion to the talent they dis-
play.   Sometimes these critics and objectors are
thoroughly in earnest.   They are seeking......How
many of them are brought back by the sermons
of one Lent?   Father Felix could tell us this
secret; preachers now-a-days deem themselves
well rewarded for their labours, when one sheep
returns to the fold.

The brave band that draws near to the altar of
Notre Dame after the retreat, is itself a noble
answer to the spirit of criticism, which no longer
attacks form, or religion, or the different ways of
worshipping God, *but God Himself.* Pure atheism
is no longer in vogue, but a system based entirely
on the discoveries of a science which, incomplete

* Perè Herambourg : Vertus.

† Perè Finet, memoires.

in itself, is necessarily incomplete in its arguments.

The servant of God who addresses these advanced, intelligent, learned men, must be yet more advanced and intelligent, if not more learned, than they are; he must know all the turns and windings of the road; he must hear everything, learn everything, see everything.

In the XVIIth century a much simpler task lay before the Christian preacher. He always needed energy, often courage; he had to try and gain an ascendancy over the masses, to awaken the faith which was dormant, not extinct, in their hearts, and to guard them against their inclination towards heresy.

"Certainly," says Mgr. Dupanloup, "although Bossuet heard from afar a dull sound of threatening impiety, he never could have foreseen the deluge of atheistical, materialist, and positivist doctrines, which sadden and alarm the present age."

"Nor could Bossuet imagine the existence of the detestable and impious romances, which now-a-days, in Germany and France, seek to tarnish the adorable form of Jesus Christ. *The good sense of the XVIIth century would not have borne such things, and I venture to say also that its noble language could not have expressed them.*"

The eminent prelate thus sums up what we have to say of Christian preaching in the XVIIth, as compared with the XIXth century.

The diocese of Coutances was the first to profit by Father Eudes' apostolic labours. He was summoned by its bishop, Mgr. de Matignon, who saw no better means of arousing faith and restoring discipline in a district where heresy had been making its way for seventy years, with little opposition from an ignorant and disorderly clergy.

Father Eudes went to Lessay, St. Sauveur-le-

Vicomte, la Haie du Puits, Montebourg and
Cherbourg. His persevering efforts were everywhere successful, and such a general change in
manners was visible, that when he went to fresh
places he was hailed as an angel sent from heaven
to help sinners.

The Carmelites of Caen joined their prayers to
his missionary labours. They visited the Blessed
Sacrament every day for his intention: "Our
Reverend Mother," they write, "having given us
permission to apply and offer all our works to
Jesus for the success of *our mission*, I use this
word, your charity having associated us with
you."

In 1634, Mgr. d'Angennes, who nine years before had admitted him to deacon's orders, claimed
his assistance. He must have felt a kind of regret
at his apparent preference for neighbouring dioceses, but soon the same good results which had
followed his other missions were seen at Benon-
ville, Avenay, Evruy and Villers Bocage.

Mgr. Harlay de Saucy, Bishop of St. Malo, and
formerly priest of the Oratory, begged for his services, and Father Eudes spent the summer of
1636 in labouring at Pleurtint, Plover and Cau-
cale.

His inclination always led him back to Normandy. He went to Fresnes, and worked wonders
there. On this occasion his special talent for the
conversion of Protestants began to appear, and he
received the abjuration of thirteen. The most
prejudiced heretics could not withstand his gentleness, simplicity, and winning manners, which
were accompanied by a most edifying and consistent life. All resistance was at an end, if once
a dispassionate hearing could be gained for his
eloquent explanations of the most difficult points.
In dealing with Protestantism, he used to pro-
pound these three questions: "*Is there a Church*

*which we are bound to believe?   Where is that
Church?   What does that Church say?"*

The annals of the congregation give a proof of
the deep impression made by Father Eudes' missions, in the fact that forty years later, when his
brethren visited the scenes of his labours, they
found the very prayers and practices of devotion
which he had taught to the preceding generation
still in use, and the forms established in the Congregation were still observed there.

Father Eudes made acquaintance with all, and
visited much, but never accepted food anywhere.

He succeeded in establishing the custom of
family prayer at Fresnes, thinking this union of
the heads and members of Christian families, before or after the toils of the day, an excellent means
of preserving the good that had been wrought.

The missionaries needed rest, especially after
their work at Fresnes; they returned to Caen,
and Father Eudes followed them there to refresh
himself by study, prayer, and the direction of
consciences.   Thus passed the greater part of the
year 1637.

A mission at Ri, his birth-place, was the only
one which he gave at this time.

He was the child of the soil; and during many
years he had only once spent a very short time
there for his health, before he went to Aubervilliers.

What joy must have filled the hearts of his
father and mother and his whole family, when the
holy priest was again seated by their fireside,
when he led their devotions, and blessed them,
after having bowed his head before the venerable
authors of his existence!   What were their
private conversations?   Perhaps, like St. Francis*

* M. de Boisy always gave many proofs of his veneration for
his son; he loved to hear him say Mass, to receive Communion
from his hands, to be present at his sermons. Yet more, *he*

of Sales, in the chapel of his ancestral castle, he
may have had to deal with Isaac and Martha in
the tribunal of penance, thus becoming at once
their father and their son.

We have knelt with a full heart at the altar,
where, with his own hands, he gave them the
Bread of Life.*

Did Francis de Mezeray manage to leave his
studies in Paris, and share the joy of his family?
We cannot answer positively, but there is a tradition at Ri that the great elm tree, still to be seen
near the church, was planted by him the day that
Louis XIV. was born. This was the 5th of September, 1638, and we may suppose that Mezeray,
who was then ill or recovering from illness, chose
the time of his brother's mission at Ri, to come
there in search of fresh strength. To use the
words of M. de Levavasseur, whom we love to
quote, " When tradition is merely a chronicle of
scandals beyond the tomb, it is almost always a
contemptible calumny; but when it gives as a fact
an occurrence in itself probable and indifferent,
we may receive it without hesitation."

What did the brothers say to each other in
those hours of open-hearted intercourse so re-
freshing to the wearied spirit? The elder was
labouring for all men, the younger for himself.
Francis could describe to Father Eudes the
rugged arena on which he would one day have to
fight. Already he saw in the distance the acade-
mic chair that he himself was ere long to occupy.

chose him for his spiritual guide. His example made the whole
family wish to go to Confession to the man of God; he was
willing, and all, from Mdme. de Boisy down to the servants,
took him for their director.—*Life of St. Francis of Sales.*

* We have never forgotten a letter from Rome, which was
read some years ago in our presence. A young priest, (afterwards Mgr. de Carcassonne,) informed the family at La Flèche,
that he had just said his first Mass, and added that he did not
know how to thank God for having allowed him to give the Living Bread to her from whom he had received life.

He was thoroughly acquainted with the men and the affairs of the day, and his information regarding the things of the world was not useless to the man of God, who was to evangelize the most demoralized parishes of the capital, and to speak in the palace of the kings of France.

Charles Eudes du d'Houny, now surgeon at Argentan, and in an official position, certainly came to Ri, to receive encouragement from the brother, who seemed already to shine with saintly glory. In the course of that very year he gave proof of self-devotion similar to that which had added such weight to the preaching of the minister of the plague-stricken in 1627.

During his short stay at home, God gave Father Eudes consolations beyond his hopes. Everyone was ready to profit by his instructions. His deeds were well known to be in accordance with his words, for Ecouché was not far from Ri. When he preached self-sacrifice, his hearers well knew how nobly he had practised it, in circumstances of the greatest danger. He never again re-visited Ri, except on the occasion of his father's death; but the impression he left behind him there was shewn, even in 1853, by the eagerness with which the inhabitants celebrated his memory, when his medallion, with that of his brothers, was placed on their school house.

Natural inclination would, no doubt, have led him to tarry for a time with his loved parents, and enjoy the fruits of his labours. But he was not his own, and he soon left them to resume his missionary work. He went to Bremoy, in the diocese of Bayeux, then, at the request of Mdme. de Budos, to Estrehan, and in the end of the year 1638, to Pont l'Evèque.

This was a fatal year at Argentan. A plague-stricken traveller had arrived there, and died at the inn of the Trois Sauciers, opposite the church of St. Martin. The contagion spread fearfully; in four months nearly 2,000 persons were carried off. All the inhabitants of the town and neighbourhood who could go, fled from the devastating scourge. Two decrees of the Parliament, commanding the public functionaries to return, were completely disregarded.

But Charles Eudes du d'Houay, the worthy magistrate, went to and fro in the deserted streets, and with the assistance of the apothecary, Thomas Prouverre, and his wife, tended the sick, and buried the dead. He thus followed the steps of Father Eudes, and gained undying glory, which descends to his posterity.

All honour then to our intrepid ancestor, and thanks to the grateful country, which, though two hundred years have passed away, still keeps his memory fresh.

The plague of 1585 had reaped a harvest in the Eudes family, but on this occasion God preserved the younger brother, as He had already preserved the elder a short time before.

The mission of Pont l'Evêque thoroughly established Father Eudes' reputation, and his success in country places now opened to him a larger field of labour.

The great cities claimed his services ; Caen had certainly the first right. Father Eudes could not refuse to go, while he felt that such a theatre taxed his powers to the utmost. He consulted with his fellow-labourers on the means to be employed, and urged them to prepare for the work as he was himself about to do.

His preparation was no common one, for although he was very learned, and was considered by those who heard him speak on the most difficult subjects, to be one of the ablest men of the age, although his natural facility had been wonderfully increased by constant practice, he never, on any occasion, ascended the pulpit without making himself ready beforehand. He thought that one who preaches unprepared tempts God even more than one who prays unprepared.*

He chose the Church of St. Stephen, the resting-place of its founder, William the Conqueror, as his centre of operations. Although this church is one of the largest in the kingdom, it could not contain the multitudes who sought to attend his daily instructions. As many of them seldom succeeded in hearing him, he was requested to preach the Advent and Lent in one of the principal churches of the city.

Renewed fervour was soon visible in every family; many Protestants, overcome by his irresistible words, returned to the bosom of the Church. His words flowed forth simply and freely, he seemed to converse with his audience, and his friends and admirers feared that this simplicity would compromise his established reputation for eloquence. But they were mistaken; almost as soon as he began to speak souls were gained; opponents were vanquished before they had had time to do battle. The following striking incident is mentioned amongst many others.

An unhappy ecclesiastic not only led an irregular life himself, but drew many young persons into similar evil courses. Father Eudes was in the pulpit; an interior voice informed him of the presence of this impenitent sinner, who had been impelled, by curiosity, or it may be, by a last effort of divine grace, to come to the church.

He suddenly cut short the thread of his discourse, and without mentioning his auditor by name, anathematized his licentious life in terms at once so strong and so measured, that the hardened heart was touched, and a few days later this

* P. Herambourg, vertus.

poor man sought one of the holy missionary's companions, and at his feet laid bare the depth of his wounds.*

The preceding pages must have served to shew that the three brothers Eudes were of the true "Norman race of conquerors and founders, a haughty, strong and dominant race, which has left a track of light and civilization wherever it has passed."

"John Eudes was of that believing pious Norman race," said M. G. Levavasseur, in 1853, when the medallions of the three brothers were inaugurated. "He was ardent and bold," to use the words of Huet, Bishop of Avranches, another celebrity of this province prolific in great men, a province which has also the honourable distinction of being specially devout to our Lady, for where have her praises been sung more than in Normandy, the sacred land of the Palinods ?†   Was not the Feast

* Chancellor Ségnier was sent to Normandy by Louis XIII., in 1640, to repress the sedition known by the name of *the Sedition of the Barefooted.* He was invested with the highest authority, and was in every sense of the word a most important person, having, for the time-being, power over life and death. A diary or journal of this mission, kept by the Chancellor's Secretary, is preserved in the Library of the Imperial Military School. The following entry appears under date 17th March, 1640. "Soon after my Lord Chancellor had dined, I brought him the petitions of the prisoners at Bayeux, and he approved all the orders, to the number of 50 or 60, including the arrest; marking with his own hand, at the side of those which had not been heard, the word 'good;' and not touching those which had been heard, for he approved them all; with regard to the general arrest, he thought it well that it should be signed in Paris, and he commanded me at the same time to do the same with regard to the prisons of Caen, as he had done for Bayeux, *a petition for the former having been made by Father Eudes, a priest of the Oratory, and a great servant of God,* who is preaching this year in the said town. I have therefore been unable to be present at the answer of the Rector, who had invited me as well as the other gentlemen of the council." (Diary or journal of Chancellor Segnier's travels in Normandy, after the rising of the Barefooted. M. de Verthament.)

† Palinods or Palinot: this name was given to poems composed in honour of the Immaculate Conception of the Blessed Virgin. Prizes were given for the best at Rouen, Caen, and Dieppe.

of the Immaculate Conception called the *Feast of the Normans?* and, but the other day, when our Lady of Victories was solemnly crowned at Paris, was it not again a Norman,* a counntryman of John Eudes, an inheritor of his virtues and apostolic zeal, who stood at the foot of her statue, and presented the dazzling diadem to the astonished people?

Father Eudes is about to enter a barren land; the men who have looked on him as their disciple, their fellow-worker, and even their example, will soon be seen opposing his plans. He will stand in the position of the accused. We are anxious to make him known beforehand, as he really was, *ever ardent and courageous*, when he looked on himself as the instrument of the Almighty; ever *simple, humble and modest*, when he alone was concerned.

Let us bear in mind that during his missions he never omitted his Mass, he considered the Holy Sacrifice as the motive power of his preaching. "When we are united to Jesus Christ," he used to say, "when He dwells within us, what a means we have of gaining hearts to Him!" As he knelt in the pulpit he humbled himself profoundly, and from the depths of his own nothingness he cried to our Lord, "*Veni, Domine Jesu, veni*," praying Him to come to him and make him nothing, and to come to others and purify them.

His mission at Caen was followed by one at Mesnil Mauger, a parish in the diocese of Lisieux. Mgr. Cospéau, the bishop, induced Father Eudes to labour for the rest of the year 1640 under his direction. This prelate was distinguished by his virtues and abilities; he shewed the greatest esteem for Father Eudes, writing to him in these

* The venerable priest of our Lady of Victories, Father Dufriche Desgenettes.

terms : "Iterum vale, *Pater, Frater ac Fili mi.*"
Again I greet you, *my father, brother, and son.*

Father Eudes only left him when called to be
superior of the Oratory at Caen. He accepted
this office under the full belief that it would not
interfere with his accustomed labours. The later
part of the year 1641 was devoted to missions at
Urville, in the diocese of Seez, at Ermilly and
Landelles in that of Coutances, at Coutances itself, and at Pont-Audemar.

Our indefatigable champion was ever to be
found in the thick of the fray, and must have
understood better than any one how much the
work of missions required the co-operation of zealous, devoted and able men.

Father Eudes must be regarded as one of the
first originators and warmest promoters of ecclesiastical conferences. From 1641 he adopted the
practice of giving these conferences at the same
time as his missions. He began at Remilly, in
the diocese of Coutances. During his mission at
Rouen, which lasted from the beginning of the
year 1642 until near Easter, he not only preached
every day to the people, but gave two conferences
each week for ecclesiastics. In his memorial presented to the Assembly of Clergy in 1645, he
mentions that two or three hundred priests used
to attend on these occasions.

While giving missions he always reserved some
hours for consultation with his fellow labourers
regarding any difficulties which might arise in
their work, and often gave them valuable advice as
to the course to be pursued.

Were not these conferences, (which have been
resumed in the present century,) like the germ of
a new congregation ? It is clear that Father
Eudes never lost sight of Cardinal de Berulle's
original intention.

CHAPTER V.

1641—1642.

FATHER DE CONDREN, SUPERIOR GENERAL OF THE ORATORY, HIS VIRTUES.—FERVOUR OF FATHER EUDES.—DEATH OF FATHER DE CONDREN.—FATHER DE BOURGOING, HIS SUCCESSOR, 1641.—FATHER EUDES ENDEAVOURS TO PROVIDE AN ASYLUM FOR PENITENT WOMEN; BEGINNING OF THE ORDER OF OUR LADY OF CHARITY OF THE REFUGE.—RICHELIEU AND THE SEMINARIES.—CONSTANTLY RECURRING DIFFICULTIES WITH REGARD TO THEIR ESTABLISHMENT IN FRANCE.—MGR. DE HARLAY, ARCHBISHOP OF ROUEN APPOINTS FATHER EUDES HEAD OF ALL MISSIONS IN NORMANDY. —FATHER EUDES' SUPERIORS ENDEAVOUR TO KEEP HIM AWAY FROM THAT PROVINCE.—PERSECUTIONS AND CALUMNIES.—CARDINAL RICHELIEU SENDS FOR FATHER EUDES.

We have spoken of the circumstances under which God had raised up Father Peter de Bérulle, to undertake among the French clergy a work of reformation similar to that carried on with such success by St. Philip Neri and St. Charles Borromeo, in Rome and at Milan. We shall see that he was the founder of a congregation, whose object, as is evident from all his acts, was not only the training of young ecclesiastics in virtue and the duties of their calling, but also the direction of devoted men who were ready to consecrate their lives to continuing this important work.

Among the latter were M. Bourdoise, instructor of the community of St. Nicholas de Chardonnet, and St. Vincent of Paul, who, being likewise called to reform the clergy, spent two years in retreat under Father de Berulle. We have seen how Father Eudes was led to place himself in the hands of Father de Bérulle, who foresaw his future usefulness to the Church, and impressed his own principles so deeply on his heart, that he never in after life deviated from the line laid down by the holy Cardinal.*

Divine Providence was secretly and silently preparing men and events for the foundation of seminaries.

Father Ollier's biographer informs us, that "although the Congregation of the Oratory had been originally intended to establish these institutions throughout the kingdom, yet it devoted itself almost exclusively to missions, to the care of parishes, and especially, as *its founder had apprehended*, to the direction of numerous schools, until at length his successor, Father de Condren, carried out the purpose of Divine Providence, not by himself founding seminaries, but by preparing those whom God selected to do so."

Of Father de Condren, M. de Berulle used to say that he had received the spirit of the Oratory from his cradle: his reputation for sanctity was very great ; Cardinal Richelieu spoke of him with wonder as a man inaccessible to the schemes of his policy. Louis XIII. venerated him as the holiest man in his kingdom.† St. Vincent de Paul said that he had never found his equal : *non est inventus simili illi.* St. Chantal's relations with him left such an impression on her mind, that she said, "If God has given our blessed founder to the

* " The progress of the Oratory, the happy effects of his instructions and his example, the signal services he had rendered to the state, by carrying on negotiations with the Pope, with the queen-mother, and with Gaston of Orleans, his difficult and dangerous mission to England, and, above all, his distinguished virtues and his reputation for piety, had long made Louis XIII. wish to obtain a cardinal's hat for the superior of the Oratory. The humble priest vainly begged the king to do nothing of the kind. Urban VIII. commanded him on his obedience to accept the dignity which was conferred on him in the consistory of August 30, 1627."—*L'Oratoire de France au xviiime et au xixeme siècle.*

† Vie de M. Ollier. Notes.

Church to teach *men*, it seems to me that He has made Father de Condren capable of teaching angels."

Father de Condren became the especial director of souls who aimed at perfection, without, however, neglecting others, for he won the title of the great converter.

He saw Father Ollier's real vocation, and kept him back from the episcopate, that he might be able to employ himself in a work which still remains amongst us, the Seminary of St. Sulpice. It is on record that when Father Ollier was presented to St. Francis of Sales at Lyons, as an *unruly child*, he foretold that he would become a great servant of the Church.

Father de Condren expected that the infant congregation of St. Sulpice would arouse the zeal of the clergy and that of the Oratory; he made over the care of the schools to one of his priests, and the government of the congregation to a vicar-general, so that he might be able to devote himself exclusively to the direction of chosen ecclesiastics, a direction of which the ulterior bearing was not yet divulged. He saw that the Oratory was not fulfilling the obligations imposed by its original rules; he saw yet further, as will soon appear.

Quite against the will of this holy priest, Cardinal de Richelieu had made him undertake the charge of the conscience of Gaston of Orleans, the lightest and most volatile prince in the world. The reconciliation between the king and his brother, at Orleans, on the 8th of February, 1639, was entirely due to Father de Condren, as Richelieu himself admits.* He was not only great in the Church, but a person of considerable importance in state affairs.

* Lettre du Cardinal de Richelieu au P. de Condren. CDXII. Lettres Missives.
5

Such, then, was the eminent priest who naturally became Father Eudes' director after the death of Cardinal de Bérulle. All these details are important; the halo that surrounded the master's head casts its brightness upon his disciple.

Father Eudes was full of fervour, his heart seemed overflowing with piety and self-abnegation.

Therefore, although the statutes of the Congregation of the Oratory did not permit either *solemn or simple vows,* and although Father de Condren himself opposed the idea, he insisted on making to him a *vow of steadfastness* and a *vow of obedience.**

Father de Condren had formed his own opinion with regard to Father Eudes and the Oratory. He knew that this disciple of Cardinal de Bérulle would carry on his work under another form, and would at the appointed moment separate himself from his colleagues. He had therefore sufficient reasons for objecting to any engagement tending to bind one who was in due time to go forth.

---

* As to the vows which Father Eudes made to Father de Condren, some time after his entrance into the Oratory, they were not solemn vows, but were made merely to satisfy his own devotion, and were of a nature from which a person could be easily released on sufficient grounds. The original is preserved in the Imperial Archives, and there is a copy in the archives of Rouen, which begins by the following words: "Extract from the official register kept at Caen, of two vows pronounced by J. Eudes, priest of the Congregation of the Oratory, in presence of the Very Rev. Father Ch. de Condren, superior general of the Congregation, and received by him, *after repeated refusals on the ground that they were contrary to the use of the Congregation,* and earnest prayers made on many different occasions in the course of several years by Father Eudes; as Father Eudes has caused to be recorded in the said register, wishing that it may have due weight, and that the said vows may be the better known to all, one of which is a vow of *steadfastness,* and the other of *obedience.*" (Above, as a heading, is J. M.) Compared with the original by me, H., priest, first general, at the Oratory, 20th September, 1656, Passot, priest.

The original of the vow of steadfastness in Father Eudes' own hand-writing, is in the Imperial Archives at Paris. We shall have hereafter to show the use made of this extract.

Father de Condren died in 1641; he had refused the cardinal's hat, and the archbishoprics of Rheims and of Lyons. "Since the days of the apostles," says Father Eudes, "perhaps no one has equalled Father de Condren in the extent and depth of his knowledge of the most sublime mysteries of religion."

He was succeeded as superior-general by Father Francis de Bourgoing, who was born in Paris in 1585, and died in 1662. Before entering the Oratory, he had been parish priest of Clichy, where St. Vincent de Paul took his place, Cardinal de Bérulle having recommended him to accept the charge. Father de Bourgoing was one of the cardinal's earliest disciples; he wrote some books of piety which were much esteemed. Bossuet preached his funeral sermon.

Let us now return to Father Eudes, whose history we have brought down to 1641, the date of Father de Condren's death; we seem indeed scarcely to have left him, so closely are these digressions connected with him; and happy is the biographer whose path is illuminated by so many glorious lights.

In his various wanderings, Father Eudes had often met with unfortunate beings, fallen angels whom want or passion had cast into the depths of depravity.

Many of them, as they heard the priest's words, had longed to return from the paths of sin; the greater their fault, the greater tenderness and compassion had he shown towards them, and he had never failed to stretch out a helping hand to them. But he knew that the world is merciless, and casts aside those who have given up domestic joys to become its playthings; he felt that he had little power to save these poor young women, whom his departure left destitute of shelter, support, and counsel; he saw that want and misery would again seize upon them, and plunge them more hopelessly into the abyss. ·Waifs and strays from the wreck, the waves seem to play with them for a while, and then dash them against the cruel rocks.

At his request some pious persons had received several of these unhappy beings into their houses, but such a plan was attended with many practical objections. Father Eudes had to try to gather them together under the same roof, and to place them under the special direction of those who would undertake to bring them back to a better life. The idea was good, but difficult of execution: however, God provided the way.

A woman named Madeleine Lamy, who was herself in great poverty, had received some of these penitents into her lowly abode; she taught them to live according to the precepts of the Gospel, endeavoured to enable them to earn their bread, and provided for their most pressing wants by means of alms, which Father Eudes and other charitable persons placed in her hands.

One day Father Eudes went with M. de Bernières and M. and Mdme. Blouet de Camilly, to visit a church in the neighbourhood. Madeleine Lamy appeared suddenly before them, and thus addressed them: " Where are you going? Wandering about churches, and gazing at the pictures, after which you think yourselves very pious ; that is not the way to do the business: you should set to work and found a house for those poor girls who are being lost for want of care and of a way of living."

These simple energetic words made a great impression on her hearers. They began to consider how they could satisfy her, and when she returned again to the charge the day was gained. One of them undertook to pay the rent of a house, another to furnish it : M. and Mdme. Camilly promised the corn required for the food of the penitents.

A house near the Millet Gate, opposite the chapel of St. Gratien, at Caen, was hired ; on the 25th November, 1641, the penitents were installed there, and, with the aid of some pious women, who had consented to take care of this little flock, all was so far arranged by the 8th of December, the feast of the Immaculate Conception, that they began to keep enclosure and to observe Rules drawn up by Father Eudes.

He often visited these poor girls, gave them instructions in private, and endeavoured to provide temporal assistance for them, in order that they might acquire a taste for a mode of life so different from the one they had given up. Mgr. d'Angennes approved of all that had been done, and gave permission for the erection of a chapel in the house, whose spiritual direction was entrusted to Father Eudes.

Much opposition was afterwards made to this work, although it was by no means a novelty ;* difficulties only served to perfect it, and led to its establishment as a religious order, which has taken root in different parts of France and in other

---

* The general idea of giving a refuge to women who had gone astray, with the hope of bringing them back to virtue, is not new. The Order of Penitence of St. Madeleine was founded in 1272, by a citizen of Marseilles, named Bernard. He was seconded in this good work by many other persons, who laboured for the conversion of the courtezans of the town. The society was erected into a religious order, under the rule of St. Augustin, by Pope Nicholas III. It is said that another religious order composed of penitent women was formed under the same rule.

The Congregation of Penitents of the Madeleine at Paris owes its origin to the preaching of Father Tisserant, Cordelier, who having converted many of these women, established this institution to receive such as after their example might wish to lead a better life. About 1294 the King of France gave them the Hotel de Bohaines, Bahaigne, or Boheme, once called the Hotel de Nesle, but latterly after the Duke of Bohemia, who spent some time there.

countries, and has always preserved its primitive fervour.

Such was the modest origin of two institutions, which, strictly speaking, are but one ; *the order of our Lady of Charity of the Refuge, and the order of our Lady of Charity of the Good Shepherd*, which branched off from it in 1827, but equally acknowledges Father Eudes as its founder.

The missive letters of Cardinal de Richelieu furnish ample proof of the extent of his genius, and of the immense amount of business of different kinds which he carried on at once, and without any very efficient assistance.

With the exception of Father Joseph, whose importance is amply shown in these same letters,* his instruments were not generally first-rate men, but he was able to give them, when occasion required, something of his own power. We have been struck with the resemblance between his correspondence and that of Napoleon the First. Each speaks with the tone of a master.

Richelieu had crushed the material power of Protestantism, and scattered its principal leaders. The taking of La Rochelle, and of the chief places occupied by the Protestants in the centre of France, had diminished their strength rather than their number. The government had not now to deal with it as a religious and political party.

But it was not enough to have repressed these innovators, and especially the ambitious nobles who made the Reformation a basis for their perpetual agitations; they must be brought back to unity, and this noble and difficult undertaking was not a work for politicians, but for holy and zealous Catholic ministers. Can it be supposed that Richelieu would have shrunk from revoking the

* To Father Joseph: "an *unlimited* power to make peace (with Germany) is sent to you." (Letter from the Cardinal, 1630.)

Edict of Nantes, if he had thought it necessary or fitting at this time to take away from the Protestants the rights of liberty of conscience, freedom of worship, and admission to public employments, which had been conceded to them? He knew that the standing of the secular clergy was not such as to make them likely to overcome the prejudices of men who had been brought up to hate priests whom they could not respect. He therefore proceeded with prudence, and restrained the zeal of the over-impetuous.* The only suitable remedy after the so-called religious wars† (from 1562 to 1598,) consisted in providing a solid education for young ecclesiastics, and training them in regularity, piety, and learning.

As early as 1625 Charles Godefrey, doctor of the Faculty of Theology of Paris, and parish-priest of Cretteville, in the diocese of Coutances, had presented to the assembly of clergy a treatise on the usefulness and necessity of seminaries.‡

* Mgr. Bertrand d'Eschaux, Archbishop of Tours, writing to Cardinal de Richelieu in March 1635, wonders that he has counted in vain on his assistance with regard to his project of *suppressing Protestant preaching at St. Maixent.* This silence of the Cardinal's proves that he was not too ready to second the over-ardent zeal of men less wise than himself in their acts of useless provocation against a religion from which he thought nothing could at that time be required save loyalty to the king and country.—He sought to combat it by other arms. (Missive letters of the Cardinal. Notes.)

† The term religious wars is generally employed in history to designate the three wars of the 16th century between Catholics and Protestants. The name is also applied to those of 1621 and 1625—1629, under Louis XIII., as well as to the war of Cevennes, consequent on the revocation of the edict of Nantes.

‡ In 1625 Doctor Godefroy suggested the idea of seminaries such as now exist; just as Captain Lanoue in Henry the Fourth's time, suggested that of military colleges. But the priest's idea was realized sooner than the soldier's. We have read with the greatest attention the analysis given of this treatise by Father Costil in the Annals of the Congregation of Jesus and Mary, and have been able to form an idea of the effect which it must have produced when presented to the assembly of clergy. We observe particularly that in conclusion he declares that he knows no more efficacious remedy for the evils which

This treatise made so great an impression on all who heard it, and especially on Cardinal de Richelieu, that they immediately sought to take measures for meeting the want indicated.

But the moment appointed by Divine Providence had not yet arrived, and there never was a case to which the proverb "Man proposes, but God disposes," could be more fitly applied.

We give the answer of the clergy, as inserted in the authentic act drawn up by the Bishop of Chartres, and read in the afternoon of the 22nd December; this document gives an exact idea of the state of things, and furnishes an answer to all the attacks afterwards made upon Father Eudes.

"The cardinals, archbishops, bishops, and other ecclesiastics of the Assembly of Clergy, wishing to see the hierarchy restored to its primitive glory, and considering the great benefits which will accrue to the whole Church from the good life and devotion of its pastors, desiring also to remedy the scandals caused by the ignorance and imperfections of some among them, have approved and authorized the plan proposed to them by Master Charles Godefroy, parish priest of Cretteville, for the formation of colleges of holy exercises throughout the provinces of the kingdom, as a sovereign and

are deplored, than the establishment of a society composed of a few very zealous persons, which will take this charge, and devote itself to the restoration of poor churches, and to the salvation of souls whose guides are unworthy; a society stable in its nature, always preserving the same spirit, the same mode of direction, and the same laws, and helping the bishops all the more earnestly because they can never be sure but that their successors may overturn what they have established. Doctor Godefroy wished that the members of this society should live as befits ecclesiastics called to labour for the salvation of others, and all were to be priests, because they were to regenerate their brethren.—(Annals.)

Father Eudes established nothing but what had here been suggested; it was Father de Bérulle's plan, not realized by the Congregation which he founded in 1611, and which did not appear to Doctor Godefroy, in 1625, to have succeeded in the regeneration of the clergy.

efficacious means for the attainment and preservation of Christian perfection. Their lordships have exhorted him, and given him power and authority, to form and establish a congregation of ecclesiastics, and to build colleges and seminaries in order to carry out and practise the articles contained in his book of Holy Exercises; in such colleges and seminaries he and his companions may celebrate holy Mass, preach, teach, and do everything else calculated to promote the welfare of the Church, or necessary and fitting in order to the perfect execution of so holy a project, subject to the good pleasure of the bishop of the diocese. And, as a token of their special approval, their lordships have promised to give him every assistance, favour, and protection, and at their visitations and synods to invite the ecclesiastics of their dioceses, and especially the parish priests, to practise these Exercises; and, foreseeing that this work will succeed, to the honour of the Gallican Church, and the satisfaction of the other estates of this realm, they order that it shall be made known throughout all the provinces by the diligence of the general agents. Given at the Assembly, 22nd day of December, 1625.

"Signed, FRANCIS, ARCHBISHOP OF ROUEN,
"President."

There is matter for serious reflection in this document: it bears date December 1625, yet it was well known to the whole Catholic world that, in 1611, Father de Bérulle had established a Congregation intended to fulfil all the above conditions. Power to make a foundation was here given to a priest, who, when he gave his solemn warning, never seems to have himself thought of carrying into execution a work already on trial under the care of one of the most eminent among the French clergy.

The essentials for this work were, men raised up by God, and the appointed time. It would therefore seem, that when the Assembly of the Clergy promulgated the preceding resolutions, they did not think that the men had already appeared, or that the right moment had hitherto arrived.

Nothing was yet done. In the correspondence of Richelieu, we find that he had another unrealized project, for the foundation of a college or society of twenty doctors.

In our work on military education before and after 1789,* we have spoken of the institution for the young nobility, established by Louis XIII.,† at Cardinal Richelieu's request. His missive letters of 1636 speak of another idea, of which this was merely the simplification, viz., an academy for 1,000 gentlemen, of whom 400 were to be destined for the priesthood, and 600 for the army. The former were to be there from the age of 12 to 20, and the latter from 15 to 18. A *seminary* and a *military school* were thus to be carried on under the same roof, united by their common patriotism ; such was the Cardinal's scheme, for at the bottom of the memorial he wrote the words, " Lilii junctæ manebunt."‡

This impracticable idea was somewhat in keeping with the position of one who was a prince of the Church, a minister of state, and, at the same time, General of the King's armies in Italy, grand master and superintendant of navigation.§

Among the same missive letters we find another

---

* Institutions d'Education militaire avant et après 1789, par M. C. de Montzey 1866-67.

† Mercure Françaús. T. xxi. page 228.

‡ Lettres missives de Richelieu, notes.

§ 10th April, 1630. " Cardinal de Richelieu, General of the King's armies in Italy. The governors and soldiers will all be hung, if they wait for the siege and the cannon." (Siege of Bagnolet.) Lettres missives.

memorial of the Cardinal's, touching the residence of bishops, and seminaries to be established in each diocese, by means of a contribution levied on the abbeys, on the organization, the working and the results of colleges.

Notwithstanding the pressure of business, which must have told on his precarious health, Richelieu never lost sight of the question of seminaries, but it was not till 1637 or 1638 that he was able to take any decisive measures. He entrusted all details to Father Joseph, who had already drawn up a plan for the establishment of a seminary in the College of Bourgogne, at Paris, and selected for its director Father d'Authier de Sisgau of Marseilles, instructor of the missionaries of the clergy, a society afterwards known by the name of Congregation of priests of the Blessed Sacrament. This Father was at the time at Valence, where he had been sent to establish a seminary, believed to have been the first founded in the kingdom. He was about to proceed to Paris with some of his companions, when he was arrested by the tidings of Father Joseph's death, at Ruet, on the 18th of December, 1638.

Father Joseph died in the arms of Richelieu, who, at this very time, was taking fresh measures to obtain a cardinal's hat for him. His removal led to the elevation of Mazarin, who now became the first candidate for that high dignity.*

It was not till two years after the death of his valued and able confidant, that Richelieu reverted

* A note added by Richelieu to a dispatch to M. de Brassac, ambassador at Rome, dated Sept. 4th, 1631, proves how much esteemed Mazarin then was at the Court of France.

"Monsieur Mazarin has shewn so much address and zeal in the negotiation of the peace, that I write you these few words to say that you could do nothing more agreeable to his majesty than to let the Pope know how well satisfied he is with him, and to use any effort in your power to promote his appointment as nuncio for France, whenever the present nuncio is recalled to Rome to fill a higher position." (Lettres missives.)

to the scheme of the seminaries, and when he did so he cast his eyes on Father Eudes. Is not the Hand of Providence visible in all these delays, these fruitless projects, these unsuccessful attempts from the days of St. Francis of Sales onwards, in the silence of Rome, and in the absence of results, as far as seminaries were concerned, from the creation of the Congregation of the Oratory? All was ordered with a view to Father Eudes and those who were being prepared by Father de Condren, who on his death-bed gave them the clue to the riddle.

We learn from Father Ollier's life that "the establishment of seminaries was generally considered an impossibility, and past experience certainly seemed to bear out the idea. During the eighty years which had elapsed since their foundation had been ordered by the Council of Trent, no fruits of so welcome a decision had been seen in France. The chapters of some dioceses had rejected the decrees, in other places they had remained unexecuted, or had only continued a short time in force."

After deliberation in the Assembly of Clergy, in 1629, it had been decided that four general seminaries should be erected; afterwards it was considered better to let each bishop take the initiative in his own diocese. But of all the abortive efforts, that of the priests of the Oratory was most worthy of notice. "Twenty-two years after the foundation of their house of St. Magloire, at Paris, as a *diocesan seminary*, it had not yet begun its exercises. The fathers merely taught theology in some of their colleges to such students as were destined for the priesthood, and gave them a retreat of ten days before ordination."*

In the mean time Father de Condren, General

---

* Vie de M. Ollier.

of the Congregation of the Oratory, was drawing to the close of his earthly career, without having explained to the disciples whom he had trained with so much care, his views with regard to the establishment of seminaries. On this subject his communications to them were obscure. In his opinion the hour had not yet come, and he thought, like St. Vincent de Paul, that a good work prematurely brought to light is half destroyed. He lived surrounded by a number of priests, whom he filled with enthusiasm by means of his own sublime ideas of the sacerdotal office; whose hearts he renewed and transformed, and whom he then sent forth full of burning zeal to the conquest of souls.*

Father de Condren was a magnificent instrument in the hands of God, whose purposes are covered with an impenetrable veil, and are generally only known by their results. His Providence did not allow seminaries to be founded by the Oratory, which was about to be tainted with the crooked and fatal errors of Jansenism, but its holiest General was chosen as the teacher and master of those who were to begin this great work, and on his death-bed he told them that "at last the time had come."

He particularly advised them only to admit into their seminaries youths of sufficient age to have their judgment already formed, so that it might be seen after a time of probation whether they were really called to minister at the altar.

" The thing that grieves me," said he to the assembled fathers, " is the schism which I foresee will come in two years."

His prediction was but too true; two years after his death the open breach between Jansenism and

* Vie de M. Ollier.

the Church was made, on the occasion of the condemnation of the Augustinus, in 1643.*

"It may seem surprising that Father de Condren, being the head of a numerous society,
founded for the express purpose of training the
clergy, should have given over its exterior government to others, and have taken so much pains to
prepare a few ecclesiastics to establish seminaries
in France ; a work which, while he recognized its
extreme importance to the Church, he neither
undertook himself, nor committed to his own Congregation. Again, it is very remarkable, that
until that time, notwithstanding the original intention of its founder, the Congregation was almost exclusively employed in missions, in the
charge of parishes, and, above all, in the direction
of colleges ; for the seminaries which it endeavoured to establish were unsuccessful. As far as
we may examine the intentions of God, it would
seem that He thus provided for the preservation
of the faith in the Church in France. It is well
known that after Father de Condren's death, the
greater portion of this congregation was corrupted
by Jansenism, which always found champions
amongst its members : if the training of the
clergy had then been in the hands of such a body,
we may easily imagine how disastrous to the

* The Congregation of the Oratory was originally connected with
Jansenius and Father de St. Cyran, by whose influence it obtained
a footing in Flanders, many of its members made common cause
with those fathers of the new heresy. After the arrest of Father
Siguenot, Father de Condren thought it necessary to make a
public declaration of the real sentiments of the Oratory, which
were open to suspicion. But after the death of this great oppo-
nent of heresy, the majority of the Congregation became tainted,
so that Father de Bourgoing, his successor, was almost without
authority, and saw the most important positions given, in spite
of his wishes, to men who had openly espoused Jansenism.
Father Amelot, who was deprived of the dignity of superior at
the house of St. Honoré, laboured and suffered till his death in
the endeavour to keep faith alive in the Oratory.—(Histoire de
M. Ollier, notes.)

whole Gallican Church would have been the consequences."*

The foregoing details, which we have borrowed from M. Ollier's life, make it clear to our mind that Father Eudes was obliged to leave the Oratory and to remain his own master, that he might use his liberty in accordance with the will of God.

From the earliest days of the Oratory, Providence seems always to have hindered the accomplishment of its founder's intention with regard to the training of the clergy. Father de Bérulle, being afraid that a taste for profane learning might divert the attention of his priests from the end of their institution, requested Pope Paul V. to forbid them, in his bull of institution, to take charge of schools; but to his surprise no such prohibition was inserted in the document. This omission, so serious in its consequences, was no doubt due to a special design of Providence, for God enlightens the Sovereign Pontiff with regard to the foundation of Religious Orders. The Oratory, therefore, instead of devoting itself to seminaries, by which means so great an influence might have been exercised on the faith of both clergy and people, undertook, as Cardinal de Bérulle had feared it would do, the care of a multitude of schools, although such a work was quite foreign to his original intention. It is also worthy of remark, that when himself making a number of small

* "Had we not the indisputable evidence of many documents before us, we should scarcely believe the persistent attachment of some of the Oratorians to the new errors regarding grace. When Father Bourgoing, the general, ordered the books of Jansenius, the theses of Louvain, and the other works on grace condemned by Urban VIII., to be brought to the library of each house, that they might be kept under lock and key, so little regard was paid to this decision, that in some houses these books were read publicly in the refectory." M. Ollier formally objected to the establishment of the Oratory Fathers in the Faubourg St. Germain. "The best friends of these fathers cannot but fly from them."—(Vie de M. Ollier, notes.)

foundations which at once exhausted the strength of the body and changed its object, he expressed a conviction that he was thereby carrying out the will of God.

In fact, as we shall soon see, the Oratory was so far from labouring to establish seminaries, that soon after Father de Condren's death it chose rather to let Father Eudes go forth, than to give him the means of realizing the cherished purpose of its founder.

God often leads chosen souls by a path invisible to others, while to them clear as a track of fire; and so it was with the disciple of Cardinal de Berulle and Father de Condren. He knew that in order to found and direct seminaries he must cease to be an Oratorian, and if the whole world had risen in arms against him, it could not have withheld him from obeying the voice that called him so powerfully. It was, no doubt, in accordance with the designs of God, that when once his future plans were known, all agreement between himself and his superiors became impossible. "God makes men," says Lacordaire; "when He means to use them, He gives them exactly what they need, by means of a series of unforeseen events, whose connection can only be perceived when they are contemplated as a whole. When I look back upon my entire life, I see that everything converges to the point where I now stand."

Ever since Father Eudes' connection with the Congregation of the Oratory, he had seen that Father de Berulle's intention was the regeneration of the clergy by the establishment of seminaries. This was the basis of the edifice, and Father de Bourgoing, who succeeded Father de Condren in 1641, expressed the same opinion some years later, in a letter to the Cardinals of the Propaganda.

"*The time has come,*" exclaimed Father de

Condren, as he died; *"men are ready and God wills it."* Such was Father Eudes' interpretation of his master's last confidence. He therefore obeyed the word of command, as our brave officers before Sebastopol cleared the barrier that separated them from the foe, when the moment appointed by their commander had come.

Meanwhile, Mgr. de Harlay, Archbishop of Rouen, summoned him to give a mission at the celebrated Abbey of St. Ouen. The Duchess of Aiguillon, niece of Cardinal de Richelieu, provided for the support of thirty missionaries from the beginning of 1642 till Lent was far advanced. They were carefully chosen by Father Eudes, each one for the functions for which he was best fitted. Great success followed their labours, and, as usual, many Protestants abjured their errors.

Mgr. de Harlay had, on the 11th January, 1642, named Father Eudes chief of the missionaries in the province of Normandy, giving him the right to choose his associates, and to confer on them all necessary powers. The document by which this was done, served as the basis of his foundations.

The prelate expressed his earnest desire that the missionary should preach Lent in his cathedral.

This would have involved such an increase of work, that he thought it right to consult his superior general, Father de Bourgoing, who immediately urged him to excuse himself on the score of his weak health.

It must have cost Father Eudes much to obey this advice, for when called to battle he never calculated the number of the enemy, nor the amount of his own strength. He could not fail to see that there was a plan to keep him away from Normandy, and that his well-known desire for the foundation of seminaries had awakened a fear that he would leave the Congregation to which

6

he was, ostensibly at least, no more closely bound
than his colleagues.

His own simplicity and humility may have
hidden from him what others knew, that the
success of his preaching, and the unusual talent
which he had from the first displayed, and the
purity and holiness of his life, had been made
known to the Cardinal, possibly by Father de
Condren, and that thus his future had been prepared. The chief cause for apprehension on the
part of the Oratorians, was that he might have to
ground his separation from them on the non-fulfilment of their illustrious founder's first project,
in furtherance of which Richelieu had entrusted
certain funds to Father de Bourgoing.

Father de Bourgoing wrote thus to Father
Eudes: "If an institution should be established at
Rouen, it would be necessary that Father St. Pé
should remain there. I have heard that funds
have been given to you for one at Caen ; let me
know, for I shall have to write to you on the subject.".........Again, with regard to a benefice
which the Archbishop wished to give to the Oratory: "If you had informed me, I should have
given my opinion that it might be attached to the
house at Rouen, in favour of a seminary."

The anxiety of the Oratorians begins to appear
in this correspondence. Nevertheless, Father de
Bourgoing's tone to Father Eudes is that of an
equal, rather than of a superior. As the gifts
and promises in question, were chiefly from the
de Répichons, benefactors of the Oratory, it was
supposed that they were all intended to benefit the
Congregation.

It was quite true that Father Eudes had
received from pious people different sums for the
foundation of a seminary. He was now required
to give an account of these sums, and to take no
further step without direction. He was even sus-

pected of self-interest in the matter, but Mgr. de Harlay answered for him in his correspendence with the superior-general.

He was placed in a difficult position; on the one hand were the claims of obedience, on the other was the will of God. But these contradictions and troubles are common, when a work is from God, and are often the means by which it is strengthened and perfected.

Father Eudes was convinced of his vocation, and nothing could make him waver; he was, as we have said, one of those Norman conquerors and founders who pursue their chosen object in spite of all obstacles.

In accordance with the request of Mgr. de Fourcy, successor to Mgr. de Harlay, he was sent on a mission to St. Malo, and thus removed from his numerous* friends in Caen and Rouen. He went, but with the conviction that a rupture was imminent and inevitable.

His next mission at St. Lo, where the Bishop of Coutances had invited him, was interrupted by a summons to Paris from Richelieu.

The order was a formal one, from a minister

---

* Father Eudes' spiritual friends were many. Besides Mgr. de Cospéan, of whom we have had occasion to speak, we may mention Mdme. de Budos, M. and Mdme. Camilly, Mgr. de Laval Bishop of Petrea vicar-apostolic in Canada; M. de Than, a religious of the abbey of St. Stephen, which he reformed; M. de Renty, and M. de Bernières, the Rev. Father John Chrysostom, of the Third Order of St. Francis, the Rev. Father Ignatius Joseph of Jesus and Mary, a discalced Carmelite, Father le Pileur, grand-vicar of Mgr. de Matignon, who left his library to the seminary of the Eudists at Coutances; several Jesuit Fathers, the Reverend Mother Mary Elizabeth of the Infant Jesus, of the monastery of St. Thomas Aquinas; the Reverend Mother Mechtilde of the Blessed Sacrament, the Reverend Mother Germain of the Nativity, an Ursuline of Bayeux, who foretold to him some of the crosses awaiting him, but did not dare to tell him the rest; and many ecclesiastics whose names are in the book of life.

Before the execution of his project, he associated himself with several religious orders, the Jesuits, Benedictins, Franciscans, &c. (P. Costil, Annales de la Congregation.)

who was not accustomed to be kept waiting, and to whom, moreover, time was now precious, for these were his last days on earth. Everything had to give way, and Father Eudes set off accompanied by Father de Jourdan, his best-loved colleague. This sudden departure, whose reason was not generally known, gave rise to many remarks. It soon transpired that he had had several interviews with the Cardinal, who had spoken of the establishment of seminaries, and enquired the reasons which had led him to devote his attention to the subject in so marked a manner.

Cardinal de Richelieu was so struck by the wisdom and decision of Father Eudes' answers, that he applied to him the words of the King of Tyre to Solomon's messengers: "Blessed be the Lord, who hath given to King David a wise and knowing son."

Here we end our first book. Father Eudes is about to leave the Oratory, and to enter on the new course which he will follow without wavering, constantly bearing the cross of Christ till he is called to receive his great reward.

BOOK II.

1642—1658.

CHAPTER I.

1642—1644.

" The cross has not ceased to be foolishness, the weakness of God is still stronger than all the power of man. He who would work for the Church, must start from this conviction, and then use every possible human means, else he will never be fit for God's service."* Where did Father Eudes, who believed himself to be the weakest of creatures, gain his immoveable firmness

* Lacordaire.

and his imperturbable serenity ? Father Lacordaire's words will furnish the answer : "There is always in the hearts of men, in their intellectual condition, in the state of public feeling, in laws, or circumstances, or times, some standing-point for God......Our great art is *to find it out and use it*, ever making the secret and invisible power of God the principle of our courage and hope."

Richelieu's last dying effort in favour of a project which had long occupied the minds of the wise, furnished Father Eudes with this standing-point, at the moment when he most wanted it. The Cardinal, who was so engrossed with the things of this world, was much less indifferent than has been generally supposed to those which affected his eternal welfare.* And he, who always dealt so severely with rebellion and insubordination, upheld the humble Oratorian, in his desire to carry out Father de Bérulle's intentions and Father de Condren's injunctions, notwithstanding the opposition of his superiors, and the dissatisfaction of most of his colleagues. He directed Mgr. de Beaumont de Péréfixe, the Archbishop of Paris, to consult with Father Eudes as to the tenor of the letters patent to be obtained, and afterwards recommended the Father to his niece,

* M. Meyster, who had taken a prominent part in the formation of the institution at Vaugirard, came to spend some days with his friends, in order to communicate to them, after his custom, the graces which God poured down on him ; he went to visit Cardinal de Richelieu, who had for many years wished to see him. The minister was delighted to make his acquaintance, and offered him 1,400,000 livres for the establishment of missions, but could not prevail on him to accept it. He was pained, and even alarmed, by this refusal, and said to M. Meyster : "But, sir, has God made known to *you that I am to be lost*, and that He will receive nothing from my hands ? Tell me, I beg of you, if you think I can be saved in my present state of life ?" "My lord," answered M. Meyster, "we have often spoken on the subject with Father de Condren." "And what conclusion did you come to ?" said the Cardinal. "We agreed that you have a means of securing your salvation, in defending the rights of the Church, and promoting the appointment of worthy men to bishoprics." (Vie de M. Olier. Notes.)

the Duchess of Aiguillon, who had already seen him at work at Rouen, and immediately gave him a sum of money for the future seminary at Caen.

Meanwhile Father Eudes was seeking the advice of his friends in Paris and in Normandy; with one voice they said, *Go forward*.

During his sojourn in Paris, all the hours he could spare from business were spent in giving conferences at the Sorbonne and at St. Magloire, where Bossuet afterwards appeared and prepared himself for victory; he took every opportunity of preaching the word of God, and the most eminent prelates of France were among his hearers; "they could not say enough in praise of his pure zeal for the beauty of God's house, and they were even more touched by his humility than by his eloquence. When the conference was over, he would often prostrate himself at the church door, and his hearers could scarcely hinder him from kissing their feet."*

Cardinal de Richelieu died on the 4th of December, 1642. It was therefore one of his last wishes to raise the clergy of France to their present high position, and Father Eudes was his chosen associate for this work; henceforth he bore the impress of his power, and Richelieu's death, instead of leaving an irreparable void, bequeathed to Father Eudes a moral support, all the more efficacious, because no influence but that of God from this time guided his acts.

Normandy, the scene of his apostolic labours, had the first claim on this son of her soil. He determined to found his first seminary at Caen.

Mgr. Beaumont de Péréfixe, and Mgr. d'Angennes, Bishop of Bayeux, acting in concert and in obedience to the orders of Cardinal de Richelieu, forwarded the letters patent in December

---

* Récit du Curé de St. Hilaire. (Diocese of Avranches, who died in the odour of Sanctity in 1700.)

1642. Power was hereby given to "the members of the new Congregation to acquire and to build the houses and places necessary for their habitation, and to enjoy each and all of the rights and privileges enjoyed by other houses and communities founded in our kingdom, and even by the missions established within the last thirty years, although not particularly expressed."

In a religious and legal point of view, the cause of the seminary at Caen was gained; but it was far otherwise with regard to those material things which necessarily hold so important a place in the history of such institutions. Are not the foundations of the most solid structures often laid with immense labour on account of the nature of the ground?

The Duchess of Aiguillon had given a thousand livres, and the de Répichons, father and son, had added two thousand more. The amount was insufficient, and the Bishop of Bayeux was anxious to have a more certain income assured before beginning, but Father Eudes, confident of success, and willing to meet the inevitable privations of the early stages of such a work, reassured and tranquillized the prelate, who relied much on his prudence. The execution of the project was delayed by various difficulties until the 25th of March, 1643.

The future companions of Father Eudes were five in number; Simon Mannoury, aged twenty-nine, and Thomas Manchon, aged twenty-six, both of the diocese of Lisieux; Peter Jourdan, aged thirty-five, of that of Coutances; Andrew Godefroy, of Caen, and John Fossey, of Thorigny. The two last did not persevere, but were very soon replaced by James Finel and Richard Lemesle, both priests of the diocese of Coutances.

On the 25th of March, 1643, they made a pilgrimage to our Lady of Deliverance, a chapel three leagues from Caen, still venerated by the faithful. On the following day Father Eudes finally left the Congregation of the Oratory, of which he had been twenty-two years a member, and took up his abode with his new brethren in a house at the end of the Place Royale, at Caen ;* he went like one of the patriarchs of old, in obedience to the voice of God, to take possession of the Promised Land, without looking back or regretting the advantages of his former position.

Let us observe with Father Costil, that the Congregation of Jesus and Mary, so called because it dates from the Feast of the Annunciation, appeared at the same time as the book of Jansénius, and in the very year when Father Hébert, theological professor of the Church of Paris, began to preach against him.

The delay of the work until 1643 was evidently permitted by Providence, in order that more means of defence might be ready for the many successive attacks which were to be made on the man of God.

Was he indeed bound to steadfastness with regard to an institution which had forsaken its own original destination ? Was he bound to remain obedient to a superior, who, notwithstanding his great virtue, was about to lose all command over his subjects ? His vows of steadfastness and obedience fell to the ground of themselves ; they even involved risk to his soul ; and, moreover, according to the statutes of the Congregation, these

---

* We have reason to believe that the fathers spent the first year in a house at Caen, whose position is unknown. Afterwards they hired one in the Rue St. Laurent, opposite the drinking-trough, and now occupied by a cooper and a farrier. The former shows a room on the second story, just under the roof, once the famous chapel, whose use Mgr. Molé prohibited. The marks of the cells, which have been thrown together to form rooms, are still visible. The Eudists left this house to take possession of the seminary at Caen, which remained in their possession until the French Revolution, and is now the " Mairie."

very vows excluded him, as Father de Condren may
perhaps have reflected, when, after long opposition,
he permitted the disciple who was, as he foresaw,
hereafter to leave his brethren, to take them.

How wonderful are God's ways! Is it presump-
tuous for weak and ignorant beings to look more
closely into them, and to venture to point out their
connection and consequences ?

We do not think it ; for if we wish to see more
it is that we may adore better, and may lead some
of the faithful, whose thoughts are chiefly turned
to temporal interests, honours and material welfare, to recognise the Hand that guides all things.

With the torch of faith in our hands, we seek
that we may love more, not that we may destroy.
St. Francis of Sales says, " He who seeks for
the true meaning of the heavenly word out of the
Church to which it has been entrusted, never finds
it ; he who would learn it otherwise than by her
ministry, will embrace vanity instead of truth ;
and instead of the sure brightness of the sacred
word, will follow the illusions of the false spirit
who transforms himself into an angel of light."

May God preserve us from the deceits of that
false angel, well-known and ably opposed in the
17th century, but still ready to take his place at
the side of many writers whose rare talents, if
guided by another light, would shine with surpass-
ing glory!

During the whole period of Father Eudes'
connection with the Oratory, all its members had
appreciated his peculiar merit, and recognized
his success. His great and ever-increasing reputation, the effects of his preaching, the results of
his extraordinary self-devotion, had done honour to
the Congregation in general.

But when he set about forming a new society, in
order to fill up a gap which the Oratory had
allowed to widen, he was looked upon as a dan-

gerous deserter, and the irritation of a great number of his former companions was betrayed by the erasure of his name from their rolls, and the deprivation of all the rights which he had acquired at the cost of so much labour and fatigue: " because he is contrary to our doings, and upbraideth us with transgressions of the law."* He was treated as our Saviour Himself had been. When he was informed of the very unusual step which had been taken against him,† he was given to understand that the Rev. Father-Superior-General would overlook the past on condition that he should henceforth render an account of all his undertakings, and that the Oratory would accept the foundations made for the benefit of the seminaries.

After much deliberation with the priests who had joined him, Father Eudes forwarded to the superior-general some very reasonable proposals, which, while they did not absolutely bind him, were sufficient to show his great respect and deference for that illustrious body, to which he always remained closely related, since his object in life was the complete accomplishment of the intentions of its holy founder.

He concluded by begging the fathers of the Oratory to lay to heart the words which the Holy Spirit spoke by Gamaliel in *Acts* v. 38 : " Discedite ab hominibus istis, et sinite illos. Quoniam si est ex hominibus consilium aut opus, dissolvetur : si vero ex Deo est, non poteritis dissolvere illud ne forte et Deo repugnare inveniamini."

They would not understand, or, rather, they

---

* *Book of Wisdom*, ii. 12.

† The famous Father Quesnel was born in Paris in 1634, and died in 1719. He became an Oratorian in 1657, and directed the institution of the Oratorians in Paris, until his attachment to the Jansenists obliged him to leave France. He was not expelled from the Congregation till he had been for years in open rebellion against the Church.

understood that henceforth they had to deal with an adversary, all the more formidable because he would never attack them, but simply defend himself; they foresaw that his increasing glory and holiness would rise above the apparent disgrace of his expulsion, and take all show of reason from that measure.

One of Father Eudes' special characteristics was his calmness in the midst of storms; he never spoke a bitter word, or gave way to recriminations, he always retained a respect for his enemies whom he merely called his old friends.

Such a disposition gave little satisfaction to the Oratory fathers, and, looking upon Father Eudes as a disaffected and rebellious subject, they determined on the most extreme proceedings. Some of the calumnies against Father Eudes having come to the ears of M. de Répichon, that gentleman wrote in the following terms to Father Bernard, parish priest of Carantilly (diocese of Coutances): "I have been astonished at the calumnies heaped upon Father Eudes, with regard to the work he has undertaken; it is said that he prevailed upon me to withhold from the Oratory the sum which I have given to his Congregation. I wish it to be known that I never had any intention of giving the said sum either to the Oratory or to any other object but the one to which I have devoted it."—25th of May, 1645.*

This letter clearly shows that the funds received by him, and of which the Oratory wished to require an account, were destined for the future institution, not given to Father Eudes as an Oratorian. We shall meet with a still more striking confirmation of this fact.

The new founder was no longer an Oratorian, and his only appeal lay to the Sovereign Pontiff,

* Annales de la Congregation. (P. Costil.)

the common father and highest judge of all the faithful.

Seminarium (semen, seminare) may be translated by the word seed-bed; hence the name of seminary is applied to institutions where young laymen are prepared for the priesthood, that they may hereafter bear to the field committed to their care, seed which never fails to bring forth fruit if only it falls on good ground.

The little seminaries are the first institutions of this kind on record; their origin is very remote, for the Council of Bazas, held in 529, during the pontificate of Felix IV., recognised their usefulness. They were probably merely schools established in the cathedral churches and the principal monasteries.

After the devastation caused by the wars and troubles of the 10th century, universities and private schools took the place of these seminaries. The bishops were for the most part obliged to rely on the heads of schools for the general learning of their clergy, and on the doctors of universities for their instruction in theology and canon law.

Nothing could be more unfavourable to unity of doctrine, or more likely to give rise to heresy. The holy Council of Trent,* (sess. 23. ch. xviii. de

---

* Trent, a town in the Austrian Tyrol, celebrated as the seat of the 19th Œcumenical Council, held there from 1545 to 1563. The Protestants had begged that this Council might be assembled, but rejected its authority even before it met. Many dogmas of the Church were defined, anathemas were pronounced against their opponents, and decrees for the reformation of the clergy were issued.

Its decisions in all matters of faith were received in France without opposition; but the Parliaments refused to admit several articles regarding discipline, being anxious to maintain the usages of the Gallican Church.

Thus, in the case of seminaries, they could not be established without letters patent from the king; this point was definitively settled by an edict, in August, 1749. The Bishops were allowed to raise the contributions from benefices without the aid of the canons, and acted with the co-operation of the syndics and deputies of the tithe-offices in their dioceses. They were also

reform.) made a decree that in all the dioceses of each province, one or more seminaries should be established, in which young men born in lawful wedlock and destined for the priesthood should be received. Those who were unable to pay were to be maintained and educated gratuitously by means of contributions collected from all the benefices in the diocese, and all religious orders, except the mendicant and that of Malta, were to bear their part. The Bishop, with the assistance of two canons, was to fix the amount of each contribution. The Council also obliged the *écolâtres*, ecclesiastics belonging to certain cathedral churches, and appointed to teach theology, themselves to undertake the instruction of the young clergy in the seminaries, or to find substitutes approved by their bishop.

The Assembly of Melun, in 1579, conformed to the decision of the Council of Trent, and added several other articles regarding the government of the seminaries. This example was followed by the Provincial Councils of Rouen, Rheims, Bordeaux, Tours, Bourges, Aix and Toulouse.

St. Charles Borromeo, Bishop of Milan, the soul of the Council of Trent, and author of its celebrated catechism, had been able, before he died, at the age of 46, worn out by the austerities and fatigues of his holy calling, to carry out the decree of the Council by opening seminaries in his diocese.

A matter of such importance to the maintenance of wholesome doctrine was not lost sight of at Rome, but the scheme entertained there was yet more general and extensive.

Has not Rome been for nearly nineteen cen-

allowed to admit clerks at a later age than that mentioned by the Council into their seminaries. (Council of Trent, 1545-1563.—*Popes*, Eugenius IV., Felix V., Nicholas V., Calixtus III., Pius II. *Kings of France*, Francis I., Henry II., Francis II., Charles IX.)

turies a diamond, whose various faces shine on the whole world ? Is not Rome a burning light which can never be quenched, because man cannot destroy what God has established ? "Instruction in truth and in morals flows with rare profusion alike from the pulpits of its universities, where learning, faith and holiness are combined, and from those where the gospel is preached to the poor. The most sublime truths are taught in its very streets and squares, and are the common property of all."*

Rome has founded seminaries, but their principal object is to convey the faith from its fountain head to distant countries.

Each nation, each diocese even, according to the law of the Council of Trent, ought to promote the development of theological science in its own sphere, but Rome is always working for all, with that maternal tenderness which would vanish from the world, could the wishes of those who dare to place his divine and supreme dignity on a level with mere human authorities be carried out, and the Holy Father be, as they say, "suppressed."

The most important and celebrated of the Roman Seminaries is that known as the Apostolic or Urban Seminary, and the College of the Propagation of the Faith.

This digression, although far too short for the importance of the subject, will have clearly shewn how good a path Father Eudes was following by adhering to the intentions of the Council of Trent, and co-operating with such men as St. Vincent de Paul, and Fathers d'Authier de Sisgau, Olier and Bourdoise, to all of whom he was ever united by the closest and most holy bonds of friendship.

We give the names of the earliest seminaries in France, in the order of their foundation. The

* Union de l'Ouest, 30th November, 1866. (Angers.)

Seminary of Valence was founded by Father d'Authier de Sisgau, in 1639, that of the college des Bons-Enfants in Paris, by St. Vincent de Paul, founder of the missionary priests, in 1642; that of Caen, by Father Eudes, in 1643; and that of St. Nicholas du Chardonnet, at Paris, by Father Bourdoise, in 1644.

At last the work was begun; but how long had been the delays! We have shewn in our work on military schools what a slow and tardy thing progress is. Seminaries for officers were only established in 1751, and then at the instigation of a clever minister of finance and a courtezan,—Paris Duverney and Mdme. de Pompadour—although the project, due to the brave Captain Lanoue, dated from the days of Henry IV., and Richelieu and Louvois had made ineffectual efforts to realize it.

Father Eudes was naturally chosen as superior by the members of the new Congregation of Jesus and Mary. They took no vows; charity was their sole bond of union; they owed entire obedience to the Pope, and were in dependence on the bishop of the diocese in which they lived.

It was decided that on Father Eudes' death a successor should be chosen, who should have the same governing powers, and assign to his colleagues the position and employment for which he considered each one best fitted by his character and capacity.

Father Eudes' system of government was based on that of Father de Bérulle; but he had merely two objects in view: 1st, to work at the training of good ecclesiastics by means of retreats and other exercises in the seminaries, and 2nd, to keep the spirit of Christianity alive among the people, by means of frequent missions.

The following words might have been taken as the motto of the Congregation: " Colere Deum et facere voluntatem ejus cordi magno et animo volenti;" or these others : " Servire Christo et Ecclesiæ, in sanctitate et justitiâ coram ipso omnibus diebus nostris."

The task of drawing up definite constitutions was put off to a future time; from the first the practice of meditation was laid down as essential, and some devotional exercises were recommended, which in course of time were generally adopted.

The Feasts of the Sacred Hearts of Jesus and Mary, of St. Joseph, St. Joachim, and St. Anne, as well as the Octave of the Immaculate Conception, were to be solemnly observed in the Congregation, which from the first moment of its existence was consecrated, 1st, to the Most Holy Trinity, as the first principle and ultimate object of the episcopal dignity and sanctity; 2ndly, to the Holy Family of Jesus, Mary and Joseph, which the order took as its model; and 3rdly, to the Divine Heart of Jesus and the most Holy Heart of Mary.

The valiant band lost no time in setting to work; as early as Pentecost, 1643, they gave a mission at St. Sauveur le Vicomte, in the diocese of Coutances, which was immediately followed by one at Valognes. Never was a mission better attended than this last. The indefatigable priests preached in the open air to thirty or forty thousand persons, many of whom came from a distance to hear them. A story of this mission is still handed down by tradition in the order. Father Eudes' hearers, alarmed by a terrible storm which seemed about to break upon them, were about to disperse, when he solemnly assured them that the thunder and the tempest would respect them. They believed him and remained, and the place which they occupied was the only one within ten miles untouched by the storm.

During this mission, Father Eudes caused some forsaken chapels to be again honoured as

7

holy places, revived failing fervour, reconciled deadly enemies, induced many persons to make restitution, and, in short, gained the most encouraging victories.

And, like St. Paul at Ephesus, he committed to the flames a quantity of hateful domestic missionaries, in the shape of bad books and licentious pictures, which his hearers gave up to him.

These glorious successes were followed by further results. Father Le Pileur, grand-vicar of Coutances, wrote as follows : " The happy change wrought in the manners of the clergy by a course of instructions and conferences lasting for several weeks, furnishes an ample proof of the importance of Father Eudes' projected seminaries." He further added, that this holy priest was specially fitted for such an undertaking, and that the approbation of the Holy Father was an essential condition of its permanent success.

The document we have quoted bears date September 3rd, 1643, and seems to have led to all the further steps taken in the course of that year. It was evidently expected that the Congregation would extend throughout all the dioceses of France, or at least all those adjacent to that of Bayeux, otherwise, according to the Council of Trent, the approbation already given by that bishop would have been sufficient. Mgr. de Matignon, Bishop of Coutances, and Mgr. d'Angennes, wrote to Rome to ask for the formal recognition of the Congregation.*

---

* The Council of Trent, and the decrees of our kings, conferred these powers and rights on the bishops, as may be seen in the twenty-fourth article passed at the meeting of the States-General at Blois, whose decisions were published in Paris in 1579; in the report of the assembly held at Melun in the same year, and in the first article of the edict of Melun in 1580 : *with this difference*, that whereas the twenty-fourth article of Blois required archbishops and bishops to establish these seminaries and schools in their dioceses in whatever form seemed to them best suited to the special circumstances, and to provide the neces-

Mgr. d'Angennes' letter of the 22nd October, 1643, was accompanied by a second, addressed to Cardinal Antonio. The letters to the Holy See produced little or no effect, for Pope Urban VIII. died on the 29th of July, 1644. They contained three requests: for the confirmation of the Congregation, for apostolic powers, and for indulgences for the missions.

Cardinal Antonio did not reply until the 2nd of July, 1644; he then informed Mgr. d'Angennes that the Congregation of the Propaganda applauded his zeal, was most desirous of assisting him, and had forwarded a summary of the requests regarding Father Eudes to the French Nuncio, in order that the customary enquiries might be made on the spot.

Father Eudes had gone to Paris with Father Manchon in December, 1643.

His principal protectors had been removed at the time when he needed them most. Cardinal de Richelieu died in 1642, and King Louis XIII. in 1643. He might truly say of his house: " Deus in medio ejus, non commovebitur : adjuvabit eam Deus mane diluculo."

But the political horizon was dark and lowering.

sary funds for foundations and endowments by the union of benefices, by the assignment of pensions, and such other means as they deemed best, and commanded His Majesty's officers, as well those of the sovereign court as all others, to give them assistance, insomuch that the parliament of Rouen enjoined on the archbishops and bishops to proceed within six months under pain of deprivation of their temporalities ; the edict of Melun admonishes bishops and metropolitans within the next six months, and again, once every three years, to assemble provincial councils to take measures for the maintenance of discipline, the correction of manners, the direction of ecclesiastical discipline, and the formation of seminaries according to the holy canons. This edict was adopted, not only by the provincial council held at Rouen in 1581, but also by a decree of Louis XIII. in 1629, to compel bishops to establish seminaries in their dioceses immediately, in accordance with the first article of Melun aforesaid.—(P. Costil. Annales.)

The importance of this note will appear in the course of our history.

The destiny of France was in the hands of a young Queen Regent, of a child-king, and of a Cardinal Minister of foreign origin, a mere effigy of his predecessor, and the troubles of the Fronde were about to break out.

In a secondary position as agent of the Holy See, and still more often of Richelieu, Mazarin had undoubtedly shown a certain amount of capacity. But if Richelieu had often urged on the chariot of the state with extreme rapidity, he, unlike his successor, had always been able to guide its course: if the nobility, the parliament, and the people had felt his power, they had bowed before his well-known high birth, they had known that they were doing homage to a Frenchman who had raised his own country to the highest place.

Honour had been his portion, but Mazarin's heritage was one of popular disquiet, of murmuring and revolt. "He was a diplomatist of the first order, his name is associated with the two most important treaties of the XVIIth century, that of Westphalia, and of the Pyrenees. He was full of resources and expedients; and he chose to corrupt parties rather than to be obliged to exterminate them."

There is a close connection between religious and political affairs, and Father Eudes could not but see that these troublous times were not favourable for religious foundations.

There was, however, a dazzling brightness about the early days of the regency. The Queen and the Minister lavished money and favours, with the hope of consolidating their power. But ere long they were obliged to resort to other expedients, and the nation, which had thought it was about to breathe more freely, soon learned to look back with regret on the yoke imposed by Cardinal de Richelieu.

A civil war was the necessary consequence of

this state of things, and it soon broke forth, spite of all the efforts of the new government. One remarkable proof of Richèlieu's skill and strength was, that he never allowed war except to the degree in which it fell in with his policy and furthered his ulterior purposes.

"It is a characteristic of Christian constancy," according to Father Eudes' biographer, Father Montigny,* "never to be deterred by any diffi-

* The first person who collected any particulars of the life of Father Eudes, was Father Finel, once a magistrate at Carentan, and afterwards a Priest and Eudist. His work, "Verba dierum," gives much information as to the early days of the Congregation. We have already spoken of that by Father Herambourg. Father Costil, by order of Father de Fontaines de Neuilly, the third Superior General, began to write the annals of the Congregation on the 22nd May, 1720. He devoted many years to this labour, and visited all the houses of the Order, and of Father Eudes' other foundations. Father de Montigny, a Jesuit, wrote Father Eudes' life in 1765. There is also a Manuscript Life written in 1778, by Father Beurier, one of the most distinguished members of the Congregation. Father Eudes deserves a place amongst his own biographers, for he kept a journal. Father Le Doré, postulator in the cause of his beatification, has lately discovered another MSS. life, which was written between 1740 and 1750, by a Eudist Priest, and is more ample than any of the others, as well as superior in style. The celebrated Huet, Bishop of Avranches, speaks of the venerable Father in his *Origines de Caen*, and in another work entitled: *Commentarius de rebus ad eum pertinentibus*.

Hermant and Heliot, in their History of Monastic Orders, have made use of these documents.

Father Tresvaux, one of the Paris clergy, reprinted Father Montigny's work, modernizing the style, and adding many interesting details. Father Blanchard, the Superior General, lent him some documents, which are believed to have been lost when the Archiepiscopal Palace was sacked in 1832.

A most interesting notice from the pen of M. Gustave Levavasseur is prefixed to the report of the inauguration, at Ri, of the medallions containing busts of the three brothers Eudes, executed by their kinsman, M. C. de Montzey.

No biography of Father Eudes has appeared in print, except that by Father Tresvaux, (1827,) M. Lavavasseur's notice, (1853,) and his Virtues by Father Herambourg, with Father Doré's notes, (1868.)

We humbly trust that God will bless our work, and permit our offering of homage to our revered ancestor to assist in promoting his beatification, by making him known throughout the world.

culties from the execution of a purpose which has good for its object."

We are about to relate the troubles which beset Father Eudes throughout life, and must again repeat that one of the marked features of his character, was the calmness with which he met ill-treatment; he bore it as Jesus bore the cowardly insults of the Jews, " he thanked Him for granting him and his brethren the favour of a share in His humiliations." His biographers tell us that he was unmoved by the calumnies which attacked his intentions and thwarted his endeavours to carry out the useful and practical decrees of the Council of Trent.

It was a matter of great importance that two false ideas which, notwithstanding their absurdity, had taken hold of the public mind, should be dispelled; one was that his project could not succeed—and yet its execution had been amongst Richelieu's last wishes; and the other, that the Bishops were opposed to the establishment of a new Order which, even in event of success, could not bring about more good than might be expected from those already at work under their direction—and yet inclination or circumstances had in most provinces directed the energy of these Orders into other channels.

A word from the throne of St. Peter was needed to silence these low-born murmurs, therefore, after having taken counsel with Mgr. d'Angennes, and the few other friends who remained constant to him, Father Eudes decided on sending Father Simon Mannoury to Rome. This priest was his faithful counsellor and one of his most devoted colleagues; the strength of his character, and the purity of his life, made him worthy of entire confidence, and he had, moreover, been the first to associate himself with him in his new work.

Father Mannoury joyfully undertook this delicate and difficult mission. He had to encounter the fatigues and perils of a long journey on foot, with the slenderest resources, and he had yet more to apprehend from the opposition of powerful enemies at Rome; an opposition rendered doubly dangerous by its apparent zeal for the cause of religion, and for the interests of the Sovereign Pontiff.

His instructions from Father Eudes were, to solicit from the Holy See the confirmation of the establishment of the Seminary at Caen, and consequently of the Congregation; and in the second place, the faculties usually granted to Apostolic Missionaries; as well as certain indulgences for those who should attend the missions. He was also to ask, in the name of Mgr. d'Angennes, for the confirmation of the Order of our Lady of Charity.

One morning, having fortified himself by offering the Holy Sacrifice, Father Mannoury bade his superior farewell, and took his pilgrim's staff in his hand: the Congregation had no resources to meet the expenses of a long journey; God was pleased to permit that poverty and opposition should be the foundation of His work.

Father Eudes's ruling passion was for the sanctification of souls; from his earliest years he had the highest idea of this object. He looked upon it as the chosen employment of God, of His angels and saints. He often repeated to his brethren the words attributed to St. Denis the Areopagite, " Omnium Divinorum divinissimum est cooperari Deo in salutem animarum." " I have no wish," he would say, " but if God commanded me to make a choice, I would live always, that I might help to save souls." His special affection was for those great sinners who were peculiarly in need of the Divine mercy and of his assistance.

He wrote to one of his spiritual children : "Since we must die, what can be better than to die for the cause for which our most dear Saviour sacrificed Himself?" "Majorem hâc dilectionem nemo habet ut animam suam ponat quis pro amicis suis." We have already seen how his love for souls impelled him to entire self-devotion at St. Christophe, at Argentan, and at Caen.*

Having heard that Father d'Authier de Sisgau was giving missions under the direction of the Propaganda, and had received ample powers from the Holy See, together with the permission to communicate them to such persons as he might select to associate with him in his labours, Father Eudes earnestly begged that his society might be united to the one already formed by this holy priest. Father d'Authier's answer bears date the 4th of January, 1644, and shows how fully he reciprocated this desire. It is not known how its execution was prevented. In the midst of all these anxieties, Father Eudes found time, after his return from Paris, to go to Honfleur, where Mgr. de Cospéau had requested him to give a mission.

This prelate had promised to assist him in the work, but was unable to do so, on account of a vexatious law-suit which had been brought against him.

He wrote to him as follows, to express his gratitude for the results of his mission : " I bless the Lord with all my heart for the favours He has shown us through you, and I beg Him to preserve you, as the greatest benefit He can bestow on me, who am entirely devoted to you. I knew well the good that you would do at Honfleur, and that God would be glorified by it to the astonishment of the beholders. God has chosen you as the organ and

* Père Hérambourg, Vertus. P. Le Doré's notes.

minister of the great graces by which He prevents and saves His children."

Almost as soon as Father Eudes and his collengues had returned home, they heard that M. de Répichon and his son, M. de Lyon, who had entered holy orders, had, by a deed executed in September, 1644, made over a sum of 14,000 livres to their house; "but," says Father Costil, "from reasons which we cannot investigate, only 3,000 were for the present forthcoming."

A few days before, on his entrance into the Congregation, M. Blouet de Than had given an income of 1,500 livres, and 3,000 livres of arrears, and thus, in a temporal point of view, he may be said to have founded the seminary at Caen.

About this time Father Eudes laid down the course to be followed in giving Missions, and the marvellous and long-continued success which attended his labours and those of his Congregation, is in great measure due to the wisdom of these rules. We regret that our space does not permit us to give them at length; an analysis would be impossible, we shall therefore merely quote the four kinds of preparation particularly recommended to the missionaries before setting to work.

The first is a pure intention to destroy sin and establish holiness in souls : the *second*, profound humiliation at the sight of their own unworthiness and insufficiency for so high a calling, and an unreserved devotion to our Lord, who is pleased to use them as the weak instruments of His grace : *the third*, complete detachment from all things that might hinder the operation of His grace, such as self-interest, curiosity, love of reputation and of pleasure : *the fourth*, a burning zeal for souls.

To these four preparations, must be added the Conferences which the missionaries were to hold once a week, with a view of keeping alive their fervour. Those who read the rules of the Missions at length, cannot fail to see how well fitted they were to produce abundant fruit, especially at a time when such means of grace were rare.

In the course of fifty-four years, Father Eudes gave one hundred and ten or one hundred and twelve Missions; others, to the number of ten or twelve a year, were given simultaneously at different places by his fellow-labourers. He also preached many Advents and Lents. How could his physical strength sustain such labours? Where did he find the time to give conferences, to travel from place to place, to look after the temporal and spiritual concerns of the Daughters of our Lady of Charity of the Refuge, as well as of many communities and private individuals, who were in the habit of applying to him for strength and for counsel? How was he able to write many books,* and to superintend their publication?

* WORKS OF FATHER EUDES.

1. Exercices piété pour vivre chrétiennement, 1636, refondu en 1638.
2. Vie et Royaume de Jésus, in 8vo, 1637, 1664, 1667.
3. Le Testament de Jésus, 1641.
4. La Vie du Chretien, in 12mo, 1641, 1669, 1695.
5. Le Contrat de l'homme avec Dieu, 1654, 1743.
6. Le Bon Confesseur, Paris, 1666, in 12mo. Rouen, 1732.
7. Le Mémorial de la Vie Ecclésiastique. Lisieux, 1681.
8. Le Prédicateur Apostolique. Caen, 1685.
9. Le propre des Offices de la Congrégation de Jésus et Marie, 1672.
10. L'Enfance Admirable, Paris, 1676.
11. La devotion au T. S. Cœur de la Mère Admirable. Autun, 1648, Caen, 1650, 1663, &c.
12. Le Cœur Admirable de la T. S. Mère de Dieu, 1682.
13. Catéchisme de la Mission.
14. 3ième partie du Sacrifice admirable—Manière de servir la Sainte Messe.
15. Manuel de piété á l'usage de la Congrégation de Jésus et de Marie.
16. Les Constitutions de la Congrégation de Jésus et Marie.

IN MANUSCRIPT.

1. Tout Jésus ou Exercices intérieures sur Jésus.
2. Viè de La ou Marie Desvallées, 2 ou 3 volumes.
3. L' homme chrétien, sur les vices et les vertues.

We cannot imagine. The secret belongs to God, who selects men for the work they are to do, and never lays a burden on one who cannot bear it. He surely must have multiplied Father Eudes' strength in a wonderful manner.

Marvellous transformations were wrought by these repeated missions in the same places; seven or eight generations have passed away, but their memory still remains fresh.

In the rocky plains of Sarthe we once stopped to watch the operations of the quarry-men on a block of granite : we thought their instruments insufficient; they had only some iron wedges, some little steel-pointed hammers, and some other tools of no great size, and the rock they had to deal with was hardened by centuries. But we were mistaken; a hole was made, a wedge was inserted, a second, and a third, some well-directed blows were struck, and then the mass gave way, and stood ready to be cut into a foundation-stone for some great edifice.

And thus the hardest hearts yielded to Father Eudes. He stood at the door and knocked with gentle force. " Ecce sto ad ostium et pulso," and souls were touched and brought back to God. He armed innocence with an impenetrable shield, and

4. Du Sacrifice admirable.
5. Ste Enfance de Jésus.
[It is not certain that this book was composed by Father Eudes himself. This catalogue, we are told by Father Doré, postulator of the cause of beatification, is as complete as he has been able to make it, but it has not been possible to find all the printed books ; and many of the manuscripts were dispersed or lost at the time of the Revolution. It will be seen that many of the published books did not appear till after Father Eudes' death.]
6. Faveurs acordées par la Ste. Vierge au diocése de Coutance (in achevé).
7. Trois volumes de meditations.
8. Sermons.
9. De l'Office divin.
10. Les Règles et Constitutions de l'ordre de Notre Dame de Charite.
11. Mémorial (avec action de grâces en Latin.)

when, alas! it had been lost under the influence
of temptations, or the oppression of power,—when
violence had ruined a life, and left those bitter
memories which time cannot efface,—fearlessly
and firmly he rescued the poor victims from the
ravishing wolves. And after conflicts which often
drew upon him the hatred of those whose evil
passions he had opposed, he would return to his
cell without any earthly reward, like our brave
soldiers, who often bring back to their huts
nothing but the memory of fearful struggles.
"Entirely for God, everything for God, glory to
God alone." Such was ever his watchword. What
a lesson to our insatiable thirst for honour and
distinction!

Nothing could lessen his zeal, and let us say it
at once, in his magnificent work of missions, as
well as in his foundations, the most determined
opposition he met with was from some of the
clergy. He was not merely a founder, but also a
reformer, and these trials were necessary in order
that his own virtue might be made perfect, and
that the glory of the word of God which he
preached might be manifested; had they been
wanting, the humility of the preacher might perhaps have been grieved by seeing men attribute to
his eloquence successes which were due to the in-
vincible power of the Cross.

A letter which was addressed to him by one
who held an exalted position in the Church, expresses our meaning perfectly: "What marvel if
our Saviour lets those who have the honour of
sharing in His great work of glorifying God and
saving souls, be also partakers of His sufferings?
God has given you uncommon zeal, therefore be
assured that you will have to bear uncommon persecution. And to make it sharper and more extraordinary, it must needs come from holy persons. If Christ was forsaken by God while He

accomplished His great work, I do not wonder that you are forsaken and persecuted by good men. When the will of God is made clear to them, they will conform themselves to it, and will be grieved at the things they have done, but in the meantime: Viriliter agite et confortetur cor vestrum et sustinete Dominum."*

God allowed His servants to make mistakes, in order that Father Eudes might be tried, and might pass uninjured through success, which St. Bernard considered the greatest peril for humility. The opposition of men of God was at once the seal of Father Eudes' vocation and the germ of innumerable fruits.

The departure of the missionaries was always marked by tears; it was the separation of fathers and children; but the children knew that their fathers were ever with them in spirit, that their prayers accompanied each step of their lives, and that they would return to give them fresh courage and strength.

What we have said applies, in a general way, to all the missions given by Father Eudes and his faithful comrades; as we continue his history, we shall give, in their proper order, some of the most striking details. When we meet with a picture painted by some great master, we begin by putting ourselves at a certain distance from it, we contemplate it as a whole, we study the broad outlines, the principal effects, the general idea, and afterwards we admire each minute detail.

Are not the Saints' Lives master-pieces painted by the hand of God?

If Voltaire and his followers had fallen upon a period like the XVIth and the early part of the XVIIth century, what irreparable mischief would have been done! though the destroying blast,

* P. Costil, Annales.

which shattered many of its branches, could not shake the immoveable trunk whose roots go down into eternity.

Father Eudes must be reckoned among the brave champions who kept alive the faith of our fathers, and preserved Catholic France, the eldest daughter of the Church.

Let us turn once more to his family.

Beneath all his firmness he bore the most tender of hearts; he had left his home to devote himself to the service of all who were in misery, but that home was ever dear to him. The news of his father's serious illness reached him suddenly; he hastened to him in the hope of being able to give him all the consolations of religion, but was only in time to close his eyes. Counting too much on his strength, he presided at his funeral, and even ascended the pulpit, and spoke to his neighbours of resignation under the afflictions which God sends; but when the service was over he hastened away to weep.

Here is another point of resemblance to St. Francis of Sales. That holy priest was about to preach when the tidings of his father's death reached him; mastering his terrible sorrow, he told his hearers of the loss he had just sustained, and begged them to pray for the departed—but soon his tears gained the victory, and all present took part in his grief, so that nothing was heard but the voice of a common sorrow, mingled with prayer for the beloved being who was gone.*

Charles Eudes being nearer at hand, had received the sad tidings sooner, and had reached home in time to watch by his father's sick bed, but Francis de Mezeray was not there. The tumults of the capital, the absorption of study, the interests of ambition, had kept the sound of the

* Death of M. de Boissy, in St. Francis' life.

passing-bell from his ears,* and he did not even come to console his widowed mother. But let us not be too hard upon him, for it must be admitted that in those days many difficulties attended the shortest journey.

In the division of the patrimonial possessions, which took place at Ri, on the 22nd November, 1644, Francis de Mezeray was, according to the custom of Normandy, represented by the attorney, Marin Guérin, who generally acted in such cases for the villagers. In accordance with another usage of the province, Charles Eudes du d'Houay, as the youngest son, made the lots, and John Eudes, as the eldest, drew first. Notwithstanding this division, the property remained entire, and the mother of the three Eudes continued to live there in some comfort, a fact which brings the celebrated author before us as a good son. After the death of Martha Corbin, Father Eudes left his share of the property to his family.

We have spoken of the celebrated author, for in 1643, Francis de Mezeray had published the first volume of his history of France, which was received with as much favour as if he had been our only historian, so completely had his predecessors been forgotten or neglected. His work was dedicated in the first instance to Cardinal de Richelieu, but this dedication was soon superseded by one to the Queen, who was by this means already favourably disposed towards Father Eudes; when St. Vincent de Paul presented him to her she at once granted him her protection, and thus Mézeray's reputation was of use to his brother.

* Notice sur les 3 Eudes. G. Levavasseur.

CHAPTER II.

1644—1648.

FATHER MANNOURY AT ROME.—JANSENISTS THERE.—AFTER INEFFECTUAL EFFORTS HE IS RECALLED BY HIS SUPERIOR IN 1645.—ASSEMBLY OF THE CLERGY OF FRANCE, IN 1645.—REQUEST PRESENTED BY FATHER EUDES TO THIS ASSEMBLY.—HE FRAMES HIS CONSTITUTIONS.—FRESH TROUBLES.—MEMORIAL AGAINST FATHER EUDES, PRESENTED TO THE QUEEN BY THE ORATORIANS.—VARIOUS MISSIONS.—DEATH OF MGR. D'ANGENNES.—SERIOUS ILLNESS OF FATHER EUDES; HIS RECOVERY.—MISSION AT AUTUN, IN 1648; ITS RESULTS.—THE GREAT MEN OF THE CHURCH, AND THE WOMEN WHO HAVE HELPED THEM.—MISSIONS.—MGR. MOLE SUCCEEDS MGR. D'ANGENNES IN THE SEE OF BAYEUX.—HIS PREJUDICE AGAINST FATHER EUDES.—CONSTANT SUPPORT OF MGR. DE HARLAY, ARCHBISHOP OF ROUEN.—FATHER EUDES PRESENTS A MEMORIAL TO THE QUEEN, TOUCHING THE TROUBLES OF THE TIME.—MEZERAY AND CHARLES D'HOUAY.

"*Ecco Roma!* People," says Mrs. Craven, "who arrive at Rome by the railway, rushing like a whirlwind into a station which has nothing to distinguish it from the most insignificant place on earth, cannot imagine the effect formerly produced by those two words, when, having reached the point from which the Eternal City could first be seen, the postillion used to stop his horses, and pointing it out in the distance to the traveller, used to pronounce them with that grave sonorous Roman accent, which is like the name of Rome herself."*

Ecco Roma! Father Mannoury also may have exclaimed, when from the same spot he looked on that beautiful prospect standing out against the

* Anne Séverin.

,clear bright sky, while before him rose the peerless dome which can never, even at first sight, be mistaken for any one of those surrounding it.

We can see the brave priest, regardless of all his fatigues, hastening on, like St. Peter of old, with his staff in his hand, to the Eternal City, to seek some place of abode, and then, after a few hours repose, to set about the business he had in hand, in the course of which he was to meet with so many difficulties.

The letters of the Bishops of Bayeux, of Lisieux, and of Coutances, had arrived before him, together with another equally important document, an attestation from Father le Pileur, vicar-general, giving a full account of the successes gained by Father Eudes. The prelates, who were anxious that Rome should merely act according to established rules, had written most urgently to the Holy Father on behalf of the Congregation. There was reason to hope for the assistance of Cardinal de Grimaldi, to whom Mgr. de Cospéan had particularly recommended the matter, and Mgr. d'Angennes wished that the same request which he had addressed to Urban VIII., at the close of his Pontificate, should now be laid before Innocent X. Everything seemed to promise success; but it was not yet to be granted, for God willed that the foundations should be dug yet deeper, in order that the holy house might be yet more steadfast.

It is said that the Jansenists of the Low Countries skilfully countermined the plans of one whom they considered a most formidable adversary.

John Sinnich, a doctor of Louvain, and Corneille Poepe, had been sent to Rome by the leaders of this sect, and had arrived there in the month of November, 1643. On their way through Paris, they had naturally made acquaintance with the Fathers of the Oratory, some of whom had embraced their doctrines. As Father Eudes had always opposed this heresy, and as its entrance into the Oratory had been one of the principal reasons which induced him to leave it, the Jansenist envoys at once made common cause with his former comrades, who were bent on his ruin at any cost.

The circumstances we have mentioned were sufficient to make the two Jansenists oppose Father Eudes by every means in their power, and they used the consideration which, thanks to their underhand dealings, they still enjoyed in Rome, to injure him.

A very strong impression was made by the reasons which they brought forward in favour of the illustrious Congregation of the Oratory. Father Mannoury at once saw how matters stood, and the Cardinals of the Propaganda could not conceal their conviction that all his efforts would be unavailing. The state of things had been made all the more hopeless by the assurance given to the Holy Father that the Congregation which Cardinal de Bérulle had founded, and Fathers de Condren and de Beauregard successively governed, had no high opinion of its expelled member.

Spite of the cup of bitterness which was his daily portion, Father Mannoury fulfilled his mission, but when he saw how effectually calumny had preceded him, he wrote to Father Eudes on the 22nd of March, 1645, begging to be recalled, but feeling certain that he would be sent back to Rome at some future time, if circumstances appeared more favourable.

Father Mannoury therefore returned, and Father Eudes, suspending all efforts to gain anything from Rome, devoted himself to his accustomed labours.

An Assembly of the Clergy was to be held in Paris in the course of the year 1645. Father Eudes thought it well to take the opportunity of seeking a formal approval for his Congregation. As a second failure would have been very prejudicial to its interests, he consulted beforehand with Mgr. d'Angennes, and Mgr. Cospéau, who advised him to make the attempt, and themselves wrote to the assembled bishops to bespeak a favourable hearing for him.

The Assembly appointed commissioners to examine the request, and, two months afterwards, having learned by their report that it contained nothing that had not already been proposed in 1625, and having debated on the advantages which would arise from the establishment of seminaries, on the means for their foundation and endowment, and on the difficulties in the way of such an undertaking; in consideration of these difficulties it decided that the project could not be entertained; by way of softening a verdict which was in opposition with all the resolutions and decisions on this subject during the previous ninety years, the assembly declared itself "nevertheless much pleased with the zeal shown by the priests of the seminary of Caen, and exhorted them to work in the other dioceses to which they might be summoned, in the same manner as they had already done in that of Bayeux."

The Bishop of Grasse was charged to answer the letters of the Bishops of Bayeux and Lisieux, and he did so in terms which at least served to testify to Father Eudes' worth. On the other hand, of what negative value were all the ordinances which we have already cited, especially that of 1629, given by Louis XIII., and apparently very explicit?

Rome had not thought fit to pronounce a decision regarding the seminaries, which, nevertheless, she must have approved, but this was on account of the man who appeared as their founder; the man was rejected, not the foundation. In France, on the contrary, the man would have been accepted as worthy of all esteem and confidence; but the foundation was rejected, a foundation which had, however, been expressly recommended by the Council of Trent, and many provincial councils, and which had entered into Richelieu's system of government.

A singular contrast is here brought before us. Father Eudes had been implicitly approved, but he felt this was by no means sufficient to give stability to his work, and therefore determined to use every means in his power to obtain a more formal decision in its favour.

He saw that he would have had a better chance of success if he had been in a position to present to the bishops the Constitutions of the Congregation of Jesus and Mary; and, accordingly, began to frame them under the direction of Mgr. de Cospéan, who was ere long to be removed from him.

It seemed as if God would deprive him successively of most of those on whom he might have leaned, and who might, by their high position in Church or state, have promoted his plans. God alone, we see, was his stay; and therefore he became more firm and resolute when difficulties appeared insurmountable. In the first surprise caused by his departure from the Oratory, three friends are said to have remained faithful to him. One of them, the Baron de Renty, who was allied by birth with the first families in France, addressed to him on this occasion a letter full of esteem and affection, expressing his conviction that the charges brought against him were entirely unfounded.

An effort was made to prejudice the queen against him, and the memorial which he had pre-

sented to her was met by another from the
Oratory, whose original is preserved in the Imperial
Archives; we quote the opening words of this
document which will give an idea of its animus:

"Father Eudes was a poor boy, of humble
birth, with small temporal possessions, and but
little learning;" it concludes by saying, "as he
will do nothing which is not done in the Oratory,
it is not necessary to divide the work, or to raise
altar against altar."

St. Vincent de Paul and Father St. John Chrysostom, of the Third Order of St. Francis, pleaded
Father Eudes' cause before the queen. It is even
said that the former laid it upon her as a matter of
conscience.

When Father Eudes had framed his Constitutions, he submitted them to his bishop, Mgr.
d'Angennes, who did not, however, give his approval, perhaps because his advanced age and continued infirmities may have made it impossible
for him to examine them thoroughly. Nevertheless, he continued to show the holy priest every
mark of affection and regard; and even granted
him for the time of his missions the powers usually
reserved for bishops.

Notwithstanding all his anxieties, Father Eudes
gave four missions in the course of this year, at
Estralts near Corbon, and Vimontier, in the
diocese of Lisieux, and afterwards at Arnay-le-Duc,
and Conches, in Burgundy: the former is a little
town about five or six leagues from Autun, and
the latter is worthy of notice on account of a
Benedictine priory, very rich in holy relics. The
two missions in Burgundy were undertaken at Baron
de Renty's request and expense.

In grateful return for his labours in that remote
part of the country, the religious of Conches gave
him a share of their treasures, which he bestowed
on the seminary at Caen.

In 1646 we find him again in the diocese of Bayeux, where he gave three missions, for M. de Matignon Thorigny, for M. de Renty at Bény, and for M. de Répichon at Lyon, near the shrine of our Lady of Deliverance.

In the following year he went through the dioceses of Chartres and Evreux, beginning by Nogent-le-Rotrou; the prejudices of the Bishop of Chartres had been overcome by the success of his conferences for the clergy, and he was pleased himself to open the mission given by request of the Duke of St. Simon, at La Ferté Vidame.

Father Eudes then went to Fouqueville, in the diocese of Evreux, where he pursued his apostolic labours under the direction of Mgr. de Perron, nephew and successor of the Cardinal of that name. The expenses were borne by Madame de Bethomas, who afterwards married M. de la Porte, counsellor of the parliament at Rouen.

Mgr. de Lescot, Bishop of Chartres, then summoned him to La Ferté, and begged him to provide the Advent and Lent preachers for the principal churches in his diocese. While Father Eudes was thus sowing abundant seed for the future, it seemed but too likely that others would enter into his labours, for, worn by fever and fatigue, he fell so dangerously ill that he received the last sacraments.

An inward voice made known to him that God would have him forsake all that might attach him to earth; he therefore made a vow to leave for a time the province of Normandy, to which he was bound by so many ties, and to devote himself to a part of France which he had only once visited. His health immediately returned, and he was convinced that he owed this favour to our Lady's intercession.

In 1648 he set off for Autun, and though he had so lately been ill, he had sufficient strength to perform a part of his long journey on foot. His preaching was ever attended with the same success; and one most remarkable result was, the abolition of a long-established amusement very dangerous to morals.

The greater number of the young men, of easy circumstances, in this place, used to form them-selves into a society of *Valentines*, so called from the name of the holy martyr honoured by the Church on the 14th of February, and whose feast, therefore, generally coincides with the carnival. On that day they used to choose a leader called the *Mad Mother*, and to follow him about the streets, committing all manner of excesses.

This lawless band came to hear Father Eudes preach, and his measured and persuasive words made such an impression on its members, that their society was broken up, and the long-tolerated disorders were for ever at an end.* This fact is full of significance; we know from experience the difficulties attending on the suppression of a usage

* By a curious coincidence, we find that forty-six years before, St. Francis de Sales had also been obliged to deal with this delicate and important subject from the pulpit. At Annecy, as well as at Autun, the members of the Society of Valentines had long been in the habit of meeting on the 14th of February. This custom, the source of many unseemly disorders, was widely spread throughout France, England and Scotland. For a whole year the young man and woman, whose names were associated by lot, became each other's Valentines. At Annecy, in particular, married people used to take part in this unbecoming amusement, which gave rise to frequent domestic jealousies. From the month of January the holy bishop set himself against it; and when his words were ill-received, gave notice that he should appeal to the secular power. He promised himself to make Valentines, by distributing in each family tickets bearing the names of different saints, followed by some striking words from Holy Scripture, or from the writings of the Fathers. These tickets were drawn by lot, and the saint whose name fell to each person, was to be honoured as his patron throughout the coming year, and the maxim which followed was to be taken as his rule of life. (Life of St. Francis of Sales.)

"To-morrow is St. Valentine's Day, when every bird chooses her mate; but you will not see the linnet pair with the sparrow-hawk, nor the robin-redbreast with the kite."—*Fair Maid of Perth.*

which time has sanctioned, and to which popular feeling has become so attached as to be blind to its dangers.*

Father Eudes obtained from the abbey of St. Symphorian portions of the bones of that illustrious martyr, and of those of St. Proculus, the bishop. The head of St. Lazarus was preserved in the cathedral, and in his ardour for relics he could not but wish to have something that had belonged to one familiar with our Lord during His mortal life. The Chapter was glad to manifest its gratitude to him by desiring two Canons, Fathers Hymblot and de Montaigu, to give him a tooth of the saint.

The commissioners, accompanied by witnesses, repaired to the sacristy of the cathedral, and endeavoured to remove the tooth from the jaw, but their efforts were ineffectual, and they were about to give up the attempt, when Father Eudes fell on his knees, and made a vow to have the office of St. Lazarus solemnized as a double in his Congregation. The tooth immediately yielded, and Father de Montaigu was so struck by what had passed under his own eyes, that he lost no time in entering a Congregation whose superior was so mighty in prayer. The original attestation made of this occurrence at Autun in 1648, is still preserved by the order.†

---

* We allude to the game of soule, in Lower Normandy. In one of the parishes of the Canton of Ecouché, the most recently married man used to ascend the steps of the Cemetery Cross on the first Sunday in Lent, after Vespers, and to throw down a purse, for which all the young men of the place scrambled on the tombs of their forefathers. The one who got possession of it took to his heels, and was pursued by the others; he had to pass through three different communes before it was considered his lawful property; on the following Sundays this game was repeated, until this condition had been fulfilled. The contents of the purse were then spent in revelry.

† Father Eudes had a remarkable devotion to the relics of the saints. It was strengthened by the consideration of the honour which the Church has always paid them, and of the fury which

The feast of the Sacred Heart of the Blessed Virgin was celebrated during the course of the mission at Autun. On this occasion, in the Abbey of St. Jean-le-Grand, one of the Benedictine nuns, who had become blind after an attack of measles, called her infirmarian, and begged her to teach her the salutation to the Sacred Heart of Mary, "Hail! Most Holy Heart." The holy Mother of God immediately answered her prayer by the restoration of her sight. "I was an eye-witness of this fact," says Father Eudes, "and have an authentic attestation of it."

The letter in which he mentions this occurrence is addressed to the Venerable Catharine de Bar, known as Mother Mechtilde of the Blessed Sacrament, and foundress of the Benedictines of the Perpetual Adoration.

The great men of the Church have generally met with pious women to assist them in their holy works.

God does not wish man to be alone, and in these holy friendships where the love of God and of souls have formed a bond between two hearts, it would be hard to say which has gained the most. "We know not whether the mother and daughter, who, under St. Jerome's direction, vied with the most mortified hermits of the desert, or St. Jerome himself, who was induced by their fervour and their entreaties to write so many immortal and ever-glorious works, reaped the richest benefits from their holy union."

Protestants have always directed against them. He not only constantly wore them, or kept them in his oratory, but once every year, on the Feast of the Holy Relics, he exposed them for the veneration of the faithful.—(Annales. P. Costil.)

Among the documents which have recently been found, and entrusted to Father Le Doré, Postulator in the cause of his beatification, is a MSS. of three pages, in which he bears witness that the Blessed Virgin had revealed to him the names of many saints, whose relics he had received without any distinguishing mark. (Communicated by Father Le Doré.)

The pious devotion of St. Paula and her daughter Eustochium, was an invaluable assistance to St. Jerome. "Amidst the troubles of the time, and the opposition of men, he found refreshment in turning to look on the picture of their virtues, and gained strength to rise to calmer regions."*

"I cannot explain to you," says St. Francis of Sales to St. Chantal, "the amount or the nature of the affection by which I am devoted to your service in spiritual things; but I must say that I believe it is from God, and therefore I will ever cherish it, and daily I am sensible of its increase. If it were suitable, I would say much more, but I must stop here."†

Again, we know how St. John of the Cross, the Reformer of the Order of Mount Carmel, caught St. Theresa's burning zeal.

From the time when Mother Agnes de Langeac was brought into contact with Father Ollier, that holy priest made wondrous advances in all those sacerdotal virtues, which he still transmits to generation after generation of worthy servants of the Church.

Mlle. Louise de Maurillac, widow of M. Le

---

* Vie de Ste. Paule, par l'Abbé Bougaud.

† In the year 1653, Queen Anne of Austria, mother of Louis XIV., wished to establish Perpetual Adoration of the Blessed Sacrament, by way of reparation for the sacrileges which had been committed during the civil wars. God raised up for this purpose a nun, who had been obliged to come to Paris with her companions. This was Catharine de Bar, of St. Dié, in Lorraine; in religion, Mother Mechtilde of the Blessed Sacrament. The Queen, by the intervention of M. Picoté, chose her as the person to carry out the vow she had made; a house was purchased in the Rue Cassette, Faubourg St. Germain, and the Perpetual Adoration was solemnly inaugurated on the 25th March, 1653. The Queen Mother, with a rope round her neck, was the first to make an act of solemn reparation to our Lord, with a devotion which edified all beholders.

On the 4th of December, 1676, Pope Innocent XI. granted a bull of approbation and many privileges. The Benedictine nuns of Caen made a vow of perpetual adoration on the 30th September, 1685.

Gras, Queen Mary de Medicis' secretary, was a fellow-labourer with St. Vincent de Paul in all his works of charity.

Similar relations existed between Father Eudes and the venerable Catharine de Bar. They gave each other mutual support, and, during his many afflictions, the priest needed the consolations offered by the holy nun, whose own troubled life must often have made her exclaim with St. Jerome, " Great toil, but a great reward."

The following circumstances enable us to ascertain the period when the friendship between Father Eudes and Mother Catharine de Bar and her nuns induced them to adopt the salutation to the Sacred Hearts of Jesus and Mary, which is still daily recited by the Eudists and the Benedictines of the Perpetual Adoration. Father Eudes used to say, "*I adore Thee, I praise Thee;*" in the year 1650, some observations were addressed to him regarding the words, "*I adore Thee,*" and he thought it well to change them. It was not till 1663 that he reverted to the orignal mode of expression, for which he had substituted, "*I praise Thee, I bless Thee.*"

It was between the years 1653 and 1663 that these relations were established, for the Benedictines still say, "I bless Thee," instead of, "I adore Thee."

"From many different directions," says Father Le Doré, "questions, and even objections, have reached me, touching the formula, *Ave Cor Jesu et Mariæ, te adoramus.* I had prepared a treatise in answer, but think it well to delay its publication until after the cause has been introduced at the court of Rome. Meanwhile a few words may suffice to remove all difficulties. The expression, *Cor Jesu et Mariæ,* like *Cor unum et anima una,* in the Acts, merely indicates a moral union ; it was also approved by the Sacred Congregation of Rites, in our Offices for the Sacred Hearts of Jesus and Mary.* With regard to the word, *te adoramus,* theologians have always used it in Latin for every kind of worship, it is only in modern French that its signification seems confined to the worship of *latria;* we may therefore fearlessly repeat with our revered Father, 'Ave Cor amantissimum Jesu et Mariæ, te adoramus.'"

The name of the venerable Mother de Bar has carried us on too far, and we must now return to the year 1648.

Ten or twelve days after the conclusion of his mission at Autun, Father Eudes recommenced his work at Beaune, at the request of M. de Renty, who contributed to the support of this mission as well as of the former one.

An ample harvest was again granted to his labours, and as nothing further detained them at Beaune, Father Eudes and his devoted companions returned to M. de Renty, the lord of the soil, who was soon to enter into his rest. "The mission here was begun at Pentecost," wrote this

* We give the prayer, Ave Cor Sanctissimum, which has been daily used in all Father Eudes' Institutions, as well as in the Congregation of the Benedictines of the Blessed Sacrament, from the time of their foundation, that is to say, for more than two centuries.

Ave Cor Sanctissimum,	Tibi gratias agimus,
Ave Cor mitissimum,	Te amamus,
Ave Cor humillimum,	Ex toto corde nostro,
Ave Cor purissimum,	Ex tota anima nostra,
Ave Cor devotissimum,	Et ex totis viribus nostris,
Ave Cor sapientissimum,	Tibi cor nostrum offerimus,
Ave Cor patientissimum,	Donamus,
Ave Cor obedientissimum,	Consecramus,
Ave Cor vigilantissimum,	Immolamus,
Ave Cor fidelissimum,	Accipe et posside illud totum,
Ave Cor beatissimum,	Et purifica,
Ave Cor misericordissimum,	Et illumina,
Ave Cor amantissimum, Jesu et Mariæ,	Et sanctifica,
Te adoramus,	Et in ipso vivas et regnes, et nunc et semper, et in sæcula sæculorum. Amen.
Te laudamus,	
Te glorificamus,	

pious nobleman to his director, Father St. Jure, a Jesuit, " and it has been attended with wonderful blessings ; hearts have been touched with contrition, so that tears have poured forth abundantly. A number of restitutions have been made, and the practice of common prayer has been established in families. Oaths and blasphemies have ceased, and people come from three or four leagues off to hear the word of God." We have reason to believe that M. de Renty's example assisted the preaching of the missionaries.

The Princess de Condé* now invited Father Eudes to la Fère-en-Tardenois; she provided the necessary funds, and Mgr. Legras, the Bishop of Soissons, followed the mission, which was given by eleven priests, under the direction of their superior; Father Dufour, the Archdeacon, mentions these facts in the honourable testimony he has rendered to the missionaries. Father Eudes' health was in no way injured by these labours, which he undertook in fulfilment of the vow he had made to preach the Word of God in Burgundy before returning to Normandy, where the reward of his labours awaited him.

The year 1648 was full of events, and brought successes which consoled him for the death of his early and constant patron Mgr. d'Angennes, which had taken place in May 1647. Mgr. Molé, his successor, proved himself the enemy of all those

* The Princess of Condé, Charlotte Margaret de Montmorency, was said to be the most beautiful woman in Europe. She had been married to Henry II., Prince of Condé, posthumous son of Henry I. His chief glory is, that he was the father of the great Condé, brother to the Prince de Conti. The Princess had been two years a widow at the time when she sent for Father Eudes. In the course of the year 1648, her son, who was already covered with glory, gained the victory of Lens over Archduke Leopold, and this victory led to peace with Germany. But the troubles of the Fronde were about to desolate France, civil war was imminent, and families were to be divided. The mother of two princes, who were to take so prominent a part in these events, had, indeed, reason to turn to God.

who had been particularly attached to his predecessor; he did not take possession of his see until 1649, but meanwhile the capitular grand-vicars were equally hostile to Father Eudes.

The storm seemed gathering on all sides. Father Eudes was obliged to content himself with merely keeping his ground, without making a single step in advance, at least in Normandy. For the present he undertook no missions in the diocese of Bayeux.

But Mgr. de Harlay, the Archbishop of Rouen, who had appointed him head of the missions in Normandy, was still there, and the kindness and confidence which he had always shewn to Father Eudes, encouraged him to address a petition to him, asking in his own name and that of his fellow-labourers, for the approval of their institution, for permission to teach young ecclesiastics, and train them in the duties of their calling, and to continue the work of missions in his province, in submission to the Ordinaries, whom he declared he should always consider as his superiors.

The Oratorians accused Father Eudes of a spirit of pride and independence, peculiarly incompatible with the state of life which he had embraced.

It was but natural that they should attack one of his dearest virtues, the virtue of humility, the chosen virtue, as St. Paul tells us, of our Lord, the foundation of our salvation, the guardian of piety, and the preparation for heavenly benedictions.

"Give me a truly humble soul," Father Eudes used to say, "and I am sure that it is a truly holy soul; if it is humble to a great degree, it is holy to a great degree; if it is very humble, it is very holy; all virtues adorn it, the Divine Majesty is glorified by it; Jesus abides in it, it is His treasure and paradise of delights; it will be very great in the kingdom of heaven, for the Gospel tells us that he that humbleth himself shall be exalted ; on the contrary, a soul without humility is the abode of devils, and an abyss of vices."

According to the teaching of the fathers, Christian humility consists of two things ; self-knowledge, and love of one's own lowness and nothingness. The first is called humility of mind, and the second humility of heart. We may safely say that no man was ever more deeply versed than Father Eudes in this important science.* His whole life was an exercise of the virtue of humility ; he was humble, in its smallest details ; he refused things naturally belonging to his position. We may observe, that in petitions where his fellow-labourers are named, he takes care to place himself the last, and uses no title or mark of superiority.

Far from seeking independence, he submitted to the authority of the Ordinaries, and we have seen how he sought to be joined with Father d'Authier de Sisgau in his labours, promising obedience to the rules which that holy priest had laid down for his institution.

Mgr. de Harlay returned a favourable answer to Father Eudes' request, and ordered his decision to be recorded in his own archives and those of the other bishops, without prejudice to their rights.

This success placed Father Eudes in a position to renew his application to the Holy See, and he turned again to Father Mannoury, who accepted this second mission with ready zeal. We shall soon see him once more at Rome.

In the course of his journeys through many parts of the kingdom, many disorders had come under Father Eudes' notice ; he had seen the effects of many abuses, he had been the confidant

* Vertus du Père Eudes. P. Herambourg.

and comforter of the afflicted, who were oppressed by these very abuses, and had no power to defend themselves.

He did not shrink from the stern duty of making these things known to the Queen Regent. The humble missionary took a high line, and at the very time when he had himself to ask for assistance against his powerful enemies, he ran the risk of alienating those who abused their position by depriving their vassals of the rights dearest to the heart of a Frenchman. Fearing that he might fail to obtain an audience of the Queen, who was at that time fully and anxiously occupied by the troubles of the Fronde,* he drew up a memorial, accompanied by a letter, which is at once a master-piece of delicacy, of respectful boldness, and of dignity. "Madame," he says, "while I offered the Holy Sacrifice of the Mass for your majesty, during your present troubles, God was pleased to send me an inspiration which I cannot reject. It is most humbly to beg your majesty, in the name of our Lord Jesus Christ, and of His Most Holy Mother, to employ the authority you have received from them in staying the impetuous torrent of iniquity, which now makes such strange ravages in France, which casts countless souls into hell, and is the sole cause of all the miseries of the kingdom.

"It is deplorable, Madame, and might make one

---

* At the time of the Fronde, (1648,) three parties existed in France, the Frondeurs, the Mazarins, and the Moderates. Bachaumont, son of the President le Coigneux, compared the Parliament to the students, who used to fight with slings, (Frondes,) in the moat of Paris. He said that the sight of the Duke of Orleans had the same effect on the Parliament as that of the Lieutenant of the town, or the archers, on the students. These youths used to disperse as soon as any of the authorities appeared, and when they had passed by, continued the fight. Bachaumont said that his father's opinion ought to be hurled as from a sling. The word took, and was the origin of the name of Fronde bestowed on the most extreme Parliamentary party, its members considered it an honour to be called Frondeurs, (Slingers.)—(L'Esprit de la Fronde.)

weep tears of blood, to see so many souls, which have cost Jesus Christ His Precious Blood, perish, and to know that the evil is constantly on the increase, and that few people lay it to heart. How much is done when some temporal interest of princes and kings is at stake! But the interests of the Sovereign Ruler are neglected. We wear out our lives in our missions, by crying out against innumerable disorders which pervade France, to God's infinite dishonour and the damnation of many souls, and He gives us grace to remedy some of them. But, Madame, I am certain, that if your majesty would use the power which God has given you, you individually could do more towards the destruction of the devil's tyranny, and the establishment of the kingdom of Jesus Christ, than all the missionaries and preachers put together. Should your majesty wish to know the means, it would be easy to lay them before you, and still easier for your majesty, with the grace of our Lord, to make use of them."

In the memorial, Father Eudes urges the reform of the clergy, the prohibition of fairs and markets on Sundays, the suppression of certain modes of recovering taxes, and of public balls. He wished to have duellists* and blasphemers brought to justice, and some bounds set to the liberty of the press and the luxury of women. Finally, he called attention to the new heresy of Jansenism, which had then begun to gain ground both in the capital and the provinces, as the evil calling most urgently for a speedy remedy.

What part did Mézeray take in the preparation

---

* Duels for the most trifling causes were of daily occurrence amongst the nobility. It is said that in a few years 900 noblemen perished in these encounters, with regard to which Louis XIII. published a terrible edict, making the sending of a challenge a capital crime. Boutteville Montmorency was beheaded, with Count Deschapelles his second, for having challenged Bourron, and fought with him on the Place Royale.

of this memorial? We do not know, but he must
certainly have been consulted by Father Eudes,
who was less conversant with the customs of the
court and capital. The Queen expressed her
satisfaction with the missionary's advice, and if
she was unable to carry it out, he, at least, rose in
her favour and esteem.

"Notwithstanding his gentleness and humility,
his priestly office, and his constant habit of obedience and charity, Father Eudes' origin betrayed
itself," M. Levavasseur tells us, "by a certain
rustic roughness of manner, and a freedom of
speech, like that which the Fronde valued perhaps
too highly in Mézeray, but which, kept within due
bounds, gave so much vigour to Charles d'Houay
and other magistrates of former days."

By this time Mézeray had published the second
volume of his History of France, and spite of his
caustic spirit he was made much of, received pensions both from France and other countries, and
occupied a high position among literary men. He
took the place of Voiture in the French Academy,
almost at the same time as Charles Eudes du
d'Houay offered a courageous resistance to the
govenor of the province, Jacques Rousel de Mé-
dave, and pronounced the noble words recorded in
our first chapter, which still make his name celebrated in the town of Argentan.

Mézeray, who has been so severely dealt with
by the author of the Spirit of the Fronde, had not
yet, rightly or wrongly, been classed amongst the
writers who kept alive disaffection, and dessemi-
nated pamphlets against the Queen, the Minister,
and the Government. The Queen's constant favour for Father Eudes tends, to our mind, to clear
his brother from the charge of disloyalty. Father
Eudes would naturally have shared in the attacks
made on Mézeray, and his ever-watchful enemies
would not have failed to turn against the holy

missionary, a weapon which might have been the more dangerous, because his holy zeal had already led him to speak openly to her majesty of the evil influences at work in the affairs of state.

Moreover, the celebrated author was not, as some have asserted, driven by penury to practise the dangerous trade of a mischief-maker and calumniator.

CHAPTER III.

1648—1651.

FATHER MANNOURY'S SECOND JOURNEY TO ROME.—SUPPORT OF THE KING, THE QUEEN, AND M. DE FONTENOY, THE AMBASSADOR.—POPE INNOCENT X. APPROVES THE SEMINARY AT CAEN.—PURCHASE OF THE HOUSE CALLED THE OLD MISSION.—MGR. MOLE PROHIBITS THE MISSIONARIES FROM ACTING IN HIS DIOCESE.—VARIOUS MISSIONS IN THE DIOCESE OF COUTANCES.—DEATH OF THE BARON DE RENTY.—ILLNESS OF FATHER EUDES, HIS RECOVERY.—MISSIONS IN 1650.—PERSECUTION FROM MGR. MOLE.—MGR. AUVRY ENTRUSTS THE DIRECTION OF HIS SEMINARY TO FATHER EUDES.—MGR. MOLE GIVES HIS APPROVAL TO THE INSTITUTION OF THE DAUGHTERS OF OUR LADY OF CHARITY OF THE REFUGE, FEBRUARY 8, 1651.—TEMPORARY DIRECTION OF THIS COMMUNITY BY THE NUNS OF THE VISITATION.—MOTHER PATIN.—MGR. MOLE DEPRIVES FATHER EUDES OF THE DIRECTION OF THIS HOUSE, AND GIVES IT TO FATHER LEGRAND, PARISH PRIEST OF ST. JULIEN, AT CAEN.

Father Mannoury having, with his habitual self-devotion, undertaken a second mission to Rome in the interests of the Congregation, left Caen on foot and proceeded to Lyons. He remained for a short time in that town to recruit his strength. After having offered the Holy Sacrifice of the Mass in the Chapel of the Convent of the Visitation at Bellecourt, he obtained permis-

sion to hold in his hands for a few moments the
precious reliquary containing the Heart of St.
Francis of Sales, enclosed in crystal.* He gained
fresh courage from this favour; nevertheless, when
he reached Rome he was half-dead with fatigue,
and quite unable to begin his business. His own
energy did more for him than any of the remedies
which were administered, and as soon as possible
he presented his requests to the Cardinals of the
Propaganda.

All the reports set on foot by the friends of the
Oratory fell to the ground before the decisive letters addressed to Pope Innocent X. and the Cardinal d'Este, by the King and the Queen Regent.
M. de Fontenay, the French Ambassador to
Rome, had received orders to use all the influence
of his high position in seconding Father Mannoury's cause.

Such protection accorded to a simple religions
at a moment when all interests centered in Paris,
and when civil war was imminent, formed an
abundant proof of the manner in which Father
Eudes' labours and their results were appreciated.

The Oratory Fathers having heard of Father
Mannoury's journey, did everything in their power
to counteract the effect of the royal sympathy.
They attacked him with a violence proportioned to
their vexation at the withdrawal of his superior;

* M. Ollier, a judge, father of the founder of St. Sulpice,
ordered that the body of St. Francis of Sales should be opened
and embalmed; the heart was found large and healthy. It was
given to the Monastery of the Visitation, and at first enclosed
in a silver reliquary, afterwards in a magnificent gold one, given
by Louis XIII., in testimony of his gratitude for his cure by
the application of this holy Heart.—(Life of St. Francis de
Sales.)
When the Revolution broke out, the Visitandines of Lyons
withdrew to Venice, where, protected by the liberty of the little
Republic, they established a Convent and built a Chapel. The
Heart of St. Francis of Sales was placed in it, under a daïs, in
a crystal reliquary adorned with jewels.—(History of St. Chantal.

that priest, who according to them was without birth, fortune, or learning.

The first two articles of this accusation were true; the humble Father Eudes was willing to let all men know that he was a peasant's son; it was well known also that he had given up his patrimony. Certainly, circumstanced as he was, he could not acquire nobility or fortune, but he had acquired learning—learning so great that he had been permitted to preach before the usual age. His spirit of self-devotion had made him brave the dangers of the plague in order to serve his brethren; he had all the qualities required in a leader, for he had been chosen to direct his equals, and to be superior of the Oratory at Caen.*

* Father Eudes was persecuted as his former master Cardinal de Bérulle had been. Richer, Syndic of the Sorbonne, endeavoured in 1613 to raise a violent storm against the new Congregation. He proposed to deprive of their doctor's degree, and expel from the Sorbonne, any of its members who had entered the Oratory.

In all Father Eudes' writings, in the Annals of the Congregation of Jesus and Mary, in the account of his virtues by Father Hérambourg, in his life by Father Beurier, etc., we meet with more facts, unaccompanied by any bitter recriminations. "Calumny went so far," says Father Beurier, "as to accuse him of having appropriated to his own infant order considerable sums belonging to the Oratory. I had rather not believe that the Oratorians gave currency to such a story, for they well knew the probity of their former colleague."

Nevertheless, it is certain that the members of the Oratory, who had been won over to Jansenism, never ceased to oppose Father Eudes in all his works. Father A. Perraud, historian of the Oratory, himself says, "We do not shrink from admitting that, from the time when Jansenism gained ground, many of the Oratory Fathers were unfortunately distinguished by a blind animosity to the Society of Jesus." Now the Society of Jesus, and the Order of Jesus and Mary, have always followed the same banner. We heartily subscribe to the sentiment expressed by the same Father: "Happily the past has carried away those obsolete traditions of antagonism between religious orders. The perils of modern society, the ever-increasing needs of the apostolate, the paramount importance of the union of all generous efforts for the defence of the Christian faith, have, we hope, rendered the return of these grievous dissensions an impossibility. Formerly, the general interests of the Church may sometimes have been forgotten for the interests of some special body; now this could not be done without treason. Now, more

The partisans of the Oratory at Rome dwelt much on the uselessness of the new Congregation which Father Eudes wished to found, and on his ambitious desire for the downfall of the Order which had originally received him as its member.

Nothing could be more unfounded than these imputations. Far from being useless, Father Eudes and his brethren were unable to get through all the work of their missions, and by reverting to Cardinal de Bérulle's original intention, they filled up a void left by the Oratory. They appreciated the greatness of this institution, and doubtless they daily prayed God to root out the cancer which was eating into its core, and which had so undermined its vital energy, that at the time of the Revolution it was not able to seal its faith by martyrdom, as did the Congregation of Jesus and Mary, on the 2nd September, 1792. Fairness is the first duty of an historian, and we must not fail to mention, that on the 10th of May, 1792, the dying Oratory "wished to breathe forth its last breath at the feet of the Vicar of Jesus Christ," and that it addressed to him a letter, which concludes with an assurance of most faithful obedience to the authority and the person of St. Peter's successor. The inroads of Jansenism, and the charge of lay schools, where its members, being too few to fill the place of the Jesuits who had been dismissed, were obliged to admit such associates as Fouché, were the principal causes of the decay and ruin of this great Order; causes fully foreseen by Cardinal de Bérulle and Father de Condren.

Jansenism has ever been fatal to its victims, and as its false maxims have made any compact

than ever, a mighty battle is being fought, and whatever may be our place in the army, we must all be united in rallying round one banner; the standard of Jesus Christ, borne by His vicar on earth, by the Head of the Hierarchy, must bring all men to Christ, and by Christ to God."

impossible, a wide breach has been opened to subversive and revolutionary principles.

Vain as were the accusations of which we have spoken, they might yet have taken effect, for Rome was unwilling to multiply foundations identical in almost everything except name.

To avoid all difficulties of this kind, Father Mannoury contented himself with merely seeking for the Confirmation of the Seminary at Caen, and the indulgences necessary for the missions.

A note from Cardinal Grimaldi, who always shewed much affection for Father Eudes, informed him that the Holy Father never gave apostolic powers to *Episcopal* missionaries, that is, to those who were simply appointed by the Bishops, but exclusively to those created by apostolic authority, who then received, as a separate matter, from the Congregation of the Holy Office, and from the Propaganda, privileges much more ample than those which Father Eudes had asked for. It was necessary to make the request for confirmation by apostolic authority by intervention of the Bishops, who, in these cases, made a statement to the Cardinals of the Propaganda, that their dioceses were infested with heresy, and that they had been satisfied with the results of the labours of such a person.

As we have seen above, Father Eudes had faithfully followed the line of proceeding laid down.

Cardinal Capponi was charged by the Pope with the examination of this matter. His judgment regarding it was most favourable, and he shewed himself ready to help Father Eudes, not only in the establishment of the Seminary at Caen, but also in regard to any other which he might be able to found elsewhere.

Cardinal Capponi's opinion received further confirmation from the signatures affixed to a decree of the 23rd of March, 1648, from which we quote the following words : " After receiving the report made by the most Eminent Cardinal Sforzia of Father Eudes' petition to the Holy See, for the confirmation of a seminary at Caen, erected under his direction, and having duly weighed the reasons to the contrary, adduced by the Fathers of the Oratory, the sacred Congregation declares that the said seminary, having been erected in conformity with the intention of the Council of Trent, the approbation of the Holy See is not required, but it ought to continue in its present form."

This conclusion is one of great importance; it justified the steps taken by Father Eudes, as well in leaving the Oratory as in founding a seminary in accordance with the principles laid down by the Council of Trent.

His enemies made a despairing effort to impede the grant of the Apostolic powers which he had sought for his missions. But, notwithstanding these new obstacles, Father Mannoury succeeded in bringing the affair to a happy conclusion, and on the 20th of April obtained a certificate couched in the following terms : " Having taken the report made by the most Eminent Cardinal Sforzia into consideration, their eminences, the cardinals, have entrusted the mission in Normandy to Master John Eudes, secular priest, and his companions, to be approved by the Nuncio in France, and proposed to the Holy Congregation ; they also have thought fit to appoint Father Eudes head of this mission, and desire him to apply to the Congregation of the Holy Office for the usual powers."

On the same day the Sovereign Pontiff issued his apostolic letters, and on the 24th of April the Congregation of the Holy Office granted the said powers.

Father Mannoury did not venture to bring forward the affair of the Daughters of our Lady of Charity of the Refuge ; he considered it more prudent to rest satisfied with the success obtained, and to trespass no further on the kindness of his zealous protectors at Rome. We shall see hereafter that the moment would not have been favourable for any attempt of this kind. Before leaving Rome he received some authentic relics, which he knew were the most acceptable gifts he could bring back to his superior.

The distinguished approbation of the Holy Father gave new warmth to the affection of Father Eudes' friends, and elicited fresh proofs of it. In 1649, M. de Quétissant bought, in the name of the Order, which gave him credit for the price, (7000 livres,) the house known afterwards by the name of the Old Mission, and hitherto merely hired by the missionaries. The deed of sale states that the donor had bought it at their request and with their funds. Henceforth they had a certain place of abode, and one serious cause of anxiety was removed.

It was not to be supposed that the enemies of the Seminary would bow in silence to the decision of the Sovereign Pontiff. They were ever on the watch, and more particularly when Mgr. Moló took possession of the See of Bayeux, on the 20th July, 1649. The prelate began by forbidding the missionaries to exercise any of their functions in his diocese. The Bishop of Coutances took advantage of this circumstance to summon Father Eudes to his assistance, and during the summer of 1649 he directed missions at St. Sauveur-Landelin, Briquebec, Allaume and St. Sever. The last of these missions was given at the request of the Baron de Renty, who had in view the reform of an abbey of the Order of St. Benedict in that town. Success attended this delicate undertaking, but death prevented the Baron from assisting at the mission.

A faithful friend was taken from Father Eudes

in this nobleman; but a few days before he had proposed to accompany him, with his wife and some pious ladies, in order to serve him during the time of his missions. "We will endeavour," he wrote, "to do it without noise and without being known, taking a separate lodging. See if you will be our father."

If we remember that the Baron de Renty, like the chosen companion of his holy life, belonged to one of the most illustrious families in France, that he had been equally distinguished at court by his virtue, his *fortune*, and his birth, and in the army by his courage and military talents; if we consider that the higher aristocracy of that period held aloof even from the mere nobility, we may well imagine what must have been the merits of the priest whom a great lord and noble ladies offered to serve as a lay-brother and deaconnesses, though despised and persecuted in his own country, and forbidden to minister in the very diocese where he had healed many bleeding wounds, dried many tears, and consoled many sorrows.

Father Eudes' soul was strong, but his body sometimes gave way beneath the burden. In 1649, he was attacked by illness, as he had been in the preceding year; his recovery is believed to have been an answer to prayer. After the mission at St. Sever, he and his companions returned to spend the winter at Caen, devoting themselves to that interior life which, while it allows necessary rest to the body, lets the soul recover its strength and elasticity in prayer and meditation.

"A thousand years of the pleasures of the world," said the venerable priest, "are not worth one moment of the sweetness which God gives to the soul that seeks her delight in conversing with Him by meditation. By this holy exercise she possesses herself, and is possessed in Him. There is no bitterness in the conversation of wisdom, nor any weariness in her company, but consolation and joy."

Father Eudes looked on prayer as his first and most important business. He would say to ecclesiastics, "If you would know what piety is, if you would possess it, practise mental prayer." No one ever worked and prayed as much as he did; no one ever knew better how to unite action and contemplation; no apostolic preacher ever conversed so much with God, and so much with man. Besides the time which he daily gave to meditation and prayer, he used invariably to make an annual retreat of ten days or more. On these occasions, laying aside all his ordinary occupations, he devoted himself entirely to the contemplation of God, to loving and glorifying Him. He looked on this time of retreat as a little portion of eternity, a foretaste of paradise, it was a spiritual autumn during which he gathered together the provisions necessary for the rest of the year. These blessed days were like those of which the prophet says, "Dies pleni invenientur eis."*

The missionaries still found ample scope for their zeal in the diocese of Coutances, where they were ever welcome. Vesly, about four leagues from Coutances, was, like many other parishes, infested by vice, and little good could be expected from the ministrations of priests who were themselves ignorant of their most essential duties. Not far from this town was the Abbey of Lessay, of the order of St. Benedict, founded in 1056.

M. de Cybrantot furnished the funds for the mission at Vesly, which was undertaken by Fathers Eudes, de Montaigu, Finel, Jourdan, Manchon, and some other ecclesiastics, amongst whom was

* P. Hérambourg. Vertus du P. Eudes.

Nicholas Paillot, priest of St. Michael of Vaucelle, at Caen.*

Our missionaries began their apostolic labours in this parish in the course of the summer of 1650; the judge of the place, an old soldier, who, on his return from the wars, had settled in the neighbourhood, gave them important assistance. Father Eudes brought back many erring souls, and induced the inhabitants to transfer to Tuesday a fair which used to take place on Sunday at Lessay, and to restore to its original purpose a forsaken chapel, dedicated to our Lady of *Sole*, or Consolation. He then proceeded with his companions to Danneville, where the concourse of people was so great, that it became necessary to preach in the open air.

Important affairs of the Congregation obliged Father Eudes to go to Paris, he was therefore only present at the opening of this mission, and entrusted its direction to Father Manchon; but before leaving his brethren he held a conference, in which he gave them the counsels which his wisdom and experience suggested. At present their course lay among thorns; and prudence was more than ever necessary. The principal subject of this conference was the instruction and education of children, and the necessity of instilling into their minds respect for holy places.

Plato said, "The happiness of families depends on the education of their children; the rise and fall of houses is in proportion to their vice or virtue."

Does not our 19th century furnish many proofs

* Father Paillot almost always accompanied Father Eudes on his missions, and had the greatest esteem and affection for him. He died at Vaucelle in Caen, on the 21st of May, 1687, aged sixty-seven. We have been unable to discover the entry of his death, the oldest registers of the parish being of a more recent date. But we gladly believe that the faithful companion of our great uncle was a member of the ancient family of Paillot, to which we are closely allied.

of the truth proclaimed by Plato, four centuries before the birth of Jesus Christ, and are not our great families taking warning by the examples of the last generation, and making the most laudable efforts to stem the torrent which was carrying them pitilessly to destruction with their children, and all their glorious recollections? God gives His messengers power to read the future, and Father Eudes believed that the only means of guarding against threatening dangers, was to inspire children with the fear of God, which is the best antidote to lawlessness, as charity is the sure pledge of salvation. And with this same conviction we entrust our sons to his successors, until the moment comes when they must be launched into public life. They may at first meet with the spectre which appeared to Bulwer Lytton when a student, the spectre of stern labour, discouragement, delay, injustice, and failure of hopes. But let them look it in the face, let them struggle, let them persevere,* and, sooner or later, they are sure to gain the day, especially if they love their calling more than themselves.

Missions at Fierville and Gatheville were given in the same year as that of Danneville.

Father Eudes' position with regard to his Bishop was of a nature to compromise him in all his proceedings, and it was therefore a duty to do everything in his power to remove the prejudices which that prelate had imbibed before his arrival at Bayeux; the task ought to have been an easy one, considering the favourable nature of Father Eudes' antecedents in the diocese. But although he went to Paris to explain his motives, and lay his

---

* Count De L——, an old Lieutenant-General officer under Louis XV. and Louis XVI., said to a young student of St. Cyr, who was joining his regiment for the first time, "My advice to you may be summed up in one word, Persevere!" .

defence before the bishop, no change seems to have taken place in his sentiments.

Providence, however, permitted that these persecutions should be the means of dispelling the principal accusation brought forward by the Oratorians.

The de Répichons had contributed to the foundation of the seminary at Caen by the gift of several pieces of ground valued at 14,000 livres; the deed of gift was made before the notary royal at Caen, on the 11th of September, 1644, under one condition, viz., that the foundation should be legalized by the registration of Mgr. d'Angennes' letters patent, at the parliament at Rouen. Father de Than had given 1,500 livres under a mortgage, and 300 of arrears, and Father Finel 300, also under mortgage, by a contract of the 2nd of August, 1644, in which the same condition was laid down. Father Ferrière, parish priest of Gacé, who had been for three years endeavouring to bring this affair to a conclusion, having answered for the integrity of Father Eudes' intentions, the president, M. d'Amfreville, was willing to let it proceed. But two difficulties at once presented themselves; the death of Mgr. d'Angennes and the expiration of the letters patent, which had been issued more than five years before. To ask for new ones from Mgr. Molé was out of the question. At length the parliament proceeded with the affair, and the letters were registered on the 23rd of March, 1650.

The lawsuit which the de Répichons had already instituted for the non-fulfilment of the required condition, was thus arrested, and the following moral result was obtained, viz., that the donations had been made, not to Father Eudes himself, but to his institution.

But the registration of the letters patent, without any fresh application to Mgr. Molé, now became the principal cause of complaint. Moreover, representations had been made to the prelate to the effect that Father Eudes had imposed upon Mgr. d'Angennes, by founding an order instead of a seminary. Now, Mgr. d'Angennes' letters of institution contain the following very explicit words: "Congregationem ecclesiasticorum sub nomine et tituli presbyterorum Congregationis Jesu et Mariæ, utpote summo Domini Jesu sancti ordinis presbyteratus sacerdotio consecratam nec non sub protectione beatissimæ Virginis Mariæ matris ejus constitutam."

Father Eudes had endeavoured, when in Paris, by an ample explanation, to lay the storm ; nevertheless, it was impossible to shake Mgr. Molé's firm conviction that contempt of his jurisdiction had been intended, while in reality the good father had only availed himself of rights which had been in his possession for years.

Louis XIII. had spoken, the Holy See had decided that the seminary had been established in accordance with the injunctions of the Council of Trent, and did not even stand in need of any *special authorization*, the Bishops of Bayeux and Coutances had done all that in them lay to obtain for Father Eudes the powers granted by apostolic authority.

In no case could a mere formal error, or a slight want of respect, have accounted for the hostile sentiments entertained by the grand-vicar of Bayeux, and consequently adopted by the Bishop. He distinctly refused to enter into any communication on the subject with Father Eudes, and at once proceeded to the most stringent measures. We have no hesitation in ascribing the bishop's anger to the terms of the ordonnance of Blois. By decree of the Parliament of Rouen,* Father

* The decree of the Parliament of Rouen, March 23rd, 1650, concludes with these words :—" With regard to the petitioners

Eudes had been legally authorized to perform and continue his functions, and the Bishop had been legally exhorted to provide for the establishment of the seminary.

Father Eudes' constant submission to the bishops was so well known, that no one could suppose him likely to compel any one of them to come to his assistance.

The cause of the difficulties which beset the foundation of these most important institutions is now before us.

Is it possible that Father de Condren's disciple, being convinced of the will of God, which always marks the fitting hour, may have wished, in the presence of a fresh obstacle, to lay up strength for the future, to determine his position, and render it impregnable? We cannot decide the question.

In any case, the prelate thought proper to convene several persons to hold council with him on this affair. God permitted that they should be adverse to Father Eudes, who was condemned on every count. It was then determined that Mgr. Molé should take every means for the destruction of the Seminary and of the infant order. These results were confidentially communicated to Father Eudes, who merely exhorted his colleagues to patience and submission, whatever steps might be taken against him or against them. "Do not wonder, my very dear brother," he writes to Father Manchon, "it is but a passing storm." He contented himself with protesting that the

under the name and title of Congregation of the Seminary of the said diocese of Bayeux, in the town of Caen, they are to perform and continue their functions in accordance with these presents and with the edict of Blois; continuing under the jurisdiction of the said Bishop of Bayeux, and of the other diocesan Bishops, who are exhorted to provide for the establishment of seminaries, each one in his own diocese, according to the said decree of Blois.

"Given at Rouen, in the said Court of Parliament, the 23rd day of March, 1650."

passive obedience of the fathers did not imply an abandonment of their assailed rights, and in particular of their right to take measures in due time and place against the said decision. This was done by a protest made on the 10th of December, 1650, before J. Campion, canon-archdeacon of the cathedral, and Apostolic-notary of the diocese of Coutances.

The decision of the Bishop's court at Caen placed the chapel under an interdict, ordered the priests of the *pretended* congregation to cast down and demolish the altar, and forbid them the exercise of their functions in any private house or other place within the range of its authority, save by permission of the Bishop of Bayeux.

A punishment of this nature seems to us, at this time, an act of persecution.

The sentence* was passed on the 29th November, 1650, and made known to Father Eudes on the 1st of December. His missionaries submitted as he had desired them to do; as for himself, calumniated and injured in that which he held most dear, in the presence of those who knew him well, he was silent......*Jesus autem tacebat.*

One of his most decided opponents died suddenly; did the others look on this event as a warning? We may assert with confidence that, far from thinking ill of him, Father Eudes prayed and had prayers offered for him. Before

* "Seeing," said this document, "that the prohibitions in our above sentence, (dated 23rd March, 1650,) were founded on the complaint made by the said Promoter, to the effect that the said Eudes and his associates in the said Congregation, lived together as a religious community, and publicly performed these functions without the permission or consent of the Lord Bishop.........."

If we observe that the prohibition to exercise their ministry bears date the 23rd of March, the same day as the contrary decree of the Parliament of Rouen, we shall not wonder that such opposing decisions perpetually gave rise to new difficulties.

his departure from Paris he was summoned by
Mgr. Claude Auvry, who had succeeded Mgr. Léon
de Matignon in the See of Coutances.

This prelate wished to establish a seminary
without delay, in his episcopal city, and had selected the holy missionary as the person to take
charge of it, thus offering an indirect, but manifest protest against the unjust persecution of which
he was the victim. Mgr. Auvry had formed an
intimate friendship with Mazarin, at Cardinal
Barberini's, had returned to France with the future prime minister, and been made bishop, first
of St. Flour, and then of Coutances ; in 1653 the
king appointed him treasurer of the Sainte Chapelle,
an important dignity, which conferred great privileges. Boileau has introduced him as one of the
principal personages in his poem of the Lutrin,
but has completely misrepresented his character.
He always preserved a sincere friendship for Father
Eudes. The life of this holy father presents some
remarkable contrasts ; one bishop destroys his
seminary another summons him to open one in
his diocese, in one place he is forbidden to preach
or to exercise his priesthood, in another he is
chosen to recall the populace to their duties, and
ere long we shall find him proclaiming the Word
of God to the great ones of the earth.

The Bishop of Coutances had such confidence
in Father Eudes that he entrusted him not only
with the foundation of his seminary, but also with
the collection of the funds necessary for its erection and endowment.

Notwithstanding the critical position in which
he was placed, he did not shrink from this undertaking, for he relied on the intervention of the
Blessed Virgin. She was considered by him, and
by those who contributed most largely to the erection of the seminary, as its only founder ; and it
was decided that the front of its church, the first

ever consecrated to God in honour of the Sacred
Heart of Mary, should bear the inscription: "Fun-
davit eam Mater Altissimi."

Mgr. Auvry's letters of institution are dated the
8th of December, 1650, just eight days after the
publication of the Caen decree. The burgesses
and authorities of Coutances met at the president's
hall to consider the project of the new seminary,
and gave it their entire consent as far as it bore
on the rights and interests of the city; nevertheless, its early existence was beset by the difficulties
common in such cases.

Father de Montaigu, the superior-elect, gave all
his patrimony to this institution, and Father
Hymblot, who had also left the Chapter of Autun
to join Father Eudes, followed his example, and
gave 6,000 livres. A similar sum was added by
two gentlemen, M. de la Boissière, and M. de
Mesle. We must not omit the offering of Marie
Desvallées, who devoted her whole fortune, 1,300
livres, to the building expenses of the new institution. We shall have more to say hereafter of the
life and death of this pious and lowly woman.

After this business was settled Father Eudes
thought it time to present a humble petition on
behalf of the Congregation to Mgr. Molé. He
hoped that the favourable opinion of the Bishop
of Coutances might tend to dispel his prejudices.

The approbation which Mgr. Molé had just
given to one of his most important foundations,
the House of our Lady of Charity of the Refuge at
Caen, might also have seemed to imply that his
anger had subsided, were it not that that very
approbation was accompanied by a heavy cross for
the founder.

This house had already passed through many
vicissitudes. One of its first superiors, under the
influence of pride and jealousy, had suddenly gone
away, taking all the moveables with her. Most

of her companions had followed her example, and Mlle. de Taillefer, a young person whom the others had not ventured to take into their confidence, and Marie Herson, a niece of Father Eudes, aged only 12 years, alone were left with the unhappy women who had been gathered together under their care.

These circumstances made Father Eudes determine, in the month of November, 1642, to ask for letters patent, authorizing the erection of a religious community, of the rule of St. Augustine, in the city of Caen, for the purpose of offering a refuge to fallen women desirous of amending their lives. Mgr. d'Angennes had patronized the undertaking, and the community had been organized. Mother Patin of the Visitation at Caen, became superior, and was joined by companions who assisted her admirably. She was afterwards obliged to return as superior to the Monastery of the Visitation, and the House of Refuge chose in her place Sister Taillefer, who had, during the troublous days of the infant community, given proof of a prudence and firmness beyond her years.

Mgr. Molé permitted many difficulties to delay his consideration of Father Eudes' petition, but at last issued the letters of institution on the 8th of February, 1651.

Let us observe that these letters were to serve as the model and guide for any future foundations. They declare that M. Jean Le Roux, knight, Lord of Langrie, King's Counsellor and President of the Parliament of Rouen, and Dame Marie Le Roux, his wife, are constituted founders, in consideration of the sum of 14,000 livres, 4,000 of which come from the Congregation. Father Eudes had thought it best to keep himself out of sight, and put forward as the ostensible founder one so high in position that he was not likely to be rejected by Mgr. Molé.

By the letters of institution the monastery was placed under the temporary direction of the Ladies of the Visitation. Here is another link between St. Francis of Sales and Father Eudes.

"We have given, and do give, permission to the said nuns, who shall undertake the direction of the penitents, to make the religious vows after a probation and noviciate of two years, and having attained the age of twenty years, under the direction of our dear daughters of the Visitation of our Monastery at Caen, or any other religious women whom we may approve, etc., etc.......We further declare that when there shall be a professed nun of the said monastery deemed by us capable, according to the Holy Canons, of being its superior, the first twelve professed nuns.........in our presence or that of our Vicar General.........may proceed to elect her as their superior.........after which the said nuns of the Visitation shall return to their monastery, unless we should see fit to detain them longer, for the benefit, utility and advantage of the said community, so that they shall not be free to retire from the said monastery without our permission."*

The Community of our Lady of Charity now anxiously desired to have Mother Patin back. She had resigned the post of superior in her own community, and had, therefore, no very serious reason for declining the charge of her former disciples. Nevertheless, she could not make up her mind to accept it, until God made His Will known to her in a miraculous manner, as we learn

---

* The Monastery of the Visitation at Caen was a foundation from the first of that order established at Paris. The community was transferred on the 16th of November, 1631, to Caen, from Dol, where it had been established on the 21st December, 1627. It was suppressed at the time of the French Revolution, and re-established on the 21st November, 1806, but not in the old monastery, which is now a barrack.

from an authentic letter of her own, given in
the Annals of the Congregation : "One evening,
after Matins, our mother having come into my
cell, and found me bathed in tears, said what she
could to console me, but without any effect. Having, as it seemed to me, passed the night without
sleep, about 3 or 4 o'clock in the morning, as I
was beseeching our Lord to deliver me from my
misery, and telling Him that I could no longer
live, I saw our Blessed Father, Francis de Sales,
with two sisters of the Visitation on his left hand,
in his ordinary habit, with a rochet and a violet
hood ; he said to me in a gentle voice : 'Yes,
you shall have the health of body and mind which
you desire, not for yourself, but for the service of
our Lady of Charity," and then disappeared. My
tranquillity of mind and health of body at once
returned, and I performed my meditation and
other exercises with great facility."

The superior put off the parting from her holy
companion from day to day, while the latter always
kept in mind the vision with which God had favoured her. She was soon attacked by a mortal
sickness, and the physician having told the superior that he saw no hope of her life, she made a
vow that if God would restore Mother Patin, she
would no longer oppose her desire. This vow was
accepted, and Mother Patin returned to the Monastery of our Lady of Charity on the 14th of June,
1651.

She was soon joined by excellent subjects, and
the future order was established on a solid basis.
Ladies of quality even sent their daughters as
boarders, that they might receive the instructions
of the Mother of the Nativity, (Marie Herson,) of
Sister Mary of the Conception, (Le Lieupaul,) and
Sister Mary of the Blessed Sacrament, (Pierres,)
etc. We must also mention the name of Mlle. de
Soullebien, who, having lost her husband, M. de

Boisdavid, captain in the French guards, took the habit in this Monastery at Caen.

The constantly increasing number of penitents made it necessary for Mother Patin to seek a larger house than that which President de Langrie had lent the community in 1649; in 1657 they therefore moved to one in the Rue Neuve, which they have occupied ever since, having bravely weathered the storm of the Revolution.

We have thought it necessary to give these details, because this house has been the fruitful germ of so many others.

When Mgr. Molé gave his approbation to this monastery, he deprived Father Eudes of its direction. This was one of the most cruel mortifications God could have permitted him to suffer, but he accepted it with his accustomed resignation : " We must follow our course," said he, "and always serve the house as well as we can, for love of our Lord and His Holy Mother." He had not even the comfort of witnessing the installation which took place on the 8th of June, 1651, in presence of Father de Bernet, the vicar-general.

Father Legrand, parish priest of St. Julian, at Caen, directed the community for twenty years with great prudence, and to Father Eudes' entire satisfaction. Providence had, perhaps, removed this burden from his shoulders, that he might be the better able to extend his order, and to continue his numerous and profitable missions.

The first death amongst his fellow-labourers was that of Father Vigéon, on the 16th of March, 1651 ; he was buried at Notre Dame, as the chapel of the Congregation was still under interdict, and even if it had not been, nothing more than the mere funeral ceremony could have been performed there.

CHAPTER IV.

1651—1658.

Father Eudes was defeated; the altar of his beloved chapel was cast down and destroyed; he was living in undeserved disgrace in the very scene of his most heroic struggles. He might say; "Inimici autem mei vivent et confirmati sunt super me: et multiplicati sunt, qui oderunt me iniquè."

Nevertheless, he was a conqueror. God had made haste to help him, and had raised him up, as He often raises up the humble; for just at this time Father Olier invited him to St. Sulpice, to second by his eloquence the holy lessons which he himself gave with such power to the young priests under his direction. Was it not likely that his voice would be drowned by the tumults of the capital, and the last murmurs of the storm which had led to Mazarin's defeat by the princes? Was not the public mind too much taken up by the conclusion of the struggle which was to make the people poorer, and give the nobility new places and fresh dignities?* But the Christian orator found his text in the circumstances of the times; he preached patience to some, moderation to others, and reminded all that, "Every kingdom divided against itself shall be made desolate, and every city or house divided against itself shall not stand." (Matt. xii. 25.)

Would that we could have listened to those eloquent words, which were so stern against wrong, so commanding, and yet so sweet; so courageous when addressed to worldly greatness, so popular when they recalled men to their duty, and to the respect they owed to the young king, who, after his troubled minority, was soon to concentrate all authority in his own person, and treat his ministers as mere messengers for the transmission of his orders.

Cardinal Mazazin, who had evaded the difficulties which Richelieu had vigorously overcome, was to govern France for ten years more, during the pupilage of the young king. Time has not yet revealed his dispositions and great qualities, but the preacher made it his business to draw all

---

* *The League and the Fronde.*—"Under the league," as M. Cousin says, "two great opinions met in conflict; therefore, by the league minds were developed and characters were tempered; it was a school of politics and of warfare; it gave strength to the vigorous generations of the first half of the XVIIth century. The Fronde is an episode in our history, divested of all grandeur; it formed neither warrior nor statesman; the nation took but little part in it, feeling that no great interest was at stake; it was the pastime of noblemen, wits, and fine ladies. The Fronde was the particular property of the ladies; they were at once its promoters, its instruments, and the most interested actors in its affairs."—Cousin, (Mdme. de Longueville,) p. 57.

hearts to him.   Is not the chief power of a king
to be found in the love of his subjects ?

Many incidents in Father Eudes' life show us
that he never failed in the duty of Christian
loyalty.

The mission of St. Sulpice occupied the Lent
of 1651; its moral effects were great, and it set
the seal to Father Eudes' still increasing reputation.

Father Olier's biographer gives some valuable
details, which do such honour to the memory of
our holy missionary, that we cannot refrain from
transcribing them.*

" A time of political trouble and its consequent
disasters had favoured the increase of disorder in
the parish of St. Sulpice.   To say nothing of the
vagabond life of many priests, who were to be seen
begging at the church doors, to the great dishonour of religion, and who were commanded by
ecclesiastical authority to return to their dioceses;
a yet more alarming and hopeless evil was to be
found in the licence of manners, in the sinful connections, which were too common, and in the complete neglect of the most sacred duties of religion;
many of the parishioners, not even at Easter, approaching the sacraments.   Father Olier had
done all that his zeal could do, and, seeing that
many persons remained unmoved alike by his
tender invitations, and the threatened judgments
of God, he implored the Prior of St. Germain† to
proceed against them with all his authority, and,
accordingly, he issued a proclamation on the 11th
of June, 1650.........Father Olier then endeavoured to bring these sinners back to God by a
means more in accordance with the charity and

* Vie de M. Olier, fondateur de St. Sulpice, T. ii. p. 50.

† St. Sulpice depended on the Abbey of St. Germain. The
prior threatened recalcitrant offenders with all ecclesiastical
censures and penalties.

gentleness of his heart, viz., by a general mission. He had long desired to give his parish the benefit of a means of grace so precious and so well-fitted to repair the ruins made by sin, and to restore fervour. In a letter to Father Conderc, one of his priests, he says, "We must reserve ourselves for the great mission which will take place next year in the parish, during the jubilee. We shall then need all our labourers, and they will be too few for a work of such importance." Considering their number insufficient, he invited his friend, Father Eudes, the founder of the Congregation of Eudists, to come and preside. He knew no one better able to preach the word of God, and to work great conversions, than this extraordinary man, whose labours had produced such abundant fruits, and whom he used to call the marvel of his age.*

This was Father Eudes' first mission in Paris. He set off with twelve of his disciples, intending to open the exercises at St. Sulpice on the Feast of the Purification, but the Seine was flooded to so unusual a degree that his journey was delayed, and Father Olier himself was obliged to take his place. He began his sermon by saying, "To speak to you worthily of Jesus Christ, our true Light, I should need the light of the great servant of God, whose place I fill. That apostolic man has an extraordinary gift for converting souls, and we feel confident that in the present favourable time, of the Jubilee and Lent together, God will,

* In his manuscript memoirs, Father Olier speaks of Marie de Gournay, widow of David Rousseau, who, notwithstanding her lowly birth, became the counsellor of the most illustrious people in Paris, and of souls who had made great progress in virtue. "Father Eudes," he adds, "the great preacher, the wonder of his age, often came to consult her."

In the correspondence between the Baron de Renty and Father Olier, which is of an earlier date, as Baron de Renty died in 1649, we find the same praise, and the same high estimate of Father Eudes' eloquence and its results.

by his means, show us grace and mercy." The mission, which lasted during the whole of Lent, had the success which Father Olier desired; according to his wishes, Father Eudes and his twelve companions lived in the presbytery, and thus did double good, for while, by their preaching, they sowed the seed of the Word of God in the hearts of the faithful, with the most abundant benedictions, by the example of their holy lives they gave another and equally successful mission to the priests of the community."

The future successor of Father Olier never forgot it. M. de Bretonvilliers, (A. Le Ragois,) some time afterwards gave a sum of a thousand livres for the erection of the chapel of the seminary at Coutances.

Father Olier had long desired to establish a Society of Charity for the relief of the distressed, and especially of many persons who had seen better days, and whose necessities were constantly increasing. The accomplishment of this purpose was one of the most lasting and consolatory results of Father Eudes' mission.

Mdme. Tronson, mother of the superior of St. Sulpice, begged him to give a mission at Corbeil; he gladly acceded to her wishes, and the mission was attended by the usual marks of divine favour; it was followed by those of Bernay and Marolles. He then went with his associates to Coutances, and in the Advent of 1651 began a mission which lasted until the following Lent.

About this time Mgr. Molé, the Bishop of Bayeux, died. Father Eudes hoped that his successor might be less ready to listen to unworthy insinuations, and immediately petitioned for the restoration of the chapel at Caen, which had been closed by the sentence of the episcopal court. The vicar-capitular opposed him, and he therefore made a direct application to Father Ste. Croix, whom the king had appointed to the see left vacant by the death of his brother, Mgr. Molé. He at once granted his request, and wrote in the strongest terms to Bayeux, but one difficulty after another prolonged, until 1653, a state of things both unjust and abnormal.

Father Finel died in 1652. He was possessor of the lands of Pondaulne, in the parish of Marchesieux, and was also known by their name. He was originally in an official position at Carentan, and received holy orders very late in life. He was buried in the choir of St. Nicholas, at Coutances, the seminary chapel being still unfinished.

The void left by his death was more than filled by the arrival of several new subjects, the most remarkable of whom was M. Blouet de Camilly, afterwards Father Eudes' worthy successor in office. We shall soon see the circumstances by which he was insensibly drawn to join him.

While the seminary at Caen was closed, the probationers were under the direction of Father Montaigu, and afterwards of Father de la Haye and Father Moisson.

On the 10th of May, 1653, the day when the community of Caen was in the habit of celebrating the Feast of the Appearance of Jesus Christ to His holy Mother, the Episcopal Court reversed the sentence of 1650, and permitted the Eudists to resume all their functions, on condition that they should always remain under the absolute direction, dependance, and jurisdiction of the Bishop of Bayeux, from which they had never thought of withdrawing.

Father Eudes, when writing to his brethren, attributed this victory to the prayers of the good Sister of Mercy in Paris, Mother Mary of the Trinity. Her monastery was situated in the Faubourg St. Germain, near the church of St. Sul-

pice, and was destined to receive persons of quality
without a dowry.   Another nun, Mother Magdalen
of the Incarnation, Carmelite of the little convent
in Paris, had also contributed much to the success
gained.

The Paris mission had then borne fruit, and the
father's joy must have been great.   But fresh
difficulties were to arise; although Father de Ste.
Croix, who had declined the bishopric of Bayeux,
had been replaced by a prelate well fitted to meet
the wants of the diocese.

Mgr. Francis Servien, formerly Bishop of
Carcasonne, translated to Bayeux in 1645, possessed the qualities which Father Eudes had ventured to mention to the queen as essential in a
bishop.   He was distinguished by his zeal and
his talents for the direction of a diocese.   He considered the training of young ecclesiastics for
their high functions a work of the first importance.
The labours of the Eudists were of a nature to
attract his special attention; and, therefore,
designing persons found means to persuade him
that they were without learning or knowledge of
of the world, and, spite of their acknowledged zeal
and virtues, were more likely to influence ignorant
rustics, than priests in any degree enlightened.

The Bishop was, therefore, inclined to give his
seminary to the Oratorians, and to order the
newly-opened chapel to be again closed.

Father Eudes received timely notice of this
state of things, and went to Paris, where he succeeded in convincing the Bishop, and opening his
eyes to the underhand proceedings of his enemies.
This success was probably due to Father Olier,
St. Vincent de Paul, and others, who knew how his
eloquence had won and charmed some of the best
judges.

It is worthy of remark, that every danger which
threatened the seminary of Caen was followed by

an increase of the Congregation; thus, a tree which has fallen beneath the woodman's axe, often sends up shoots which cover the field where it stood.

Mgr. Léonor de Matignon had been transferred from the diocese of Coutances to that of Lisieux. He had already often asked Father Eudes' assistance, and invited him to come and give a mission in his new episcopal city, immediately after his installation. Father Eudes went as soon as he could to fulfil the wishes of the kind patron who had supported him in days of persecution. He had first to give a mission at Pontoise, which had been asked for by Mother Anne of Jesus, a Carmelite nun, sister of Chancellor Séguier, and aunt of Cardinal de Bérulle, whose mother had also entered the same order, under the name of Sister Mary of the Angels.

Two promised missions in the diocese of Coutances also claimed him before that Lisieux.

There was a school at Lisieux, but it had fallen into ruin for want of money.

It was evident that a seminary became daily more and more necessary. The chapter and the town agreed with the bishop on this subject, and Father Eudes brought things to a point by a most generous sacrifice.

Many instances of remarkable disinterestedness on his part make the accusations brought against him quite inexplicable. On one occasion he refused a considerable donation, because the heirs of the donor complained of the diminution of their future fortune; he paid a sum which a nun in the monastery of Caen claimed from him, although he had never received anything from her; he gave the Oratorians a chasuble which had belonged to Cardinal de Berulle, and to which they maintained they had a right, though it was a present made to him by Mgr. de Harlay, Bishop of St. Malo, when he was giving a mission in that diocese. At a later period, when the seminary at Evreux was established, he learned that the Chapter of the Cathedral contested a pension which had been granted to that institution on the revenues of the clergy of the diocese. He wished to give it up, but the bishop forbade him, and his rights were maintained. He preferred peace to any possible advantage, and always feared that a lawsuit would sow hatred and disscusion among Christians.

He immediately sent Father Manchon as superior of the seminary at Lisieux, and with him men fitted to fill different posts in that foundation.

By the request of the Ursulines of Lisieux, and with the bishop's consent, he undertook the direction of their house, and this he did the more gladly, because in the spiritual relations he had already had with these nuns, he had learnt to admire their zeal and regularity.

They had, moreover, supplied the fathers, on their arrival, with everything they required, and had thus preserved them from many privations.*

Many pious persons contributed to the establishment of the school and seminary. The letters of institution for the seminary of Lisieux were given on the 8th of June, 1655.

In 1654 St. John the Evangelist was chosen patron of the Congregation. In the same year, Father Eudes bought, for the sum of 23,000 livres, an estate situated in the parish of Hérouville, and belonging to the lord of that place.

* In a visit which Father Eudes paid to the Convent of the Ursulines at Lisieux, in 1670, as he was conversing with the superior, Mother Rénée St. Agnes, on the favours of the Blessed Virgin, he fell into a sort of ecstasy, which lasted about a quarter of an hour. She made a formal declaration to this effect in 1692. Father Eudes admitted to this nun that whenever the Mother of God appeared to him, he lost consciousness for some time. His humility led him to fear that he had spoken too freely, and he begged her not to mention what had passed. She obeyed as long as he lived.—(Annales.)

A mission was given at Réville, near Barfleur, and the fathers of the Bayeux seminary also laboured at St. Etienne de Lailles, Beuzeville, and Pont-Audemer. Father de Léthumière, who had in 1650 witnessed the results of the mission of Gatheville, induced the Coutances Fathers to give another in that town in 1655. He had himself established, and amply endowed, a seminary near Valogues, which was afterwards suppressed by Mgr. de Loménie, as tainted with Jansenism.

M. d'Amfréville, a benefactor of the Congregation, was anxious that his dependants should have the blessing of a mission, which he himself also meant to attend. Father Eudes therefore went to Cisey to open it as soon as his business at Lisieux was concluded.

Immediately afterwards he returned to Caen. As his Congregation increased in numbers and in reputation, it became necessary to lay down fuller rules for its guidance, and this work now claimed his uninterrupted attention. He framed the plan of his constitutions in the year 1654, but went on perfecting them until his death. Distrustful of his own judgment in so important a matter, he studied most of the existing constitutions, and in many cases merely developed or modified them, according to the exigencies of the times. He was also guided by his recollections of the lessons of those great masters in the science of intellectual and Christian life, Cardinal de Bérulle and Father de Coudren.

The choice of a successor is naturally a subject of the greatest anxiety to every founder, for, however deep may be his humility, he knows that his successor ought to be a second self, and, doubtless, this care often weighed on Father Eudes' mind.

But Providence was preparing one who would fulfil all his desires, and who, by his example as

11

well as by the influence which he justly exercised in the Congregation, would promote the observance of all his rules.

Father Eudes had long enjoyed the esteem and affection of M. and of Madame Blouet de Camilly, people of distinction in Normandy.

Madame de Camilly, whose maiden name was Anne Le Haguais, had often sustained him in his labours, and accordingly, when she was left a widow, with three sons and a daughter, he did not fail to console her. Her eldest son was gifted with all that promised to make a man distinguished, and seemed likely to follow the steps of his forefathers, and fill some high military position.

He was tenderly attached to his sister, but when he returned home he no longer found her there. She had entered the monastery of the Visitation at Caen, and was only waiting for her mother's consent to take the religious vows. Notwithstanding Madame de Camilly's eminent piety, she could not make up her mind to this sacrifice. Her eldest son, moved by her tears, and himself in despair at seeing his sister renounce all his views for her happiness, made up his mind to force the enclosure of the monastery, and, with the assistance of one of his younger brothers, to carry her off. To avoid such a scandal, the nuns induced Mlle. de Camilly to return to her relations, hoping that time, and this token of her submission, would calm their excitement. She understood that she had a mission to fulfil, and, without neglecting any of her practices of piety, she lived with her brothers, whose religious sentiments had been impaired by their contact with the world, and employed all a sister's power to win them ; a power so well described by one of our most amiable poets ;* "If her brother is younger than her, she

<hr>

* Legouvé, 1861.

is almost a mother to him, but if he is older,
she is like his daughter :. new virtue animates
him; he becomes pure while he watches over
her, and she in her turn is a support to him,
making him love what is beautiful, guiding him
towards what is good, and urging him on to win
a place amongst those who are worthy of renown."

Mlle. de Camilly's constant efforts to overcome
the opposition of her brother were at length successful, and he accompanied her to the gate of the
enclosure, from which he had intended to carry
her away by force. But Mlle. de Camilly, this
fair lily-bud as Father Eudes called her, only
entered it to die, at the age of 23, to the sorrow of
the community, whom she had edified by her
virtues.

Her brother was overpowered with grief. God
was calling him to come to Him by the same
rough and thorny way which his sister had chosen,
and he promptly obeyed, giving up the world, with
all its charms and honours.

The joy which filled Father Eudes' heart when
young de Camilly told him of his resolution, did
not make him forget the prudence necessary in
dealing with so ardent a soul. He sent him to
Coutances, and after a strict probation the neophyte was admitted into the Congregation on the
8th of February, 1655.*

Father Eudes saw his foundations flourishing;
the numerous subjects who flocked to them made
him think of sending out swarms from these overcrowded hives, to establish new colonies ; he was
obliged, however, to proceed step by step, for his
detractors were ever on the watch for any act of

* His second brother also entered the Congregation, and sub-
sequently became Canon and theological lecturer of the Chapter
at Bayeux. The third was Counsellor in Parliament. Mlle. de
Camilly had taken the name of Anne Jesus in religion.

imprudence. The affair of Marie Desvallées furnished them with a pretext for animadversions, though it is no more true that he wrote the life attributed to him, than that he instituted a Feast in her honour.

In 1641, during the Mission at Coutances, he had been her director, and had been convinced that her state was an extraordinary one; the most enlightened ecclesiastics of Rouen and Coutancés entertained the same opinion. She died a very holy death on the 25th of February, 1656, and must evidently have been regarded as a person of eminent sanctity, for the Canons of the Cathedral, and the priest of the parish where she died, were alike anxious to obtain possession of her remains; they were buried quietly by the latter in his church.

The body remained there until the 4th of December following, when, in virtue of a decree of the Parliament of Rouen, President de Langrie caused it to be exhumed and transported to the seminary. It was found to be perfectly free from corruption, and a very sweet odour exhaled from it.

Soon afterwards the dispute regarding the place of burial was revived; attacks were made on the memory of Marie Desvallées, and consequently on Father Eudes. These unfounded and unworthy annoyances lasted until 1658, when the bishop, wearied by their continuation, took the affair into his own hands, and caused it to be investigated by an assembly composed of three doctors of the Sorbonne and three Jesuit Fathers. He invited the members of his episcopal court, formerly antagonistic to Father Eudes, to be present, as well as Fathers de Montaigu and Blouet de Camilly, the latter of whom had arranged the materials for this singular trial. The doctors were Father Morel, Father Cornet, (whose funeral oration was afterwards pronounced by Bossuet,) and Father Séguier, theological lecturer in Paris. All things having been scrupulously examined, the Bishop paid honour to Marie Desvallées' memory in the strongest terms. "I feel obliged to say what I now say," added the Bishop, "and God is my witness that I speak from no particular affection for this person, for Father Eudes, or for the missionaries, but simply from a sense of justice."

Ten days later, on the 14th of September, the prelate published his judgment; the sentence was as clear as possible, and two copies of it were sent to Father Eudes.

We have given these unimportant details because the subject has been often revived, as is not unusual, when enemies are at a loss to shew cause for their attacks. Twenty years after the death of Father Eudes, whose holy life had given no pretext for malice to fasten on, a Jansenist author dared to say that he had "seen and read all the folios written by Father Eudes' own hand, regarding his pretended saint, Marie Desvallées.*

Successful missions at Lingèvre and Léthanville, in 1656, and 1657, gained the complete confidence of the Bishop of Bayeux for the Eudists; he authorized them, as Mgr. d'Angennes had formerly done, to preach in all parts of his diocese. It was decided, notwithstanding the proceedings of their enemies, that the seminary for candidates for orders, and for the retreat of ecclesiastics who might wish to follow the spiritual exer-

---

* In 1674, the priest of Aulnay, Father Dufour, a well-known Jansenist, published a libel, in which he accused Father Eudes of thirteen heresies. The venerable founder had been, like St. Bernard, deceived by a young secretary, whom Father Dufour bribed, by a promise of a benefice, to give up the notes written by his superior on Maria Desvallées' case. These notes had not been collected with a view to writing her life, but merely for the guidance of his priests in such matters.

Father Launay, by request of Father du Val-Richer, answered this libel. Father Eudes thought silence his best defence.—(Account of Brother Richard, Father Eudes' faithful servant.)

cises, should be re-established in Father Eudes' house at Caen.

In order to give it all possible stability, Mgr. Servien thought it well to obtain new letters patent, which were granted in the month of December, 1657. His letters of institution were registered on the 9th of November; they contained some clauses difficult to be observed, which were afterwards modified by his successor.

As a reparation for the past, he wished that all possible splendour should attend the re-opening of the seminary. The parish priests were ordered to give notice of it beforehand in their Sunday sermons, and to explain to their congregations the advantages which the institution would confer, not only on priests, but on the younger clergy. The ceremony took place in the very chapel which had been closed in Mgr. Molé's time; solemn Mass was sung, the whole town took part in the rejoicings, and one of the Vicars General was appointed to do the honours.

Father Eudes was at this time almost alone, most of his comrades being engaged in a mission at Honfleur. When he imparted these good tidings to them, he did not fail to warn them against any feeling of pride in the preference shewn by Mgr. Servien to them, above another congregation to which he was much attached, and from which he had received many good offices.

The Oratory had spared no efforts to carry the day.

On the 15th of November, 1657, Father Eudes gave the following rule of conduct, in a letter to the directors of the school at Lisieux. "Avoid the reproach, "thou therefore that teachest another, teachest not thyself;" imitate the Saviour, who began to do and to teach; let these words be fulfilled in you, "he that shall do and teach, he shall be called great in the kingdom of heaven." He concludes his important advice in the words of St. Paul, "whatsoever things are true, whatsoever modest, whatsoever just, whatsover lovely, whatsoever of good fame...think on these things...and the God of peace shall be with you;" his modesty did not permit him to add, "the things which you have both learned, and received, and heard, and seen in me, these do ye."*

Alas! would that all who direct our youth could say, as this holy priest might certainly have done, "the things which you have both learned, and received, and heard, and seen in me, these do ye." His government was remarkable for its gentleness, he devoted himself to his brethren, he did not claim anything by authority; "I write, not as your superior, but as your brother." His charity was so tender and compassionate that he used to make all possible concessions; it was manifested most particularly with regard to the sick; "Let everything be sold," he would say, "rather than that they should want and suffer." He made it a point that the exercises of the community should be finished before those of simple devotion were begun. If he felt angry at some infraction of rule, he did not reprove the delinquent until after he had regained his habitual serenity. Finally, he exhibited unequalled prudence in his dealings with the superiors of the different houses.

Let us glance for a moment at Mézeray. The contrast between these two lives tends to make each appear remarkable. A sort of family likeness may be traced in the minds as well as in the countenances of the three brothers: "Non facies una, nec diversa tamen, qualem decet esse fratrum."

In 1649, on the death of Vaugelas, the Academy

* St. Paul to the Philippians, iv. 8.

chose Mézeray, already celebrated by his great work on the National History, to prepare for its discussions the materials of the dictionary which has done so much to elevate the French language.

The meetings of the Academy were held at that time in the Hotel Seguier, afterwards known as the Hotel des Fermes, 55, Rue de Grenelle, St. Honoré, and 24, Rue du Bouloi. It was built by the Chancellor Pierre Séguier, from a plan of Andronet du Cerceau, the celebrated architect of the XVIth century, who, having been engaged by Henry IV. to complete the Louvre, was obliged, on account of his attachment to Protestantism, to leave France while his task was yet unfinished.

For thirty years the Academy met in this hotel.

Here the visit of Queen Christina of Sweden was received. After she had listened with attention to some compositions in prose and verse, she expressed a wish to have an idea of the great Dictionary then in progress. Mézeray proceeded at once to satisfy her desire, and it so happened that he took up the portion of the manuscript in which the word *Game* occurred; among the proverbial expressions adduced to illustrate its meaning was the following: "Princes' games please none but the players." No one present could refrain from a smile, as these words were pronounced by Mézeray, and it was seen to play for a moment, accompanied by a look of constraint and a sudden blush, on the cruel lips which had a few months before pronounced Monaldeschi's death-warrant.

"This striking anecdote," says M. Patin, "more authentic than many that have been handed down, brings before us the thing represented as far as art can represent it, in the principal figure and the allegorical accessories of the monument which we are inaugurating; the moral physiognomy of Mézeray; the love of truth, the uprightness, the sincerity, the freedom of thought and expression ; distinctive and prominent characteristics, which, not always, it may be, kept within due bounds, set their stamp on his manners, his genius, and his works. This monument shews us that such were, if we may so speak, the features of his race and family. Mézeray had them from his father, the loyal servant of Henry IV. ; he shared them as an undivided inheritance with the pious and eloquent missionary, the indefatigable apostolic labourer, who has sanctified the name of Eudes; and with the upright and courageous magistrate who gained honour for that same name by his bold assertion of municipal liberties."*

We could not but transcribe this portion of the speech of one of Mézeray's successors in the French Academy, M. Patin, the present director of that illustrious assembly, who has already, in the presence of all Normandy, bestowed the name of *Saint* on Father Eudes. May those who have to judge the cause do the same.

* Mézeray bore no malice against the Congregation of the Oratory. He was, as M. Patin has said, upright and sincere. In 1674, the illustrious Oratorian Malebranche printed his book on the Search after Truth. Father Pirot, doctor and professor of the Sorbonne, considered it tainted with Cartesian errors, and refused his approbation. Father d'Aligre, son of the keeper of the seals, and a friend of the author, caused it to be examined by the historian Mézeray, and the approbation was granted gratis. The Assembly of the Oratory which met in 1675, passed a resolution thanking Father Malebranche for the honour which his book brought to the Congregation.—(L'Oratoire de France du XVIIième au XIXième siècle.)

At this very time many members of the Oratory were perse-cuting Father Eudes with great vigour.

BOOK III.

CHAPTER I.

1658—1660.

After martyrdom comes triumph; not a triumph leading to indolent repose, but one ever ready for fresh combats.

This is the case in religious foundations; but, especially at the time of which we are speaking, the persecutions which beset them were often raised by men who themselves bore the priestly character, and even by those whose intentions were good, and who were therefore all the harder to convince.

Father Eudes and his adherents were considered mere Utopians ; and as the needs of the age often required speedy and active measures, self-love was in some cases wounded, and long established customs were attacked by them. Irritation arose, and before the evil could be arrested it had gained strength ; for it was impossible in those days to be in time to know the means of attack, and the motives of false judgments ; years passed away before decisions were given, and if, unfortunately, they were adverse to a foundation, there was nothing to be done but to wait in all humility, and to draw new energy from the sentiments of faith which never forsake the true servants of God.

When we see the venerable Father Eudes beset by so many cruel misunderstandings, bowed down, calumniated, misjudged, and, nevertheless, keeping his eye ever fixed on heaven, we feel for him that deep and sincere admiration which real greatness alone calls forth. He seems to rule his enemies from the cross, which is the first step to the throne of the Eternal.

Our readers will have observed that this work is divided into three parts.

In the first book we have given Father Eudes' history from his birth in 1601, until he left the Oratory in 1643 ; in the second we speak of him as a founder, during the years between 1643 and 1657 ; in the third we shall have to narrate the progress of his Congregation, his seminaries and other establishments, until his death in 1680.

Mgr. Harlay, the Archbishop of Rouen, determined to offer Father Eudes the means of founding a house in the very capital of Normandy. In mentioning this intention to him, he recommended him not to speak of it, as he well knew what opposition was likely to arise.

Jansenism was gaining ground, " that disloyal heresy," as Father Lacordaire calls it, " which never dared to attack the Church openly, but hid itself in her bosom like a serpent." It was well known, that, when once the Church had spoken, Father Eudes would never admit the possibility of a compromise, or to use Father de Condren's words, of disobedience "to the Church of the present day, in which we live, which baptized us, which teaches us, which leads us ;" and therefore these new sectaries looked on him as a constant adversary. He let every one know that he and his colleagues were as far removed from Jansenism as heaven is from hell.

The celebrated Rohrbacher speaks of Father Eudes as one of the best priests of the Oratory, and attributes his departure from that Congregation to the "Jansenist spirit which had invaded it ;" and he bears witness that the Society of Jesus and Mary, "faithfully kept the spirit of its pious founder until the French Revolution."*

St. Simon speaks of Mgr. Harlay's skill in selection and talents for the direction of his diocese. This prelate was well aware that every effort would be made to thwart a project which he considered most important for the future of his clergy. Father Dufour, Priest of Aulnay, and a Jansenist, had, by deceiving Father de Barbery, a Cistercian and Superior of the Ursulines of Caen, succeeded in gaining permission to celebrate Mass in the church of the nuns, and was now endeavouring to introduce his new ideas amongst them, but they were more alive to his schemes than he had supposed, and therefore carefully removed everything requisite for the Holy Sacrifice, just as he came forth vested for Mass. He was obliged to send into the town for what he needed. This affair made much noise at Caen, and especially among the Jansenists ; it was brought before the judge, and he pronounced a decision requiring the Chaplain and the Sister Sacristan of the Monastery to appear before him. The king himself wished to take cognizance of the case, and Father

* Histoire universelle de l'Eglise Catholique, 1. 88.

Dufour, foreseeing serious results, declared "that
he had never shared the sentiments of those persons called Jansenists." Father Eudes was a
friend of M. de Bernières, who occupied an apartment in the court of the Ursuline Monastery, and
Father Dufour therefore feared that his disgrace had
come to his ears. Under this impression, he lost no
time in allying himself with the adversaries of the
the holy priest, and endeavoured to impede his
designs when he heard that a new Seminary at
Rouen was in contemplation.

A proposal was made to Mgr. Harlay, that the
direction of the Seminary should be entrusted to
the priests of the parish of St. Patrick, formed
into a community.

Seeing that the prelate's intentions remained
unaltered, the Chapter presented a memorial containing all the former accusations against Father
Eudes.

Father Eudes' answer bore only on the alleged
material impossibility of supporting his Seminaries, whose downfall, it was said, would be dis-
advantageous to the Archbishop and his Chapter;
as to that which concerned himself, as a man, as a
priest, or as formerly an Oratorian, he was silent :
"Jesus autem tacebat." Mgr. Harlay cut short
all further opposition, by the publication of his
letters of institution, on the 30th of March, 1658.
The next month he obtained letters patent, which
were registered in Parliament on the 14th of
January following, and on the 15th of February,
1659, the Octave of the Feast of the Sacred Heart
of Mary, the Seminary was opened with a solemn
Mass. Father Eudes appointed Father Manchon
its superior, and placed under him five of the
best subjects in the Congregation. He himself
directed the first retreat, as well as the conferences given for those about to be ordained.
His care could not guard them against many pri-

vations; all, however, preferred to suffer, rather than to claim the assistance to which they had a right, according to the prescriptions of the Council of Trent, confirmed by different decrees which we have cited.

The Eudists triumphed while they suffered in patience, supported by the Right Hand that never fails. They knew that God places in every crown some of the thorns that pierced the Brow of His Divine Son.

The Jansenists, though for the present they remained hidden, were ever on the watch. In 1650, Mgr. de Harlay had made a proclamation, threatening with all the severity of the law any one who should put forward or defend Jansenist doctrines.

Father Eudes recommended his brethren to use the greatest moderation, and to abstain from all intercourse with the professors of these errors. He thought it useless to speak in public of a heresy of which the people were almost entirely ignorant, fearing that their curiosity might be excited by the mention of it; and this fear was not unfounded, for many years afterwards Massillon wrote, "I believe that one of the greatest wounds that Jansenism has inflicted on the Church, is, putting the highest and most incomprehensible mysteries of religion into the mouths of women and lay people, and making them a subject of ordinary conversation and discussion. This has promoted the spread of irreligion; in the case of the laity, there is but a step from discussion to doubt, and another from doubt to unbelief."

Father Eudes' counsels bore fruit, but if external peace seemed to be restored, discord broke out in an alarming manner in the very bosom of his Congregation. His great wisdom, and the veneration which his colleagues felt for him, enabled him from the first to master it.

Considering the seminary of Rouen, on account of its position in the archiepiscopal city, suited to hold the first place among his institutions, Father Eudes had transferred Father Manchon, the priest of his Congregation in whom he placed most confidence, from the direction of the house at Lisieux to that of the new foundation.

The sorrow of his disciples at Lisieux degenerated into open revolt, but it soon yielded to the rebukes of Father Eudes, whose severity was tempered by a tenderness manifest in every line of his admonition. Full of contrition, they acknowledged their error, and promised entire submission for the future. Nothing disturbed the unity of the Congregation after this incident, which gave the superior an opportunity of taking the reins more firmly in hand.

For some time Father Eudes had been looking for a site in the town of Caen, where he might, with the help of God, build a house suitable to the greatness of his work there. For fifteen years the community had been established in an abode too small for them, situated between the Rue St. Laurent, and the little river Odon. In front lay a waste place, with buildings on three sides, the present Place Royale of Caen. Father Eudes cast his eyes on this plot of ground, but before he could obtain it, the self-interest of many people had to be overcome, others had to be induced to co-operate, and it was necessary to do everything skilfully and secretly, for fear of attracting the attention of his enemies, who looked with little favour on the growth of a plant which they had endeavoured to crush in its germ.

Mgr. Servien took a personal interest in this project, and Father Eudes had also the support of the Duke de Longueville, who had already granted him, from his forest of Briquebec, a considerable portion of the wood required for the construction.

of the church and seminary of Coutances. M. de la
Croisette, governor of the town and castle of Caen,
gave his assistance, and Father Eudes became
possessor of the ground, on condition that it
should be used for no other purpose than the one
specified; that the building should be begun
within the next six years, and that a rent of 369
livres 15 sols, should be paid in perpetuity to the
town, unless this rent were redeemed.

The conditions were onerous, but all things are
easy to God, and, trusting in His assistance,
Father Eudes accepted them, and he was not dis-
appointed, for in 1662, a person in Paris, who
concealed his name, sent him first 10,000 livres,
and soon afterwards 4,000 more, part of which
served to pay his debt to the town, and the rest to
begin the buildings. Father Eudes knew by experience that the first stone attracts others, and
that the intentions of benefactors are more
likely to be carried out when they see a definite
prospect of the speedy employment of their gifts.

He contented himself with a very simple plan
for his church, hoping that the means necessary
to carry it into execution would, by and by, be
forthcoming. In the meantime he was anxious to
institute a Feast in honour of the Sacred Heart of
the Mother of God. Mgr. Servien gave his approbation on the 17th January, 1659, and the 8th of
February was fixed as the day. It was solemnly
kept in the old Chapel of Caen, which had undergone so many vicissitudes. This Feast, and that
of the Sacred Heart of Jesus, are the principal
solemnities of the Order, which is under their
patronage.

Mgr. Servien died a few days after he had given
Father Eudes this last proof of esteem. He was
succeeded by Mgr. de Nesmond, who closed his
long and holy career in 1715, having been a bishop

54 years.* This prelate was not nominated until 1661; two years therefore elapsed between his predecessor's death and his entry into the diocese. During this interregnum affairs were managed by the vicars-general, but the time was not favourable for the conclusion of Father Eudes' arrangements, and as the ordinary exercises of the Seminary at Caen were necessarily suspended, he employed himself in giving missions in the diocese of Coutances.

The first took place at Vasterville, in June and July, 1659. Its effects were glorious, for even Father Eudes, accustomed as he was to these things, could not help exclaiming, "O! what a benefit missions are! How necessary they are! What an evil deed it is to oppose them! If only those who have prevented our giving several in this diocese knew the harm they have done! My God! forgive them, for they knew not what they were doing!"

The little town of Villedieu soon shared the same blessing; it was a commandery of the Order of Malta, held at that time by Father de Caillemer, of the Order of Jerusalem, Doctor of Theology of the Roman College. That no rights might be infringed, Father Eudes wrote to him about this mission, and on the 15th of September he issued a proclamation authorizing it. Father Eudes afterwards went to Rouen to prepare some young ecclesiastics in his seminary for priests' orders.

He here heard of an affair, for which his oppo-

---

* Mgr. de Nesmond considered the annual visitation of his diocese as one of the most imperative duties of his office. To another prelate who asked for tidings of him, he invariably answered: "I am making my pastoral visitations;" thus giving a charitable lesson not always appreciated. His brother was President Theodore de Nesmond, the Frondeur who had the courage to head a deputation from the Parliament to the King at Compiègne, requesting that Mazarin might be dismissed. In 1660 his nephew married Mlle. de Miramion, whose mother was well known by her piety and good works.

nents would fain have made him appear responsible. As he never gave any ground for accusations, it became necessary to attribute to him acts in which he had had no part. He was thus unable to prepare himself beforehand, or to obviate the harm which might result; like Jeremy, he might have said: "Et non cognovi, quia cogitaverunt super me consilia."

In 1624, Jourdaine de Bernières had founded the Ursuline Monastery at Caen, and brought the first three nuns from Paris. Her brother, M. de Bernières, Father Eudes' faithful and constant friend, retired to a house which was situated in the court of this monastery, and came to be called the Hermitage.

"The little house of the Hermitage," says Mgr. Huet,* "became celebrated on account of the eminent piety of Jean de Bernières, brother of the foundress, who, forsaking the world, chose it as his retreat and that of several holy persons whom he had drawn round him, and who, after they had there made great progress in virtue, dispersed to many places, and were the means of great good."

M. de Bernières died on the third of May, 1659. His companions had lost their leader, and although they placed themselves under the direction of Father Guillebert of the parish of St. Ouen, where they had taken a house, they soon proceeded to acts of such religious eccentricity that the civil authority interfered.†

As Father Eudes was known to have been the

---

* Huet, the learned Bishop of Avranches, published, during his Retreat at the house of the Professed Jesuits, in Paris, his "*Origines de Caen;*" a work of far greater erudition than its title would seem to imply, and which must have been to him a remembrance of his travels among the Scandinavian nations.

† They went through the streets of Caen like inspired persons, praying God to save the town from the hands of the Jansenists.

(For further details, see the Life of Mgr. de Laval, first Bishop of Quebec, who had himself belonged to this body.)

friend of M. de Bernières, and had often visited him at the Hermitage, he was accused of having called forth this public exhibition of feeling against the Jansenists. The fact was, that he had, on this occasion, acted with his usual prudence, and had approved the conduct of Father Dupont, in refusing to open the door of the seminary at Coutances to several of this band. He lost no time in directing all the superiors to take the same course.

We have already observed that each fresh attack of calumny was followed by some special mark of confidence shown to Father Eudes.

The opposition at Rouen, and the endeavour made to compromise him with the civil authority at Caen, were soon followed by an urgent invitation to give a mission in Paris at the hospital of the *Quinze-Vingts*,* founded by St. Louis.

This mission was opened on the Vigil of the Ascension, 1660, and lasted seven weeks. At its conclusion, twelve bishops were present in the church, and during the last four weeks, as it was too small to contain the audience, Father Eudes and his brethren were obliged to preach out of doors. To the immense effects of this mission St. Vincent de Paul thus bears witness : " Father Eudes, with some priests, whom he has brought from Normandy, has been giving a mission at Paris, which has made much noise, and borne much fruit. The crowds have been so great, that the court of the Quinze-Vingts could not hold them.......We have no share in these good things, for the poor people of the country are our portion ; we have only the consolation of seeing that our small efforts have aroused the emulation of many

* Fifteen score. A hospital founded by St. Louis for 300 poor blind people, about the year 1260.

good men, who carry on the work with far more grace than we do."*

It will be remembered that the special object of St. Vincent de Paul's missions was to evangelize the country districts.

In the same spirit Father Bourdaloue answered one of his brethren, who asked him his opinion of Massillon, as he came down from his pulpit: "Hunc oportet crescere, me autem minui."†

At the conclusion of the mission, the queen-mother expressed her desire that Father Eudes should undertake the spiritual direction of the hospital of the *Quinze-Vingts*, and establish a certain number of his colleagues there. Mgr. Auvry, formerly Bishop of Coutances, was at this time treasurer of the Sainte Chapelle;‡ and in his capacity of Grand-Vicar of Cardinal Mazarin, High Almoner of France, also superior of the hospital. He already knew and venerated Father Eudes, and lost no time in preparing the first clauses of a contract by which the Eudists would have been settled at the Quinze-Vingts. How it came to pass, that notwithstanding the expressed desire of Anne of Austria, Father Eudes' enemies were able, not only to hinder the execution of a plan which would have given his Congregation so advantageous a footing in the capital, but, at the same time, themselves to gain possession of Mount Valerian,§ is a thing which we are unable to explain.

* Esprit de St. Vincent de Paul, chap. 20.

† Massillon, an Oratorian, Bishop of Clermont. (L'Oratoire de France.)

‡ This was the Palace Chapel; the present building dates from 1240, and is due to St. Louis.

§ Mount Valerian, a hill in the department of the Seine, above Suresne, near the left bank of the river, was, from time immemorial, a place of pilgrimage. It is said to have been sanctified by the presence of St. Genevieve, and was long the abode of anchorites, who, about the middle of the XVIIth century, were

In 1610, Father Hubert Charpentièr, of Coulommiers, had formed a society of priests to receive the pilgrims who came every year to Mount Valerian to honour the mysteries of Jesus Christ.

These priests needed a firm and continued direction; after many combinations had been tried, and a rich person had offered an endowment of 2,000,000 francs yearly, the Queen-mother herself proposed to Father Eudes that he should undertake the direction of this work. But, although the Queen's good intentions were frustrated by the schemes of his opponents, it must not be forgotten that a great number of restitutions were made, many bad books were burned, many heretics were converted, and many sinners brought back from their evil life by the power of the missionaries, whose efforts God so constantly blessed.

In the early days of St. Sulpice, Cardinal de Richelieu had openly expressed his high veneration and esteem for Father Olier and his companions. These sentiments were shared by the whole court, and many young ecclesiastics of distinguished families joined them, that they might learn the practice of apostolic virtues. We find the names of de Pardaillan, de Gondrin, de Thubières de Quaylus, amongst those of the seminarists first received at Vaugirard. M. Ragnier de Poussé soon followed their example, and ultimately became parish priest of St. Sulpice.

The labours of Father Eudes and his twelve companions had left deep traces in this parish, and

gathered into a community. In 1640, Hubert Charpentièr, a priest of Paris, founded a Calvary there, with representations of the different circumstances of the Passion; twelve priests were connected with it. The Calvary was demolished at the time of the Revolution, but restored under Louis XVIII.; it was again abandoned in 1830. In 1841 important fortifications were erected, and Mount Valerian is now one of the strong places which surround Paris.

Father Poussé begged that a second mission might be given to his flock in the celebrated abbey of St. Germain.

The Queen and the French court crowded round the pulpit where the poor son of Normandy, now a distinguished orator, was about to preach.

In presence of an audience so different from those which he usually addressed, and so little accustomed to hear the truth, the holy priest retained his self-possession, and, at the conclusion of the mission, which the Queen had followed with the most edifying piety, he ventured to recall to her mind in public the memorial which he had addressed to her some years before. He conjured her to lay to heart the eternal welfare of her son, and constantly to keep before him the maxims best fitted to promote the growth of national and religious sentiments in France.

The Queen was not offended by the holy missionary's words, and, with all her court, followed the procession of five hundred priests which went through the streets to a magnificent *Reposoir*,* erected at the seminary of St. Sulpice. M. Levavasseur tells us that Father Eudes, with the Blessed Sacrament in his hands, ready to give solemn Benediction, addressed the nobles who surrounded him. Louis XIV. had just made his entry into Paris, after his marriage with Marie-Theresa† of Austria. Father Eudes congratulated his hearers warmly on their love for their king, and commended the acclamations and shouts of joy which had greeted his entrance, concluding by these words: " You all who know so well how to shout, ' *Long live the King !*' before your earthly

---

* A resting-place for the Blessed Sacrament.

† Marie Theresa of Austria, daughter of Philip IV., King of Spain, was married to Louis XIV. in 1660, and died in 1683. She was distinguished by her gentleness and piety, and bore her husband's many infidelities without murmuring.

monarch, will you not pay the same homage to the King of Heaven, by crying out with me, ' Live Jesus !'" And now it was not, as it had been twenty years ago, a cry of mercy that the missionary elicited from the poor, but a cry of enthusiasm and love from the mighty of the earth. The queen burst into tears, the cry of "Live Jesus !" broke from her lips, and was often repeated by the courtiers and the people.

Anne of Austria promised her constant protection to Father Eudes and his missionaries. The holy founder endeavoured hereafter to turn it to account in obtaining an authentic approbation for his new Congregation, and the erection of the Community of the Daughters of our Lady of Charity of the Refuge into a religious order, a preliminary step necessary before solemn vows could lawfully be taken.

CHAPTER II.

1660—1666.

The holy founder had already, as we have
related in the preceding chapter, taken preliminary measures at the court of Rome, and, under
the protection of the king and queen, with the
French ambassador ready to forward his claims,
he might have confidently expected the success
of the two affairs he deemed so important, were
it not that those whom he called his *former
friends*, had said, " Circumveniamus justum, quoniam inutilis est nobis, et contrarius est operibus
nostris."

We must remember that all he had hitherto
obtained from Rome was the simple approbation

of a seminary established in conformity with the
prescriptions of the Council of Trent; the Congregation of the Eudists did not, therefore, yet
rank as a religious order.

Some years had passed since Father Mannoury
had treated with the prelates of the Court of
Rome, who had shown great esteem for him, but
those two journeys had injured his health, and his
presence was most necessary to the Seminary of
Lisieux.

At Paris Father Eudes had met a Flemish
priest named Boniface, who was very ardent in
everything he undertook, too active, perhaps, but
bore an excellent reputation. He had entered
the Congregation of the Oratory when quite
young, had left it early to take the parish of
Douay, and, having resigned this benefice, spent
some years in Rome, where he formed many valuable friends.

After his return to Paris, he diligently followed
Father Eudes' missions, and, the latter having
often met him, and knowing him to be conversant
with affairs in Rome, spoke to him of his projects.
Father Boniface seemed certain that if the conduct of the business in question were entrusted to
him, he could soon bring it to a happy conclusion.

Father Eudes, who had been much perplexed
by the choice of an envoy, was struck by his confidence, and proposed to him that he should undertake a mission to Rome in his name, and at
the cost of the Congregation; the proposal was
eagerly accepted, and Father Boniface received
Father Eudes' instructions. He was, in the first
place, to solicit the erection of an order of women,
who, in addition to the three ordinary religious
vows, should take a fourth, of labouring for the
salvation of women who had gone astray; with
regard to the second matter, he was to begin by

requesting the continuance of the apostolic powers
granted to the Congregation, and then to endeavour to keep alive any kindly feeling towards
it which he might find existing at the Court of
Rome ; Father Eudes had other means in view
for obtaining, either then or at some future time,
its definitive confirmation from the Holy See.

The new envoy arrived in Rome on the 17th of
May, 1661, and he soon learned that the cause of
the failure of the affair of the nuns, in 1647, was
the fourth vow proposed, it being considered that
the constant and obligatory contact with women
who might be more or less penitent, was likely to
endanger the salvation of young persons. One of
the Roman cardinals said to Father Boniface,
"Rem magnam petisti, et periculi plenam pro
istis monialibus." "You ask a great thing, and
one full of danger to these nuns." In Italy, where
passions are so intense and excitable, it was not
thought possible that it could be otherwise, and it
was considered well to give the new Congregation
a longer trial.

Father Boniface, therefore, was at once checked
by an unforeseen difficulty, and as he did not wish
to return to France empty-handed, he went completely beyond Father Eudes' instructions, and set
to work to obtain from the Holy See the approbation of his other institution.

To accomplish this point, he committed a great
imprudence, which, although at the time it passed
unobserved, was cleverly discovered some years
later, and became the basis of an apparently valid
accusation against Father Eudes, of a nature, like
everything affecting the liberties of the Gallican
Church, to make a deep impression on Louis
XIV.

We shall speak more at length of this matter
in its proper place; no satisfactory result was
obtained, and Father Boniface failed to fulfil the

hopes of Father Eudes, who, however, had not the pain of foreseeing the adverse consequences of the measures taken.

About this time three colleagues, whom he numbered among the founders of his Congregation, were removed by death, and a void was made which could not easily be filled up.

Father Eudes was still in Paris, when part of the Louvre was destroyed by fire. Two days after this catastrophe he was preaching in the church of the Benedictine convent of the Perpetual Adoration, where he is said to have lodged during his visits to the capital. The queen, with all her suite, entered the church; ever ready for action, the gifted missionary at once changed his subject, and, addressing Her Majesty with all his characteristic force and energy, alluded to the recent disaster, saying it was a judgment sent from Heaven, because the works at the palace had been carried on on Sundays and feast days. "I am but a poor man," he said, "and a miserable sinner; nevertheless, standing here in the place of God, I may say with St. Paul, and with all those who have the honour of preaching the word of God, I perform the office of an ambassador of Jesus Christ, bearing the message of the King of kings to a great queen, and I pray her to accept it as such."

The sermon was not such as the courtiers were wont to hear, and when some of them expressed their astonishment at it, the queen answered, "It is a long time since I have heard preaching, but to-day I have heard it; this is what a sermon ought to be, instead of the sweet things which others tell us."

Pope Alexander VII. had just appointed three French ecclesiastics to go as bishops and vicars-apostolic to China and the neighbouring countries. They were Pallu, Bishop of Heliopolis, de la

Motte-Lambert, of Berytus, and de Cotolendy, of
Metellopolis.   Father Eudes consented to let
three of his priests, Fathers le Meunier, Dam-
ville, and Brunel accompany them, and they went
resolved to show themselves worthy of their
master.   But they never reached their destination;
one letter was received from them, dated on the
20th of March, 1662, from Aleppo, where they were
waiting for a caravan to proceed to Ispahan.
Four great caravans used to leave Aleppo at different times of the year, and were the means of com-
munciation with Persia, India, Constantinople,
Diarbekir, and Armenia.

This letter from Aleppo is the only memorial of
the enterprise and its devoted priests. *

* These short details are taken from the Annals of the Congregation, but we have just read with great interest some further particulars given by M. Alfred Bonneau, in his history of
the Life and Works of Mdme. de Miramion.   It was of great importance to found a Seminary, and to have bishops who could
admit men to the priesthood, in a part of the world where priests
were hourly in danger of exile, imprisonment and martyrdom,
so that, uno avulso, non deficit alter, and this consideration no
doubt made Father Eudes all the more ready to send his three
brethren; they sank before they reached their journey's end,
but their sacrifice was not in vain.   We quote Alfred Bonneau's
words:
"A Jesuit Father, Alexander de Rhodes, celebrated for his
devotion to the service of religion, proposed this undertaking to
the Pope, in 1653, but without effect.
"Some years later, several French ecclesiastics of great merit,
led by Father Pallu, went to Rome, and offered to set off as
simple missionaries to India and China.   The Holy Father was
so touched by their devotion, that he not only gave them the
authorization they asked for, but was pleased to confer on three
of them the dignity of Bishop and Vicar Apostolical.   He furthermore chose Father Pallu to be elevated to the Episcopate in
his presence and at his cost, and had him proclaimed with great
pomp in Rome, under the title of Bishop of Heliopolis, by his
Eminence Cardinal Antonio, head of the Congregation of the
Propagation of the Faith.   Mdme. de Miramion, full of admiration for these future martyrs, undertook to defray the expenses
attending the consecration of Father de la Motte Lambert, with
whose family she was well acquainted.
"Thinking the quiet and solitude of the country better fitted
than the tumults of the capital for the necessary preparatory
consultations between the new bishops and their missionaries,
she gave them the use of her Chateau of Couarde, ten leagues
from Paris.   The three prelates, with twenty other ecclesiastics,

While Father Eudes was still mourning their loss, Father Manchon died at Rouen on the 6th of February, 1663, aged forty-six. His death was soon followed by that of President Le Roux de Langrie,* who had appeared as founder of the monastery of our Lady of Charity at Caen, and was united by the closest bonds of friendship with Father Eudes and his Congregation. He expressed a wish to be buried in the seminary of Coutances, near Marie Desvallées.

After many difficulties with regard to the superiors of the reformed Carmelites, who had been invited to come to France by Blessed Marie of the Incarnation, and Cardinal de Berulle, Pope Alexander VII. definitely deprived the Carmelite Fathers of jurisdiction over these nuns, who were left free to choose superiors and name visitors for the preservation of regularity.

The monastery of Caen accordingly elected Father Eudes as superior, and while he lived the nuns would take no other director. Other houses of the same order often availed themselves of his light and guidance.

He was now advancing in years, but his courage

took up their abode there for eighteen months, during which time she provided for all their wants.

"It was from this Chateau, and loaded with the bounties of this pious lady, that the worthy ambassadors of the Word of God set off on their mission. The outset was disastrous, for the ship which had been chartered in Holland to take them to India, went down on leaving port, before they had embarked."

The Duchess of Aiguillon cooperated with Mdme. de Miramion in repairing this great misfortune, and some months later the expedition started by land, and after many difficulties reached its destination. Unhappily, Mgr. Cotolendi, the Bishop of Metellopolis, whose health was already delicate, died on the shores of Bengal, from the effects of the journey. But the Bishops of Heliopolis and Berytus reached Siam in good health, and soon, with the assistance constantly furnished by these ladies, they were able to establish a Seminary, which flourished, and afterwards supplied other missions."

* The son and daughter-in-law of M. le Roux de Langrie, were buried in the Monastery of our Lady of Charity, at Caen, in front of the altar.

was ever fresh. He was about this time attacked by an illness, the consequence of his incessant labours, which, however, he resumed as soon as strength permitted him. We find him again at St. Germain, in the diocese of Lisieux, and at Léthanville, where the Bishop of Bayeux joined in the labours of the mission.

A third mission at St. Lo checked the course of Jansenism, whose partizans had not ceased to oppose him.

A false doctor named Charles, who had come from Paris to Lower Normandy, sought to prejudice the public mind against the missionaries before their arrival at St. Lo. But he met with his match in Mgr. de Lesseville, Bishop of Coutances, who desired him to leave his diocese.

The six years within which the municipality of Caen had required that the construction of the seminary should be commenced, were fast passing away. Notwithstanding the small means at his command, Father Eudes decided to begin by the church, which he intended to consecrate to the Sacred Heart of Mary. In concert with Mgr. de Nesmond, he fixed a day for the laying of the foundation stone. Madame de la Croisette, wife of the governor of Caen, performed this office, in presence of the prelate, who gave all possible solemnity to the ceremony. But want of money soon brought the works to a standstill; they were resumed and abandoned several times within the course of the next twenty years, and were ultimately concluded by means of the donations of the Duchess of Guise and Father Blouet de Camilly.

Mgr. de Marca, formerly Archbishop of Toulouse, and successor of Mgr. de Retz in the see of Paris, wished to give the Eudists an establishment in the capital, and, before his death in 1662, had applied for the necessary letters patent from the king.

Mgr. de Péréfixe, the next Archbishop of Paris, seeing his seminaries overcrowded, and insufficient to contain the numerous subjects who offered themselves, reverted to his predecessor's project. M. de Langrie had offered an endowment of 1,500 livres a year as a beginning. We are unable to say whether the failure of this scheme was due to the opposing influences to which we have already often had to allude.*

On the return of spring the Eudists gave a mission at Meaux, by the request of the Bishop of the diocese, Mgr. de Ligny, who defrayed the expenses. While Father Eudes was directing it, he received letters from Cardinal de Grimaldi, Archbishop of Aix, sending him from the Congregation of the Propaganda a renewal of his apostolic powers, and asking him to draw up a memorial explaining his mode of governing his Seminaries and his Congregation. He fulfilled the Cardinal's desire without interrupting the exercises of the mission, and after its conclusion returned to Normandy, and gave three others at Ravenoville, Cretteville, and Granville, all in the diocese of Coutances.

In 1665 our indefatigable preacher was summoned to Châlons-sur-Marne by its Bishop, Mgr. Vialar de Herse, a disciple and chosen friend of Father Olier. This prelate had found his diocese in a deplorable† state, and from the time of his

---

* Annales de la Congregation. P. Costil.

† Henri Clausse de Marchaumont, Bishop of Chalons-sur-Marne, had long mourned over the fearful state to which the relaxation of discipline had reduced his diocese. His grand vicar wrote to M. Bourdoise, that the most ordinary ecclesiastic of Paris would be worth his weight in gold in Champagne. He had long intended to establish a Seminary, and with this view he begged Cardinal Richelieu to give him Father Olier as his co-adjutor. The holy priest refused this dignity, to the great vexation of his family. The Bishop of Chalons wishing at least to have one of Father Olier's fellow labourers, begged the king to appoint Father Vialar, who soon succeeded him in the See,

arrival he had endeavoured to revive religion and to convert the Protestants by means of missions directed by the Fathers of the Oratory. Father Eudes' fame had reached his ears; perhaps he had even heard him preach in Paris. He hoped to reach the very root of the evil by inviting this celebrated missionary and his colleagues to come to his diocese, and, giving them the assistance of thirty or forty priests, Oratorians and Doctors of the Sorbonne, in their labours: with this unlooked-for aid Father Eudes worked wonders. The co-operation of the Oratory Fathers is a happy proof that *all* did not take part in the constant persecutions which have filled our pages; but that the greater number proved worthy sons of Fathers de Bérulle, de Condren, de Bourgoing, Senault, &c. A success so extraordinary, and gained under conditions so remarkable, suffices to prove the often-questioned eminence of Father Eudes' talents and virtue.

Mgr. de Vialar expressed the greatest satisfaction at the results of this mission, and knowing that Father Eudes wished to visit Clairvaux,* he lent him his carriage for that purpose.

This visit was the fulfilment of a long-cherished hope. Father Eudes had already become intimately acquainted with the Bernardins of Val-Richer, in the diocese of Bayeux,† and their abbot had given

for Mgr. Marchaumont died before his co-adjutor's Bulls arrived.

* Clairvaux, (clara vallis,) is about six miles to the south-east of Bar-sur-Aube, in a valley, and near a fine forest. The abbey buildings have been turned into a prison.

† It is on record that when Father Eudes visited this monastery, now the abode of M. Guizot, he used always to say his Mass at the Altar of St. Mary Major, above which the Holy Picture is to be seen. The abbot permitted him to have a copy taken, and he wished the painter whom he employed to go to Confession and Communion before beginning his work. This is in keeping with his love for the virtue of chastity, which was such that a veil seemed to cover his eyes when he had to con-

him letters of association, the monks of Clairvaux therefore received him as a brother, and gladly answered all his questions regarding their holy founder. He had the happiness of wearing the saint's cowl for a few moments, and received a small portion of it as a precious relic.

Some misunderstanding had arisen between the abbot of Citeaux, general of the order, and Fathers de Rancé and Georges, abbots of la Trappe and Val-Richer. The two latter were therefore going to Rome, and they undertook to ask for the confirmation of the institute of our Lady of Charity of the Refuge, and its erection into a religious order. Fears had been always entertained at Rome regarding the contact of the nuns with fallen women; but Cardinal de Retz, who had left France in consequence of the troubles in which he had taken so prominent a part, said that this objection could not stand, seeing that for twenty years this Congregation had been engaged in the care of penitents, and that, although most of its members were young, no one of them had deviated from the line of duty; and that the fourth vow, considered so full of danger for them, would only tend to confirm the regularity of their life.

The commissioners appointed by Alexander

verse with women. St. Francis of Sales was distinguished by the same virtue.—(Annales P. Costil.)

This Holy Picture was a copy which the Abbot of Val-Richer had caused to be made, with Pope Alexander VIII.'s permission, from one at St. Mary Major, at Rome, said to be the work of St. Luke. The tradition that St. Luke was a painter, though not in itself improbable, has been questioned, and some say that the pictures of our Lady and the Infant Saviour attributed to him at Rome and Bologna, were painted by Luca, called *il Santo Luca*, a Florentine artist of the IXth century, who embraced the religious life, and was celebrated for his piety. On entering the nave of St. Mary Major by the great archway, with its two beautiful pillars of Oriental granite, the Chapel of Paul V. Borghèse is in front, and opposite that of Sixtus V.; it is only equalled in splendour by the Corsini Chapel at St. John Lateran. The picture of the Blessed Virgin with the Infant Jesus in her arms is in this church.

VII. gave a favourable report, and the Holy
Father, on the 2nd of January, 1666, issued a bull
erecting the new order under the rule of St.
Augustin, and approving the constitutions drawn
up by Father Eudes, and presented by his diocesan, who was authorized, if necessary, to add new
regulations.

As soon as he received this bull, Mgr. Nesmond
hastened to take it himself to the monastery,
whose inmates were anxious, without delay, to
pronounce the solemn vows now permitted by the
Head of the Church; this was not to be done by
any one under twenty* years of age, so great was
the apprehension still felt at Rome regarding intercourse with the penitents.

On the Feast of the Ascension, after a retreat,
during which their dispositions were carefully
examined by Father Legrand, their director,
sixteen religious made, in presence of the prelate,
the usual vows of poverty, chastity, and obedience,
and a fourth which bound them to work for the
salvation of penitent women.

Father Eudes had borne the toil, it was meet
that he should have the honour, and he preached
on the occasion of this long-expected event. "I
speak to you, my dear sisters: I would say to you,
O, daughters of the Sacred Heart of the Mother of
Fair Love, here is the long-expected day, when you
are about to renew your holy vows; do it with a
large heart, *corde magno et animo rolenti.*

"You, like other nuns, will make the vows of
poverty, chastity, and obedience, but you will be
distinguished from them by a fourth vow of labouring for the salvation of souls purchased by the
precious blood of the Son of God. Remember,
dear daughters, that this is the object for which

* The Council of Trent allows religious vows to be taken at
the age of 17.

you have been founded, that the town has received you on this condition, and that at the hour of death God will require of you an account of the manner in which you have fulfilled this obligation. Woe to the daughter of our Lady of Charity who has no soul to present to God at that day! Think of this, my dear daughters in Christ. Be firmly persuaded that you are absolutely bound to do all, that care, diligence, and prayer, and above all the example of a holy life can do, to win for your Spouse the souls that He has redeemed with His blood. Such is your bounden duty. Bear it constantly in mind. Oh, if it is possible that you should ever be so unhappy as to neglect it, I now pray with all my heart that the Heavenly Father may chasten you so severely as to compel you immediately to return with fervour to your divine and only work."

Father Eudes had never entered into the uneasiness of the Court of Rome in regard to the fourth vow. He used to say that " purity, united with true charity, cannot be sullied, any more than the sunbeam is sullied by the mire. God has so manifestly protected this holy Order from its origin to the present day, that no one of the nuns has suffered any harm."

The same thought is expressed by M. Arlincourt : " The sunlight which shines upon corruption returns to heaven as pure as it came down."

Mother Patin, the superior, shared Father Eudes' joy, as she had shared his labours, but it was only for a short time. She was soon attacked by a mortal illness, and after having, *under obedience,* given her blessing to all her daughters, and taken a blessed taper in her hand to make an act of *honourable reparation,* she died on the 31st of October, 1668, at the age of sixty-eight. For two days her body remained as flexible as during life, and gave forth a sweet odour which was long retained by the linen she had used during her illness.

After her burial, Father Legrand, the rector of the parish of St. Julian, assembled all the nuns in the community-room, where some of the Visitandines also were present, and asked them if they intended again to choose a superior from the Monastery of the Visitation. Sister de Balde, who was only twenty years of age, answered with decision, that after the Order of our Lady of Charity had been so well directed, it would be little to its honour if no religious could be found fit to be named superior. Her words were so calm and reasonable, that Father Legrand advised the community to do what seemed to them best. It was therefore decided that henceforth the superiors should be elected from among its members, and the first choice fell on Sister St. Peter of the Blessed Sacrament. The nuns of the Visitation returned to their monastery, notwithstanding the desire expressed that one of them should remain to assist the new superior.

God often makes use of the lowliest instruments to carry out His designs. The beginning of this order was due to Magdalen Lamy, and another poor woman was to promote its growth. Mary Heurtaut, who was born at Estraham, near Caen, was miraculously preserved from death two or three times. It is said that on the first of these occasions she was devoted to our Lady of Deliverance, and that the Blessed Virgin had often condescended to appear to her, and had taught her to say the Rosary.

She became a postulant in the monastery of our Lady of Charity, and was immediately employed in the most servile work; it is believed that the submission with which she undertook these labours was rewarded by special divine assistance; in 1658 she was allowed to take the habit, under the name of Mary of the Trinity, and she soon became a lay-sister. She gained the confidence of the penitents, and used to exhort them and induce them to go to confession ; her continual ecstasies compelled Mother Patin to dismiss her, but this holy superior expressed her belief that Mary Heurtaut would die a choir-sister. She then went to the Capucines, but, having heard that she had left another religious house, they refused to keep her, and in 1663 she returned to her family, having spent five years in the convent of our Lady of Charity. In 1666, Mother Patin was requested to send a nun to take charge of a community newly-founded at Rennes, for the care of penitents; she had no one to send, the Bull constituting the order had not yet arrived, and the nuns had not yet taken the fourth vow. Under these circumstances Marie Heurtant occurred to her mind. She, being seriously ill with dropsy, prayed God to cure her, if He willed that she should undertake this journey; wonderful to say, the following day she was able to receive the superior's orders, and to set off for Rennes, where the little community received her with open arms. This house had been established in 1659, by Mlle. Du Plessis. Mgr. d'Argouges had given 16,000 livres, and Madame de Brie 1,500. Mlle. Ménard had succeeded Mlle. Du Plessis as its head.

Marie Heurtaut at once looked into every detail; she began by establishing enclosure, and introducing the black habit. Gentleness was her rule, even with the most refractory penitents, and she soon won their hearts.

A pious tradition relates that on one occasion, when Marie Heurtaut had given all the money in the house to the poor, an unknown person brought a hundred crowns; and that a cask into which she had caused holy water to be poured, with this intention, supplied wine for a whole year. We see no reason to doubt these anecdotes, which are taken from the Annals of the Congregation of Jesus and Mary. Many of a like nature are to be found in the process of canonization of St. Jane Frances de Chantal.

By the 14th of May, 1673, the house at Caen was able to send some nuns to Rennes. Sister St. Julian was appointed superior, and, according to Mother Patin's prediction, Marie Heurtaut took the solemn vows. The Bishop of Rennes formally recognized this establishment, which took rank as a religious house on the the 11th of November, 1673, having existed as a charitable institution from 1659. Rennes has still a convent of this order, though no longer in the house then occupied.

Madame de Brie had given a house and a small piece of ground for a similar foundation at Hennebon, and had invited nuns from Caen to establish themselves there; but the Mother of the Nativity, (Herson, Father Eudes' niece,) had not at once sent them, and on the death of Madame de Brie, her relations, who were Protestants, raised many difficulties. In 1687 this house was given up, and the nuns who had been there went to the convent at Guingamp, founded in 1676, and then ruled by Marie Heurtaut, Mother Mary of the Holy Trinity. This foundation was afterwards transferred to St. Brieuc, where it still exists.

The good mother received these poor sisters, fourteen in number, with the greatest charity, although they were a serious charge to a house whose own resources were the smallest.

The house of Guingamp was founded at the earnest request of Mother Mary of the Holy Trinity, by the Viscountess des Arcis, and M. de Kervégan; Mgr. Grangier afterwards granted letters of institution.

This good mother had directed it for six years, when she was invited by M. d'Argouges and his wife to take charge of the house of St. Pelagia, Faubourg St. Marcel, Rue-de-la-Clef.* She went through Caen to take some nuns from the convent there, who were to accompany her; but some differences with the parliament, on account of having permitted a novice to take the veil without its authorization, led to her return to Guingamp in 1684, accompanied by her nuns and this novice, not, however, before much good had been done at St. Pelagia.

The order founded another house at Vannes in 1683; some nuns from Hennebon were sent there in the first instance, but they were afterwards replaced by three from Rennes. The first superior of this house was Mother Mary of the Sacred Heart (Bedaud). She sought the assistance of Mother Mary of the Holy Trinity, whose experience and talents were considered indispensable in making new foundations.

This institution owed its existence to M. de Kerlivio and M. de Francheville, formerly advocate general in the parliament of Brittany, and ultimately Bishop of Perigueux. Mlle. de Francheville, M. de Kerlivio, and Father Huby, also laboured to establish in the same town two houses

---

* Mdme. de Miramion had, with the consent of the magistrates, gathered together six or seven unfortunate women in a private house in the faubourg St. Antoine. Encouraged by the success of her effort, this pious lady, of whom it might well be said, "A law of gentleness guided her tongue, and a spirit of prudence and discernment ruled all her words," resolved to found a house of correction for abandoned women. Many charitable ladies seconded her efforts, and considerable sums of money were placed at her disposal. In 1665 the king granted letters patent for the establishment of a refuge in buildings belonging to the house called la Pitié. But Mdme. de Miramion did not succeed in this larger undertaking, and we cannot wonder that in 1632 she gladly committed the work to Father Eudes' community.

of retreat, which have been a means of untold good.

Mother Bedaud's second three years of office having expired, Mother Mary of the Trinity (Heurtaut) was chosen to succeed her, and ruled the house for six years. She died there in 1709, aged seventy-five, after a life full of good works.

The name of this lowly maiden, who became so eminent in religion, is now perhaps forgotten. It is a pleasure to us to bring it again to light, and to apply to her the words, *Maxima in minimis.*

Two more houses were founded about this time, one at Tours, on the 28th of October, 1714, (still in the same place,) and one at La Rochelle, on the 21st of November, 1715, (afterwards transferred to the ancient convent of the Recollects.)

Six choir and two lay-sisters from Guingamp began the first, in a house situated in the parish of Notre-Dame de la Riche, the most ancient in Tours, where St. Gatian first celebrated the holy Mysteries. This house had formerly been occupied by nuns of the Order of the Annunciation, one of whom had, fifty years before, foretold the arrival of devoted sisters in white habits.* In 1722, this community contained twenty-two members.

M. Etienne de Champflour was Governor of La Rochelle when the house there was founded, and, at the request of Madame Desconhel, he endowed it with 30,000 livres. This lady had been in the habit of living at the Monastery of Vannes, while her husband was at sea. Many difficulties were overcome by the influence of the Comte de Chamilly, and M. de Beauharnais, steward of the province, and nuns were invited to come from Vannes. Madame Desconhel did everything in

---

* Annales de la Congregation. P. Costil.

her power to establish them in their new abode, gave them all she had, and ultimately joined the Order.

We shall soon have to speak at greater length of a monastery founded in Paris, in 1724.

A general assembly of the nuns of the different houses of the Order of our Lady of Charity of the Refuge was held in 1734, in the Monastery at Caen, which was considered as the Mother-House, although possessed of no jurisdiction over the others. Many difficulties required discussion, and it was considered necessary to revise the constitutions.

The houses of Vannes, la Rochelle, Rennes, and Paris, sent their Superiors, each accompanied by a nun, and under the obedience of their respective Bishops. The communities of Guingamp and Tours did not think it well to send any of their number to this assembly, and therefore begged Father Martine, assistant of the Superior General of the Eudists, and director of the seminary of Coutances, and another priest, to give them the benefit of their advice, and to represent them at these deliberations, which occupied a month.

It was decided that measures should be taken to have the constitutions definitely approved by the Holy See; and as the Bull of Alexander VII., erecting the Congregation into a Religious Order, authorized the Bishop of the diocese in which it had taken rise, to add whatever regulations circumstances might seem to require, a revised copy of the constitutions was laid before Mgr. de Luynes, Bishop of Bayeux, who sanctioned them without any difficulty.

Let us return to the monastery in Paris. In 1720, Cardinal de Noailles summoned several nuns from Guingamp, to re-establish order in the house of the Madelonnettes, where it was

greatly needed. The task was as irksome as that
of reformers generally is, but they remained there
until 1734, when the Ursulines took their place.
They had long felt the necessity of some alteration in their position, and in 1724, requested permission to form an establishment in Paris, not
with any intention of leaving the Madelonnettes,
but in order to supply subjects formed and accustomed to life in the capital, and thus to avoid
the constant difficulties of bringing sisters from a
distance of eighty leagues, and sending them back
again, if they proved unsuited.

Cardinal de Noailles recognized the importance
of the proposed foundation, and conjointly with
Marie Le Petit Verno de la Chausseraie, bought
on the 3rd of April, 1724, a large house, (Rue des
Postes, 40, now the College Rollin,) and established the nuns from Guingamp in it. In 1764,
the chapel was consecrated under the invocation of
St. Michael. The penitents who sought admission into this house, or who were transferred
to it, occupied buildings separate from those of
the nuns and the boarders. In 1792, the nuns
were driven out of it, but they preserved the
spirit of their vocation, and in 1806, they re-
assembled in the old Convent of the Visitation,
Rue St. Jacques.*

Father Eudes great work was begun as a private
institution in 1641, became a canonical institution
in 1651, and a Religious Order in 1666. At the
time of the Revolution it numbered houses in
the following towns: Caen (founded in 1651);
Rennes (1673); Guingamp (1676); Vannes (1683);
Tours (1714); La Rochelle (1715); Paris
(1724).

The Convent at Hennebon, founded in 1676,

---

* All these details are taken from the " Annales de la Congregation de Jésus et Marie."

was given up, as already related, in 1687. We give the history of the Order from the time of the Revolution to the present day, in an Appendix.

Mézeray was now a gouty bachelor, and had become peculiar in his manners. "Mézeray at the Academy," wrote M. Levavasseur, "looked like an ancient soldier of Henry IV. amongst the courtiers of Louis XIV. He persisted in singing old airs of the Fronde, never perceiving that the age cared not for songs, or for the Fronde. His disgrace, and the cessation of his pension, embittered him yet more." The two brothers often met in Paris; they were tenderly attached to each other, and Father Eudes helped to keep alive in the heart of the Academician the sentiment of faith, which was, by and by, to be aroused.

As for Charles d'Houay, the quiet tenor of his life was little broken by the duties of the public offices which he filled; his two sons were united with the best families of the province; and he was passing into a happy old age, while his two elder brothers were gaining fresh glory on two very different battle-fields.

CHAPTER III.

1666—1677.

We must go back a little in our history, to say that in Advent, 1665, Father Eudes opened a mission in the beautiful church of St. Peter, at Caen, which lasted till the following Lent. It was succeeded by those of Mesnil, in the diocese of Lisieux; Cerisy, Montpinson and St. Esny, in the diocese of Coutances, and by another at Caen, for the garrison of the Castle.

Mgr. de Maupas, Bishop of Evreux, next summoned Father Eudes, and he was so satisfied with the results of the mission of 1666, that he wished to secure a seminary in his episcopal city for the Eudists. He bought a site, furnished the house, gave it his own library of six hundred volumes, and many relics which he had brought back from Rome, where he had twice journeyed to promote the beatification and canonization of St. Francis of Sales.

M. Le Doux de Melville, Dean of the Cathedral, accepted the title of founder of the Seminary, resigning in its favour the priory of Our Lady of the Desert. Father Mannoury was the first Superior.

The letters of institution of this Seminary bear date, January 14th, 1667. It was necessary to obtain the consent of the Duke de Bouillon, who was also Count of Evreux. Richard Le Queux, a burgess of Rouen, gave the lands of Aulmay, and donations were also made by Claude de Villiers, Barbe Outon, Pierre de la Barre, and Guillaume de Vaucel. The year 1667 was spent in a mission at Rouen, and the zealous band there underwent a persecution, whose authors were well known to them.

In the following year the plague re-appeared in the country, and Father Eudes, who had long since shown, by his example, how this terrible foe should be met, now wrote a long letter full of wise and holy advice on the subject, to Father Bonnefont.

The Rouen Mission had been preceded by one

at Besneville, and was followed by others at Persy and Brucheville, and by a third, which lasted from the end of 1667 till the following Lent; these missions, as well as others given within the next two years at Carentan, Moufurville, Plessix, de Serilly, and de Queteben, all took place in the diocese of Coutances.

In 1669, we find the missionaries working at Rennes, by the request of the Bishop, Mgr. de la Vieuville; their mission in this city lasted four months, and was one of the longest undertaken by Father Eudes. It brought its reward, for the Bishop was so delighted with its results, that before its conclusion he gave the direction of his Seminary to Father Eudes, and begged for three other missions in his diocese, one of which was at Fougères. The letters of institution for the Seminary are dated the 8th of March, 1670. The Bishop gave the Congregation the house and garden bought for this purpose, situated in the Rue St. Etienne, near the parish church of that name. He authorized the priests of the Congregation to celebrate solemnly the Feast of the Adorable Heart of our Lord Jesus Christ, on the 31st of August, with an Octave, and that of the Heart of the Blessed Virgin, on the 8th of February, in the same manner. Let us remark that this is the first mention of the Feast of the Adorable Heart of our Lord in an episcopal document.

The first Superior of the Rennes Seminary was Father Blouet de Camilly; Mgr. de Vieuville afterwards made him Canon of his Cathedral, but he was recalled to occupy the theological chair at Coutances, and thus became permanently connected with that city.

At the close of the Mission of Rennes, Father Eudes established in the principal church the Confraternity of the Sacred Heart of Jesus, which

still exists. Another Confraternity was also erected
in this diocese, though not at the same time; it
is known as the Society of the *Children of the
Admirable Mother of the third order of our Lady
of Charity of the Refuge*, and spread into the
dioceses of St. Brieuc and Vannes, where it is still
in being. Some of its members have formed a
Community at Paramé, in the diocese of Rennes,
with the object of training female teachers. This
institution, which bears the name of the Congregation of the Sacred Hearts of Jesus and Mary,
was set on foot by Mgr. Maupoint, Bishop of St.
Denis, (Ile de Réunion,) and formerly Vicar-general of Rennes.

At the end of each of his missions, Father
Eudes generally established the Confraternity of
the Sacred Heart of Mary; but seeing that it was
not sufficient to meet the needs of some souls
called, while living in the world, to a higher degree
of perfection, he instituted on their behalf this
Society of Children of the Heart of the Admirable
Mother. He does not appear himself to have
composed the rules, but they are so full of his
spirit that it is evident they were drawn up by one
of his Congregation.

In 1668 Father Eudes consecrated himself and
those belonging to him to the service of the
Blessed Virgin; he signed the act with his blood,
carried it about him until his last day, and, after
the example of St. Edmund, Archbishop of Can-
terbury, desired that it should be buried with him
in his coffin.

Having finished his labours at Rennes, he returned to Caen, and was engaged in examining
the younger brethren of the Order, from the house
at Coutances, when the interests of the Congregation required his presence in Paris. This was in
1671; Mgr. Harlay de Chanvalon had just been
transferred from Rouen to Paris, and Father Eudes

lost no time in going to see this prelate, who had always proved his protector.

Louis XIV. had desired Mgr. de Harlay to choose four priests fitted to give a mission of some weeks' duration, at Versailles; when Father Eudes appeared, the bishop at once thought that Providence had saved him from the embarrassing duty of making this selection, and without further delay he requested Father Eudes to summon three of his missionaries, and to hold himself ready, with their assistance, to begin this important work in Holy Week.

The age was an age of orators, and our humble missionary was now to take his place as the king's preacher.

Louis XIV. was only thirty-three years of age; the priest was a septuagenarian; he had to speak to a young and handsome monarch, whose idea of his own importance was so high, that his policy might be summed up in the three words, "*the State is myself*," and to youthful noblemen who could ill brook any restraint. The truth which he had to bring before a brilliant court was the same which Massillon pronounced forty-four years later, beside the coffin of the same great king, "God only is great, my brethren!"

How were Father Eudes and his colleagues to face so imposing an audience? They were priests from the country, the scene of their labours had been for the most part in lowly parishes; was not the change from such obscurity to such splendour too sudden and too dazzling? But they retained their calm and lofty bearing; they rose to the occasion; they were its masters. They could not fail in a trial to which it pleased God to call them. The illustrious Oratorian Mascaron had but lately left the pulpit they were about to occupy. He had preached the Advent of 1666, the Lent of 1667, the Advent of 1668, the Lent of 1669, and the Advent of 1670.   The Bishopric of Tulle becoming vacant, Louis XIV. gave it to him, and he returned to court to preach the Lent of 1671.*

Bossuet, by Louis XIV.'s desire, had preached at the chapel of the Louvre during the Advent of 1661, before the court in the Lent of 1662, at Val de Grace, before Anne of Austria in 1663; again in the chapel of the Louvre in Advent 1665, at St. Germain-en-Laye in Lent 1666, and and in Advent of 1669, in the same palace before the king.

Father Eudes was about to subject himself to dangerous comparisons when he arrived at Versailles on Palm Sunday, 1671.

Mgr. de Harlay must have felt the greatest confidence in his choice, when he called the Eudists to succeed the Oratorian preacher, "whose very failings had made him popular, who was subtle and pompous, but grave and dignified, with flashes of wonderful eloquence."

The court had but lately listened to another celebrated Oratorian, Father le Boux, "whose reputation had even borne a comparison with Bossuet in his prime."† The day after Father Eudes arrived, he was presented to the king, who received his thanks with much affability. "I am very glad," said His Majesty, "that the Archbishop has chosen you for this mission; you will do a great deal of good.   Continue as you have begun.   You will convert many, you will not convert everybody, but you will do your best." The king was pleased to command M. de Bonte-

* On Mascaron's first appearance, the learned Tanneguy-Le-Fèvre, Mdme. Dacier's father, said, "'This young orator is most eloquent.   His appearance is in keeping with his office.   He teaches, he pleases, he touches the heart.   Alas for the preachers who will come here, (to Saumur,) after Mascaron."
  Mascaron was then thirty.

† Jacquinet.   Les prédicateurs au XVIIieme siecle avant Bossuet.

14

ras, the governor of the palace, to take the greatest care of the missionaries. What did he imply by those words, " you will not convert everybody" ? The Duchess of la Vallière had just retired from court, the Marquise de Montespan had taken a place very near the throne, the Duke of Maine, who was declared legitimate, had lately been born, but titles, riches, and honours could not cover the disgrace of his birth.

Father Eudes, who had never made any compromise with sin, who looked on chastity as a priceless virtue, was thus brought face to face with open wickedness.

To gain a hearing from a prince who knew no control, he must needs temper the firmness of the missionary with the address peculiar to Normans.

He adopted the plan which Mascaron himself had chosen ; he gave his noble and mighty hearers to understand, that if he spoke the truth to them under a certain disguise, if he did not bring it into the fullest light, their penetration must surpass his courage.*

The king came from the court at St. Germain to Versailles, to follow the mission for three days. The queen herself rewarded the children whom the missionaries pointed out as most pious and best instructed.

The king gave proofs of his satisfaction by offering Father Eudes a donation of 2,000 livres for the construction of the seminary chapel at Caen, and by retaining one of the missionaries to take charge of the sacristy of his chapel. The remembrance of this mission also induced him to use his authority in favour of the establishment of a house of the order in the capital.

The opportunity seemed favourable, but God willed that Father Eudes, like Moses, should

* Mascaron à Versailles.

behold the horizon of a land of promise which he could not enter.

Madame Petau, widow of M. de Traversay, counsellor of parliament, was devoted to good works, and intimately acquainted with St. Vincent de Paul, in obedience to whose wishes she had become guardian of the nuns of the Order of the Cross, established by Madame de Villeneuve, for the care of schools in hamlets and country places.

This lady gave Father Eudes and his Congregation two-thirds of a house, since occupied by the Priests of the Community of St. Josse,* in case it should be found impossible to settle some of the Order there, they were free to sell it and employ the money in the purchase of another house for the same purpose. Father Eudes obtained letters patent enabling him to accept this donation, and it was this affair which had required his presence in Paris in 1671.

But the rector and the wardens of the parish of St. Josse were adverse to the establishment of a community of strange priests close to their church, and notwithstanding a letter which M. de Colbert wrote to the parliament by the king's order, their opposition kept the matter pending until 1703, when an arrangement was made enabling Father Eudes' successors to carry out Madame de Traversay's intentions by buying another house.†

---

* St. Josse was a Parish Church, at the corner of the streets Aubry le Boucher, and Quincampoix. It was destroyed during the Revolution. When Philip Augustus built a wall round Paris, part of the parish of St. Lawrence was included within it. The inhabitants of this portion found themselves placed in a difficult position for the performance of their religious duties, and begged that the chapel of St. Josse might be made a parish church.—*Dulaune.*

† This house was near Estrapade, and at no great distance from the Church of St. Geneviève; the Eudists remained there until the Revolution, and the last Superior was Father Hébert, whose glorious death we shall have to record. It was seques-

In 1704, Father Legrix, a Eudist, was appointed to the parish of St. Josse; he was unhappily led away by the novelties of Quesnellism to such a degree that he, as well as Father Bournisieù, who replaced him, appealed against the constitutions of Clement XI. The Order of Jesus and Mary at once gave up all intercourse with St. Josse.

Mgr. de Maupas, Bishop of Evreux, being attacked in 1672 by a tedious and painful illness, and fearing that he could no longer do justice to his diocese, wrote to Father Ferrier, a Jesuit, confessor to Louis XIV., and begged him to use his influence in favour of a petition which he was sending to Paris by M. Durancel, one of his vicars-general. In the petition, he begged the king to appoint Father Eudes his co-adjutor, because, as he said, he knew no priest more worthy of this position, or in whom he could place more entire confidence.

The episcopal dignity had no attractions for the humble priest, and he lost no time in writing to desire that Father Mannoury would declare to the bishop and the grand-vicars, that he wished for no promotion but that which his Saviour had chosen for him, the cross. He repeated in other words his constant sentiments, " Mihi confusio et ignominia, tibi autem honor et gloria." " Confusion and shame to me; honour and glory to God."

Father Ferrier told Mgr. de Maupas that the proposed step was out of the question, as Father

trated at that time, like all other religious houses, and afterwards became the property of the Sisters of the Monastery of the Visitation, Rue du Bac.

At a much later period it was bought by the Jesuit Fathers, and became the seat of their celebrated school. Every year, sons of the most noble families in France seek to prepare themselves by its high course of studies for the duties of their position, and to escape the inaction which honourable scruples have often imposed, but which our dearest interests now require us to shake off.

Eudes was already fulfilling a great mission, and ought not to be fettered by any obligations which would interfere with his presence in any place to which Providence might call him. We see that the refusal, no less than the selection, added fresh laurels to his crown.

After the mission at Versailles, he gave one to the nuns of the Congregation of our Lady, recently established at Vernon. This institution, founded at Nancy, by the Blessed Peter Fourrier, must not be confounded with the Order of our Lady, established by Madame de Lestonac.

His missions followed one another in quick succession; he often chose the most deserted places. He was obliged also to take charge of the daily business of his different foundations, as well as of many religious houses, which had placed themselves under his direction.

Amongst these we must mention the celebrated Abbey of Montmartre, at that time governed by Madame Françoise Renée de Lorraine. Ten years previously, this Princess had begged that her Community might be associated in prayer with the new Congregation. No surer means could have been found of gaining Father Eudes' affection, and the Abbess ere long perceived the advantages which her nuns derived from this holy union. The good priest, notwithstanding his infirmities, and the many urgent claims on his attention, spent three months in regulating the spiritual concerns of this important Abbey.

The Abbess, in her gratitude, begged her relation, the Duchess of Guise, to contribute handsomely to the Church of the Caen Seminary, and at once adopted the Feast of the Sacred Heart of Mary, which had been instituted in Father Eudes' Congregation, and seemed to have won for it blessings from heaven. This Feast was celebrated at Montmartre for the first time in 1673.

A Mass and Office for the Feast of the Sacred Heart of Jesus, composed some years before by Father Eudes, had been approved by several Bishops. We read the following words in the letters of institution granted to the great Seminary at Rennes, in 1670, "We permit the said priests, of the said Congregation, to celebrate solemnly every year.........the Feast of the Adorable Heart of our Lord Jesus Christ, with an octave, and to use for this purpose the proper office and mass, and to say the same double office, on the first Thursday of every month, if not already occupied by a double or semi-double Feast; and to do the same with regard to the Feast of the Heart of the Blessed Virgin, &c."*

* Father Le Doré writes thus to us on the 28th November, 1868. "I have found some very valuable documents at Caen; those to which I attach most importance are original letters authorizing Father Eudes to solemnize the Feast of the Sacred Heart of Jesus; which enable me to prove that he has the glory of being the first Apostle of this Devotion."

Father Doré says again, (Vertus du P. Eudes,) "A man of himself may doubtless do great things; but the establishment of a glorious devotion, the introduction of a solemn Feast into the Church, is not the work of any mere man;" in such a fact we cannot but acknowledge the immediate action of God, and say, "Digitus est Dei."

We can confidently assert that Father Eudes was the first person entrusted with the mission of making devotion to the Sacred Hearts of Jesus and Mary known in the Church, and establishing its public and solemn celebration. It is generally believed that the Venerable Mary Alacoque, a nun of the Visitation Convent at Paray-le-Monial, in the diocese of Autun, was the first to make known the devotion of the Sacred Heart of Jesus. This holy religious induced her sisters at Dijon to adopt it, and the Feast was celebrated in their church for the first time in 1686, under Mother Saumaise.

Mgr. Languet, Archbishop of Sens, author of the Life of Mary Alacoque, was made aware of the priority of Father Eudes' claim, by Father le Moine, prefect of the Seminary at Caen, and added a note to his book rendering him justice. Mary Alacoque was born at Lauthecour, in 1647. On the 8th of February, 1648, Father Eudes, with the sanction of Mgr. de Ragny, solemnized the Feast of the Sacred Heart of Mary, with extraordinary pomp, in the Cathedral of Autun. We must here admire the secret designs of Providence, which, but a short time before, and in the very neighbourhood of this city, had caused Mary Alacoque, the future chosen apostle of the Sacred Heart, to be born. She

Father Eudes considered it wiser not at once to establish this devotion, but in 1672 he thought the fitting moment had come, and ordered that the Feast should be celebrated by his Congregation on the 20th of October, each year, with permission of the Ordinary. On this occasion he published a circular from which we give an extract. "If objections should be raised on account of the novelty of this devotion, I reply that novelty, although most pernicious in matters of faith, is very good in matters of piety; otherwise we should condemn all the Feasts of the Church, because they were once new." The Feast was henceforth kept in all houses of the Congregation, with the exception of those at Rouen and Rennes; the latter, as we have seen, had the necessary permission; at Rouen some difficulties had been raised by Mgr. de Médavid.

Father Eudes always associated the two Sacred Hearts; indeed this union is one of the special characteristics of the new devotion. "Nevertheless," as Father Le Doré remarks, " he began by the Heart of Mary. In so doing he only conformed his practice to the admirable order of the counsels of Providence; as God has given us Jesus by Mary, Father Eudes wished first to present to us the Heart of the Mother, that we might find a freer and more easy access to the loving Heart of her Son."

The nuns of our Lady of Charity immediately adopted these feasts established by their holy founder, and their example, (with some alterations in the rite,) was followed by the Ursulines, the Benedictines, and the Visitandines, whose special intention was to offer reparation to the Heart of Jesus outraged in the Sacrament of the Altar.

On the 11th March, 1673, Father Eudes re-

died in 1690, celebrated for her virtues and for the extraordinary graces bestowed upon her.

ceived a letter from Father Hubert, the priest of his Congregation whom the king had detained at Versailles, for the service of his chapel, ever since the mission given there two years before. This letter contained an order from their majesties that Father Eudes should come at once to St. Germain-en-Laye, with as many of his companions as he required, and begin a mission. Amongst others he chose Father Blouet de Camilly, to preach before an assembly, in the midst of which, but for his vocation, he might have claimed a distinguished place. Father Delaunay Hue, a missionary of rare merit, who afterwards became canon of the cathedral of Bayeux, and Father Paillot, of whom we have already spoken, also accompanied him.

The King and the Duke of Orleans received Father Eudes at St. Germain with tokens of sincere affection. Sermons were preached every evening for a fortnight; the King often heard them with pleasure, and the Queen said to a Carmelite in the Rue St. Jacques, that the sermons generally preached before her were only words, but that those of the Eudists went to the heart.

Missions in country places are generally fruitful, the seed springs up at once, and the missionary is rewarded for his toil, when he can himself appreciate its results. But things are different at court; if the master does not set an example of piety, the courtiers are apt to remain cold and unmoved.

The cares and business of the state, which the king never neglected, were relieved by the pleasures of a court whose magnificence was only equalled by the obsequious flattery of its atmosphere.

The king at this time found his only consolation in the society of Madame de Maintenon, who gained such power over his heart and mind, that she shared the throne more really, it may be, than if she had borne the title of queen. And, at last, the seed sown by Father Eudes brought forth fruit, and if his life had been prolonged, he would have rejoiced to see the monarch, to whom he had at two different periods preached the Word of God, win fresh esteem and love from his subjects, by a regular and truly christian life.

The success which Providence had granted to the missions at Versailles and St. Germain, and the assurances of protection from their majesties, encouraged Father Eudes to resume his efforts to obtain from the Holy See the confirmation of his institution.

He began to feel the weight of years, and wished to give all possible stability to his work, before leaving it to his successor. He chose Father de Bonnefont, in whom he had the greatest confidence, as his messenger to Rome on this occasion. This father's virtues and learning had won for him the esteem of the Congregation.

He set off on the 5th of June, 1673. The French prelates who had most credit at the Court of Rome gave him letters to several of the Cardinals; the king also wrote in favour of the new institution, and the Duchess of Guise specially recommended him to the Grand Duke of Tuscany, through whose territories he had to pass.

Father Eudes' enemies were roused to fresh activity at the sight of the powerful means now brought to play for the attainment of his long-desired end. He was personally known to the king; he had passed through a serious ordeal with honour; any blow must now be aimed at the height where his virtues and talents had placed him. Libel after libel, calumny after calumny, reaching even to Rome, everything was tried. " Crosses are not wanting," wrote Father Eudes, " crosses of many kinds. I heard yesterday of a

new libel and new calumnies, thank God for
them; I pray Him, with all my heart, that my
calumniators, or, I should say, my great benefactors, may all become great saints."

These persons had succeeded in gaining over
to their views the Lazarist priests, by persuading
their superiors that the approbation of the Eudists
would injure them.* They had also obtained a
decree from the Propaganda, against the erection
of new Orders.†

But this arrow missed the mark; the Congregation was not new; it could count thirty years of
toil; the king had called it to proclaim the Word
of God in his very palace. Furthermore, the
self-abnegation of the holy founder, the untold
fatigues which were day by day undermining his
vigorous constitution; his constancy, his calmness, his admirable resignation in the hour of
adversity, his humility in success, all these things
seemed to give little colour to the attacks directed
against him.

The Court of Rome was about to proceed, and
Father Bonnefont's journey was drawing to a
happy conclusion, when an unforeseen circumstance changed the whole state of the case.

Father Boniface, in despair at his inability to perform the promises he had made to Father Eudes,
had determined, as we have said, at any price,
to obtain the approbation of the Holy See for the
Congregation of Eudists. Going beyond his instructions, he took, on his own responsibility, a step
which Father Eudes would never have sanctioned,

---

* The Missionary Congregation of St. Lazarus took the three
vows of religion; it was instituted with a view of promoting the
salvation of the poor peasants by missions *out of towns*, according to the brief of Alexander VII. (1632.) This brief exempts
the Congregation from ordinary jurisdiction. It was thus essen-
tially different from the Congregation of Jesus and Mary, whose
members make no vows, and work only under Episcopal jurisdiction.

† Annales de la Congregation. (P. Costil.)

and addressed the following petition to the Holy Father. "Most Holy Father, a Congregation of secular priests, which has been formed in France, has been approved by some of the Bishops, and has had the honour of being recommended by the most Christian King. For twenty years or more it has laboured with zeal and diligence for its own perfection, and the salvation of others, and it now earnestly entreats the Holy Apostolic See to confirm its way of life. But as it too often happens that many heresies, springing up at different times, corrupt ecclesiastical communities, and lead them, by specious pretexts, to calumniate the Sovereign Pontiff, who is the Vicar of Christ, and to offer open opposition to his decisions; this Congregation, desiring ardently to have its members ever united by indissoluble bonds to the Roman Church, begs for permission to bind itself by a vow, from which no dispensation can be granted, to be ever submissive to the Sovereign Pontiff, and always to defend his authority, even in doubtful matters."

This document was without a date, and did not bear the name of any Congregation; but unfortunately on the other side of the page, Father Boniface had written the words, *Pro Joan. Eudes,* and at the bottom of the petition, the Holy Father's refusal was expressed by the term: *Sanctissimus abnuit.**

How did his enemies contrive to get possession of a document so likely to injure Father Eudes, although it was not even from the pen of a member of his Congregation?

---

* The following answer to Father Boniface's petition is preserved in the Imperial archives: "In parvo registro rescriptorum et resolutionum S. Cong. Episc. et Reg. negotiis præpositæ, sub die 2 Junii, 1662, ad ante scriptas preces ita reperitur decretum: Ex audientiâ SS. 31 Maii, 1662, Cong. de Seminario in Franciâ. Ludovico Boniface. SS. abnuit. In quorum fidem. Romæ, 4 September, 1662.—G. Epus. Com. Secret."

He alone, in the name of his brethren, had the right to make a proposal such as it contained. Had it long been suspected in France that the Archives of the Roman Chancery contained matter so certain to compromise Father Eudes seriously in the king's eyes? Are we not obliged to believe that the Oratorians took measures to possess themselves of this paper, which was refused to them?* Was a copy procured from the agent of the Chancery? or was it found among the papers left by Father Boniface with a priest† who lived at Cardinal F. Barberini's, and to whom he entrusted the conclusion of the affairs of the Congregation? Be this as it may, this petition reached France towards the end of the year 1673, and was immediately placed in the hands of his majesty, who indignantly ordered Father Eudes to leave Paris for Normandy.‡

He obeyed, and on the 27th of November, 1673, made a formal act disavowing Father Boniface's petition; a copy of this act is in the Imperial Archives; it was made in presence of Nicolas de Montier, lord of La Motte, councillor of the king, lieutenant of the bailiwick, and president of the court at Caen; of J. de la Menardière, esquire, king's councillor and advocate, and of Messire d'Auge, clerk of the said bailiwick. In this act

* The Imperial Archives contain a bundle of fifty letters from Father Amy, (an Oratorian) written in 1673, and 1674, to Father de Saumaise, assistant to Father de Ste. Marthe, the General of the Oratory; in these letters he speaks of efforts made to obtain the above authentic document; after a copy had been promised it was refused to the Oratorians, on the ground that they wished to use it against the Holy See.—(Annales de la Congregation.)

† Annales de la Congregation. (P. Costil.)

‡ "Boniface's petition had no effect," says Mgr. Huet, "and it would have been completely forgotten, but that some French ecclesiastics in the suite of Cardinal d'Estrées, who was then at Rome, happened to hear of it. It was thus brought to light, and soon came to the king's knowledge."—*Origines de Caen, ch.* xxiv. p. 634.

Father Eudes disavows all those who put forth the aforesaid document in his name, and renounces for ever any further proceedings under the conditions there laid down. "Moreover, he informs us, that not only was this petition presented without his order or consent, but that such a proposal is entirely contrary to his feelings, and to the spirit of his Congregation."

A similar circumstance had occurred in the case of the Carmelites of the great convent of Paris, who were accused of having presented to the king a petition prejudicial to the interests of other houses of their Order. The king answered that their denial must be believed; why then did he not take that of the holy priest?

Father Eudes also said in a memorial on this subject: "If I had written the petition in question, (a thing which I would simply admit, if I remembered it), I should not have inserted the words touching the authority of the Pope, nor these, '*even in doubtful matters*,' except with regard to things bearing on the faith and decided by His Holiness, such, for example, as those connected with the five propositions which at that time many persons wished to rank as doubtful; not admitting that they were to be found in a certain author, but openly contradicting the decision of the Holy See." In vain Father Boniface declared that he alone was the author of this petition, and that Father Eudes had known nothing of it. He even proposed to give the latter a sum of money by way of reparation for the harm done by his imprudence; this was declined by Father Eudes.

The bishops who had so often given him proofs of their esteem and affection, did not forsake him in this cruel disgrace. Five of them wrote on his behalf to Pope Clement X. on the 10th of February, 1674.

As the king continued inflexible, credit and reputation fled together. The hope of an establishment at Paris was at an end; the house at Versailles was given to the Lazarists, to the great injury of the Congregation, which was now accused of having failed in its duty to the sovereign, of having betrayed the interests of his crown, at the very moment when he had loaded its founder with favours, and finally, of the unpardonable crime of having declared against the so-called liberties of the Gallican Church.

The position was a desperate one: this blow had indeed struck home; but Father Eudes did not lose heart. He drew up a document in justification of his conduct, and begged the king to defend him. The queen had the greatest confidence in his words and acts, and herself presented this memorial to her august husband, who answered: "I have the greatest good will towards Father Eudes, but here is a petition against my state, he must justify himself, and after that his affairs can be looked to."

But, in order to justify himself, it would have been necessary to act on the offensive; to attack, as he had been attacked; to cite his accusers before the throne. His friends, and the principal members of his order begged him to take the most rigorous measures to stop the progress of this wrong, which they attributed to the Jansenists. His answer was, "Perhaps God will raise up some one to answer the libel. In any case, I embrace the crosses He is pleased to send me with all my heart, and I most humbly beseech Him to pardon those who persecute me."

Father Boniface's proposal, although not accepted by the Court of Rome, was not of a nature to give offence there. But Father Eudes' open disgrace became known, and all Father Bonnefont's efforts for the recognition of the Congregation failed; he was not, however, discouraged, for he remained in Rome until the 30th of March, 1675. He had told Father Eudes of all the difficulties that met him, and he had replied, "I rejoice in all the favours God shows you, being assured that Ubi abundavit tristitia, ibi superabundat lætitia."

Father de Bonnefont, however, obtained many benefits for the Congregation, and, amongst others, a bull permitting Father Eudes to give missions in all parts of France, with plenary indulgence; this grant was renewed in the name of the Congregation, and with the privileges of prelates, according to Father Eudes' hope. Although the Court of Rome did not formally confirm the Congregation, its name was allowed. Father Bonnefont also brought back six bulls of indulgences for the establishment of the Confraternity of the Sacred Hearts of Jesus and Mary in the six seminaries at Caen, Coutances, Lisieux, Rouen, Rennes, and Evreux. The Holy Father, moreover, granted indulgences in favour of the priests or clerks of the Congregation, to the exclusion of the rest of the faithful, and even of the serving brethren. This bull accorded a plenary indulgence on entering the Congregation, at the hour of death, and for visiting the church of Caen on the Feast of the Sacred Heart, 8th February, also four indulgences of seven years on special days, all in perpetuity. In 1688 Mgr. de Laménie, Bishop of Coutances, declared in the act of verification of this brief, that he wished his name to be the first on the list of the Confraternity of the Sacred Hearts, and that he permitted all priests and all laity in his diocese to belong to it.

Father Bonnefont's journey was not therefore fruitless.

During his exile in Normandy, Father Eudes continued to labour as an evangelist; he spent the year 1674, and the two following years, in

going through the dioceses of Bayeux, Evreux,
Lisieux, and Coutances.

His last mission was given at St. Lo; tradition
says that he preached from the stone pulpit in the
outer wall of the church of Notre Dame. The
crowds that came to hear him were so great, that
notwithstanding the intense cold, he was obliged
to preach out of doors. He did not appear at the
time to suffer from it, but in 1677 his strength
manifestly gave way. He was advised to settle at
Caen, and to occupy himself merely with the
affairs of the Congregation. For twenty-five
years he had been suffering from a rupture; no
one had known of it, for he had always preserved
a calm countenance and cheerful manner. He
now fell into a serious illness, which was no doubt
aggravated by the grief his unjust accusation
had caused him. But the danger passed away for
a time, and he said to his anxious brethren,
that God was giving him time for conversion;
"For I do not know," he added, "if I have yet
begun to love our Lord and His holy Mother."
So far did he deem himself from perfection.

CHAPTER IV.

1677—1680.

During Father Eudes' weary hours of suffering,
that which weighed most heavily on his mind
was not his own approaching death, but the
failure of all his endeavours to set himself right
with the king, and the fear of leaving his beloved
Congregation under the cloud which had already
weighed upon it for years, and which, with the
aid of fresh calumnies, threatened its entire
ruin.

When strength returned in the measure permitted by his great age, he set to work again, and
on the 7th of November, 1678, addressed to the
king a touching petition for restoration to favour.
In a spirit of perfect Christian charity, he seeks
justice for himself, without so much as naming

15

his accusers. "I beg your Majesty to observe that it is a priest who has the honour of addressing you, one who for more than fifty years has daily offered to God the Adorable Sacrifice, and the Precious Blood of Him who is the Eternal Truth, and that it is the part of Christian charity to give him credence, rather than to. judge and condemn him as an impostor; I am ready to affirm, by every means permitted to a Christian, that that petition never entered into my mind, that I disavow and detest it with all my heart, and I protest that I had rather die a .thousand times than do anything against the interests of your Majesty, whom I implore to forget that unhappy document, as you desire that our Saviour may put away everything that could oppose your eternal happiness, and to allow me the honour of casting myself at your feet," &c.

Such was his noble protest. He was a *priest*, therefore he could not lie; he was a Frenchman in heart and soul, therefore he could not betray his king. There is no return to the past; no direct reply to the calumny. And is it not remarkable that in 1674 the Court of Rome was enquiring the reason why Father Eudes. had left the Oratory in 1643 ?*

We have fully answered the question; it was the duty of the historian, charity could not be wounded by the expression of truth, but he, the accused, was silent, "Jesus autem tacebat."

Father Eudes wrote to Mgr. Auvry, former Bishop of Coutances, who had supported him under all circumstances, and against all adversaries. He also wrote to Mgr. de Harlay, Archbishop of Paris, and to Father Lachaise, the king's confessor. In his letter to the prelate, he calls to mind all the favours he had bestowed

* Annales de la Congregation.—(P. Costil.)

upon him while he occupied the see of Rouen, and
to the celebrated Jesuit he spoke of the affection*
which the Society of Jesus had ever shown him.
Both were perfectly convinced of his innocence,
and took means of seconding his ardent desire to
see the king.

Four months elapsed, and it was not till June
1679 that he had reason to hope for a restoration
of the king's favour. Three days before he had
made a vow to dedicate one of the principal
chapels of the seminary to the Blessed Virgin, in
honour of her Immaculate Conception. Mgr. de
Harlay charged Mgr. Auvry to let Father Eudes
know that the king was no longer under the influence of the painful impressions which had caused
him so much suffering and anxiety during the last
six years, and to urge him to come to Versailles as
soon as possible and thank his Majesty.

He had hardly recovered from his illness, and
was still very weak, the journey was long and
irksome, but nothing could keep him back; he
left Caen by the coach, and immediately on his
arrival, June 16th, 1679, was presented to Louis
XIV. by the Archbishop of Paris. He gave the
following account of the interview in a letter to
Father Dufour: "Yesterday I had the honour of
seeing the king at St. Germains, which came to
pass in this manner: I was ushered into the
king's chamber, where I found myself in the
midst of a great number of bishops, priests, dukes,
marquises, counts, marshals of France, and king's
guards. The Archbishop of Paris made me take
my place in a corner of the chamber; when the
king entered he passed through all the great lords

* Not long ago, when on a pilgrimage to Notre Dame du
Chêne, near Sablé, we met the venerable missionary, Father
Chaignon, of the Society of Jesus, an old friend of Father Louis,
Superior General of the Eudists, who died in 1849. He told us
he had read in Father Eudes' statutes an article concerning the
reception of any Jesuit who might visit a house of his order.

and came straight to me, with a countenance full
of kindness. Then I began to speak to him of
our business, and he listened to me with much
attention, as if he was very glad to hear what I
was saying.........When the king had heard these
things, he said to me, 'I am very glad to see you;
I have heard of you; I know that you do a
great deal of good in my realm. Continue your
work; I shall be very glad to see you again, and I
will serve and protect you whenever an opportunity
arises.' Those were the king's words; they filled
me with unspeakable joy, and they were heard by
the Archbishop of Paris, and by all the noblemen
present."

The echo of these words doubtless reached the
enemies of Father Eudes, as they were planning
further attacks; but he was about to appear before
God, the only Judge of our souls; and if he
rejoiced at the royal favour, it was not because
they were discomfitted, but because he was enabled
to put his cherished institution under the protection of a sovereign whom all Europe has called
great.

His journey had been a martyrdom, for the
motion of the coach had seriously aggravated the
infirmities which had already brought him to the
gates of death.

He saw that he had not much time before him,
and that it would be well to choose an associate
on whom the chief care of the Congregation might
devolve.

Soon after his return from Paris he heard of the
serious illness of his brother Charles Eudes du
d'Houay. No family tradition tells us whether
Father Eudes assisted our ancestor in his last
moments, but we love to think that this sweet
consolation was granted to him. He died at
Argentan, in the parish of St. Martin, not far
from the inn of the Trois Sauciers, where, in

1638, that plague broke out which first called his heroic virtue into action.

Father Eudes had cast his eyes on Father Deshayes de Bonnefond to fill the office of vicar. As far back as 1673, he had named him to the Holy Father as his probable successor.

In an assembly held at Caen in the month of October, 1679, he made known his intentions. It was decided that he should continue to govern as before, Father Bonnefond being only entrusted with the details. But the state of his health soon made him unable to do more than regulate some complicated accounts between the Caen seminary and the community of our Lady of Charity. These serious difficulties were brought to an end by a compromise which both parties accepted on the 14th of November, 1679.

As Father Eudes could no longer really direct the Congregation, and Father Bonnefond's powers as vicar were limited, complaints began to arise.

To put an end to all difficulties, the Superior-General resolved to let his brethren choose his successor.

Every house of the Congregation was to send its superior and one of its members to Caen, on the 26th of June, 1680.

On the following day, after each had said Mass, Father Eudes, the fourteen deputies, and the three members of the Caen Seminary entitled to vote, met together. The Venerable Superior laid before the assembly the position of the Congregation, and the motives which induced him to resign the post he had filled for thirty-seven years. One of the fathers, answering him in the name of all, said that they accepted his proposal, but only on certain conditions, which their respect for him rendered indispensable; 1st, that the new superior should take no important step without his consent; 2nd, that in the event of the new superior's

death, during Father Eudes' life-time, all authority should revert to him, and be exercised by him
as he might think well ; 3rd, that two assistants
should be chosen by the assembly, and that the
superior should make no serious change in the
temporal concerns of the Community without their
consent.

Father Eudes made no objection to these conditions ; he knew that as far as they concerned
him they would not long remain in force.

Father Blouet de Camilly, grand vicar of Coutances and a benefactor of the Order, was then
elected by ballot, sixteen out of eighteen votes
being in his favour. Father Eudes at once left
the place of honour, and went slowly to the new
superior of his Congregation, he uncovered his
head and fell at the feet of his own spiritual child,
humbly asking his blessing, and promising him
obedience in all things.

This humility was the crown of his long and
holy life. We have now only to learn the lessons
of his death-bed.

He spent his little remaining strength in consoling some persons who needed his advice, put a
finishing stroke to his treatise on the admirable
Heart of the Blessed Virgin, and then retired to
his cell, whence the tumults of earth were for ever
shut out. He left his defence to others, he only
thought of forgiveness, and of leaving his last instructions to his brethren. He had made a will
in Paris, on the 24th of April, 1671, concluding
with the words, "Amen, amen ; fiat, fiat, veni,
veni, veni, Domine Jesu !" He mentioned the
Church of the Seminary as the place where, if he
were allowed to have a desire, he would choose to
be buried, and named some objects of piety to be
placed in his coffin.

He soon asked for the Holy Viaticum, which he
received kneeling on the floor, supported by two

of his brethren; all present were touched by the words which he spoke on receiving the Blessed Sacrament.

Some days went by without any great change; he received visits from some of his old friends, amongst others from Mdme. de Camilly,* to whom he made a promise that he would pray God to grant her a calm and peaceful death. Such was not his own lot, his agony was long and sore. The violence of his sufferings soon reduced him to a state of such extreme weakness, that his brethren thought he had but a few moments to live, and gathered round him to receive his last breath. The sight of so many whom he loved seemed to call him back to life, and he spent his remaining moments in strengthening them in those sentiments of piety, of which his life had given the holy example. At length, after having received Extreme Unction, he breathed his last, about three o'clock in the afternoon of Monday, the 19th of August, 1680.

When his death was known, the concourse of people who came to look on his remains was so great, that it was difficult to preserve order amongst them. The poor had lost a benefactor ever ready to seek out and relieve their misery with his own hands, or by means of the rich who had taken him into their confidence. Sinners had lost a minister always willing to listen to them and to reconcile them to God; pious souls, an enlightened director; priests, a pattern; the Church, a zealous champion of her faith.

He was one of those men "invented by reli-

---

* Some months afterwards, as Mdme. de Camilly was leaving the Church of the Seminary of Caen, where she had received Holy Communion, she felt herself stricken to death; she had only time to kneel down, and immediately expired without any agony, according to Father Eudes' promise. She was buried in the new church, near a pillar which separates the choir from the nave.

gion," to use M. Cochin's happy expression, a friend and benefactor of children, a counsellor of the doubtful, a repairer of our faults, a pilot for the last voyage. Wherever Providence led his steps, he was a man of duty and of truth, at once the minister and the example of Faith and Pardon.

Therefore the mourning for him was general.

The nuns of our Lady of Charity of the Refuge did everything in their power to obtain possession of their founder's heart; but the Eudists opposed their desire, believing it contrary to his own wishes, and the body was watched until Father Mannoury and Brother Richard laid it out. It was exposed in the Seminary Chapel. The faithful crowded there to kiss his feet. On the morrow all the parish priests of the city came with their clergy to the funeral. The Jesuit Fathers sent several of their number, thus giving a public token of the esteem and veneration they had long entertained for this holy minister of the Gospel, once their pupil.

After the funeral ceremonies had been performed with all possible solemnity, the body was enclosed in a leaden coffin, and buried in the middle of the place destined for the Choir of the new Church of the Seminary. A white marble tomb was afterwards erected, with the inscription: "Hic jacet venerabilis sacerdos Joannes Eudes, seminariorum congregationis Jesu et Mariæ institutor et rector. Obiit die 19 Augusti 1680, ætatis suæ 79."

The cities of Caen and Bayeux paid homage to the holy priest's memory; the members of the Cambremer conference composed an epitaph setting forth the virtues which so eminently distinguished him. They form the subject of a separate publication from which we have often had occasion to quote, and in which the faithful will find further and valuable information.*

We have related all that is known of the deeds of this venerable Father; they bear the impress of ardent faith, hope and charity towards God; they manifest his submission to the Divine Will, his tender love to the Blessed Virgin, his peculiar devotion in celebrating the Holy Sacrifice of the Mass, his charity to his neighbour, his self-devotion and courage, his humility and detachment from earthly things, his scrupulous chastity, his extreme modesty, and his spirit of mortification.

Father le Beurier gives the following description of Father Eudes: " He was rather above the middle height, the natural gentleness of his character was depicted in his features, his fiery but modest eye shewed at once the keenness of his mind and the calmness of his soul. His originally delicate constitution gradually became so strong that he was capable of the most difficult undertakings and the most fatiguing labours; witness his fifty years of missions, some of which lasted two or three months, and during which he preached every day, or even two or three times a day. His faith, far more than the natural strength of his mind, supported him in the midst of opposition of all kinds, which he had to encounter for at least forty years. He had almost ruined his health in early life by excessive mortification, but happily the danger was perceived before the case became hopeless, and by means of much rest in the first instance, and a little care afterwards, he completely recovered his strength. At sixty years of age his fresh and healthy look was that of a man in the prime of life. It may be remembered that when he was seventy he preached almost every

* Des Vertus du Serviteur de Dieu, Jean Eudes, prêtre missionaire. Imprimerie P. Hauvespre, Rennes.

day in the Cathedral of Rennes, during a mission
which lasted three months.

Mgr. Huet, a friend of Father Eudes, wrote of
him :* "His remarkable virtue and ardent piety
won my love and admiration. It would be useless
for me to praise him. His innumerable labours
for the glory of God and the salvation of souls,
his pious and useful writings, have made him dear
to God and venerable in the Church."

We lay particular stress on the testimony of
this celebrated prelate, because a passage rather
different in its nature occurs in his book on *Origines de Caen:* "No consideration could hold
him back when the interests of God were in question, and his zeal, which was not always kept
within due bounds, being without *right, mission,*
or the *character of authority,* sometimes led him
to rash actions whose consequences were unfortunate. No one, however, can deny that he was a
great servant of God, who from his childhood
walked in His ways and devoted himself actively
to the salvation of souls. He published several
works of piety full of the sentiments which animated his own heart."†

. Some parasites have crept in among the sweet
flowers which the distinguished bishop has laid on
our ancestor's tomb. We would fain remove
them, although it may seem fool-hardy to enter
into collision with such an adversary.

It is our bounden duty, and, besides, we know
that in order to take a fair view the eye must be
at a certain distance from the object. Mgr. Huet
was Father Eudes' cotemporary, and perhaps he
was brought too much into contact with his opponents to be altogether uninfluenced by them.

* Huet, Evêque d'Avranches : Commentarius de Rebus ad
eum pertinentibus, page 352. Latin.

† Origines de Caen. Mgr. Huet, ch. xxiv. page 635.

Father de la Rue* tells us, that "the nuns of our Lady of Charity of the Refuge were much displeased by some expressions in the 'Origines de Caen,' relating to Father Eudes. The superior complained bitterly of them, and begged Mgr. Huet to modify them ; but the prelate refused to make any alteration."

We can now affirm that Father Eudes possessed *right, mission*, and the *character of authority.*

Right.—Father Eudes was born, as we have seen, at the beginning of the XVIIth century ; the preceding age had been a time of destruction ; disorder was general. No one can deny that he was one of those men whom Providence raises up at epochs of calamity. Therefore he had a *duty* to fulfil. His vocation was so marked, that, notwithstanding all their objections, their plans and projects, his parents† felt obliged to let him follow it ; and after he had entered the Oratory Father de Bérulle made him preach even before he had received Holy Orders. During the fifty years that he performed this *duty* he was never seen to fail ; he assisted in raising up the priesthood ; he admonished the nobles and the people ; he stretched out a helping hand to those poor fallen women, who had forfeited domestic happiness, who were dead like lepers ; "homines ante mortem extincti."

Now *Duty* constitutes *Right:* there are no duties without rights ; no rights without duties.

Mission.—If Mgr. Huet alludes to divine mis-

---

* Essais historiques sur la Ville de Caen, par l'Abbé de la Rue, page 165.

† "It belongs to none but God," says Mascaron, "to dispose absolutely of the vocation of men ; men can merely decide each one in the sight of God, concerning their choice of a state and their vocation. This principle is one of the most unquestionable in Christian morality. Therefore I conclude that a father cannot absolutely control the vocation of his children without two evident acts of injustice, *one against God*, and the other *against his children themselves.*"

sion, we answer that no one is in a position to pronounce a decision on the subject. It is a secret between God and Father Eudes; nevertheless, his works are so numerous, and so marked by the apostolic characteristic of constant persecution and constant success, that we are firmly convinced that God, whom he loved so much, and in whom he trusted so fully, had given him a mission to fulfil on earth, before calling him to heaven.

As for his Ecclesiastical Mission; we have seen that he made no foundation without letters of institution from the bishops, who had the legal sanction of Parliament; that he was constantly summoned into other dioceses, and was unable to accomplish all the works entrusted to him by the bishops of those dioceses. And when it was proposed to raise him to the Episcopate, we know that Father Ferrier, a Jesuit, and Louis XIV.'s confessor, answered that he must be allowed to fulfil his *Mission,* for the regeneration of the people.

The character of authority.—From *mission* directly emanates the character of authority necessary for the fulfilment of that mission. Religious foundations are made by divine inspiration; otherwise they have no firm basis and no duration, for human authority has no creative power. God often uses the weakest and most despised instruments. The sanction of the Vicar of Christ is no doubt necessary; in the year 1666 it was given to the Order of our Lady of Charity of the Refuge, and although only formally accorded to the Congregation of Jesus and Mary in the present day, we know that the Popes who have had this Congregation brought before their notice have always declared that it was carrying out one of the principal decisions of the Council of Trent.

We have now only to point out the three principal characteristics of the useful and laborious life of the holy founder.

1st. The multiplicity of his works.

2nd. The unchanging unity of their object.

3rd. The firmness of their foundation.

The multiplicity of his works.—It is inconceivable how the life of one man sufficed for so much toil. A hundred and twelve missions, exclusive of frequent ecclesiastical conferences, and many courses of Advent and Lent sermons; the affairs of his two principal foundations, and of all the monasteries of various orders under his direction; his printed and manuscript works; his constant journeys; his daily correspondence; his habit of consecrating each year, each month, each day and each hour, to some special act of mental prayer. In addition to which he was often laid aside by dangerous illnesses brought on by excessive fatigue. Alas! what are our lives compared to his!

The unchanging unity of their object.—From his childhood Father Eudes had the most tender devotion to Jesus and Mary; afterwards, when under the spiritual direction of Fathers de Bérulle and de Condren, and intimately acquainted with Father Olier, he learned to set before him in all things the Person of the Son and that of the Mother. This holy education soon led him to find in the teaching of St. Gertrude, St. Mechtilde, and St. Bridget, a new object of devotion;— the Sacred Hearts of Jesus and Mary. Henceforth, guided by divine light, probably even by heavenly revelations, he sought no other object for his love and worship. He made the honour of these Divine Hearts the chief end of his two institutions, the Congregation of Jesus and Mary, and the order of our Lady of Charity of the Refuge. Works with such an origin could not die. No one can deny the solidity of the foundation on which Father Eudes built.

What a lesson for those who live without any definite occupation, and die leaving to their successors nothing but the sad and useless memory of an idle, and, it may be, a guilty life!

Francis Eudes de Mezeray, the last surviving son of the surgeon of Ri, soon felt his end approaching. He had retained the most tender affection for his eldest brother, and in his will he left a sum of money towards the erection of a monument to him. "Art. XIII. I give and bequeath the sum of 120 livres to assist in the erection of a monument to my brother, the Reverend Father Eudes, although, indeed, his virtue and his fame have already raised one more beautiful than can be made by human hands."

In the early days of July 1683, death came to Mézeray. He asked for the last Sacraments, and received them with piety which touched all present. "My friends," said he, "a great change has taken place in me; now that I am about to die I confess the errors of my life; I firmly believe all that the Catholic Apostolic and Roman Church teaches; I believe the truth of its mysteries, and the efficacy of its sacraments. I am about really to receive Jesus Christ my Saviour. If by my words or deeds I have given scandal to any of you, forget what I have said or done, and only remember that Mézeray dying is more worthy to be believed than Mézeray living."

Father Eudes could not have asked more from his brother if he had lived to watch his last moments, and certainly, in the sight of the Judge of all, this noble profession of Faith is worth more than all the works which have made his name celebrated.

Some years ago, a Eudist, Father Coubard, had the happiness of a private audience of Pius IX. "You belong," said he, "to the Congregation of

Eudists.* I know your Father Eudes; I am reading his life just now; he was a great servant of God, a worthy son of the Church; science and virtue met together in him."

No higher testimony can be given on earth, unless the same Vicar of Christ, from the Chair of St. Peter, pronounces a solemn sentence of beatification.

Will that sentence one day be pronounced in favour of this son of Ri, to the eternal glory of those who claim kindred with him, whether by natural or spiritual ties?

We venture to hope that it will; but whatever may be the result of the active efforts made by the venerable Fathers of the Congregation of Jesus and Marie, and the pious Daughters of our Lady of Charity of the Refuge, and our Lady of Charity of the Good Shepherd, we cannot but believe that from the day when he was called away from earth, their venerable founder has been enjoying eternal happiness in the ineffable presence of the Son of God, and of His holy Mother, who was, during the days of his weary and toilsome pilgrimage, his life, his hope, and his consolation. We believe that he shares the power of the saints, and that we may confidently turn to him and seek the aid of his intercession, in those dark days when

* The volume of Constitutions approved by the Holy Father was received at Redon, on the 17th of July, 1864; but it was in an audience on the 19th of February, that the Sovereign Pontiff Pius IX., gave his consent to a report made by the Secretary of the Sacred Congregation, which led to the approbation of these Constitutions. And it was on the 2nd of February, Feast of the Passion of our Lord, that the Pope, in a farewell audience, told the Very Reverend Father Gaudaire that the Constitutions would be approved, and that he might go without uneasiness.

The approbation given is not definitive, "Sanctissimus dominus noster Pius Pape IX., per modum experimenti, ad decennium approbavit atque confirmavit;" that is to say, that if, in 1874, the Congregation is satisfied with these Constitutions, it will then take rank in the great family of approved Congregations; otherwise it will make a fresh application to the Sacred Congregation for future modifications.

our soul seems to be without strength, and we feel alone and forsaken.

As we have written these pages, as step by step, and day by day, we have traced the life of Father Eudes, we feel that it has done us good; we seem to have gained new strength to meet difficulties and endure reproaches.

May many who read them, say with us, "Nonne Cor nostrum ardens erat in nobis, dum loqueretur in viâ, et aperiret nobis scripturas ?"*

God grant us, as well as every member of our numerous posterity, grace to imitate the ancestor, of whom we may say what was said of his Example and Master; "Qui pertransiit benefaciendo, et sanando omnes oppressos à Diabolo : quoniam Deus erat† in illo."

* St. Luke xxiv. 32.　　　† Acts of the Apostles, x. 38.

APPENDIX I.

1680—1782.

SUPERIORS-GENERAL FROM 1680 TO 1792.—THEIR GOVERNMENT.
—THE CONGREGATION OF JESUS AND MARY AT THE TIME OF
THE FRENCH REVOLUTION.—FATHER HEBERT, CO-ADJUTOR
OF FATHER COUSIN, SUPERIOR GENERAL, AND DIRECTOR OF
THE HOUSE IN PARIS, IS NAMED CONFESSOR TO LOUIS XVI.
—IS MARTYRED WITH NINE OF HIS BRETHREN AT THE
CARMES, ON THE 2ND OF SEPTEMBER, 1792.—DIFFERENT
FOUNDATIONS IN WHICH MEMBERS OF THE CONGREGATION
HAVE CO-OPERATED.

We have already seen how M. Blouet de Camilly was led to place himself under Father Eudes' direction, and to enter the Congregation of which he became a distinguished member and a great benefactor, and which he governed for thirty-one years. It was no easy task to fill Father Eudes' place; but Father de Blouet inherited his virtues as well as his office.

The celebration of the anniversary of the holy founder's death was delayed until the 31st of February, 1682, on account of the absence of Mgr. de Nesmond; and, as the chapel of the seminary was not yet finished, the ceremony took place in the church of Notre Dame, at Caen. The following notice occurs in the "*Mercure Français*," published at the time: "You must long since have heard of the death of the Reverend Father Eudes, one of the most celebrated missionaries who has appeared for a long time, and a most

16

useful servant of the Church.............The Bishop of Bayeux, wishing to honour his memory, caused a most solemn service to be performed last month in the church of Notre Dame, which, large as it is, could not contain the crowds gathered together to hear the praises of the great man who is gone."

The church of the seminary was not finished, and the general opinion was that it never would be. The Jesuits accordingly proposed to purchase the establishment, but Father Blouet refused to sell it, and having consulted with a skilful architect, completed all the works, to the great astonishment of the bishop, and the church was consecrated on the 23rd of November, 1687.

The superior-general resigned his theological chair as soon as possible, and settled permanently at Contances.

From the first he laboured to extend the Congregation. He bought for the seminary of Coutances the estate of Manoir, situated at the end of the faubourg, at the side of the Avranches road. He set on foot ecclesiastical conferences in his archdeaconry of Cotentin, and obtained new letters patent, which placed all the establishments under his care on a more solid basis, and gave new strength to the existence of the Congregation.* He pro-

---

* A letter written by the Bishop of Rodez to the "*Univers*," on the 15th of January, 1868, in relation to the future council, gives a clear explanation of the registration of religious deeds in general.

"The object of the registration by the parliaments of pontifical decrees and decrees of councils was not, strictly speaking, to authorize their publication in the kingdom, nor to constitute those bodies judges of Faith and ecclesiastical discipline, but to adopt the dogmatic and disciplinary decisions of Popes and Councils as *laws of the state*. As soon as these decisions were known they were binding on the conscience, which is the domain of the Church, but they had not the force of civil laws until received by the state with the usual formalities, that is, by parliamentary registration. It then became illegal to write or to act in any way against what was thus sanctioned by the civil power, and authors could not evade these decisions inasmuch as

moted the publication of Father Eudes' works with filial zeal, endeavoured to bring about a union between his Congregation and that of the Foreign Missions, and took special care that the Eudists should carry on their missions as they had done in the life-time of their founder. He gave one himself at St. Lo, on which occasion he received from Father La Chaise the following testimony of the king's regard for the Congregation; "I have given the king an account of the letter which you were good enough to write to me about your mission at St. Lo, and his Majesty is much gratified by its good results. I hope you will be equally successful at Sainte-Marie. It would give me pleasure to be able to second your zeal..." In 1684 Father de Bonnefont was sent to take the direction of the community of St. Josse, in accordance with the offer of Father Hamelin, to whom this benefice belonged.

Father Eudes' death had calmed the irritation of his adversaries, and his successor was distinguished by fortune and high birth, as well as by great virtues and devotion to the Church.

Father de Blouet endeavoured to bring about the union with Mgr. de Sisgau's Congregation of the Blessed Sacrament, which Father Eudes had wished to establish forty-four years before; but this effort was fruitless, as it was found impossible to agree on the principal heads of an act of union.

In 1688 the direction of the chapel of St. Anne de la Bosserie, near Fougères, was entrusted to the Eudists. This chapel was much visited by the inhabitants of Normandy, Brittany, and La Manche, because of the miracles wrought there,

they were not at liberty to publish anything without Royal permission."

Communities used, therefore, to take the precaution of asking for letters patent in confirmation of the constitutions framed or approved by the bishops, and these letters patent were registered by Parliament.

twelve of which were carefully verified by Mgr. de Cornullier, Bishop of Rennes.

On the first of September 1691, Mgr. de Nesmond laid the foundation-stone of the Seminary at Caen. Father Pinel took charge of this institution, which was completed in 1703, and blessed by the same prelate. The Priests of the Congregation had now a suitable place of abode.

The Maréchal de Bellefonds did everything in his power to establish the Eudists on his property of Sainte-Marie; but notwithstanding all the care and attention bestowed on the three fathers who were sent there, the place proved so unhealthy that they were unable to remain.

In the same year Mgr. Huet gave the Eudists his seminary at Avranches. We must not omit to mention a mission which Father Damesme gave in 1692 to two regiments encamped on the plain of Courrouze. These troops formed a part of the force sent by Louis XIV. to the frontiers of Normandy under command of his brother, with a view of assisting James II. to recover his throne.

The beginning of this mission was attended with great difficulties, but its results were most satisfactory.

In accordance with the resolution passed in 1679, Father Blouet called together in 1693 the members of the Congregation in whom he had most confidence. This second assembly consisted of eleven priests, the superior-general, Fathers Esnouf, Jagan, Norgeot, Bence, Lefèvre, Roger, De Fontaines, Trochu, Le Gravois, and Hérambourg. Nineteen new regulations were made, five of which related to the rule, three to the brethren, two to the habit, and the three others to different details.

The seminary at Avranches was bought in 1693, and letters patent were granted in 1695.

The superior-general was always anxious to

have a foundation in Paris, the centre of religious
and civil concerns. In 1697 he made a fruitless
effort to obtain one by proposing to pay the debts
of a man named Gervais, who had a school there.

In 1701 the Congregation undertook its eighth
foundation, the Seminary of Dol. Mgr. de
Chamillard the Bishop of Dol, himself came to
the Priory of Notre Dame, to make over his
seminary to the superior, Fathers Esnouf and de
Mauny, as representatives of the Congregation.
At length, in 1703, Father Blouet was able to
gain a footing in Paris, and bought a house called
les Tourettes, (rue des Postes,) in the parish of
St. Etienne du Mont, behind the gardens of the
church of Ste. Geneviève. A garden was attached
to this house, and the price was 3,000 livres.

This purchase was made in the name of the
priests of Caen and Coutances. About the same
time Mgr. de Chamillard's successor, Mgr.
d'Argenson, gave the Eudists the charge of the
retreats in Dol.

Fresh marks of esteem were shown to the Congregation by the king, Father La Chaise, and
Mgr. de Chamillard; and its members took the
place of the priests of the Congregation of the
Blessed Sacrament in the seminary of Senlis.

In 1704, a mission at the College of Avranches
was attended with such success that the Congregation of the Blessed Virgin was in consequence
established there.

We have already said that Father Legrix was,
in 1704, appointed parish priest of St. Josse, and
have spoken of his conduct and that of Father
Bournisien.

Father Blouet's incessant labours and his great
natural ardour, now so useful in the service of
God, gave reason to fear that his career would
soon come to its close. In 1705 he was seriously
ill ; many prayers were made to our Lady of La

Roquette, and the venerable superior recovered
suddenly while the holy Sacrifice was being offered
on his behalf.

He knew, however, that God had only granted
him a respite; he had always retained the direction of the seminary at Coutances, and now named
Father Hérambourg as his successor there in the
event of his death. He then summoned the third
general Assembly of the Congregation to meet on
the 1st of August, 1705. All the deputies were
to be empowered by their respective houses to
elect a superior-general; the result was that Father
Blouet was induced to continue in that office, and
the proceedings were terminated on the 8th of
August.

A plot of ground named Bosillé, at the end of
the faubourg Saint-Helier, near the gate of Rennes,
was bought with a view to the establishment of a
little seminary there.

The fourth general Assembly took place in 1708.
Mgr. Loménie honoured it with his presence, and
before the beginning of the deliberations blessed
all the fathers as they knelt at his feet.

A fifth Assembly was convened on the 1st of
May, 1711, with the object of electing a new
superior-general. Mgr. de Nesmond had previously made Father de Fontaines his grand vicar,
and given him one of his richest canonries; his
position had therefore kept him aloof from the
Congregation, and he found some difficulty in
accepting Father Blouet's invitation, which was
delivered to him by Father Legrand, superior of
the Seminary of Avranches.

The choice of a superior-general was a matter
which caused some perplexity; Louis XIV. was
growing old, difficulties were likely to arise, and
it was necessary to find one who, in addition to
the qualities always required in such a position,
had a certain amount of knowledge of the world,

good connections, and the kind of authority given, especially in those days, by high birth.

The appearance of Father Guy de Fontaines put an end to all uncertainties, and he was elected by 19 votes out of 24, as successor to Father Blouet, who at once threw himself at his feet, saying: "Hitherto we have looked upon you as a dear brother, but henceforth we shall consider you as a beloved and honoured father."

The new superior, son of M. Simien de Fontaines, Lord of Neuilly and Vicomte of Caen, was born in 1664, and had entered the Congregation in 1691.

Father Blouet lived a life more and more hidden from sight, until he died on the 11th of August, 1711, at 8 o'clock in the evening, at the age of 79. Like his master, he had been for 56 years a member of the Congregation.

The chapter wished to bury him in their church, but the fathers foresaw this intention, and laid him in their chapel. Solemn offices soon made up for the deficiencies of his funeral.

His family approved of all he had done for the Congregation, and it was decided that two candidates from the Seminary of Coutances, and two from Caen, should appear as his heirs.

Father de Bonnefont soon followed Father Blouet to the tomb; he was a native of the parish of Cuye, near Argentan, and entered the Congregation in 1658. Father Eudes loved him as a son, and employed him in the most delicate affairs.

We have been led to dwell at some length on the history of the second superior of the Congregation, because he and its holy founder were united, as closely as two different natures could be, by their common ardent love of God.

Father Blouet completed Father Eudes' work; on his death the Congregation possessed thirteen establishments in the nature of greater and smaller seminaries, and enjoyed the king's protection and favour. Good was wrought wherever the fathers appeared; private foundations rose up under their care; and we may here remark that the contagion of Jansenism attacked only three members of this compact body, and they at once openly or actually left it, finding it impossible to propagate their opinions in its bosom.

When Father Guy de Fontaines was named superior-general, he made no change in his place of residence, nor in his mode of life, which was somewhat more luxurious than that of his predecessors.

His direction was zealous and able, but it was that of a general obliged to remain at a distance from his army, rather than that of a leader who shares the perils and fatigues of his soldiers. Perhaps circumstances made it necessary that the superior should stand, as it were, on a height, in order the better to guard against the coming storm.

Father Perraud says that " the promulgation of the bull Unigenitus (1711) provoked the passions of the Jansenists to the greatest degree, and thereby placed the Oratory in a difficult position. At this period all the religious orders, except the Jesuits and the fathers of St. Sulpice, carried away by a kind of irresistible excitement, ventured on open opposition to the authority of the Holy See, and sacrificed the peace of the Church to some few sectarians; a strange manner of defending what they believed to be the true doctrine of Jesus Christ."

Father de Fontaines' chief care was the preservation of tranquillity in the minds of his brethren; and this gives a special character to his generalship.

The sixth Assembly met at Caen on the 20th

September, 1715. It was there decided that new buildings should be erected at the Seminary of Caen, and that persons wishing to enter the Congregation should spend their time of probation there instead of at Launay, as had been done for 36 years.

Nearly 10,000 persons died of dysentery at Rennes and in the diocese, in the year 1719 ; and some of the candidates in the seminary being attacked, made a vow to have Mass said every week at the altar of the Holy Family, to give a dinner to a poor person, and to say the *Memorare* of the Blessed Virgin every day. The malady immediately ceased.

In the course of the deliberations of this council, the superior spoke in an admirable manner on the state of public opinion, and on the deplorable error of those who were induced, by ignorance or by obstinacy, to appeal from the Bull Unigenitus to a council. He made it his great object to convince his brethren that, during this grievous conflict, their proper attitude was one of patient waiting for the decision of the bishops.

Father de Fontaines had means of seeing further than his brethren, and perhaps he knew already that the Abbé de Lorraine, whose faith was doubtful, was to succeed to the See of Bayeux. This high-born ecclesiastic had, in fact, already been nominated to the Bishopric, but the Court of Rome being uneasy as to his sentiments, kept him waiting for his bulls two years, and he only entered into possession in 1720.

Many difficulties were therefore imminent, and the superior had thoroughly foreseen the consequences of this appointment.

Mgr. de Lorraine made an ineffectual attempt to give the direction of the Seminary of Caen to M. Legrix, formerly priest of Saint-Josse,* and

* Father Legrix, once a Eudist and parish-priest of St. Josse,

separated from the Congregation by his adhesion to Jansenism ; " You know," he wrote to Father Damesme, " that it is my intention, if possible, to preserve peace, and not to allow any one, by his own authority, to venture to apply false and opprobrious epithets to those who think differently."

By an ordinance of the 6th of April, 1720, Mgr. de Lorraine revoked all powers granted by his predecessors. This act did not include the Benedictins, the Jacobins, or the Oratory fathers.

The eighth general assembly of the Congregation was held at Caen in 1722. The twenty-seven articles of the institutions of the Eudists were approved by the first council of conscience, at which the Regent, Cardinals d'Estrées and de Bissy, and Mgr. de Fleury, formerly Bishop of Fréjus, were present. Some difficulties raised by Cardinal Dubois were referred to the Parliaments of Normandy and Brittany.

In 1724 Father Creully was appointed superior of the Seminary at Caen, which Mgr. de Lorraine had long regarded with so little good-will. He had to present himself to this prelate, who demurred about granting him the necessary powers. " My lord," said the old Eudist, " for more than

in 1715 resigned his office to Father Bournisien, with whom he continued to live until his death on the 11th February, 1729. The *Nouvelles Ecclésiastiques*, a Jansenist publication, speaks of him in the following terms : " Spite of all the prejudices which he had imbibed against Jansenists and Jansenism, the uprightness of his heart and the warmth of his piety had guarded him from the extremes usual among ecclesiastics in such communities, and allowed a ray of light to enter. The Unigenitus completely opened his eyes, and, notwithstanding his unbounded respect for the Holy Father, and the blind obedience which these gentlemen pay to their superiors, he had the courage to take part in the protests made, at different times, by the priests of Paris against this bull."

Father Legrix appealed in 1717, and again in 1720, on the occasion of the famous accommodation. His name appeared in the lists printed afterwards. In 1721 he was summoned before M. de la Vrillière, (minister to the Regent,) and banished from Paris. He settled at Corbeil. Such was the man to whom Mgr. de Lorraine wished to entrust the Caen Seminary.

thirty years I have had the honour of working
under the direction of bishops. The only favour
which I ask from your Lordship is that, when
complaints are made of my conduct, you will not
condemn me unheard."

The prelate was satisfied, and gave him the
most ample powers; he even wished him to be
associated with those of his own party who were
giving missions, but the father declined on account
of his advanced age.

These details bring before us the state of affairs.
Although Mgr. de Lorraine did not venture to
deprive the Eudists of their powers, he continued
firm in his resolve that his clergy should not perform their studies under their care. Moreover,
on the 17th of July, 1724, he was induced to publish a pastoral, in which he engaged to appeal to
a Council against the " *Unigenitus*," and condemned a catechism written by the Jesuits, in
order to defend the faithful against the novelties
of the day.

Father Le Fèvre, dean of the faculty of theology, gave information of this proceeding to Cardinal de Billy, and the pastoral was condemned.
The prelate could not have brought forward his
opinions, which unfortunately were not singular,
in a more public manner.

At the ninth general assembly, in 1725, the 27
articles already approved by the Regent were formally adopted. A school at Domfront, which had
originally been directed by priests, was made a
seminary in 1719, and given to the Eudists in
1727.

On the 19th of January in this year, Father
Guy de Fontaines de Neuilly died, having governed
the Congregation for sixteen years; during which
he had summoned seven general assemblies.
Missions had not been neglected, but we observe
that Father de Fontaines had been anxious rather

to maintain the Congregation in its position, than to enlarge its sphere of action. He never retreated, but he did not deem it prudent to advance. The death of Louis XIV., the government of the Duke of Orleans with Cardinal Dubois for his prime minister, the minority of the king, the dissolution of manners which opened so wide an entrance to new opinions, the results of the publication of the bull Unigenitus, the efforts of its opponents, among whom were members of the higher clergy, were all exceptional circumstances, fully justifying the language used by the superior-general in 1718.

He remained unmoved in presence of his bishop, who was at once a temporal and spiritual prince. When this prelate wished to depose Father Le Fèvre, that Father Legrix, priest of Saint-Josse, might fill his place, he wrote to him as follows : " My lord, the council has desired me to inform you of the sentiments of the Congregation ; it believes that your lordship will be pleased to know them, and it speaks with perfect openness to a person of your rank. Every one of its members, my lord, feels bound to submit to the *Unigenitus;* almost all are Thomists* or Congruists, and reject the medium course. I do not know one who would not be ready ty adopt another system were the Bishop of his diocese to think it advisable."

Father de Fontaines had continued to live at Bayeux, and to keep up an intimate intercourse with the constitutional ecclesiastics, notwithstanding the bishop, who, however, never openly

---

* *Thomists* was the name given to those who adhered to the doctrine of St. Thomas ; they teach that efficacious grace is, by its own nature, effective ; and (by virtue of that nature,) infallibly produces certain results.

Congruists were those who maintained that God gives grace so proportioned to the state of the will, that with His grace the will surely, but freely, performs that which God wills.

attacked him. He died at the age of 64, having spent 40 years in the Congregation and 17 as superior-general.

His heart was placed at Caen beneath the tomb of Father Eudes. His highest praise is contained in the words spoken of him by his relation and predecessor, Father Blouet de Camilly, in allusion to his personal sacrifices: "Father de Fontaines does not do good like other people; *he devours it.*"

The tenth general Assembly met on the 10th of February, 1727, and Father Cousin was elected superior by ten votes out of eighteen. Father Cousin returned to Father Eudes' mode of life; he visited all his houses on horseback, accompanied by a brother on foot. He only consented to be served apart from the others in the common refectory, when it was represented to him that this was done with a view of honouring the Son of God, first superior of the Congregation. By the entreaties of distinguished friends of the institution, he was at last induced to keep a small carriage.

The new superior thought it necessary to take up his abode in Paris, where the community had not yet been organized, although the house in the Rue des Postes was bought in 1703; it was entirely destitute of the most necessary furniture, and contributions came in from many quarters. The Communities of Saint Sulpice and Saint Nicolas de Chardonnet took the greatest interest in this establishment.

The fathers who accompanied Father Cousin used to say Mass at the Convent of the Visitation, in the Chapel of the English Seminary, and of the nuns of our Lady of Charity of the Refuge.

Good is often brought out of evil. The persecution undergone by the Congregation in the days of Mgr. de Lorraine, made many persons anxious to become acquainted with its members.

The superior always kept at least one priest in the house in Paris, and he admitted three students, to whom he gave as much attention as possible amidst the pressure of business.

Such was the beginning of the Paris establishment.

Mgr. de Lorraine, Bishop of Bayeux, died in June, 1728. He had gone to Paris for the recovery of his health, which was, as he told Mdme. de Camilly, superior of the Refuge at Caen, impaired by grief. He joined eleven other prelates in a protest against the Council of Embrun. He is said to have had confidence in the relics of the deacon Pâris, and to have put on one of his shirts.*

The Chapter of Bayeux was placed in an embarrassing position by publishing a document which, although expressing respect for the episcopal dignity, did not appoint any public prayers for the deceased.

The parish priests and superiors of religious houses understood that they were not called upon to celebrate any service for a bishop who had died excommunicate.

The first care of the vicars-general was to send back to the Seminary at Caen the students on the foundation of M. de Condom.

On account of the erroneous doctrines held at Caen by Father Buffart, and the Dominican Father Drouïn, the students of the Congregation had been

---

* It is almost impossible, in the present day, to realize the excitement caused by the disputes about Jansenism and the *Unigenitus*, which condemned 101 propositions taken from a book by Father Quesnel, an Oratorian. François de Paris, who was born at Chatillon, (Seine) in 1690, was an ardent Jansenist, appealed against the Bull, and refused a benefice rather than sign the required formulary. His austerities were very great, and the Jansenists declared that miracles were wrought at his tomb.

entered at Coutances. But these professors had
been removed in 1722, and in 1728 some of the
students were sent back to Caen, and others to the
house in Paris, to pursue their studies at the
Sorbonne, under the care of the superior-general,
who was anxious to disprove the assertion of the
Jansenists, that the subjects of the Congregation
were wanting in ability.

The eleventh Assembly took place in 1729. It
decided on accepting an establishment at Valognes,
and transferring the Seminary of Senlis to the
Abbey of Notre Dame des Victoires, which was
now made the noviciate.

Deliberations were held with regard to the house
in Paris. Should it be continued? Was it well
to seek for the registration of the letters-patent
granted in 1722? Should students be sent there?
What funds should be employed for their support?
How was the necessary furniture to be provided?
Should the superior still continue to reside there?

All these questions were answered in the
affirmative; the funds required, to the annual
amount of 3,000 livres, were to be furnished by
the other houses; the care of providing furniture
was left to these houses and to the generosity of
the public.

Strengthened by these decisions, Father Cousin
increased the number of his students; they
attended the Sorbonne, and were under the care
of masters and of the superior himself. In order
that everything might be done according to rule,
he applied to M. Joly de Fleury, procureur
general, for letters patent in favour of the Paris
establishment. Meanwhile, he obtained permission to erect a chapel, which was blessed by
Father de Romigny, the grand vicar, on the feast
of St. Francis of Sales, the fourth Sunday after
Epiphany, 1729.

Father Cousin's application for letters patent

met with a refusal, based on the calumnies which had constantly accused Father Eudes of want of sympathy with the Gallican Church, Ultramontanism, &c.*

There were persons who watched the progress of the Eudists with dissatisfaction. In 1733, Cardinal de Fleury, to whom Father Cousin had presented a petition, referred the matter to M. de Brissac; he was already prejudiced, and the answer received by Father Cousin was in these terms: "We do not know you: when the Archbishop of Paris gives you a seminary, we will take your case into consideration......There is nothing to prevent your building......and settling as private individuals, &c."......"Toujours le janénisme," as Mgr. Languet wrote to Father Legraud.

Mgr. de Luynes was named Bishop of Bayeux in 1729. He showed much kindness to the Congregation, which now contained 250 candidates for Orders.

The twelfth general assembly met at Caen, on the 30th of September, 1733. The affairs of the houses of Caen and Coutances were discussed, and it was decided that they should furnish funds for the establishment in Paris, without, however, thereby acquiring any right of property.

The thirteenth general assembly was opened at Caen, on the 28th September, 1738.

Father Cousin, either from humility or because of failing health, wished to resign his office of Superior General, but was induced to remain.

Like his predecessor, he recommended prudence in all works of piety; the enemy to be dealt with was no longer open heresy, but a powerful schism, which, hidden like a snake in the grass, threatened with its venom all who opposed its progress.

In this same assembly it was decided that a

* Cardinal de Noailles only signed the Bull Unigenitus in 1728.

white marble slab should be placed over the spot
where the hearts of Fathers Blouet and de
Fontaines were laid; and that the seals of the Congregation should be engraved. Around them was
to be put the inscription : "Sigillum seminarii
Cadomensis, Rothomensis," or whatever the name
of the seminary might be.*

It was also decided that the fourteenth assembly should be convoked in 1739, with a view of
making arrangements for the celebration of the
centenary of the Congregation, in 1743.

In 1739 the young probationers were moved
from Launay to Caen, where they occupied the
first and second storeys of the new building
erected for their use; a gallery was assigned to
them so that they might adore the Blessed Sacrament, and take part in the offices of the church
without any intercourse with the public. Launay
had been occupied by the probationers for sixty-
two years.

At the fifteenth general assembly, (at Caen in
1742,) Father Cousin, then eighty-seven years of
age, again vainly sought permission to resign.
He gave a long address to his brethren on the
approaching centenary of their institution, and
doubtless recalled to their minds the virtues of
their holy founder. He advised the assembly to
ask the Holy Father for the indulgence of the
forty hours on this solemnity.

The Venerable Father Cousin, fourth Superior
General of the Congregation, died on the 14th of
March, 1751, at ninety-six years of age.

His direction had been prudent, zealous, and simple. He seems to have followed the steps of Father

* Father Eudes' seal turned on a pivot, and had three sides.
It was found at Caen by one of the priests of the place, who
values it as a precious relic, and will not part with it. The
Very Rev. Father Gaudaire has had one made after the same
pattern, one side of which serves as the seal of the Congregation.

Eudes and Father Blouet more closely than his immediate predecessor. He and his Congregation had been often attacked by an infamous newspaper, called "*Nouvelles Ecclesiastiques*," first published in 1727. A Jansenist priest, named Fontaine, was its original editor. After being condemned by the Holy See and the Paris Parliament, it still continued to appear, and it was impossible to discover its author or printer.

The sixteenth general assembly having been convened at Caen, on the 10th of June, 1751, named Father Auvray de Saint André Superior General. He was admirable in his observance of the rule, and gained the sympathy of all members of the Congregation.

It is evident that the Eudists were faithfully performing their mission. They did not, indeed, lead the van of the army; but they were never in the rear. The seventeenth, eighteenth, and nineteenth general assemblies met at Caen, in 1754, 1759, and 1763, and on each occasion the perils of the time furnished matter for consideration, for France seemed now threatened by Jansenism as seriously as she had been by Protestantism in the XVIth century.

The "*Nouvelles Ecclesiastiques*," represents the Eudists as defending the breach in 1750. "The Eudists," to quote its angry words, "a sort of congregation of priests established during the last century by Father Eudes de Mézeray, an ex-Oratorian, distinguished by his ignorance, his visions, and his fanaticism, and whose rule is but too widely spread in Normandy, have furnished an impious and scandalous spectacle at Avranches."

These invectives were aimed at the fathers who had given a retreat at the school of Avranches, in 1760.

In 1762, the Eudists took the place of the Jesuits at Seez, and the priory of Livré, near

Rennes, founded by Geoffrey, Duke of Bretagne, in 998, and united in 1604 to the Jesuits' college, was made over to the great seminary of that town.*

The successful preaching of the Eudists filled their opponents with dismay: "Jansenism is losing ground in the diocese of Blois," said its organ, the "*Nouvelles Ecclesiastiques.*"

This cry of alarm was elicited especially by the zeal and ability of Father Beurier. He was born at Vannes, on the 5th of November, 1715, and became one of the most remarkable preachers of the XVIIIth century. Before beginning his sermons, he used to beg his audience to join with him in saying a Pater and an Ave for the salvation of sinners. On the 22nd of July, 1776, as he was about to preach before Mgr. de Trimont, Bishop of Blois, he asked him to make this request of the congregation; when the prelate left the church he was struck by apoplexy.

The "*Nouvelles Ecclesiastiques*" paid Father Beurier the honour of attacking him in the most virulent manner on occasion of the mission which he opened at Caen, on the 1st of May, 1768. He died at the seminary of Blois, on the 2nd of November, 1782; many miracles bore witness to his sanctity. He wrote some sermons, and a manuscript life of Father Eudes. His remains have been taken to Redon, where they will soon be

---

* The removal of the Jesuits was a serious blow to the many establishments which they directed with equal perseverance and talent; and the Protestant historian, Leopold Ranke, looks on the dispersion of this society, which made the instruction of youth its chief means of success, as an event calculated to shake the Catholic world to its very depth. It was evidently most difficult to replace them; Father Perrand, of the new Oratory, considers one cause of the decay of the old Oratory to have been the necessity of associating with its members, who were too few for the care of all the new schools offered to them, many lay-persons whose conduct ultimately brought discredit on the Congregation.

placed in the Seminary Chapel of la Roche du Theil.

In 1769, Father de Saint André convoked the twentieth general assembly, in order to tender his resignation, which was accepted on the 9th of October, and Father Michel Lefèvre, Superior of the Rouen Seminary was chosen in his stead. Father de Saint André died on the 20th of January, 1770.

Father Michel Lefèvre summoned the twenty-first general assembly to treat of sundry affairs on the 24th of October, 1774.

His colleagues remonstrated with him on account of a work which he had written while superior, in favour of lending money on interest, a practice at that period generally condemned. He was even threatened with deposition, unless he would retract. He did so, and died soon after having given this proof of obedience. In the same year, Mgr. de Beaumont, Archbishop of Paris, obtained the registration of the king's letters patent for the Paris foundations. It will be remembered that these letters had been refused when Cardinal Fleury was in power.

Father Lefevre died while on a visitation at Rennes, about the year 1775. He was buried in the seminary church, and in 1799 his body was found to be in perfect preservation, with the sacerdotal vestments entire. The following epitaph was engraved on his tomb: "Vir amoenitate et prudentiâ commendabilis, scientiâ et fide conspicuus, salutis fidelium ac præcipue clericorum indagator assiduus." On the 3rd of October, 1775, at the twenty-second general assembly, Father Peter Lecoq was elected superior. He had written a clear refutation of his predecessor's book. The question on which Father Lefèvre had spoken prematurely was afterwards settled by the Court of Rome ; and money being considered as an article of commerce, its loan for a certain fixed interest was authorized. Father Lecoq wrote several highly esteemed works on law, especially one entitled "De l'etat des personnes et des choses," which was quoted as an authority by the celebrated Thouret, president of the Constituent Assembly, while a lawyer at Rouen.

The time of his generalship was short; for he had a paralytic stroke, and died at Caen, on the 1st of September, 1777, and on the 1st of October, in the twenty-third general assembly, Father Dumont was chosen as his successor.

This Superior was revered by all who knew him. His intellectual gifts were accompanied by solid learning, and his life was most edifying. Every Bishop who had a seminary under the direction of the Congregation appointed him grand vicar. After he had been some years in office, he also was attacked by paralysis, and though his life was prolonged, it was deemed necessary to summon the twenty-fourth general assembly, by which Father Francis Louis Hébert, Superior of the Paris house, born at Croupte, in the diocese of Lisieux, was named his coadjutor and successor in the event of his death.

Dark clouds were lowering on the horizon; a sullen calm foretold the coming tempest, and the Eudist Fathers felt that at any moment circumstances might require to be met by exceptional measures. It was therefore most necessary that a strong hand should guide the helm. The Congregation could not have made a better choice than that of Father Hébert. We have been sustained in a tedious analysis of the history of the Congregation since its founder's death, by our desire to show it standing firm in the midst of the fearful devastation and dissolution of French society, and defending to the last, in the person of its chief, the banner of our holy ancestor.

The Congregation continued its missions, and led back to the foot of the altar many who had been beguiled by Jansenism, and had then fallen victims to philosophy. It always inculcated calmness, union, and that Christian fraternity of which so strange a parody was soon shown to the world. In 1784, nine bishops, full of gratitude for the assistance afforded them by these vigorous evangelical labourers gave their attestation to this effect.

The part taken by the Eudists was less prominent than that of the Jesuits, with whom they continued the closest relations, and for some time direct attacks had ceased. Under a direction at once zealous and prudent, they did a great work for God during the 18th century.

At this critical period it was necessary to keep the ground they had gained, rather than to go forward. But at the decisive moment we shall see the Congregation of Jesus and Mary fighting valiantly and winning the martyr's crown.

On the 4th of August, 1789, the National Assembly declared that ecclesiastical property belonged to the nation, and on the 2nd of November a decree was passed placing it at the disposal of the nation. On the 13th a further decree required superiors of religious houses, and all who held benefices, to make a declaration of their possessions.

These measures were followed, on the 13th of February, 1790, by the suppression of the religious orders, on the 12th of July, by the civil constitution of the clergy, and on the 25th of September by a decree requiring all priests to take a schismatical oath of fidelity to the nation.

Having taken their goods, it was proposed to take their consciences, but this was not so easy.

Such was the state of affairs; the head of a Congregation which had never deviated from the course pointed out by its holy founder was placed in a terrible position. Father Hébert, who must be considered as the real superior-general, no doubt often implored Father Eudes to gain for him all that he needed in the struggle; and doubtless it was heard, for he left this world with the martyr's palm in his hand.

Father F. Louis Hébert belonged to a respectable family, one of whose members was employed in the office of M. Bertin, minister to Louis XVI. He was too disinterested ever to ask anything for his own advantage, and only used the credit given him by this alliance for the good of others.

One of his relations was carried away by his passions to the commission of a fearful crime, which brought upon him the punishment of death. He had the courage to assist him on the scaffold.

Many distinguished men showed him by their marked attention the sympathy generally felt for so great a misfortune.

He wished to resign his office, but his colleagues would not hear of it. Mgr. de Juigné, and all his vicars-general, went to visit him on this occasion.

The king's confessor, Father Poupart, parish priest of St. Eustache, having taken the constitutional oath in 1791, his Majesty's confidence in him was gone, and he turned to Father Hébert, at that time superior of the Eudists in Paris, and co-adjutor of the superior-general.

Father Hébert was fully aware of the dangers of such a position; to accept it seemed equivalent to signing his own death-warrant, but he did not hesitate for a moment, for where could he have found greater sorrows to soothe?

It is said to have been at his request that the king made a vow to the Sacred Heart of Jesus for the restoration of peace, and such a request, although not absolutely proved, is not improbable from a child of the Congregation of Jesus and Mary. The prayer and the vow must have been made early in the year 1792. The "Ami de la religion," says: "the king's choice of Father Hébert was denounced to the Legislative Assembly as an act of opposition to its decrees." Complaints were made of the favour shown by the court to the ministers of illegal worship.

Father D——, assistant priest of St. Louis in 1814, who had often been in communication with Father Hébert, was employed by him to transcribe the prayer and the vow. He told her Royal Highness the Duchess of Angoulême, that these two documents had been placed in his hands by the king's confessor, with whom he was intimate. They gave a high idea of the king's piety, and might, as the priest said, be put side by side with his admirable will. Father C., parish priest of Bonne-Nouvelle in 1792, was requested by Father Hébert to make a novena in the name of Louis XVI. in relation to this vow.*

In the second volume of the history which we have already quoted, we read, "The queen, with her daughter and Madame Elizabeth, used to spend their evenings listening to the religious consolations which Father Hébert offered to them. The words of this good man gave the royal family strength to resign themselves to all the troubles that threatened them."

We give a further testimony, which cannot be looked upon as partial, seeing that it emanates from Henry Grégoire, a regicide and schismatic Bishop of Loir-et-Cher; "Father Hébert spent the night of the 10th of August with the king; he did not accompany him to the assembly where his downfall was pronounced."

* We are sorry not to be able to give the names of these two priests; they are merely designated by their initials in the Annals of the Congregation, whence we take these particulars.

Father Hébert had summoned Father Pottier, the superior of Rouen, Father Lefranc, superior of the great seminary at Coutances, and several other members of the Congregation to Paris.

Father Pottier expiated by his death the constitutional oath which he had taken, and which two days afterwards he retracted in the cathedral of Rouen. He published his retractation under the name of a "Cry from the heart."

At the tidings of the apostacy of his colleague, Father Hébert at once set off for Rouen, in order, as he said, to bring back his wandering sheep. He brought him back to Paris, and Father Pottier devoted himself with fresh ardour in the midst of peril to preaching and the other duties of his ministry. Father Tresvaux tells us that he knew the whole Scriptures by heart; his conferences at the Carmelite church in the Place Maubert, and at the Irish Seminary, attracted large congregations. He was arrested on the 26th of August, 1792, and taken to the seminary of St. Firmin, rue Saint Victor, where he and most of his fellow captives were massacred on the 3rd of September.

Father Lefranc had said before leaving his disciples, that a good priest ought to die rather than show the least weakness. He was about to preach by example as well as by words. In 1792 he published a book called "Conspiracy against Sovereigns and the Catholic Religion;" this was followed by another, "The Veil removed," in which he revealed the secret of the admission of Free-Masons.

After the king and his family had been induced by Rœderer to take the fatal step of leaving Paris, the palace of the Tuileries was attacked by a blood-thirsty mob, and most of its inmates, and of those who had gathered there for the defence of their king, were put to death.

We are unable to say how Father Hébert

escaped. He entered by one door of a house where he was known and loved, at the same moment that the son of its proprietor, who had joined the revolutionary troops under pretext of going to defend the king, and had afterwards managed to elude the observation of the assassins, entered by the other. We owe the following details to this young man. Fearing immediate arrest, he threw himself into Father Hébert's arms, and begged him to hear his confession. After this was done, Father Hébert begged him to go to the Eudists in the rue des Postès, and tell Father Pottier that he was in a place of safety, and that the king was perfectly resigned to whatever might be the will of God in regard to himself and his family.

When he had delivered this message, the young man returned to his father, who had been unable to persuade Father Hébert to remain for the night in his house. He insisted on being taken to the Convent of the Recollects, rue du Bac, where his trunk was brought to him. Afterwards, that no one might be compromised, he took a room in the Hôtel de Provence, (in the street which now bears the name of Servandoni,) where he was soon discovered and arrested with two other priests, Father Rosey, of Emableville, and Father Berton, ex-canon of Lyons, who escaped from the massacre at the Carmelite monastery. Soon after midnight, on the 12th of August, 1792, Father Hébert and his two companions underwent a long examination, and were then taken to the convent of the discalced Carmelites, rue de Vaugirard, which had been turned into a prison, and was soon to become a slaughter-house.

"I might have seen the man of God every second day," says the young man whom we have mentioned, "but on Sunday, the 2nd of September, I was afraid of disturbing him, and therefore did not speak to him, but contented myself with looking at him, and admiring him ; he was on his knees in the sanctuary of the convent church, with his hands crossed on his breast. He seemed to be offering his life to God. At half-past three in the afternoon, I saw him in this humble attitude ; at five he was dead."

The Annals of the Congregation inform us that Lacretelle (Histoire de France, tome 9, page 309,) is mistaken in stating that all the priests had received communion, and that many masses had been said, inasmuch as the church had been devastated, and the prisoners had only been permitted to assist at the masses of priests who had taken the oath, a permission of which they refused to avail themselves.

When the assassins who were looking for the Archbishop of Arles arrived, Father Hébert's post of confessor to the king made his destruction certain. On his demanding a trial according to law for the prisoners, the only answer was a shot, which shattered his shoulder.

It is said that he was one of the first struck down in the oratory of the Carmelites, now known as the Martyrs' Chapel, and that when he fell on the step of our Lady's altar, one of the assassins, raising his sword, called on him to take the oath. " No," replied the generous confessor, " I will not deny my faith." The monster immediately murdered him, killing him with fourteen sword thrusts.

M. Anne Guillot, in a work published in 1824, tells us that when Father Hébert's turn came to appear before the commissary, and to go into the corridor, at the end of which he knew the murder of the priests who refused the oath was going on, he walked with his eyes cast down, with a heavenly tranquillity, never saying a word, and went to his assassins as a lamb to its slayer.

In his heroic death Father Francois Lefranc, superior at Caen, and Fathers Nicholas Beaulieu,

Berauld Duperron, Bousquet or Du Bousquet, Dardan, Durvé, Grasset de St. Sauveur, and Lebis, bore him company. Lacretelle also mentions three other fathers, named Blamin, Saurin, and Grasset. M. Camoussary, a layman who had been with the Eudists, and had shared the imprisonment of the priests, was among those who escaped from the massacre. He was naturally able to give many particulars regarding the last moments of the venerable superior.

It seems probable that Father Pottier, the Rouen superior, who was at Paris when these terrible events took place, met his death there. His name does not occur in the list of those put to death at the Carmelite convent, nor of those who escaped.

Most of the Eudists emigrated from France, and little is known of the greater number during the persecution.

Such was the glorious fall of a Congregation which had lasted one hundred and forty-nine years, and which, to use the words of Mgr. Bruté of Rennes, the learned and holy Bishop of Vincennes, (North America,) "had been the nursery of the heroic clergy of Rennes and Normandy, who who were well known before the Revolution, and better still during its worst troubles. It had gained ground and strength during the 18th century, says the editor of Father Eudes' life, and its primitive spirit was never impaired. It was always devoted to the bishops, and was never involved in any trouble with them or the other clergy."

The following words were written at Rouen in 1866 : "Father Eudes' Congregation was ever humble, modest, attached to wholesome doctrine, and opposed to Jansenism. It did good quietly, never seeking praise or fame."

And so it works on still, always faithful to the traditions of its founder, but it is more in conformity with his spirit and that of its venerable fathers, to let their merits be guessed than to try to describe them, as our heart would dictate and as justice perhaps requires.

VARIOUS FOUNDATIONS IN WHICH MEMBERS OF THE CONGREGATION OF JESUS AND MARY HAVE CO-OPERATED.

The Eudists provoked others to good works when they were themselves unable to carry them out.

1669.—*Schools at Rouen.*

Mdlle. Houdemare founded a school for poor girls, in the parish of St. Denis, in 1669; she also founded one at St. Sever, a very bad part of the city.

By and by the number of children at these schools increased, the principal one was transferred to a more spacious building than it had formerly occupied, and Father de Montaigu, superior of the Rouen seminary, was requested to take their direction. He framed a rule for their work and their exercises of piety. A kind of community was formed under Mdlle. Louvel, who had been won for God by Father de Montaigu in one of his missions, and its five schools in the town, and two in the neighbourhood, did an immense amount of good.

1674.—*School of Perriers.*

Father Dupont, superior of the Coutances seminary, endeavoured to perfect this institution, which had been put under the charge of the Congregation, and made rules for it. Father Blouet, superior-general, afterwards took great pains with it, and went to visit it in 1690.

1708.—*House of the Good Saviour at St. Lô.*

Father Hérambourg, (who was born in the parish of St. Vivien, at Rouen, in 1661,) during one of his missions at St. Lô, organized a society of unmarried ladies to take care of the sick, of poor persons who had seen better days, and of fallen women who wished to reform their life.

Some of the ladies who composed this society belonged to the best families of the province. By Father Hérambourg's advice, several of them lived in the general hospital, while others remained in the town and devoted themselves to those in reduced circumstances and to prisoners.

God seems to have prepared the way for this good father to establish at St. Lô a monastery of our Lady of Charity of the Refuge; the house at Caen contributed the ample dowry brought by Mdlle. Le Boucher; but the intention of God was that the new establishment should be occupied by persons who, under a secular exterior, observed the rule of the order. Mdlle. de Surville directed this community.

After many difficulties she went to a house which Father de Goney, canon regular and parish priest of Notre Dame de St. Lô had bought, and in which he had made a chapel.

This became the abode of the Sisters of the Good Saviour, founded by Father Hérambourg. They still occupy their original house at St. Lô, and take care of the insane.

About 1718, or 1720, the Ursulines of Caen, in obedience to the command of Mgr. de Lorraine, Bishop of Bayeux, dismissed a lay-sister, named Anne Le Roi, who, as well as her companion, Madeline Le Couvrier, had openly expressed her horror of the new doctrines favoured by the bishop.

They both went to live in the neighbourhood of

the Place Royale; soon, however, Anne Le Roi was seized with an earnest desire to enter the community of the Sisters of the Good Saviour. She was admitted, and adapted herself to their mode of life, although she did not feel inclined to remain there permanently. One day during prayer, she heard a voice say to her, "There is a house for you at Caen," and thought it her duty to obey this inspiration. It seemed little likely that a poor unknown lay-sister was to be the foundress of the important and well-known convent which still exists. She returned to Caen, and with her old companion Madeline Le Couvreur, lodged in a small house, (faubourg de Vaucelles,) where she received some little boarders. As the number increased, she hired a more commodious abode, with a garden, near the Quarries, in the same parish, and Anne Pannier and Isabelle Loriot having joined her, community life was begun. Besides taking charge of their boarders, they directed a lace manufactory, which gave employment to the poor children of the parish.

They soon adopted a black habit, and took the simple vows, in accordance with the advice of their diréctor, Father Creully, a Eudist.

The rising institution attracted the notice of Mgr. de Luynes, Bishop of Bayeux, and its solid usefulness ensured his protection.

These pious women not only went out to nurse the sick in their own houses, but had a ward where they received them temporarily. The Bishop gave them permission to have a private chapel, and came to consecrate it on St. Thomas' Day, 1731.

At first, he had given them the name of Daughters of the Association of Mary, but on the 20th of June, 1731, they were definitely united to the Sisters of the Good Saviour, at St. Lô, and took the same name. This change was made with the sanction of Mgr. de Luynes, who wished them to apply for letters patent, not only for the instruction of poor children of their own sex, but also for the reformation of any unfortunate girls who might be sent to them by the authorities. But as the Procureur-General wished to take advantage of this last clause to remove them from episcopal jurisdiction, it was abandoned.

The present importance of the house of the Good Saviour at Caen is well-known. It is connected with Father Eudes' great family through Father Hérambourg and Father Creully, and the venerable Father Dumont, superior-general, was received there when struck with paralysis, and remained till his death in 1794.

It has a branch-house at Pont Labbé, and another at Alby, which contain asylums for the insane and for orphans, boarding schools, schools for the deaf and dumb, &c.

1762.—*Schools at Caen.*

Father Damesme supported these schools, which were established in the house of M. Davyot, rue du faubourg St. Gilles, and placed under the direction of the superior of the Eudists' house. Father Creully also provided for the necessary repairs, and in 1730 brought about the union of this institution with the Brethren of Christian Doctrine, founded by Father de la Salle.

1724.—*Sisters at Caër.*

The Sisters at Caër, in the diocese of Evreux, were placed under the direction of Father James, a priest of the Congregation at the Seminary of Evreux.

These Sisters had been brought together in 1750, by Father Duvivier, parish priest of Caër who in the following year asked to be associated to the Congregation; his sister was first superioress of this community, now known as the Providence of Evreux. Father James is considered as its founder.

The sisters bought the ancient abbey of St. Tourin from Father Lerossel, an old Eudist, who died vicar-general of Evreux. They take charge of hospitals as well as of schools.

1724.—*Society of the Sacred Hearts at Rouen.*

Father Legrand established this society at Rouen; it has thirty-three members in honour of the thirty-three years of our Saviour's life.

1725.—*The Retreat of Massillé, and Community of the Daughters of Wisdom at Rennes,*

Established by Father Vannier, in the faubourg St. Cyr, at Rennes, also bears witness to the zeal of this worthy Eudist.

APPENDIX II.

FATHER EUDES' FOUNDATIONS.

1792—1869.

EXHUMATION OF FATHER EUDES.—HIS REMAINS TRANSFERRED
TO THE CHURCH OF LA GLORIETTE, AT CAEN.—DESTINATION
OF THE OLD EUDIST ESTABLISHMENTS.—THE CONGREGATION
RECONSTITUTED BY THE EFFORTS OF FATHER BLANCHARD,
AN OLD EUDIST.—ITS PROGRESS SINCE 1826.—SUPERIORS-
GENERAL. — INSTITUTIONS DIRECTED BY THE EUDIST
FATHERS IN 1869.—ORDERS OF OUR LADY OF CHARITY OF
THE REFUGE, AND OF OUR LADY OF CHARITY OF THE GOOD
SHEPHERD, FROM 1791 TO 1869.—CONCLUSION.

The Revolution having swept away all old institutions, society had to be formed anew. Meanwhile the nation had taken possession of all
religious establishments, and of their landed
property.

The house of the Eudists at Caen was successively used as mayor's offices, magistrates' court,
post office, and communal school.

In the worst days its church served for popular
meetings and the celebration of decades and civil
marriages; the laws and decrees of government
were publicly read there. Afterwards the fire
engines were kept there, an exhibition of pictures
was to be seen in the left wing, and the public
library occupied the upper story. In 1836 or
1837, part of the nave was fitted up for the concerts of the Philharmonic society.*

* Notice historique sur l'Hôtel-de-Ville, par Bévithe, 1861.

The Caen newspaper of the 17th of February, 1810, gives the following account of Father Eudes' exhumation, and that of the other superiors-general.

" The upper part of the church belonging to the Eudist Seminary is now one of the finest libraries in France; its interior being destined to another use, (balls or concerts,) it was thought well to exhume the mortal remains of Father Eudes, and the superiors-general who succeeded him, and to transfer them to the chapel of Notre Dame de la Gloriette, attached to the Jesuit College, which is now the Hotel de la Prefecture. The Community of our Lady of the Refuge, of which he is the founder, and which still occupies the original house in Caen, have obtained possession of his skull, and of a reliquary found in his coffin. Some other portions of his bones have been removed with a view of distributing them among the houses of the same order."

On Tuesday, 20th of February, 1810, the ceremony of the translation of these venerable remains was performed in presence of Mgr. Brault, Bishop of Bayeux, and all the clergy of the city, followed by part of the population. They were borne in procession to the church of Notre Dame de la Gloriette. A discourse was pronounced by Father Boucher, chaplain of the college, and the prelate himself buried them. Father Eudes' coffin was laid in the choir, and those of his successors in the body of the Church. The nuns of our Lady of Charity of the Refuge placed the relics they had obtained in a shrine below the grille of their choir, with a suitable inscription. They could not get possession of their founder's heart, as it was reduced to dust. Other portions of his flesh, his bones, his hair, and his coffin, have been preserved. The Congregation of the

Eudists has a reliquary given by the nuns of St. Cyr, at Rennes.

At the request of the clergy at Caen, M. Ch. Cafarelli,* prefect of Calvados, caused a white marble slab, with the following inscription, to be placed on Father Eudes' tomb.

"D. O. M.

" Hic è sacello quod olim erexerat, asportatæ et repositæ jacent reliquiæ venerabilis presbyteri Joannis Eudes, Congregationis Jesu et Mariæ et monialium a Charitate fundatoris et primi superioris. Ecclesiasticæ scientiæ propagator fuit indefessus et clericalis disciplinæ exemplar. Qua in Deum et SS. Virginem Deiparam ardebat charitate, verbis et scriptis prædicavit. Piè vixit, sanctè obiit, die 19 Augusti, 1680, anno ætatis suæ 79."

And so Father Eudes rests in the church where in former days his piety had edified his schoolfellows.

The house of the Eudists in Paris, rue des Postes, was bought by the Visitandines, who, after having

---

* M. Cafarelli had been ordained priest in the end of Louis XVI.'s reign, but when the Revolution broke out he followed the example of many members of his family, resumed the dress of a layman, and entered the army of the Republic, in which he served with distinction. His brother, General Cafarelli, fell at the siege of St. Jean d'Acre.

The regularity of his conduct, and his protection of the clergy, seemed to imply that his heart was still influenced by religious sentiments. We are even told that he said his Breviary every day. In 1807 he caused the remains of M. de Bernières, and his sister Jourdaine, foundress of the Ursulines, to be exhumed and transferred to the Church of St. John, where they were buried near the altar of St. Barbe. In 1810, after having paid the solemn honours we have mentioned to the remains of Father Eudes, he threw himself at the feet of the bishop of his former diocese, who, after a time of probation, wished to make him vicar-general. But he begged to be appointed to the poorest benefice, and having laboured for thirteen years, died, followed by the blessings of those whom he had led back to God. May we not attribute the remarkable conversion of this priest to the intercession of Father Eudes?

considerably enlarged it, sold it to the Jesuits in 1818. It is now a famous school.

The seminaries of Valognes and Honfleur were turned into schools. That of Evreux is a prison, that of Avranches was thrown down in 1800, its chapel shared the same fate in 1806, but the school still remains, and serves its former purpose.

The Blois seminary is now a private house, some remains of its chapel are to be seen in the garden of the normal school.

The Seminary of Dol is the town hospital, that of Senlis a cavalry barrack ; at St. Vivien, (Rouen,) the church has been thrown down and a cotton factory established ; that of Séez, with its beautiful chapel, has been gradually rebuilt since 1865, and is now the Seminary of the Immaculate Conception ; the site of the old church of the mission being occupied by school-rooms.

The great Seminary of Rennes is the military hospital, and the little Seminary an asylum for old and infirm women.

The great Seminary and school at Lisieux are occupied by the Sisters of Providence, and the little Seminary is now the school.

An unsuccessful attempt was made to establish a factory at Garlière, formerly a possession of the Eudists ; its chapel was destroyed in 1798. This house, of which hardly two-fifths are now standing, still goes by the name of the Seminary.

Father Dumont, the last superior-general, having become paralytic and childish, was received in the house of the Good Saviour, at Caen, and died there in 1794, two years after his heroic co-adjutor.

It was the lot of an old Eudist to restore the Congregation which had left so many holy and noble memories.

Father Pierre Charles Toussaint Blanchard, was born at Carentilly in 1755. After having

received deacon's orders, he entered the Eudist
noviciate at Valognes on the 1st of June, 1779,
received the priesthood on the 23rd of September,
1781, and went to Rennes in 1782. Here he
became prefect of studies in the little Seminary,
and afterwards superior. When the Revolution
broke out, he emigrated, in the first instance, to
Jersey, and afterwards to Spain, where he and
other priests were generously received and entertained by Mgr. Benedict Uriay Valdès, Bishop of
Ciudad Rodrigo.

In 1797 he returned to France, and remained
for five years in concealment at Rennes, first with
the brothers Hermann, then with Mdme. Dupont
des Loges, grandmother of the present Bishop
of Metz, and lastly with M. de Talhouët-Brignac,
formerly counsellor in Parliament. Religious persecution had broken out again, and Father Blanchard narrowly escaped arrest, when the police
made a domiciliary visit to Father de Léon, in
the very house he inhabited.

He retired to la Mettrie, a property near Rennes, belonging to M. de Talhouët, and endeavoured
to gather around him some ecclesiastical students.
He was still animated by the spirit of the Congregation, and never gave up the hope of re-establishing it. In 1802 he hired la Hautière, that he
might have room to lodge his pupils. M. de
Talhouët then gave him the garrets of his hotel,
place du Palais, and he succeeded in maintaining
thirty young men there.

Two old serving brothers of the Congregation,
Peter and John Guénard, became cook and steward.
A little chapel was established, and it was the
first in which the Divine mysteries were celebrated
at Rennes after the Revolution.

M. Brossais Saint-Marc, father of the Archbishop of Rennes, having bought from the nation
the old Convent and Church of the Cordeliers,

with a view of restoring them to their original
destination, allowed Father Blanchard and his
pupils to occupy them, and on his death, 26 floréal
year XII. (1803-4), left them to Father Blanchard.
This Convent had been the place of meeting of the
States of Brittany, and afterwards of the club of
Cordeliers. Father Blanchard established the
great and little Seminary, that is to say, courses
of philosophy and theology; the students were
installed on the 24th June, 1802, under the direction of Father Blanchard, who was assisted by
Fathers Morin, Beuchère, Teissier, Gabaille and
Marie, all old Eudists.

Many pious persons followed the example of
M. Brossais Saint Marc, in contributing to this
good work. Mgr. de Maillé de la Tour-Landry,
first Bishop of Rennes after the Concordat, when
vicar-general at Dol had witnessed the important
services rendered by the Eudists. On the 18th
October, 1813, he made Father Blanchard his
honorary vicar-general, and gave him the most
ample powers; powers whose exercise was, however, restricted by a decree of the Imperial Government, on the 9th April, 1808, requiring ecclesiastical students to follow the course of studies in
the state colleges, if any such existed in their
neighbourhood. They were to take the degree of
bachelor of arts before commencing their course of
theology.

The imperial government further required, from
all institutions for secondary education directed by
priests, an engagement to teach all the doctrines
it might impose. Father Blanchard refused to
bind himself in this manner, and accordingly his
little seminary was closed on the 11th December,
1811. He left Rennes and built a house on the
estate of St. Martin, which he had bought. He
gave the Cordeliers to the See of Rennes, on condition that, if sold, the price of the house should

be expended in furtherance of his object; and in
1827, with his consent, the monastery of the
Carmelites, where the great seminary had been
established since 1808, was bought.

Having heard that the new government seemed
disposed to restore to communities any part of
their property which was still unsold, Father
Blanchard went to Paris in 1814, and presented a
petition in favour of the Congregation of Jesus
and Mary, to Mgr. Talleyrand Périgord, high
Almoner of France; he received an encouraging
answer, but no result followed.

In 1815 Father Blanchard was appointed head
of the school at Rennes, and in 1820, on account
of the marked success of his pupils, he received
the Cross of the Legion of Honour.

He had established a small school on his property of St. Martin; the pupils were under the
care of M. Louis, a pious layman, who took them
every day to attend the classes at Rennes. From
this period Father Blanchard's efforts to re-establish the Congregation of Jesus and Mary were
incessant. Another project for its restoration in
the diocese of Bayeux was set on foot by Father
Guérard, a Eudist, formerly Superior of Garlière,
and now parish priest of Hottot, near Tilly-sur-
Seules. He meant to provide an income of 1,500
francs, and this circumstance hastened its re-
organization. Father Blanchard invited the most
distinguished among the clergy of Rennes, many
of whom had been his pupils, to meet at Pont-
Saint-Martin. They could not come to an agreement with regard to Father Eudes' constitutions,
some thinking them good, while others looked on
them as unsuited to the existing state of affairs.

Mgr. de Lesquen, who had no great affection
for the Eudists, took advantage of these differences, and formed the Diocesan Missionaries into
a Congregation, under the direction of Father J.

de la Mennais, founder of the Brothers of Christian Doctrine, who bear his name. They were to be exclusively employed in missions, and in the care of the diocesan seminaries.

Father Blanchard could now look merely to the co-operation of the old Eudists, whom he at length succeeded in assembling.

The twenty-fifth general assembly of the Congregation met on the 9th of January, 1826. Before its formal opening, Father Louis, Father Blanchard's fellow-labourer, who had studied theology and been ordained at Saint-Sulpice, was elected a member of the Congregation. The following priests were present: Father Blanchard, canon of the Cathedral Church of Rennes, ex-superior of the little seminary, vicar-general, rector of the academy, and chevalier of the Legion of Honour; Ch. Fleury, formerly missionary of la Garlière, (in the ancient diocese of Avranches); René-Marie Beuchère, formerly professor of theology at the great seminary of Rouen; Jerome-Julien-Marie Louis, missionary of the diocese of Bayeux, and professor of rhetoric in the school at Rennes; and J. B. Guérard, missionary of the diocese of Bayeux. Fathers Fleury and Guérard were empowered to act as deputies by their colleagues, in Caen, Bayeux, Coutances, and Avranches, and especially by Father Pierre-Noel Guérard, formerly superior of the seminary of La Garlière and the missions; Father Lequettier, formerly professor of theology in the school at Avranches; Father Cardet, formerly professor of theology in the seminary at Rennes; Father Bosvy, formerly director of the Caen seminary and professor of theology, and at this time canon of the Cathedral Church of Coutances, vicar-general, and head of the conferences in the diocese; Father David, formerly director of the Dol seminary; Father Beaumont, formerly professor of theology

in the great seminary of Rennes, and now canon
of the Cathedral Church of Bayeux, and vicar-
general; Father Hebert, formerly director of the
seminary at Rennes, now parish priest of Saint-
Gilles, at Caen; Father Langevin, formerly prefect of the seminary of Caen, and many other old
Eudists.

This assembly made no change in Father Eudes'
constitutions. It appointed Father Blanchard
superior-general of the Congregation, Father
Fleury his coadjutor, and Fathers Benchère,
Boisnet, and Guérard, assistants.

If the coadjutor should live at an inconvenient
distance, Fathers Bosvy, Beaumont, and Hébert,
were also to act as his assistants, giving the superior-general an account of their proceedings.

The Congregation was now re-constituted, but
it had not yet assumed a tangible form; the superior-general was like a chief without an army,
each of the fathers continuing, for the time-being,
his ordinary mode of life. It regained possession
of the constitutions which had been copied out by
Father Dufour, secretary to Father Eudes, and,
like many interesting parts of the Annals of the
Congregation, corrected by the holy founder's own
hand.

In 1826, Father Tresvaux, canon of Paris, was
entrusted with the task of drawing up a life of
Father Eudes, from the Annals, the manuscript
of Father Beurier, and that of Father Montigny,
of the Society of Jesus, great-uncle to admiral
Trublet, who lent this document to Father Blanchard, in 1823. We have made use of Father
Tresvaux's work, which was revised by Father
Mollevault of Saint-Sulpice, and printed in 1827,
in Father Montigny's name.

About this time Father Tresvaux sent his book
to one of the advocates in causes of canonization
at Rome, who, after reading it, expressed his sur-

prise that no effort had yet been made to promote the beatification of Father Eudes. There is a manuscript life of Father Eudes in the Rennes Library. (No. 11,879.)

The Eudists recommenced their missions in 1826; they were principally employed by Mgr. Saussol, Bishop of Seez. Father Louis preached a retreat at Domfront; the jubilee was preached by some of his colleagues at Rennes, and by Father Guérard at Tinchebray.

To Mgr. Saussol's great regret, Father Louis declined the little seminary at la Ferté-Macé. In consequence of a bankruptcy, he bought for 8,000 francs the old Capucin Convent, rue d'Antrain, Rennes, with its chapel, garden, courtyard, and another house adjoining it.

In 1828 Mgr. Feutrier, Bishop of Beauvais and minister of public worship, required all clergy engaged in instruction, to make a declaration that they did not belong to any religious Congregation which had not been recognized.

The Eudists declined to make this declaration, but they spoke openly to the minister, who told them to continue their labours in peace.

The Revolution of 1830 deprived Fathers Blanchard and Louis of their university distinctions and offices.

The former died on the 14th September, 1830; his heart was taken to the Capucin Church, and a large concourse followed his remains to the cemetery.

Father Louis was then named superior-general, and the missions were continued.

Father Louis, himself formerly a student of Saint-Sulpice, sent all young men who meant to enter the Congregation there for their time of probation and their noviciate. This custom continued until 1852, when the Congregation bought the estate of la Roche-du-Theil, a league from Redon.

This Father also carried into effect a projected establishment in Cincinnati, but its results have not been great.

Mgr. Poirier, a Eudist, is Bishop of Roseau, (English Antilles,) and has lived in that Colony since 1856; in 1867, 34,000 francs of the alms contributed for the Propagation of the Faith were assigned to his diocese.

In 1839, when the arch-confraternity of the Sacred Heart of Mary was founded in the church of Notre Dame des Victoires, at Paris, its venerable director, Father Desgenettes, asked that the whole Congregation might be admitted, which was done.

The lay-school at Redon had occupied the buildings of the ancient Abbey of the Benedictines, founded by the Blessed Convoïon, of which Cardinal Richelieu had been commendatory-abbot. It had lost ground completely when the Congregation bought it in 1839; Father Gaudaire was appointed director, and enlarged and improved it considerably.

The Rev. Father Louis, like Father Blanchard, was removed from the government of the Congregation just as a revolution was about to break out. He died in 1848, and from that time Father Gaudaire has been superior-general.

The three assistants are not allowed to remain in office for more than six consecutive years. One of them, Father Doré, has been obliged to give up the direction of the Seminary of St. Gabriel, in order to attend to the labours necessary to prepare for the beatification of Father Eudes.

We earnestly trust that our present work may contribute to the success of this holy cause.

It can indeed weigh but little in comparison to the many services rendered by the sons of that holy priest, whose pupils have become worthy members of society, devoted priests, courageous champions of the Holy Father, martyrs at Castelfidardo and Mentana, brave and loyal officers in the French army and navy.

We conclude with a short account of the institutions at the present moment under the superintendence of the Eudists.

1st. About the year 1815, Father Blanchard, who had been superior of the little Seminary of Rennes from 1782 to 1792, and of the diocesan Seminary at the Cordeliers, from 1802 to 1808, opened a boarding-school in his own house at Pont-Saint-Martin, Rennes, now occupied by the normal school. It was very successful, and he continued to superintend it, even after he had been made master of the Lycée at Rennes, and rector of the academy.

On the 2nd of June, 1828, the old Capucin convent was purchased, and a portion of the school of Pont St. Martin transferred there. The rest followed in 1832. Father Blanchard died September 14, 1830. The higher classes of pupils follow the course of instruction given at St. Vincent's institution, which was founded by Mgr. Brossais St. Marc, Archbishop of Rennes.

The old Capucin convent now goes by the name of St. Martin, and most of the students admitted are destined for holy orders. The building has been gradually altered, and a beautiful chapel is now in course of erection. The hearts of Fathers Blanchard and Louis are to be placed in it.

2nd. *Redon.* On the 25th of August, 1838, Father Louis de la Marinière, superior-general of the Eudists, and successor to Father Blanchard, bought the ancient abbey of St. Saviour, at Redon. It had been founded about a thousand years before by the Blessed Convoïon, archdeacon of Vannes. In 1839 classes were opened there, and five or six former pupils of the communal school were admitted. This institution was in full working order before the promulgation of the law of the 15th of March, 1850, on secondary instruction. It is the usual residence of the Very Reverend Father Gaudaire, superior-general. The staff is composed of a certain number of Eudist priests, with some assistant masters; and the servants of the house are religious. Four sisters (Sœurs de l'Esperance,) belonging to a branch of the Holy Family* at Bordeaux, live in a separate wing, and take charge of the linen and the infirmary. All the details are carried out with that attention to cleanliness so much recommended by the venerable founder, and the sanitary arrangements are perfect.

"When this ancient monastery came into the possession of the Eudists," says Dom Jausions, (a Benedictine father, and former pupil in this house,) "it was repaired and considerably enlarged......They also built a large and beautiful chapel in pure ogival style, which is pronounced to be a master-piece of elegance, originality, and victory over difficulties.

"But the material restoration of the monastery is the least part of the work of the Eudists. The real merit of their institution, and the secret of

---

* The Holy Family was founded at Bordeaux, in 1820, by Father Nouilles, priest of that diocese, and Apostolic Missionary, who died a few years since, director-general of the association. This singular and sublime order is divided into several branches, wearing a different habit, but remaining closely united. The Sisters of the Immaculate Conception are devoted to the education of young girls of the higher classes of society; the Sisters of our Lady of Loretto to that of poor children in the country; the Sisters of St. Joseph preside over work-rooms, and take charge of the young people employed in them; the Sisters of Hope nurse the sick; those of St. Martha are entrusted with the care of household concerns in schools. The Daughters of God or Solitaries form the inward part of the association, which has been canonically approved.

This mention is due to the good Sisters who co-operate so zealously in the work of the Eudist Fathers at Saint Sauveur.

their quiet success, is to be found in the excellent organization of the school, as regards solid learning and a Christian and paternal education.

"The part of the building most interesting to the antiquary is the cloister of the Benedictines, which has been carefully restored under Father Gaudaire's direction. Its great extent, its height, and the majestic proportions of its dark granite arches, make it one of the most beautiful architectural monuments of the 17th century.

"The cloister runs all along the south side of the abbey church; the western wing, which has been almost entirely rebuilt by the Eudists, was, until the year 1790, the hostelry of the monastery. The east and south wings remain much as they were before the Revolution. They contain, on the first and second storeys, the dormitory and cells of the monks, now occupied by the masters; the pupils' dormitories are in the new part. Along the whole breadth of the building is a glazed cloister, now divided by partitions into class-rooms. It is in no way remarkable, but the Benedictine sacristy, used as a chapel for confraternities, is well worthy of a visit.

"Its four arches meet in a central marble pillar, and each one of them bears a shield.* The wooden altar is a work of some merit. A picture painted in Rome, and brought by Father Louis, represents an apparition of the Blessed Virgin to Father Eudes.

"The abbey enclosure, much diminished by the opening of the rue du Moulin, is now divided

* The coats of arms on these shields were spared in the Revolution; they are repeated on several doors opening into the cloister. The first shield bears the Lilies of France, Redon having been a royal abbey; the second, the Ermines of Brittany; the third, Pax, the motto of the Order of St. Benedict; the fourth, the Breton motto, "Potius mori quam fœdari." In the XVth century the arms of the Abbey were two crosiers face to face; in the XVIIth and XVIIIth they were turned back to back.—*Dom Jausions.*

into large play grounds. They are gravelled and planted with trees, excepting the cloister meadow, which is assigned to the day-boys.

" The terrace to the west of the new chapel is a part of the rampart constructed in the 14th century by the Abbot Jean du Tréal. The wall still remains, and the porticullises are preserved."

We could not do better than borrow from Dom Jausions the description of the school of his youth.

3rd. *Noviciate and College of St. Gabriel of Roche-du-Theil.*—The noviciate of the Congregation had been at St. Martin, Rennes, and the students had followed the course of studies at St. Sulpice, in Paris, until the month of October 1852, when the noviciate and college were opened near Redon.

The situation is one of the most beautiful in that part of the country. The burying-place of the fathers and brethren is in the park; Fathers Blanchard and Louis are laid there. The remains of Father Beurier, who died at Blois before the Revolution, in the odour of sanctity, are to be placed in the seminary chapel. When they were exhumed, an old man said that he had heard from his father that the venerable Eudist had all his teeth perfect, and in fact only one was wanting, which was found amongst his bones.

4th. *Ecclesiastical College at Valognes.* — In consequence of an agreement made on the 28th of May, 1855, with Mgr. Daniel, Bishop of Coutances, the Eudists, in the following October, took possession of the ecclesiastical college of Valognes, (Manche), which had been one of their seminaries from 1730 to 1792.

5th. *Richelieu Institution at Luçon.*—By virtue of an arrangement made with Mgr. Delamarre, Bishop of Luçon, (Vendée), the Eudists in October

1856 assumed the direction of this institution,
which had not as yet received any pupils.

6th. *Missions in the Diocese of Coutances.*—
In the end of August 1856 the Coutances Diocesan
Missions were entrusted by Mgr. Daniel to the
Eudists.

7th. *Mission of Roseau.* — In 1858, Mgr.
René Charles Marie Poirier, a Eudist, vicar-
general of the Port of Spain, (Trinidad), having
been nominated by the Holy See to the Bishopric
of Roseau, (Dominica), the Propaganda proposed
to the Eudists that they should furnish priests for
this diocese. Mgr. Poirier has, under his direction in Dominica, a house of our Lady of Charity
of Bayeux. This Congregation was founded in
1750 by Mgr. Servien ; the house at Bayeux was
the only one until about the year 1831, when
two others were established at Delivrande, three
leagues from Caen, and at Norwood, near London.
Mgr. Poirier's predecessor in Dominica had been
chaplain to the latter house, and had taken with
him some of the Norwood nuns, who devoted
themselves chiefly to the education of poor orphans.

8th. For the last four years two Eudist priests
have had the spiritual charge of a young men's
society at Marseilles, founded in 1799 by a holy
priest named Jean-Joseph Allemand. This most
important and useful institution has a house and
garden, (rue Savournin 25,) a chapel, a gymna-
sium, and everything calculated to promote the
innocent amusement of the young men who come
to receive religious instruction from its directors.
Many of them grow up excellent Christians, and
about two hundred have become priests or religious.

9th. The same thing has been set going at
Rennes. Father Bourdon, honorary canon of the

cathedral, is its patron, and the Eudist Fathers of St. Martin are his fellow-labourers.

One word more. For twenty-six years one of the fathers at St. Sauveur, Redon, has been at the head of a confraternity established among the pupils in honour of the Immaculate Virgin Mary. On the death of a member, his family return to Redon his letters of admission in order that prayers may be made for him by the rest of the Confraternity. A few days ago, one of these letters bearing a date many years old, made known that a lawyer in a town of Brittany, once a student at St. Sauveur, had died; of his fellow students, who in the capacity of prefect, assistants, and secretaries, had signed this document, one is now a naval engineer, one an infantry officer, the third a regular, and the fourth a secular priest.

Is not this fact full of significance? But we must conclude, for perhaps we have already over-stepped the limits of the reserve which, from the days of Father Eudes, has been the law of the Congregation of Jesus and Mary.

SUPERIORS GENERAL

OF THE CONGREGATION OF JESUS AND MARY, CALLED EUDISTS, FROM 1643 TO 1873.

I.—1643—1680.—Jean Eudes, died August 19, 1680.

II.—1680—1711.—Jean - Jacques Blouet de Camilly, died August 11, 1711.

III.—1711—1727.—Guy de Fontaines de Neuilly, died August 11, 1727.

IV.—1727—1751.—Pierre Cousin, died March 14, 1751.

V.—1751—1769.—Jean Prosper Auvray de
        Saint André, resigned 9th
        October, 1769, died Janu-
        ary 20, 1770.

VI.—1769—1775.—Michel Lefèvre, died Sep-
        tember 8, 1775.

VII.—1775—1777.—Pierre Lecoq, died Septem-
        ber 1, 1777.

VIII.—1777—1796.—François-Pierre Dumont,
        died January 8, 1796.

„   1782—1792.—François-Louis Hébert, co-
        adjutor, fell in the massa-
        cre at the Carmes, Septem-
        ber 2, 1792.

IX.—1826—1830.—Pierre - Charles - Toussaint
        Blanchard, died September
        16, 1830.

X.—1830—1849.—Jerome-Julien-Maria-Louis
        de la Marinière, died Janu-
        ary 30, 1849.

XI.—1849—1873.—Louis-Alexis-Marie Gau-
        duire, died 1873.

XII.—1873.—Ange Le Doré, present Superior
        General.

ORDERS OF OUR LADY OF CHARITY OF THE REFUGE, AND OUR LADY OF CHARITY OF THE GOOD SHEPHERD.

"In vain," says M. de Montalembert, "do spoilers constantly recommence the work to which revolutionary writers incite them; devoted charity is ever ready to begin anew. In the garrets or the cellars of palaces inhabited by the successful men of the future, beneath their feet or above their heads, virgins will be found who have vowed to belong to none but Jesus Christ, and who are ready to keep their vow, if need be, at the peril of their life.

"In the present age of great luxury, and of universal feebleness, they have preserved the secret of strength and of victory; notwithstanding the weakness of their sex, they manifest that masculine and persevering energy which we want, in order to enable us to meet and overcome the egotism, the cowardice, and sensuality of our day. They perform this task with a chaste and triumphant boldness. All that is noble and pure in human nature, is arrayed in battle against our meannesses, and brought to the aid of our miseries. Let us say no more of the contemplative life, of the sweet joys of meditation and of solitude; these things are the portion of few; the greater number of devoted souls have found another path. They hasten to lavish their indefatigable care on the most prolonged infirmities of poor human nature, they break up the desert soil of ignorance, and of that childish stupidity which is often so wayward and restive. In spite of all difficulties and hardships, of opposition and ingratitude, they press on by thousands unconquerable in their courage and patience, to honour, caress, and comfort suffering and want of every kind."*

We regret that our space does not permit us to give at full length the words written by M. de Montalembert, at the moment when the cloister hid from his sight a daughter on whom his dearest hopes were centred.

In the second chapter of the third book of Father Eudes' life, we have spoken of the early days of the Order of our Lady of Charity of the Refuge.

From time to time some of the nuns detached themselves from the existing communities, and, taking with them their constitutions, established

---

* Les Religieuses d'autrefois et leurs Sœurs d'aujourd 'hui'
M. le Comte de Montalembert. (Annales religieuses d'Orleans.)

new foundations. Each house was independent
of all others, and elected its own superior, but the
same observances and traditions were common to
all.

The bull of erection of the Order conferred on
the bishop of the diocese the right of adding new
rules, according to the necessities of different times
and places.*

This Order continues its course, and God alone
knows the good that has been done by it, since
the day when poor Magdalen Lamy called upon
Father Eudes to provide fitting places of abode
for the women whom he had rescued from degra-
dation and misery.

At the time of the French Revolution, seven
houses were at work, at Caen, Rennes, Guingamp,
Vannes, Tours, La Rochelle, and Paris.

That at Vannes was not re-opened after the
Revolution, and the Community of Guingamp was
transferred to Saint-Brieuc; the Paris nuns re-
assembled in 1806, in the old Convent of the
Visitation, rue Saint-Jacques, which they bought;
they were approved by the government in 1810,
and in 1821 Louis XVIII. generously gave them
the funds necessary for building within their enclosure the Convent of La Madeleine, for the
penitents who wished to enter religion. The
other houses resumed their functions, that of
Caen always holding its position as the parent
stem.

Eighteen new foundations were made in the
following order: Versailles, 1804; Nantes, 1809;
Lyons, 1811; Valence, 1819; Toulouse, 1822;
Le Mans, 1833; Blois, 1836; Montauban, 1836;
Marseilles, 1838; Besançon, 1839; Dublin, 1853;
Buffalo, (United States,) 1855; Loretto, (Italy,)
1856; Bilbao, (Spain,) 1857; Bartestree, (Here-

* Book III., ch. 2.

fordshire, England,) 1863 ; Marseilles, (second house,) 1863 ; Ottawa, (Canada West,) 1866 ; Valognes, 1868.

We are well acquainted with the house of Caen, the first of the Order ; to speak of it is to speak of all ; and we gladly take this opportunity of thanking the holy daughters of Father Eudes for the kindness with which we were received by them when summoned to appear before the Commission of enquiry, appointed by Mgr. Hugonin, Bishop of Lisieux and Bayeux, to begin the process of the beatification of Father Eudes. The hospitality shewn to us in the monastery, and the attention of the two chaplains Fathers Pépin and Delaunay, were such that we felt treated as members of the family.

On Monday, the 31st of August, the day fixed for the enquiry, Mgr. Hugonin, after receiving the vows of several sisters, allowed us to accompany him in his visit to the monastery. We felt deeply moved as we passed through the buildings in which the great servant of God had installed the first nuns, and our emotion reached its height on entering the Chapter-hall, where were assembled all these holy sisters, in the white habit, which is at once imposing and symbolical.*

* As a mark of devotion to the Blessed Virgin, who is the Patroness and Mother of the institution, and in order to keep the symbol of purity constantly before the nuns, they are dressed in white ; even their shoes are not blackened. The choir sisters only wear a black veil to remind them constantly that they must pray and do penance for their adopted daughters.

Inside the habit, over the heart, a blue cross is worked, in remembrance of the Passion of our Saviour, and of the duties they have taken upon them. Above the tunic, (which is white for the choir-sisters and brown for the lay-sisters,) are worn a habit and scapular, blessed on the day of clothing, as is also the long white cloak. A silver heart about an inch and a half long, blessed on the day of profession, is worn round the neck. On one side of this heart is the figure of the Blessed Virgin with the Infant Jesus, surrounded by a branch of roses and one of

The first wards which we visited were those of the *preservation*, occupied by young girls, who have not given open scandal, but whose position was such as to expose them to great danger. They are completely separated from the penitents, and are divided into different classes according to their age.

The second part of the establishment is devoted to women who have forsaken the paths of virtue, and who have entered the house by their own free will, if they are of age, or have been sent there by their relations, if still minors. They listened with attention to the words of the bishop, and their bearing was modest and becoming.

They are called Penitents, or Refugees, and are divided into different classes, according to their antecedents and their conduct after admission. The remedies employed in the case of these wounded souls consist in retirement, silence and frequent confession, and, above all, a singularly gentle guidance and supervision. These poor creatures, who have often been previously treated with great harshness, find themselves all at once surrounded with a care and consideration quite new to them, and many are full of grief when the moment comes for leaving this place of protection.

The relations of the nuns with the penitents are carefully guarded. Only the sisters who have the care of the classes hold communication with them. The oldest and most prudent are selected for these duties : they never leave the penitents; at night they retire to their cells, and a grating, which commands the dormitory of the Penitents, is closed and sealed.

lilies ; on the other side are engraved the words, " Vive Jesus et Marie."

The nuns wear a large ivory chaplet at the right side; a linen band on the forehead; a linen wimple encircling the face and covering the bosom. All the other garments are woollen. The lay-sisters' dress is the same as that of the choir-sisters, except that their tunic is brown, and their veil white.

A number of the rescued women, fearful of their own weakness, beg to remain for ever in the Refuge. In the ward of *Perseverance* we saw some whose heavenly lives are the blessed fruits of the fourth vow imposed by Father Eudes, and so long disallowed by the Roman Curia. They are all clothed in black, and wear a cross on the breast; their countenances are calm and peaceful. Many, we were told, are highly favoured by God, their souls, like those of Magdalen and Thaïs, are visited by torrents of grace. Such miracles are of constant occurrence in these blessed abodes; Father Eudes seems constantly to watch over transformations exceeding all expectation, and moral recoveries in cases that might well be deemed hopeless by the world. "The most perverse are won," said the Very Reverend Mother Superior, "as soon as we can prevail on them to seek the intercession of our revered founder and father."

The inmates of this monastery number from four to five hundred; it has recently been enlarged by the purchase of the hotel of the military division, formerly the residence of the Bishop of Bayeux during his visits to Caen.

The chapel of the monastery is the same as in Father Eudes' days; the holy relics are in the choir, beneath the place where the nuns kneel to receive Communion. In the nave, near the steps, are the tombs of M. and Mdme. Leroux de Langrie, the son and daughter-in-law of the founder.

The commission of enquiry held its first sittings in the choir of this chapel. "On the 29th of August," says Father Doré, the postulator of the cause, "all the witnesses were assembled.* The members of the tribunal took their seats in front of the high altar of the Church of our Lady of Charity at Caen. On the right and left of the

* We speak of such as had received the summons.

choir were placed the priests invited as witnesses. The nuns were behind their grating, and near the Holy Table were many pious lay-persons, anxious to give their testimony in support of the cause. Every one knelt and took an oath on the Holy Gospels, to speak the truth and to preserve the most absolute secrecy with regard to the enquiries addressed to them. This oath was inserted in the acts by the notary of the cause, and was signed by each one. Amongst those who signed were many worthy priests of Caen, chaplains of communities, a monk, seven nuns of our Lady of Charity, sisters from various houses, and the Reverend Mother Superior of the Hospital of St. Louis, whose foundation two hundred years before had been assisted by Father Eudes' sermons. Among the laity, we remarked M. de Montzey, formerly an officer of the French army, and allied with the family of Father Eudes. Many peasant women were there to give their simple depositions. One thought animated each mind ; all hearts beat with the same hope ; each one looked on it as an honour to have been chosen to promote the glorification of a man whom all loved as a father, and revered as a saint."

On Monday, the 31st of August, we were the first summoned to appear alone before the judges. The doors were closed, and the interrogation occupied five long sittings, and lasted fully fifteen hours ; hours marked in our life, and of which we shall always retain a sweet and holy memory. We were able to appreciate the special care with which the Church proceeds in the canonization of a saint. And in the name of Father Eudes' family, we thank the members of the commission, the promoter of the faith, and the priest who acted as notary, for their patient zeal in fulfilling the mission, whose object is to place our ancestor on the holy altars.

We shall now give a rapid sketch of the history of the house at Caen, from the 14th of August, 1790, to the 29th of June, 1811. A similar tale of persecution might be told in regard to most of the other monasteries.

The last act of the Chapter of the Monastery at Caen, was the election of a Sister-Assistant, on the 14th of August, 1790.

On the 22nd of the previous January, the government agents had taken an inventory of the possessions of the Community, and the sisters were forbidden to dispose of their income without special permission.

On one occasion these gentlemen visited the convent, and endeavoured to persuade the penitents that they had been forcibly detained, and that they had now come to give them liberty. But these supposed captives, to the number of 52, obstinately refused to avail themselves of the proferred freedom.

On the 20th of April notice was received that the possessions of the Community were advertised for sale, and on the 17th of December the magistrates of the town ordered the suppression of the house; but, on the 4th of January, 1793, a fresh decree maintained it as a charitable institution. The same magistrates required the nuns to appear in the chapter-house, and take the oath of allegiance to the Constitution.

But, notwithstanding all offers of favour, they followed the example of their chaplain Father Godefroy, and declined to take it.

In consequence of a decree of the Assembly for the evacuation of all suppressed convents before the 2nd of October, worship was discontinued; the house was occupied by soldiers, and the sacristy was made their guard-room.

On the 16th of August the commissioners of the district summoned the nuns, and informed them of the decree by which they were required to leave their house. There was no alternative but submission, and on the 19th, the anniversary of Father Eudes' death, these holy women departed.

The community at the Hôtel Dieu subsisted for some time longer, and several of the Caen nuns found a shelter there; others returned to their own families, or took lodgings in private houses, and waited for better times.

The superior, Mother Mary of St. Michael Picard, had obtained permission to undertake the care of the aged and infirm nuns, who were without relations or means of support, and to keep with her as her assistant one of the young sisters. She selected Sister Mary of Saint Dosithéa Bourdon, who continued to devote herself to her beloved companions, and at last succeeded in bringing them back to their former home.

The superior and the remnant of the community took refuge in an apartment on the third floor, rue du Puits-es-Bottes, and notwithstanding the cruel hardships they had to undergo, continued, as far as possible, faithful to their rule.

So passed the year 1793.

In 1794, having received information that they had been denounced to the club, and would soon be imprisoned, they accepted the hospitality offered by a farmer living at Lébisey, a hamlet near Caen. He had already rendered them service, and was considered a good patriot. They left their furniture in the charge of some friends, and the poor infirm nuns were carried one by one on a donkey to their asylum, a miserable barn where their only bed was straw.

Young Sister Dosithéa laboured night and day with redoubled care and zeal to procure means of support for her companions; to make matters worse, it was a season of dearth; God only knows how she was able to accomplish her task.

By and by, the death of Robespierre gave breathing-time to these poor sufferers. The community returned to Caen, and hired a house in St. Gilles, where some more of the dispersed sisters of the order joined them.

In 1795 the persecution again broke out, but the courage and presence of mind of the good Sister Mary of Saint Dosithéa saved the community. She not only contrived to conceal the priests to whom the convent from time to time gave shelter, but also saved the sacred vestments, although the nuns were suspected of having hidden them.

The cross was very heavy at this period. The prioress and one of the nuns were imprisoned, but after three months Sister Mary of Saint Dosithéa succeeded in obtaining their liberation. For this purpose she had recourse to the most extreme measures. She persuaded the poor old nuns, who looked on her as their guardian angel, to get into a cart, and took them to the municipal court, once a Eudist seminary; presenting herself to the astonished authorities, she said: "I have brought your our infirm sisters; I am no longer able to provide for them; after removing the two sisters who assisted me, you have sent me soldiers to lodge. Being alone, I am not able to take care of them and earn bread for them."

"Very well," answered the municipal authorities, "we will put them in prison."

"So you may, citizens, for at least you will feed them there." The authorities, embarrassed by the young sister's answers, and perhaps touched by an involuntary sentiment of admiration for her courage, ended by saying, "Take back your good women, citizen, we will attend to your request."

The soldiers were sent away, and the imprisoned nuns soon rejoined their companions.

In 1796, the pensions promised to the sisters

were paid, and several families who were anxious that their children should receive a Christian education, urged them to open a small boarding-school. For this purpose they hired a second house, the first was called la Grande Charité, and the second, which was very near it, la Petite Charité. The sisters of our comrade, General de Malherbe de Bayeux, who distinguished himself at the siege of Sebastopol, still cherish the memory of this establishment and of their former teachers.

In 1800, better days dawned upon the good sisters. The boarding-school at la Petite Charité flourished, and some worthy priests who had returned from exile assisted them in their work and gave lessons to their pupils. They thus fulfilled, as far as in them lay, that fourth vow by which they are distinguished from all other religious orders.

In 1802, Father Cousin, an ancient Eudist, and superior of the house at Lisieux, was chaplain to la Grande Charité, and another priest, uncle of the first mistress, lived at la Petite Charité, and was most useful in arranging the difficulties which constantly arose in those days. In the same year Mgr. Brault having been appointed to the bishopric of Bayeux, came to visit them, and promised to protect them in every way.

Correspondence with other houses of the order had been entirely interrupted during the troubled days of the Revolution, it was now resumed, especially with those of Paris, La Rochelle, and Guingamp.

The approbation of government was given to the monastery in Paris in 1803. The Caen sisters hoped now to enter into the promised land, but the good Mother Mary of St. Michael Picard was only allowed, like Moses, to see it in the distance.

Mgr. de Bayeux consented to a new election.

Mother Mary of St. Aloysius Desbouillons

had returned to her family in 1790. She was much beloved, and employed her fortune in assisting her poor companions, and relieving the many miseries common in those sad times. She was chosen superior, and as soon as the tidings of her election reached her, she left the comforts of her home and went to share the poverty and trials of her sisters in religion. Many subjects presented themselves, and she soon formed a noviciate. At the same time she took measures for the legal re-establishment of the order, which was attended with many difficulties, inasmuch as the government wished to impose statutes which might clash with the rule.

The old convent, in the rue des Quais, had been turned into a barrack, and was generally occupied by 1,500 or 2,000 soldiers. The superior was advised to seek to settle the community elsewhere; many old religious houses then vacant were inspected with this view, but it seemed as if the good mothers could not sing the songs of Sion in a strange land.

They therefore waited.

In 1805 and 1806 many efforts were made to obtain the restitution of the old house and legal approbation; but, notwithstanding the good will of the authorities, fresh difficulties constantly arose.

1807 was an eventful year. In 1805 vows had been prohibited, nevertheless, the superior and the council did not think it right to dismiss their novices, and in January three professions took place, the first made since 1785.

Sister Mary of Saint Dosithéa was sent to Paris to make fresh efforts. She was furnished with many letters of recommendation; M. Portalis, the minister of worship, had a great esteem for her, and the emperor's mother took her under her special protection; it also happened at this time, by the permission of Providence, that some of the soldiers occupying the convent at Caen fell ill, the minister of war therefore decided that it should be abandoned; and on the 18th of September, 1807, the emperor signed a decree which restored to the community as much of the ancient building as had not been sold. It was in a state of complete dilapidation, when twenty-nine sisters returned on the 29th of September, 1808; sixteen had died during the Revolution, and a few never rejoined the order.

The great question of legal re-establishment still remained.

The government wished to form all religious women into two great orders, each of which was to be ruled by a superior-general.

The communities then in process of reconstruction were invited to send representatives to a chapter-general, to be held on the 13th of October,* 1807. Sister Mary of Saint Dosithéa Bourdon was again chosen to maintain the rights and interests of the house at Caen. The mission was a delicate one, but she performed it with a wisdom and firmness which influenced her most obstinate opponents.

At length, on the 29th of June, 1811, Napoleon signed a decree re-establishing the order, and authorizing its statutes as drawn up by the venerable founder. Successful opposition was made by

* By a decree of the 30th of September, 1807, Napoleon summoned a general Chapter of all the religious orders devoted to the care of the poor. This Chapter was to be held in Paris, in the palace of his mother, who was to preside, and to be assisted by the Abbé de Boulogne, high almoner of the Emperor, and secretary. Each establishment was to send a representative well acquainted with its circumstances and requirements.

The Emperor's principal ostensible object was the adoption of the best means for the spread and efficiency of these institutions.

The *hidden object* was to establish *unity of direction;* a unity incompatible with some of their constitutions.

the nuns to certain articles contrary to the primitive constitutions of their order.

And so, notwithstanding the fearful storm which had changed the whole face of society, the first Community of Our Lady of Charity of the Refuge lived on, preserving the precious trust committed to it by Father Eudes, and showing what can be done by perseverance founded upon faith and confidence in God.

Sister Saint Dosithéa Bourdon, the heroine of these troublous times, was superior of the convent at Caen from 1819 to 1821.

One spirit animates all the monasteries of the order; the other houses constantly turn to the one founded by Father Eudes himself for support and advice. If space permitted us to quote largely from their annals, we could give many most interesting details.

A new building was necessary at the convent of St. Cyr, at Rennes, but the community had no funds to undertake it; the parish priest made the matter known, and immediately a poor woman came to the Reverend Mother Superior, Madame de Saint Pierre, with an offering of *ten centimes,* (about one penny). Encouraged by this circumstance, she sent for the architect and the builders, and soon their labours were completed and all expenses paid.

The order of our Lady of Charity of the Refuge is known and respected throughout the world.

After an existence of one hundred and ninety-four years it sent forth a vigorous shoot, which has since borne many branches; we allude to the Order of our Lady of Charity of the Good Shepherd, formally recognized on the 16th of January, 1835, by the Sovereign Pontiff, Gregory XVI. It possesses 110 monasteries in different parts of the world, of which we shall give a list.

There are some exceptional natures which would

be stifled in a narrow circle, for their moral force requires an extended sphere of action; when this exuberant moral force is curbed by the great virtue of charity, it becomes a mighty agent for the regeneration of lost souls.

Rose-Virginie Pelletier, called in religion Mary of Saint Euphrasia, was born at Noirmoutiers, on the 31st of July, 1796. Her father died during her early childhood, and she was placed by her mother in an excellent school at Tours, kept by Madame Choblet, and situated near the monastery of our Lady of Charity of the Refuge, which had been founded in 1714, and restored after the French Revolution.

She was soon remarked for her goodness, and spent a year under the care of one of the principal mistresses, Mdme. de Lignac, afterwards Superior of the Ursulines at Tours. This venerable nun has kindly favoured us with the following letter, regarding the youth of the pupil whom she survives:

"I did not know Sister St. Euphrasia in her very early childhood; her good mother Madame Pelletier, brought her at the age of 14 to Madame Choblet's; one or two years later I was appointed mistress of her class, and it was easy to see that she was a most promising pupil. She told me of her desire to be a nun, and I advised her to weigh the matter well before speaking to her guardian and her sister, for by this time she had lost her pious mother. Soon afterwards I left this house to become an Ursuline, and young Virginie Pelletier went to the Sisters of the Refuge, who then lived very near Mdme. de Choblet's house. This dear pupil was only a year under my care; but I had time to observe that her chief attraction was burning zeal, and I saw the beginning of her apostolate. While her companions were thinking but little of preparing for the great feast of Pentecost,

20

she begged my permission to speak during recreation to some of the most thoughtless; she then took two of the best girls into her confidence, and the three began their mission. I admired their work in silence, and encouraged them privately; at the end of a week the whole household saw a wonderful change in many young persons, who were much older than the three apostles. I really believe that the grace of their Confirmation then took its full effect, and their good dispositions continued throughout the whole year. From this time I foresaw that Mlle. Virginie Pelletier might do wonderful good; therefore, I was by no means astonished at the success of her undertakings, and to the end of her life we were united by the closest friendship. I pray most earnestly for the continuance of her good works, which have hitherto been so flourishing and so much blessed by God."

This testimony is of great value; Mdme. de Lignac is a venerable religious, whose pupils form the joy of their families, and as matrons are distinguished by their Christian virtues.

She was persuaded that Virginie Pelletier was gifted with that genius which, when devoted to God, produces great things.

This young girl had been brought up by the sea-side, and the conflicts of the elements seem to have left their impress on her imagination. She soon learned to look upon life as a battle, in which those who would be victorious must never look backwards, never be discouraged, and must, after any check, resume their task with the calm tenacity characteristic of great founders.

Mdme. de Lignac has told us, that while yet a young girl Virginie Pelletier longed for cloister-life, little as it seemed in accordance with her natural disposition. She was attracted by the white sisters, whom she had seen from time to time, and on the evening of the 20th of October,

1814, at the age of 18, she left her school, and went to seek admission into the Community of our Lady of Charity of the Refuge. Mother Mary of St. Joseph, the superior, received her gladly, but her guardian, not approving her decision, or at least wishing to put it to the test, her clothing was delayed until the 8th of September, 1815. She took the name of Mary of St. Euphrasia, was professed on the 9th of September, 1817, became mistress of the penitents, and before she had reached the age required by the constitutions, a dispensation was granted enabling her to succeed Mother Mary Saint-Hippolytus de Bottemillieau as superior.

She was only twenty-nine, and her election was unanimous. She soon set to work to increase the number of penitents, and founded in her monastery a class of Magdalens, which still continues to produce most abundant and happy results.

What were, at this time, the projects and thoughts of the remarkable woman, who had so wondrous a power of forming other souls after her own likeness?

They travelled through the whole world, and turned with special interest to countries where new sects were proclaiming those principles of liberty and communism, which bring man, the image of God, down to the level of irrational animals.

She could do anything inside the cloister walls, but beyond them she had no power.

It seems probable that she now conceived the plan of a vast system for the diffusion of divine mercy, by means of a *Generalate*, although she knew not whether it would ever be in her power to carry it out.

The work of the Good Shepherd was among those which occupied the last years of Mgr. Montault-des-Iles, Bishop of Angers. In 1829, he sent several of his priests to Tours, to beg Sister Mary of Saint-Euphrasia to come and found a refuge for penitents in his episcopal city; she gladly acceded to his wishes, and went with some of her nuns to Angers for the purpose.

Madame Innocente-Jeanne-Baptiste de Lentivi, widow of M. Le Roy de la Potherie de Neuville, was well known at Angers for her inexhaustible charity. She felt for every kind of distress, but none touched her heart more than that of poor women, who had been led astray by weakness or by want.

Her experience coincided with that of Father Eudes; isolated cases of success were followed by hopeless relapses, and at last she became anxious to restore the ancient establishment of the Good Shepherd, which had existed before the Revolution in the rue Saint-Nicolas at Angers. God called her to Himself before she had been able to carry her design into execution, but she left a sum of 30,000 francs for the purpose. This money was immediately paid by her son Comte Augustin de Neuville, to Mgr. Montault, and the priests of the town, who hoped much from the effects of this good work, added their contributions.

An old manufactory, situated on the banks of the Maine, near the parish church of St. Jacques, was bought, and here Mother Mary of St. Euphrasia established her companions. After having set things in order, she returned to her monastery at Tours to finish her second triennium as superior. The priests of Angers, who had had the opportunity of appreciating her great virtues and her uncommon administrative abilities, were averse to her departure; three of them even went to Tours to obtain the bishop's permission to keep her, but his vicar-general represented to them that the

Community there had a right to reclaim her, as she had not completed her period of office.

Mother Mary of St. Euphrasia established enclosure at the monastery of Angers, on the 31st of July, 1829, her birthday. The direction of the house was then entrusted to Mother Mary of Saint-Paul Baudin, who, while acknowledging the inferiority of her abilities to those of Mother Mary of St. Euphrasia, continued the work she had begun.

Mother Mary of St. Euphrasia completed her second term of office as superior at Tours, on the Feast of the Ascension, 1831.

Mother Mary of Saint-Paul Baudin was elected as her successor, and she was appointed Superior at Angers.

Accordingly, the Archbishop of Tours desired his vicar-general to draw up an obedience for her; this holy priest predicted that the house at Angers, whose situation was then so precarious, would become the most considerable of the order. The Archbishop of Tours signed the *exeat* without reading it; it was given for an *unlimited time*, and became a valid title* and principle of prosperity. Mgr. Montault was now able to keep the good mother without infringing the prerogatives of the Archbishop of Tours, who, however, could hardly be brought to believe that he had implicitly and actually given up his rights over her.

·But the parting was bitter; Mdme. de Lignac, at this time Superior of the Ursulines, witnessed the anguish of her former pupil, who was almost ready to draw back when Father Pasquier summoned her, and admonished her in words which seemed inspired by God, to restore her strength and courage. "Go to Angers," he added, "God

---

* This obedience is preserved in the Mother-House, at Angers.

will perform great things for His own glory by your means."*

On the following day, May 21st, 1831, Mother Mary of St. Euphrasia, accompanied by Mother St. Philip Mercier, went to the monastery of Angers, never more to leave it.

The intelligent direction of the new superior gave fresh life to the house. Penitents came in such numbers that the holy daughters of Father Eudes were obliged to suffer the greatest privations. One day they had nothing for dinner until one of the priests of the town sent them his own repast.

Their generous devotion did not remain unrewarded; the Comte de Neuville, who had no direct heir, determined to devote his whole fortune to the furtherance of this noble work.

Madame Cesbron de la Roche, a widow lady who lived at Angers, entered the order, and was followed by the Countess of Couespel. They both were appointed assistants, and became benefactors of the house, and valuable supporters of Mother Mary of St. Euphrasia.

Among the greatest friends of the monastery of Tours was the Countess d'Andigné-Villequier; she had a special affection for Mother Mary of St. Euphrasia, and on the 21st of November, 1833, settled at Angers near her chosen friend, and thenceforth was of the greatest use to the Community.

The Count de Neuville erected five distinct buildings, for the Community, the penitents, the Magdalens, the children of the class of preservation, and the little orphans; these buildings are separated by walls, and with their gardens and enclosures, and the additions since made, form the largest religious establishment in France.

* From notes furnished by the Monastery of Angers.

Meanwhile, by request of the bishops of the several dioceses, Mother Mary of St. Euphrasia had sent nuns to make foundations at Poitiers, Grenoble and Metz.

Father Eudes' writings quickened the zeal of his holy daughter; she sought to gain a share of his creative spirit; she invoked him with confidence, and a story is still told that while she was at Tours, mistress of the penitents, a wreath of nasturtiums, which she put round his picture on the day of his fête, retained its freshness for a whole month. It must have seemed to her that the revered father was exhorting her to persevere in the purpose which was gradually taking possession of her heart; she waited with a zeal and humility like his own, to see if our Lord would use her as the instrument of His divine mercy.

But when she had seen the working of His Hand at Angers, she formed the plan of a generalate, the only means of turning the material progress and rapidity of communication of the present day, to account in promoting the glory of God and the salvation of mankind. She prayed fervently, and distrusting her own self, she consulted her sisters, her friends, and all who were fit to give her advice.

Indications of the Divine Will were not wanting; on one occasion a Jesuit Father, preaching in the Convent Chapel, suddenly exclaimed, "O thou little Bethlehem of Judah, thou shalt send forth numerous branches which shall cover the whole world."

At last, fearful lest she might be resisting grace, she opened her mind to Mgr. Montault, who fully entered into her ideas, and in conjunction with his venerable colleagues, the Bishops of Poitiers, Grenoble, and Metz, presented to his Holiness Pope Gregory XVI., a petition for the erection of the generalate. At the same time Mgr. Cesbron

de la Roche, the Count de Neuville, and the Countess of Andigné, wrote to Rome supporting this
petition, and promising to contribute to the expenses of the work in hand.

The Generalate was viewed by different Cardinals, Counsellors of the Sacred Congregation, and
Religious deeply versed in the things of God, as a
most powerful means for the salvation of thousands of souls.

On the report of Cardinal Sala, a favourable
decree was issued by the Sacred Congregation, on
the 9th of January, 1835, and on the. third of
April this was followed by a pontifical brief, signed
by Cardinal Gregorio, of which we give an analysis.

The first article decides that the house at
Angers, and all houses founded by it, shall observe the rules laid down by Father Eudes, and
approved by the Holy See.

The second establishes a Superior-General.

The third defines her position.

The fourth requires a nomination to be made
every six years, and permits the same Superior-
General to be re-elected indefinitely.

The fifth lays down the form of election.

The sixth empowers the Superior-General, assisted by her council, to nominate local superiors.

The seventh ordains that the Congregation of
Angers shall continue to wear the habit used in
the old monasteries of the Refuge, but that a blue
cord shall be substituted for the white girdle, and
the figure of the Good Shepherd engraved on the
silver heart worn by the nuns.

The eighth and last confirms in favour of the
Congregation of Angers, all privileges and favours
granted by the Holy See, to the old monasteries
of the Refuge.

The new order was now established under the
name of **Our Lady of Charity of the Good Shep-**

herd of Angers, having for its protector Cardinal Odescalchi, who was succeeded by Cardinal Patrizzi.

But never while she lived would Mother Mary of St. Euphrasia allow herself to be called a foundress; she said that her mission had merely been to develop the work of Father Eudes; she never thought of assuming any authority over the order she had left, and continued until her last breath attached to it by sentiments of the most ardent and pious affection; in speaking of the religious life, she constantly reverted to the origin and the traditions of our Lady of Charity of the Refuge.

Her words came from a heart overflowing with respect, love, and veneration for the good mothers who had guided her first steps in that life, and she has bequeathed the same sentiments to the daughters who now deplore her loss. We have been deeply touched by their words, and would gladly transmit to others the impression left on our own minds.

The foundation at Angers comprises eight different departments; the Community, the Magdalens, the Penitents, the class of Preservation, the Orphans, Boarders, Prisoners, and those whose term of imprisonment has expired, and who live in the house of Nazareth, near Angers.

1st. The Community numbers 300 between nuns and novices; they are French, Italian, Belgian, German, and Irish. Spiritual assistance in their native language is provided for all, and there is a novice mistress for each nation.

2nd. However great the virtue of a penitent may be, the rule never permits her to enter the Order, but many of these rescued ones long to spend the remainder of a life, whose beginning has been so stormy and troubled, in the peace and quiet of the cloister. For their sakes Mother Mary of St. Euphrasia opened within the monastery-enclosure a charming asylum for Magdalens, that is to say, for those who, having spent some time among the penitents, or coming from a distance, wish to devote themselves entirely to God. They make the three vows of religion, say the little Office of the Blessed Virgin, wear a habit of the same colour as that of the Carmelites, sleep on a mattress, are cloistered, live as religious, and employ themselves in needle-work.

3rd. The system pursued with regard to the Penitents is the same which we have already described in speaking of the monasteries of the Refuge.

4th. The class of Preservation consists of young girls, who would have been in danger of losing their innocence had they remained in the world.

5th. The Orphans are little girls from four to twelve years of age, and are formed into two classes.

6th. Some young persons who have been admitted as boarders, receive a simple but most careful education in the monastery.

7th and 8th. As the rule permits the religious to labour for the conversion of penitents, and also of women entrusted to them by the civil authority, the worthy superior obtained permission to extend her charity to young girls undergoing imprisonment. In conformity with the views of the minister, she established an agricultural colony near the town ; the young prisoners are occupied in field and farm work, the care of the poultry-yard, and household duties. At certain hours they receive instruction from the choir-sisters.

But many of the poor girls, on the expiration of their sentence, were not considered thoroughly reformed, others had no relations, or would have had to return to depraved homes, therefore Mother Mary of St. Euphrasia, in her inexhaustible charity, gave them a refuge in the beautiful old abbey of St. Nicholas, bought by the Community in 1854.

Every member of each of these eight bands is taught to venerate Father Eudes ; the good done and the benefits received are all ascribed to him, and his picture hangs in the chapter houses and community rooms.

Let us add that twenty negresses have received holy baptism, and the most affectionate and judicious care in this house ; some of them have died holy deaths, and those who remain are leading good and industrious lives.

Before we speak of the death of Mother Mary of St. Euphrasia, Superior of the Order of our Lady of Charity of the Good Shepherd at Angers, we will give a list of her foundations.

IN FRANCE.

Angers, 1829. — Poitiers, 1833. — Grenoble, 1833. — Metz, 1834. — Sanmur, 1835. — Nancy, 1835.—Amiens, 1836.—Lille, 1836.—Le Puy, 1837.—Strasbourg, 1837.—Sens, 1837.—Reims, 1837.—Arles, 1837.—Chambéry, 1839.—Perpignan, 1839.—Bourges, 1839.—Nice, 1839.—Avignon, 1839.—Paris, (Conflans-Charenton,) 1841.— Toulon, 1841. — Lyons, 1842. — Dôle, 1844.— Loos, (near Lille,) 1845.—Saint Omer, 1845.— Moulins, 1845. — Angoulême, 1846. — Annonay, 1850.—Arras, 1852.—Nazareth, (near Angers,) 1852. — Cholet, 1859. — Orleans, 1860.—Bastia, 1860.—Ecully, (near Lyons,) 1867.—Total, 33.

IN OTHER COUNTRIES.

Rome, (via Lungara,) 1838.—Mons, 1839.— London, (Hammersmith,) 1840.—Namur, 1840.— Munich, 1840.—Rome, (alla Lauretana,) 1840.— Algiers, 1843. — Louisville, (Kentucky, United

States,) 1843.—Turin, 1843.—Montreal, (Canada,) 1844.—Imola, 1845.—Cairo, (Egypt,) 1846.—Limerick, 1848. — Aix la Chapelle, 1848.—St. Louis, (Missouri, U. S.) 1849.—Philadelphia, (U. S.) 1850.—Münster, 1850.—Glasgow, 1851. — Miserghin, (Oran,) 1851.—Bristol, 1851.—Neudorf, (near Vienna,) 1853.—Mayence, 1854. —Bangalore, (Mysore, East Indies,) 1854. — Bologna, 1854.—Constantine, 1855.—San-Felipe d'Aconcagua, (Chili,) 1855. — Baumgartenberg, (near Linz, Austria,) 1856.—Santiago, (Chili,) 1857.—Modena, 1857.—Cincinnati, (U. S.,) 1857. —Genoa, 1857.—Trèves, 1857.—New York, 1857. —Reggio, (Emilia,) 1857.—Berlin, 1858.—Waterford, 1858.—Liverpool, 1858.—Forli, (Italy,) 1858.—Malta, 1858.—Gratz, (Austria,) 1858.—New Orleans, (U. S.,) 1859.—Chicago, (Illinois,) 1859.—Breslau, 1859.—Valparaiso, (Chili,) 1860. —Leyendorp, (Holland,) 1860.—New Ross, (Ireland,) 1860.—Capua, 1860.—La Serena, (Chili,) 1861.—Ettmansdorff, (Bavaria,) 1861.—Viterbo, 1862.—Cologne, 1862.—Faënza, 1863.—Cinciunati, 1863.—Monza, 1863.—Port-Saïd, (Egypt,) 1863. — Melbourne, (Australia,) 1863. — Talca, (Chili,) 1863.—Santiago, (Chili, monastery of St. Rose,) 1864.—Baltimore, (U. S.,) 1864.—Louvain, 1864. — Columbus, (Ohio, U. S.,) 1865. — Suez, 1865.—Vellore, (Madras,) **1865.**—Rangoon, Birmah.—Cincinnati, Louisville, (U. S.) — London, Brook Green, 1866.—Brussels, 1866.—Manchester, 1867. — Boston, (U. S.) 1867. — Vienna, 1867.—Belfast, 1867.—West Philadelphia, (U. S.) —Aden, (Arabia.)—Altstetten, St. Gall, (Switzerland.)—St. Paul, Minnesota, (U. S.)—Brooklyn, (U. S.,) 1868.—Tertibut, near Namur, 1868.—Colombo, (Ceylon,) 1869. — Cleveland, (U. S.,) 1869. — Finchley, (near London,) 1869.—Montreal, (Canada,) 1870.—Cork, 1870.—Montreal, 1870.—Quito, 1871.—Lima, 1871.—Cardiff, 1872.

Indianapolis, (U. S.,) 1873. Total, 89. The number of monasteries of the order throughout the world is 122.

With such antecedents the nuns of the order of Our Lady of Charity of the Good Shepherd, represented by the general chapter convoked at Angers for the election of the second superior-general, have presented to the Sovereign Pontiff a petition for the introduction of the cause of their founder, Father Eudes.

The mother-house of Angers, so small in its beginnings, has made 122 foundations, 33 of which are in France, 5 in Holland and Belgium, 14 in Italy, 12 in Germany and Austria, 12 in England, Ireland, and Scotland, 9 in Asia, 8 in Africa, 29 in North and South America; its inmates are 1,100 in number, and 2,000 nuns belong to the order.

The day of rest and reward was at last drawing near for Mother Mary of St. Euphrasia. Notwithstanding all her manifold labours, she made two journeys to Rome, where Gregory XVI. granted her a private audience; she afterwards visited all the houses of the order in Europe. Since the Holy Father has authorized the formation of provinces subject to the mother-house, the mothers-provincial, appointed by the superior-general, visit the houses in their respective provinces.

In 1868 it was seen that the Reverend Mother was suffering more than commonly; but her courage gave false hopes to the nuns. Her weakness increased, and she was hardly able to take any nourishment; nevertheless, on the 13th of March, her fête, she made an effort and joined them in the refectory. She went out the next day for the last time, in a little invalid chair, to visit her favourite haunts; the hand of death was upon her, and day by day she faded away. It was vain to beg her to take care of herself, she was determined to keep up to the last and to die in harness. As long as it was possible she took her place in the community-room in the midst of her children, exhorting them and speaking to them of things past, present, and future.

She used to gaze on them long and earnestly, as if to take a last farewell. Soon her sufferings became so great that she was unable to leave her room. But her heroic courage, sustained by the Holy Father's blessing, never failed for a moment.

A few hours before her agony began she blessed a colony of her daughters who were setting off for Aden, and sent the following message to Mgr. Callot, Bishop of Oran : " One of the last sighs of my heart sends you a superior for our dear monastery of Miserghin."

The Bishop of Angers pronounced the last blessing, and, surrounded by her sorrowing daughters, the superior-general expired on the 24th of April, 1868, aged almost seventy-two years.

She was buried within the monastery enclosure. Sixty ecclesiastics and representatives of all the communities in the city, assisted at her funeral, which will long be remembered by all who were present.

Great during life, she was yet greater in death, and on her entrance into her heavenly home she might have said : " I have glorified Thee upon earth, I have finished the work which Thou gavest me to do."

The chapter-general for the election of a new superior-general met at Angers on Thursday, the 8th of October ; it consisted of ninety-five members, amongst whom were provincials and superiors from all parts of the world, Mgr. Angebault, Bishop of Angers, presided, and Mother Mary of

St. Peter Coudenhove, who had been first assistant to the late superior-general, and had enjoyed her confidence, was chosen to succeed her.

The prioresses present at this chapter were anxious to draw yet closer the links that bound them to the mother-house, where the remains of her who had trained them all, repose. They wished to bear their part in the work undertaken by Father Eudes' sons, and, thanks to their care, prayers for its success arise to heaven in many different tongues. We may truly say now, when all earthly powers are threatened, when thrones are tottering, when all that is not God's, or supported by God, is passing away: "Deposuit potentes de sede, exaltavit humiles."

The limits of our space have obliged us to omit much; we have had to choose among the sweetest flowers, leaving many ungathered.

Nevertheless, we hope that we have given ample proof that the same characteristic marks Father Eudes' works and those of his spiritual children; they are all alike durable, for they fulfil the three necessary conditions on which we have enlarged at the conclusion of his life; they are manifold in their nature; they are one in their object; they have a solid foundation, being founded on the divine Hearts to which we have dedicated this book, the Hearts of Jesus and Mary.

CONCLUSION.

Our task is done, our readers will judge if we have that love for our saint, which Mgr. Dupanloup declares is necessary in a hagiographer. But our love has not led us in any way to depart from truth.

We have related the deeds of this valiant son of the Church, and if we had ever seen weakness in him we should have said so.

Moreover, falsehood betrays itself; the story becomes confused; the facts do not hang together; the brush trembles in the painter's hands; his touch loses its boldness, and his work becomes mediocre because nature has not been his model.

Truth is the very essence of everything pertaining to religion; "to veil it, to withhold it, to desert it under pretence of serving religion, the supreme truth, would be," says M. de Montalembert, "adding sacrilege to falsehood......A lying panegyric is hateful as an invective calumny."*

These words fully express our sentiment, and we conclude with the humble and fervent prayer, Nos cum Prole pia benedicat Virgo Maria.

* Moines d'Occident.

PRINTED BY RICHARDSON AND SON, DERBY